SECURED BY THE SEAL

CAROL ERICSON

RANGER DEFENDER

ANGI MORGAN

MILLS & BOON

First Published in Great Britain 2018
by Mills & Boon, an imprint of HarperCollins*Publishers*
1 London Bridge Street, London, SE1 9GF

Secured By The Seal © Carol Ericson 2018
Ranger Defender © Angela Platt 2018

ISBN: 978-0-263-26557-6

39-0218

Printed and bound in Spain
by CPI, Barcelona

Carol Ericson is a bestselling, award-winning author of more than forty books. She has an eerie fascination for true-crime stories, a love of film noir and a weakness for reality TV, all of which fuel her imagination to create her own tales of murder, mayhem and mystery. To find out more about Carol and her current projects, please visit her website at www.carolericson.com, "where romance flirts with danger."

Angi Morgan writes about Texans in Texas. A *USA TODAY* and *Publishers Weekly* bestselling author, her books have been finalists for several awards, including the Booksellers' Best Award, *RT Book Reviews* Best Intrigue Series and the Daphne du Maurier. Angi and her husband live in North Texas. They foster Labradors, love to travel, snap pics and fix up their house. Hang out with her on Facebook at Angi Morgan Books. She loves to hear from fans at www.angimorganauthor.com.

Also available by Carol Ericson

Also available by Angi Morgan

Visit millsandboon.co.uk
for more information

SECURED BY THE SEAL

CAROL ERICSON

Prologue

The sun shimmered across the water of the Black Sea, but Alexei had his Dragunov pointed at the land, specifically a patch of emerald green lawn that rolled down to the beach. Alexei's lip curled at the deadly irony of training his Russian-made sniper rifle on…Russians.

The boat bobbed, and Alexei widened his stance, speaking into the mic clipped to his T-shirt. "We'd better get a signal here soon before the wind kicks up any more."

From another boat, his team leader's voice crackled. "We're waiting for one more member to show up— the most important one, an old-style gangster from the *Vory v Zakone*."

A muscle in Alexei's jaw jumped at the name of the gang that used to be the most feared and influential criminal organization in the old Soviet Union. New gangs had cropped up since the breakup of the Soviet Union, but the *Vory* would always be revered by the criminal world even as its relevance slipped away.

Slade, the team member sharing Alexei's boat, hunched forward slightly. "Why do we have to wait for him? We're not shooting any of the mob, right?"

"Nope." Alexei licked the salt spray from his lips.

"But he's going to lead his terrorist friends into position on the lawn. I guess it's his house. He's their host."

Slade whistled between his teeth. "Who said crime didn't pay?"

"Not me." Alexei swept his scope along the large, rambling summer mansion perched at the edge of the sea in the Bulgarian Riviera.

Their team leader issued a command. "Get focused. We have movement."

Alexei tracked the new arrival through his scope. He focused and his heart slammed against the wall of his chest. A flood of adrenaline coursed through his body. He lined up the owner of the extravagant home in his crosshairs—the face older, puffier, but unmistakable.

He swore under his breath.

Slade shifted beside him. "You okay? You got your guy?"

Tracking his rifle from the old gangster to the Chechen terrorist walking toward the sea, Alexei said, "I do now."

The countdown started. "Five, four, three, two..."

Alexei squeezed the trigger of his sniper rifle and dropped the target. His sniper teammates had hit the other terrorists at the same time, but, as Slade had pointed out earlier, the mobsters were off-limits. They'd set up the Chechens for the US military to take out.

Fighting terrorists sometimes led to strange bedfellows—despicable bedfellows.

Slade crouched on the deck of the boat and began to break down his rifle. He nudged Alexei, who was still hunched forward in his sniper posture. "You didn't get a clean shot on your target?"

"He's dead." Alexei swung his rifle from the lifeless

body of the Chechen in the sand and zeroed in on the old *Vory v Zakone*, now laughing and smacking the back of one of his fellow gangsters, celebrating their safety.

Alexei's pulse ticked up a notch. His breath hitched in his throat. His trigger finger contracted a centimeter.

Slade hopped to his feet and jabbed Alexei's back. "Let's go, man."

Releasing a breath, Alexei lowered the Dragunov and rolled his shoulders.

You escaped this time, Belkin, but next time I have you in my sights you'll be a dead man.

Chapter One

Three Years Later

"Britt, I thought you were coming out here for a visit. I'm...in a bit of trouble. Call me."

Britt Jansen cut off Leanna's voice-mail message and stuffed the cell phone into her purse. Dragging the back of her hand across her nose, she blinked the tears away. She flipped down the car's visor and dabbed her pinkie finger at the edge of her heavily made-up eyes. She couldn't afford to lose this job before she started.

The Tattle-Tale Club was her only link to her missing sister.

She slid from her car, an old compact she'd bought from a private party when she got to LA. Although she'd parked outside the Tattle-Tale's lot, she didn't want to be tooling around in a rental car. She'd gone through too much trouble setting up a fake identity.

In the alley behind the club, she stepped around a transient's grocery basket to make her way to the back door beneath a red-and-black-striped awning. As she grabbed the handle of the metal door, the owner of the basket approached her.

"You got any spare change?"

"Sorry, no." She held up one hand as she yanked open the door and slipped into the back hallway of the club.

Irina Markov, the manager, had shown her the ropes yesterday, and Britt plucked her fresh time card from the rack and inserted it in the clock, stamping her arrival time. As she placed the card back in her slot, Irina bustled down the hallway, her dyed blond hair floating around her face.

"Right on time. Go introduce yourself to the bartender, Jerome Carter. We open in thirty minutes. Once the show starts, it'll get packed." Irina patted Britt on the back and then disappeared inside the owner's office—the owner, Sergei, who'd lied to the police about Leanna.

Britt squared her shoulders and blew out a breath. She could do this—she'd put herself through college working as a waitress. The harder part would be getting into Sergei's office after hours, but she had a plan for that, too.

She strode up to the end of the bar and waved at the bartender setting up. "Hi, I'm Barbie Jones. This is my first night."

Jerome wiped his hands on the towel tucked into the waistband of his jeans and leaned forward, hand outstretched. "Nice to meet you, Barbie. Jerome."

"Good to meet you, too." She grasped Jerome's hand. "Do you need any help back there?"

He shoved a tray of small candles and cards printed with drink specials toward her. "If you could set up the cocktail tables with these, that'd be great."

Britt hoisted the tray and started depositing candles and cards at the tables closest to the stage.

Leanna had mentioned a nice bartender in her infrequent phone calls, but Britt had no intention of revealing herself to anyone—nice or not—until she could get a handle on the situation. Anyone in this club could be complicit in Leanna's disappearance.

The cops had just done a cursory survey of the employees and had come away satisfied with Sergei's explanation that Leanna—or Lee, as she was known here—had quit to take off with a boyfriend. As flaky as Leanna was, there was no way she would've taken off like that without telling her big sister—and there was that voice-mail message.

As Britt moved to the second row of tables back from the stage, a woman approached her and tapped her on the shoulder.

"You really shouldn't put those candles on the tables ringing the stage." The woman, outfitted in the waitresses' uniform of short black skirt and white blouse, scrunched up her nose, shaking her head.

"Why?"

"Because when the show starts, those guys in the front row might start a fire when they reach for the dancers."

"Oh." Britt squeezed to the front line of tables and grabbed one of the candles. "Jerome didn't tell me that, but it makes sense."

The woman shrugged. "What does Jerome know? He's stuck behind the bar. I'm Jessie Mack, by the way."

"Hi, Jessie. I'm Barbie Jones."

Jessie narrowed her heavily lined eyes. "With a name like that, are you here to be a waitress or do you wanna be one of the dancers?"

"Oh, no, waitress only. Barbie's my real name, and I can't dance."

Jessie snorted. "If that's what you wanna call it."

"Are you here to waitress or dance?"

"I'm a waitress…for now, but I'm trying to get on the stage." She flicked her fingers at the stage. "You make more money shakin' your stuff, and I'm all about the dollar bills."

"Do you have to audition or something?" Britt transferred another candle from the front row to the second row of tables.

"Or something." Jessie grabbed two candles and two drink cards from the tray and placed them on the tables behind her. "There's a vacancy for sure. One of the dancers left recently, and I know Sergei wants to replace her."

Britt's heart took a tumble. Jessie couldn't be talking about Leanna. Her sister had assured her she was waitressing, not stripping, but then, Leanna didn't always tell the truth.

"Have you talked to Sergei about replacing her?"

"Have you met Sergei yet?"

"No. I interviewed with Irina." She'd wanted to meet Sergei, but Irina told her he interviewed the dancers only and left the cocktail waitresses to her.

"Yeah, that explains why you think it's so easy to talk to Sergei." Jessie put her finger to her lips as more women entered the bar. "Just stay on his good side…or stay out of his way altogether."

As the waitresses and the dancers flooded the bar, their chatter filled the air. Britt noted the heavy accents of some of the women and figured them for Russians since both Irina and Sergei were Russian, too.

When she found herself alone with Jessie again at the end of the bar minutes before opening, Britt asked, "Why do so many Russian women work here? Is it because of Sergei?"

"Sergei's father. He owns the place, along with a few others in the Valley. He has a Russian restaurant with a banquet hall in Van Nuys, so sometimes we work out there for events."

She touched Jessie's arm. "What you said before about auditioning for Sergei. What does that entail?"

"You mean what do you have to do for the audition?" Jessie rolled her eyes. "Use your imagination. That's why I haven't applied yet. I'm trying to get my courage up."

The bar opened for business, and Britt didn't have time for any more conversation or snooping. The customers kept her hopping with drink orders.

She bellied up to the bar for another order, reading off a slip of paper on her tray where she'd scribbled the drinks. As Jerome hustled to fill her order, Britt turned and wedged her elbows against the bar, watching the topless women undulate under colored lights.

"You want chance on stage?"

Britt jerked her head to the side, almost colliding with a dark-haired man with glittering eyes and a smirk on his lips.

She tucked her hair behind one ear. "God, no. I'm perfectly happy being a waitress. I can't even dance."

The man's eyes tracked down her body, and Britt craved a shower. "You have body of dancer. Maybe one day."

A chill pressed against her spine as Britt realized

the identity of the man. "You must be Sergei. I'm Barbie, the new girl."

"Barbie, Barbie Doll." He touched his fingers to his forehead. "Welcome to Tattle-Tale."

He sauntered off toward the stage, his tight shirt clinging to his taut frame, and Britt sagged against the bar behind her, puffing out a short breath.

With a clenched jaw, Jerome placed the last bottle of beer on her tray. "First time meeting Sergei?"

"Yeah. He seems…okay."

Jerome's fingers tightened around the long neck of the beer bottle before releasing it. "Just don't get on his bad side."

"That's the second time tonight someone has warned me about one of Sergei's sides." She lifted the tray. "I can handle Sergei."

"That's what they all say." Jerome turned away without further explanation.

Britt couldn't stay out of Sergei's way if she hoped to discover why he'd lied about Leanna leaving her job and town with a boyfriend. Why would he say that? Unless that was what Leanna had told him.

She needed to get into Sergei's office, the sooner the better. She'd already discovered he left before closing time, so she'd have to figure out a way to stay behind after everyone left.

As Britt launched into the crowd of thirsty customers, Jessie grabbed her arm. "When you're done with those, can you hit a table in the front row at the end of the stage? Guy's been sitting there alone for a while, and I haven't had a chance to get to him."

"Sure. Which side?"

"On the left, facing the stage." Jessie jerked her thumb over her shoulder as she scurried to the bar.

Britt peered over her tray of drinks at a single man reclining in his chair—long legs stretched out in front of him, head tipped back, watching the woman on the pole. She mumbled under her breath, "Great—a weirdo by himself."

She scurried among her tables, delivering drinks and picking up a few tips. On her way to the lone guy up front, Britt stopped at a few tables along the way, scribbling drink orders on her pad. When she reached his table, she flicked a cocktail napkin down. "What can I get you?"

The man turned his head and pinned her with a gaze from a pair of the bluest eyes she'd ever seen. "Two shots of vodka and a glass of water, please."

"Hope you weren't waiting too long. The waitress at this station is really busy tonight, and she asked me to take care of you." Britt bit the inside of her cheek. She had no idea why she'd engaged this weirdo—maybe so she could stare into his eyes a minute or two longer.

He shrugged, his black leather jacket creaking with the movement. "I didn't notice."

Of course he didn't notice. He'd been too preoccupied ogling the topless dancer, who was still trying to get a tip out of him.

Without breaking eye contact with Britt, he reached into his front pocket, withdrew a bill and tucked it into the dancer's G-string.

Britt felt a hot flush creeping up her throat and spun around before a customer could wonder why a cocktail waitress at a topless revue would be embarrassed by a common method of tipping.

She hightailed it back to the bar and smacked her order on the top. "I'm up, Jerome."

The antics of the dancers and the customers hadn't bothered her at all. As a therapist, she'd heard all kinds of stories from her clients and had learned to keep a straight face through all of it.

There had just been something so personal about what that particular customer had done—as if he wanted Britt to witness him touching the dancer in that intimate way.

She pushed her hair back from her face and fanned it with a napkin. She'd imagined it. The guy's appearance had just taken her by surprise, since she'd expected some dweeby loser to be going to topless bars by himself. That man still may be a dweeby loser, but he was one hot dweeb.

Jerome's dark face broke into a smile. "It does heat up in here pretty fast, and I'm not just talking about the girls."

"Busy place."

He tapped the last order on her list. "Is this a specific vodka on this order?"

"I forgot to ask, and he didn't say." She'd been too mesmerized by his eyes.

"Okay, I'll pour him the house brand. Ask next time, since Sergei stocks all the best vodkas. Even the house brand is decent."

"Will do. Thanks, Jerome." She picked up her tray and waded back into the mayhem. She delivered the drinks and then returned to her loner, still sprawled in his seat as if he hadn't moved one muscle.

She dipped beside his table. "Sorry I didn't ask you before, but is the house vodka okay?"

"It's fine." He shifted his body away from the stage, making a slight turn toward her. "How much?"

"Do you want to run a tab?"

"No." His long fingers were already peeling bills from a wad of cash.

"That's twelve dollars. The water's free." She giggled.

His lips, too lush for his lean face, quirked up at one corner, and he handed her a folded twenty. "Thanks."

As she reached for his change, he held up a hand. "Keep it...for the added comedy."

"Thanks." She backed away from his table and then spun around, nearly colliding with Jessie.

"Whoa." Jessie raised her tray of drinks above her shoulder.

"Sorry, just looking after your customer. He paid for his order already."

"Thanks, sweetie. Although from the looks of him, I'm sure you didn't mind waiting on him. I wouldn't." Jessie winked and squeezed past her.

Okay, so her reaction to the loner hadn't been completely out of left field—and Jessie hadn't even experienced his magnetism up close and personal.

She let Jessie handle him the rest of the night, although she tried to catch glimpses of him on her drink runs until he left. She had more important issues to deal with than men hitting up topless clubs on their own. The guy probably had a wife and three kids at home waiting for him.

After making two trips to the supply room, Britt figured out a plan for the evening. She could slip into the supply area instead of leaving for the night, wait for everyone else to take off and then search Sergei's office.

She'd already shoved a wad of chewing gum into the lock on the doorjamb of Sergei's office. Of course, if someone discovered that the door wouldn't latch completely, she'd have to figure out another way to get into his office. The plan sounded easy in her head until closing time approached and she got an attack of butterflies.

All the waitresses had to participate in closing down the bar. Irina had left at midnight, leaving Jerome in charge, which soothed Britt's nerves a little. If Jerome discovered her in the supply room, he might not even tell Sergei—it didn't seem like Jerome had much loyalty to Sergei.

After wiping her last table, Britt saw her opportunity. She tossed her dishcloth into a basket of dirty ones behind the bar. "Anything else, Jerome?"

"You can leave. You had a great first night."

"Thanks." Britt waved to a couple of the waitresses gossiping near the stage and turned down the hallway to the back of the club. She clocked out and then shoved open the back door. Before it closed, she tiptoed past the dressing room, where a few of the women were still chatting, and backed into the supply room. She crouched behind a stack of boxes.

About fifteen minutes later, the door to the supply room opened, and Britt held her breath. She didn't move one eyelash as the stacking and shuffling noises moved closer to her hiding place. It had to be Jerome finishing up, but even Jerome finding her hiding out would most likely end badly.

When the light went out and the door closed, Britt finally let out a long breath. She waited several more minutes until she heard that back door close for the last time.

Her muscles aching, Britt unfolded her body and peeked around the boxes. She crept forward and pressed her ear against the door. After the noise of the voices and the music, the silence pulsed against her eardrum.

Swallowing hard, she turned the door handle and stepped into the dark hallway. A few low lights from the bar area kept her from complete darkness, and she sidled along the wall to Sergei's office.

Biting her lip, she gave the door a bump with her hip. It didn't budge. She dug her feet into the carpeted floor and put a little more grit into it. The door popped open, and she grinned as she tapped the chewing gum wedged in the lock. The things you learned from clients, especially the juvenile delinquents mandated for therapy.

She took a step into the room, her fingers hovering over the light switch. She didn't want to announce her presence, but she couldn't see a thing.

She whipped out her phone and flicked on the light. Sergei's desk beckoned, and she accepted the lure, creeping around the back as if she wasn't the only inhabitant of the club. She tried the first drawer and gulped. She didn't have any tricks to break into a locked desk, especially inconspicuously. If she forced anything, Sergei would know someone had been snooping.

Gathering her hair in one hand, she leaned over the desk and shuffled through a few papers—orders for supplies and bills. Sergei didn't have a computer on his desk. He must take that home with him.

She put her hands on her hips and swiveled left and right, taking in the small office. Her gaze tripped over a filing cabinet, and she crouched in front of it, yanking on the handle. Locked.

What could be so private in a topless bar that everything had to be locked up like Fort Knox?

A sound from the back door had her blood running cold. Had Jerome forgotten something? A million stories started running through her brain in case he walked through that door. She wanted to change something in her employee file. She didn't have a place to live yet and figured she could crash here.

Her ears picked up movement in the hallway, a whispering sound. She dived beneath Sergei's desk, killing the light on her phone. Why had she left his office door ajar?

The floor beneath the carpet creaked, and Britt squeezed her eyes closed with the childish hope that if she didn't see him, he wouldn't see her.

The soft footsteps continued to the office, and she curled into herself, drawing her knees to her chest. Her stomach knotted and her lungs burned as she took tiny sips of air.

Her nostrils flared at the smell of leather and a faint odor of motor oil invading her space. Before her brain had time to fully process the smells, the chair she'd tried to pull back beneath the desk slowly eased away from her.

She wouldn't be yanked from a cowering position under this desk like some kind of thief. She rolled from beneath the desk and jumped to her feet. She gasped as her gaze locked with a pair of blue eyes.

The loner from the club stood before her…and he had a gun.

Chapter Two

Alexei clenched his jaw, stamping out the surprise from his face. He'd never expected that cute blonde American waitress to be hiding beneath Sergei's desk.

She obviously didn't have the same need to school the surprise from her face, and her big eyes got rounder and her jaw dropped.

He'd better be the one to gain control of this situation and go on the offensive. He tucked his weapon into the back of his waistband. "What are you doing in here?"

"I—I…" She ran a hand through her blond hair, and then she snapped her mouth closed and narrowed her eyes. "What are *you* doing here? At least I work here."

He couldn't bluff the previously giggly, apologetic waitress so easily, so he let his lashes fall half-mast over his eyes and growled, "How do you know I don't work here?"

She flinched, and he felt a stab of guilt. He'd laid it on too thick.

"I was just… I don't have a place to stay, and I thought I could crash at the bar for a few nights."

The back door of the club scraped open, and Alexei lunged for the office door and pulled it closed.

The waitress hissed at him. "It's not going to lock."

He put his finger to his lips as he took a step forward. Placing both hands on the waitress's shoulders, he pushed down, urging her back beneath the desk.

She scrambled for cover.

Alexei pulled out his weapon. Coiling his muscles, he flattened his body on the other side of the door and waited. If the door wouldn't lock, he'd better be ready for whoever came through it.

A man's footsteps thumped against the carpet and then scuffed on the wood floor in the bar area. The footsteps seemed to recede or had stopped altogether. Soft clinking noises carried down the hallway, and then a few minutes later the man's boots clumped on the wood again and were muffled by the carpet as he walked toward the office.

Alexei watched the door handle, his hand wrapped around the barrel of his gun, ready to strike. The steps carried on. The back door opened and shut.

The woman beneath the desk sighed and whispered, "Is it safe to come out now?"

"For now, unless he comes back in."

She crawled from beneath the desk and brushed off her short black skirt as Alexei averted his gaze from the smooth expanse of her thigh.

Wedging her hands on her hips, she said, "You don't work here."

"Maybe not, but Sergei's not going to be happy when he finds out you were searching his office."

"You can't tell him that without revealing you broke into the club." She jutted out her chin and crossed her arms, daring him.

"An anonymous phone call would do the trick. He's a suspicious guy."

She tossed her head, flicking a swath of hair over her shoulder. "I won't tell on you if you don't tell on me. I don't care why you broke in here tonight, but I'm not going to be blamed if you decide to rob the place."

"That's where we differ." He raised one eyebrow. "I *do* care why you're here after hours, and don't give me that story about needing a place to stay. You didn't need to be in Sergei's office for that."

"I—I thought he might have a couch in here."

Alexei held up his hand. "Save it. You do realize we're both on camera, don't you?"

"Where?" The waitress widened her eyes and cranked her head back and forth. "How?"

"I'm not sure where all the cameras are, but he has one in that corner." He pointed to a camera perched on top of a tall bookshelf. "He probably has one at the back door, too."

"Then we're both in trouble if Sergei decides to review the footage." She twisted her fingers in front of her. "I *can't* lose this job."

Alexei tilted his head, his gaze sweeping the woman from head to toe. Why did she care so much about a job as a cocktail waitress in a dumpy topless bar in Hollywood—or did she care about being in this club specifically? If so, he needed to find out why.

"I have no intention of either of us being caught." Alexei pulled his phone from his pocket and accessed the club's video files that his friend at the CIA had hacked for him. A few taps later, he accessed the night's footage. He paused it as an African American man used a key to get through the back door.

"This is the guy who was just in here." He held out the phone for the woman. "Do you recognize him?"

She nodded. "That's Jerome Carter, one of the bartenders. How did you get—"

"Never mind." Alexei tapped into a different camera and dragged his finger along the counter until Jerome appeared at the bar. "What do you think he's doing?"

Leaning in, her hair tickling the back of his hand, the waitress squinted at the display. "He's doing something behind the bar. The camera isn't picking it up."

"Do you think he's stealing something?" He jabbed his finger at the screen of his phone. "Looks like he's shoving something in his pocket, but that might be his phone."

"If Jerome has keys to the bar...and Sergei's office, I'm pretty sure he knows about the security cameras." She circled her finger above his phone. "I'm also pretty sure he doesn't have the ability to hack into the security footage. How—"

"You're right. Maybe he just forgot something. Has Sergei had any problems with Jerome in the past?"

"You're asking me?" Her voice squeaked as she drove a thumb into her chest. "This is my first night working here."

Alexei's pulse jumped. A cocktail waitress snooping around her boss's office her first night on the job?

"Well, whatever Jerome was doing here, it's his lucky night. Sergei's not going to find out about it." He selected each of the four camera views and deleted the footage.

"Isn't Sergei going to be suspicious that he has no footage from tonight?"

"But he will." Alexei made a few more selections on his phone. "Just none showing any activity in the club after hours."

"Whew." She hugged the small purse hanging across her body. "Then I guess I'm glad I ran into you tonight. Thanks."

She made a move toward the door, and Alexei put his hand on her arm. "Not so fast. Since I saved your... behind, I want something from you in return."

A pink flush crept into her cheeks as she glanced at his fingers curled around her upper arm.

He released his hold and cleared his throat. "I want to know what you were doing here tonight. You already know I'm not going to rat you out to Sergei... or the police."

"Police?" She put a hand to her throat. "I wasn't here to steal."

"I believe you."

"Why should I tell you anything?"

"Because I hold all the cards."

She opened her mouth and then snapped it shut. A furrow formed between her eyebrows. "I'm not staying here another minute."

"I agree. It's Hollywood. There's a twenty-four-hour diner halfway down the block. Let's talk there."

Taking a step back, she reached for the doorknob behind her. "I'm not going anywhere with you. You could be some crazed killer or something."

"If I'd wanted to kill you, I would've done it already." He touched the gun in his waistband. "What reason would I have to kill you? As far as I can tell, we're on the same side."

"Side?" Her gaze flicked to his weapon and back to his face. "There are sides?"

"If you're worried, you drive over in your own car

and I'll meet you there. Do you know the restaurant I'm talking about?"

"Half a block down on this side of the street." She dragged a keychain from her purse and dug some putty out of the lock on the doorjamb with a key.

He raised his eyebrows. "Is that how you got into the office?"

"Yep." She squeezed past him into the hallway, and her light perfume lingered beneath the smells of the club that still clung to her clothes and hair.

She turned suddenly, bumping his shoulder as he locked Sergei's office. "What would stop me from driving right home?"

"The fact that I can still call Sergei and tell him to keep an eye on his new waitress." He watched her green eyes darken to chips of glass. "And your own curiosity."

A pink flush washed into her cheeks. "You're mistaken. I don't care what you were doing here. I was just trying to find a quick place to bunk tonight."

"Really? You just asked me what would stop you from driving home." He touched the end of her pert nose with his finger. "If you're going to be in the espionage business, you're going to have to learn to lie better, *moya solnishka*."

FIFTEEN MINUTES LATER, Alexei pushed through the glass door of Mel's 24/7 Diner. The homeless guy in the corner nursing a cup of coffee didn't even look up. The couple at the counter, who looked as if they'd stumbled in after a bender on the Sunset Strip, gave him a quick glance and went back to stuffing their faces.

Only the cocktail waitress looked up and eyed him as he approached her table. He'd need to get a name out of her before the end of the evening…and the truth. If she were actively working against Sergei, he liked her already. He also liked the way her green eyes glittered and changed color with every passing emotion. And that hair, like a mass of sunshine.

He slid into the vinyl booth across from her and extended his hand. "I'm Alexei Ivanov."

Those eyes widened, and her mouth formed an O. "You're Russian."

"I'm American, born and bred. My parents are Russian."

"Is that why you're sneaking around the club?"

"Yes and no."

"Are you KGB?" She put a hand over her mouth. "Is Sergei some kind of criminal?"

Alexei toyed with the edge of the plastic menu. She was figuring this out a lot faster than he wanted her to, and he still didn't know why she'd been hiding in Sergei's office.

He tapped the edge of the menu on the table. "The KGB doesn't exist anymore."

The coffee-shop waitress parked herself next to their table, raising her brows and the coffeepot. "What can I get you?"

Turning his coffee cup over, Alexei tipped his head across the table toward the other waitress.

"Umm." She ran her finger down the breakfast side of the menu. "Two eggs, scrambled, bacon and wheat toast…and coffee, please."

Alexei ordered some French toast, and when the waitress left, he hunched forward. "What's your name, and what were you doing in the club after hours?"

She searched his face as if trying to read signs there.

"My name's Britt Jansen, but the club knows me as Barbie Jones."

His pulse jumped. She'd lied to the club about her identity. Anyone who could put one over on Sergei had his respect.

"And?" He circled his finger in the air.

Once the waitress had poured the coffee and left, Britt dumped three packets of cream into her cup and watched the milky swirls create a pattern on the surface of her coffee. "I'm looking for someone."

"At the club?"

"Yes—no." She picked up her cup with a trembling hand and slurped a sip. "I'm looking for someone who worked at the club but doesn't anymore."

"That doesn't make sense."

"I'm looking for someone who—" Britt leaned forward and whispered "—disappeared."

The one word, hissed at him in the nearly empty coffee shop by a woman clearly afraid, made the hair on the back of his neck stand up and quiver.

"You're looking for someone who worked at the Tattle-Tale, and you think the club holds some key to her disappearance?"

"I do, only because Sergei told the police that my... the woman quit, left LA with a boyfriend."

"Maybe she did. She's an adult, and people do quit jobs and move, sometimes without telling their friends."

Britt smacked the table, and his spoon jumped from the saucer. "She wasn't just a friend. She was my sister, and there's no way she would leave for parts unknown without telling me first. I tried to communicate that to the police, but they just shrugged their shoulders and said there was no foul play."

Alexei picked up his spoon and drew invisible patterns on the Formica tabletop. He had no doubt women in Sergei's employ vanished occasionally, but usually not American women with families who'd notice their absence.

"You called the LAPD when you couldn't reach your sister?"

Britt nodded, and her green eyes shimmered with unshed tears.

"What did they tell you?"

"First they told me I had to wait because she was an adult. When they did a welfare check at her apartment, they told me that while she had left some personal items at her place, it looked like clothes were missing and her car was gone. Then they talked to Sergei, and he claimed she'd told him after work one night that she was finished, leaving town with a boyfriend, and the cops told me it was over. They had no reason to investigate further."

"But you did. Is it just that she didn't tell you she was leaving? Are you and your sister close?"

"We…" Britt dragged a hand through her hair. "We weren't that close. We'd just gotten back in touch."

"So she could've left without telling you."

"French toast and eggs." The waitress delivered their food with a clatter of plates.

Britt waited until the waitress ambled back to the couple at the counter. "She could've, but I don't believe it. In the last voice mail she left me, she talked about being in trouble."

"What did the cops make of that?"

She lifted her shoulders and poked at her eggs. "My

sister had some financial issues—unpaid bills, delinquent rent. That's what they interpreted as her trouble."

Alexei spread his hands. "You have to admit, the police make sense on this one."

"I know, and yet…"

"What?"

She patted a place right above her heart. "I know right here my sister needs me. I can feel it."

Alexei let out a breath and sawed into his French toast. Britt's sister was a flake who took off, leaving her sister to deal with her debts. Although Sergei was a dirtbag, he probably wasn't involved in the disappearance of Britt's sister—other things, but not this.

"What do you hope to discover skulking around Sergei's office?"

"I'm not sure. Personnel files, my sister's name somewhere."

"It's a dangerous game you're playing. Sergei is not someone to cross."

"I know. I sense that, too. I'm pretty good at reading people." She slumped back against the seat and broke a piece off the end of her bacon. "So, you don't believe he had anything to do with my sister or even that she's missing."

"I understand why you're worried, but I can see why the police declined to investigate."

"Now it's your turn, Alexei Ivanov."

"My turn?"

"Why did you break into the club, how did you erase that footage and how do you know Sergei?"

"I'm doing a sort of…investigation." Now that he'd determined Britt didn't have anything on Sergei, he regretted inviting her into his world.

"An investigation?" She crumbled more of her bacon between her fingertips, dropping it into her eggs. "Is that why you're so quick to side with the police? You're a cop?"

"Something like that." He had no intention now of telling Britt anything resembling the truth. She needed to get out of that club and go back to her life.

"After I gave you my life story, that's rather vague on your part."

"Just trying to protect you." He took one of her hands in his and felt her wild pulse beneath his thumb. "You should quit the job at the club and go home. Wait for your sister to call you. She'll probably contact you the next time she's in trouble or needs money."

Britt jerked her hand away from his, her bottom lip trembling.

"I'm sorry. I'm a jerk." That same guilt he'd felt before lanced his belly, and he wanted to press his thumb against her mouth to stop the quivering.

"You're just telling it like it is, and you're not wrong about Leanna." Britt sniffed and dabbed her nose with a napkin. Then she dragged her purse into her lap and pawed at the contents inside. "There is something else. Can you read Russian?"

"Yes."

"Maybe you can at least help me with this." She waved a Tattle-Tale cocktail napkin at him. "I found it with my sister's bills. I'm pretty sure she didn't learn Russian while working at the club."

He held out his hand, and she dropped the napkin. It fluttered and landed in his palm. He flattened the napkin on the table. "It's written in Cyrillic."

"Yeah, I have no clue."

Alexei ran his finger beneath the symbols, and when he reached the end of the note, he curled his fist around the napkin, crushing it.

"What's wrong? What does it say?"

"You were right, Britt. Your sister is in very big trouble…if she's even alive."

Chapter Three

A chill raced through her body, leaving a pebbling of goose bumps across her flesh. She swallowed hard and met the unflinching gaze across from her, as Alexei's blue eyes darkened to midnight.

She started to speak, her voice raspy. She cleared her throat and tried again. "What does the note say? Who wrote it?"

"A woman named Tatyana. She's a victim of...rape, of slavery."

"Slavery?" Britt wrapped her hands around her coffee cup, trying to warm them, but little heat remained in the lukewarm liquid. "Who? Does she name her rapist?"

Alexei released the crumpled napkin, and it fell to the table in a ball. "She doesn't name names, but I think it's clear who's behind the human trafficking."

Britt smoothed out the napkin on the table and read the black-and-red lettering of the club's logo in the corner. "The Tattle-Tale Club? Sergei?"

"A good assumption."

"Why would my sister be in danger?" She flattened her hands against her belly to soothe the butterflies swirling inside. "D-do you think they tried something on her?"

"I think they're too smart to try to enslave an American with a family, but your sister must've known Tatyana. Maybe Tatyana was reaching out to her for help. If Sergei knew about the note, that would be enough to put Leanna in danger."

Britt chewed on her bottom lip. She and Leanna didn't have much family to speak of—just each other, and they'd done a poor job of having each other's backs up to now. *She'd* done a poor job.

"I don't understand." The strange characters of the note blurred before Britt's eyes, which were puddling with tears. "I work at the club of my own free will. I witnessed a bunch of women coming into work—some waitresses, some dancers—nobody forcing them."

Alexei drove his finger into the napkin on the table. "Maybe this Tatyana worked at a different place. They have more than one."

"They?"

"Sergei's family. They own a restaurant and banquet hall in Van Nuys. There could be other activity going on there."

"One of the other waitresses mentioned a banquet hall tonight."

Alexei's lean jaw tightened, and Britt could almost imagine smoke coming out of his ears from the anger that kindled in his eyes. He'd done his research. He knew these people. Maybe he could help her find Leanna.

"Is that why you were in the club? You're investigating human trafficking?"

He blinked once, his heavy lids shuttering the blue depths of his eyes. "No."

"But now that you know about this—" she poked at

the napkin on the table between them "—you can bring charges against them. You can tell the police about my sister."

"Now that I know about this aspect of their operation, I can use it to further my own investigation. It's not a good idea to involve the police at this stage. That will just alert Sergei and his family and drive them further underground. We don't even know who or where Tatyana is."

Since she'd hit her own brick wall with the police, she wasn't anxious to return to them for help. She'd rather put her money on this blue-eyed stranger who seemed to understand the seriousness of her sister's predicament.

Drawing in a breath, she folded her hands on the table in front of her. "If you help me find my sister, because I refuse to believe she's dead, I'll help you."

He raised one eyebrow. "You'll help me?"

Her gaze dropped to his mouth—no twitching or smirking. At least he hadn't laughed at her. As she took in the soft sensuousness of his lips, at odds with the intensity of his face, she had a hard time dragging her gaze away from them.

"That's right." She blinked and swept her hair back from her face. "I'm inside the club, and I plan to stay there. I can find out who Tatyana is and how my sister knew her. I'll give you everything I have…and you'll return the favor by using your resources to look for Leanna."

Steepling his long fingers, he said, "You're putting yourself in danger by working at the Tattle-Tale. How do you know Sergei and Irina haven't already discovered your identity?"

"You *have* done your research. You know about Irina, too?"

He waved one hand. "Answer my question, Britt."

Alexei didn't have a detectable accent—after all, he was a born-and-bred American—but he pronounced her name with a long *e* sound, like *Breet*. She liked it. She liked everything about him.

"For one thing, Irina doesn't know me as Britt Jansen. Like I told you before, I'm Barbie Jones from New York, nice and anonymous."

"And if they do a search for Leanna Jansen, are they going to find her sister, Britt, who looks a lot like their new waitress Barbie?"

"Leanna went by Lee, and we have different last names. She's Leanna Low."

"She's Chinese?"

"Half. After my mother split from my father, she… ah…played the field. Let's just say that the only reason she knew Leanna's father was Mr. Low was because of Leanna's features." Britt flicked her fingers in the air. "But that's another story."

"So the two of you don't look much alike?"

"Not to the casual observer. Believe me, Irina has made no connection between me and Lee-Low."

This time Alexei's lips did twitch. "Is that why your sister uses the nickname of Lee?"

"Yes." She tapped her phone and skimmed through several pictures with the tip of her finger. "Leanna has a quirky sense of humor and lives kind of a Bohemian lifestyle."

She spun her phone around on the table to face Alexei. "That's my sister. That's Lee-Low."

"They'll never guess you two are sisters, not by appearance, anyway." He studied Leanna's picture for a few seconds, running his finger down her sister's tattooed arm. Then he smacked the table next to the phone. "Delete this photo from your phone and any others you have of your sister."

Gasping, she scooped up her phone and held it to her heart. "I can't do that. I have so few pictures of her."

"Download them to your computer and then delete them. If someone at the club finds your phone, or snoops through it or even if you're showing them something else and they see any pictures of Lee, you've blown your cover."

"My cover?" She grabbed his hand. "You're going to take me up on my offer?"

He shrugged quickly. "I figure you're not going to leave that club just because I tell you to, so we might as well make this deal. I don't want you putting yourself in harm's way—no more skulking around. The cameras are going to catch you anyway. Don't ask any questions about Tatyana or Lee, but keep your eyes and ears open."

She was still in possession of his hand, so she squeezed it. "I can do that. And you'll help me find my sister?"

"I will, and I'm going to start by searching through her belongings. Do you have them, or are they still in her apartment?" He drove the heel of his hand against his forehead. "Don't tell me you're staying in Lee's apartment."

"I'm not that stupid. I did pay her past-due rent and a few months in the future…just in case she comes back, but I rented myself a little bachelor in West Hollywood. I left Leanna's apartment as I found it, except for this."

She pinched the Tattle-Tale napkin between two fingers and then stuffed it into her purse. "Like I said, it was with her bills that I took with me."

"Have you been back to her place since?"

"No."

"Anything else?" Their waitress had returned with a coffeepot and their check.

Alexei glanced at Britt, and she shook her head. "We're good, thanks."

As Britt ducked beneath the strap of her purse, she watched Alexei peel off a few bills from the same wad he'd used to tip the Russian dancer. His strong fingers moved with deftness and confidence, and for the first time since coming to LA to look for Leanna, Britt *was* good.

While Alexei had confirmed her worst fears about her sister, Britt now had someone on her side—a mysterious Russian American with acute knowledge and vast resources.

"Let's go, *moya solnishka.*"

That was the second time he'd called her that. She had no idea what it meant and didn't want to know, but Alexei Ivanov could call her anything and she'd follow him anywhere.

As BRITT DROVE through her sister's seedy neighborhood looking for a parking spot, she continued to keep one eye on her rearview mirror. Nobody at the Tattle-Tale had any reason to follow her, but she didn't want to tempt fate. With that in mind, she drove around the block from her sister's place and parked in front of a different, although just as crummy, apartment building.

She exited her car and scanned the block, her gaze

sweeping past an older couple walking a dog and a young Latino waiting for someone at the curb, his car idling and his music thumping through the open window.

She didn't even know what Alexei was driving. He'd walked her to her car in the diner's parking lot and watched as she drove away. Maybe he had a gadget to materialize and then disappear. She wouldn't put it past him after watching how he'd altered Sergei's security footage from his phone.

Hunching into her sweater against the gloomy late-June marine layer that had spread inland, Britt loped down the sidewalk. She turned the corner and made a beeline for Leanna's pink stucco apartment building.

She jogged up the steps to Leanna's place on the second floor and held her breath as she peered down the row of doors leading to about six apartments. She stopped midway at Leanna's door and inserted the key into the dead bolt first and then the door-handle lock.

Her heart skipped a beat at the whisper of movement behind her, and she spun around, her nose meeting Alexei's chest.

"Hurry, before someone sees us." He reached past her and pushed open the door, crowding her inside from behind.

She closed it and locked the dead bolt. Turning to face the room, she slipped the key into the pocket of her sweater.

"Is this how you left it?" Alexei took a turn around the small living room.

"Yes." Britt's gaze darted among Leanna's sparse furnishings, lingering on a row of oil paintings propped up against the wall. A dark piece with red swirls was still clipped to the easel in front of the window.

Alexei pointed to the painting. "Your sister was an artist?"

"Yes, and I'm pretty sure she wouldn't have left her work behind."

"Is it worth anything?" Alexei cocked his head to the side as if trying to make sense of the chaos on the canvas.

"They could be. She told me she sold a few pieces on the street at an art fair."

"Where did you find the bills with that note on the napkin?"

Britt crossed the room and rapped on the kitchen counter that doubled as a table. "Right here. There were three bills, and the napkin was stuffed inside one of the envelopes."

Alexei squeezed past her into the kitchen, his leather jacket brushing her arm. While the hot summer weather hadn't yet descended on Southern California, the jacket and his motorcycle boots seemed like overkill—unless he rode a motorcycle.

He pulled open drawers and cabinets. "Looks like she took most of her kitchen stuff."

Britt snorted. "That's what the cops said even though I tried to tell them my sister wouldn't have had much of that stuff to take. It's not like she had a set of matching china to pack. Besides, I thought you believed my theory after finding Tatyana's note."

"Maybe she knew she was in danger and got out."

"That's what I've been hoping ever since you translated that note, but why wouldn't she contact me?"

"Fear? Doesn't want to involve you?"

"That would've been the old Leanna, but I made her promise me at the beginning of this year to call me if she needed anything."

Crossing his arms, he wedged his hip against the counter. "Why weren't you two close? Is it because you're half sisters?"

"We didn't grow up together." Britt traced the dingy grout lines on the tiled countertop. "My mother was a drug addict and lost custody of us when we were little. My father's family took me in, but they didn't want Leanna. She went to foster care."

"Your father?"

She shrugged her shoulders, hoping to convey everything, knowing it conveyed nothing at all. "Do you want to search the rest of the place?"

He pushed off the counter and returned to the living room in a few steps. He pulled the cushions off the couch and held up a quarter. "Payback for taking care of her bills and rent."

He tossed it to her, and she caught it in one hand. "My sister doesn't have to reimburse me. I just want her back."

He continued to go through Leanna's belongings in the living room, flipping through her pieces of modern art. "These aren't half-bad. They convey a range of deep emotions—rage, terror, hopelessness."

"You see all that in those swishes of dark, heavy strokes of paint?"

"Must be my Russian heritage." He twisted his mouth into a smile—of sorts. "Anything else you can tell me about this room? Nothing missing from the last time you were here?"

"Not that I can tell. You think someone searched her place?"

"They may have done that before you or the police got here. It's a good thing she hid that note in her bills. I guess she was pretty sure nobody would want to look through those."

"Nobody but me." Britt caught her breath. "Maybe that's why she put the napkin with her gas bill. Leanna knew I'd grab all that stuff and take care of it for her. She put it someplace where she could be sure I'd find it."

"If Sergei's people never saw Tatyana's note, maybe they don't know anything about it. Although you can bet if Tatyana and Lee were close, they noticed."

Britt clasped her hands together. "Oh, God. I hope Leanna got out of Dodge on her own, sensing danger. But why won't she call me?"

"Did the police ever ping her phone?"

"Turned off. My sister used cheap burner phones anyway. She was always calling me from a different number."

Alexei gave the living room a last look before heading to the back of the apartment. He poked his head into the empty bathroom, where a lone towel was hanging unevenly on a rack. "Anything in here?"

"No, and the police clung to that fact." She nudged him out of the way, liking the feel of his solid shoulder beneath her hands. She yanked open the medicine cabinet above the sink. "All cleared out. Nothing in the shower. As if some…kidnapper couldn't have swept all her toiletries into a plastic bag and hauled them out of here."

"Same story in the bedroom?" Alexei jerked his

thumb over his shoulder at the final room in the dinky apartment, already making his way toward it.

"There are no suitcases." She followed him into Leanna's bedroom. "But honestly, I don't even know if Leanna had any suitcases."

He flung open the slatted closet doors, and the empty hangers swayed on the wooden rod. Grabbing a handful of clothing on the other side, he pulled them forward for a closer look.

"These aren't all the clothes she had, right? I mean, most women—" he released the clothes and they rustled and whispered back into place "—have a lot more than this in their closets."

As she stood beside Alexei, relishing his shoulder wedged against hers, drinking in the way his dark stubble outlined his lean jaw, a horrible thought hit her right between the eyes. What if he had someone in his life? A wife? A girlfriend with a bunch of clothes?

"Sh-she wore a lot of different outfits with quirky accessories—hats, scarves." Britt tipped back her head and squinted at the shelf above the hangers. "I don't see any of that stuff here."

Alexei stepped back, and she was able to think again without all that masculinity crowding her. She didn't even know who or what Alexei Ivanov was. After her internet search for him this morning, she was pretty sure he wasn't a photographer living in Algeria or a boxer. He was probably FBI, and she planned to ask to see his badge or credentials or whatever before she traveled much further down this rabbit hole with him.

He sat on the edge of the bed and yanked open the single nightstand drawer. He reached inside and held up his find, letting several connected foil packs of condoms unfold from his fingertips. "Would a woman take off with her boyfriend without these?"

"Exactly." The sight of Alexei brandishing an accordion of condoms did funny things to her insides, so she charged forward to prove otherwise, hovering over his shoulder to peek into her sister's drawer. She wished she hadn't.

"And those?" She jabbed her finger at the sex toys stuffed in the drawer. "A woman wouldn't take off with her boyfriend without packing *those*."

"I guess not." Alexei's eyebrows formed a V over his nose as he tilted his head to the side.

Britt nudged the drawer shut with her knee and brushed her hands together. "I think we pretty much put to rest the boyfriend story, although I'm hoping she hightailed it out of here on her own. Of course, that brings me back to the question of why she hasn't contacted me. She has to know I'd be worried."

"Did worrying you bother her before?" Alexei pushed up from the bed and whipped back the covers.

"Not really. Why are you doing that? What are you looking for?"

He flicked the covers back into place. "Bloodstains."

Britt sucked in a breath, and she plopped down on the edge of the bed. "If somebody did take Leanna, they grabbed her somewhere else. There was nothing out of place here when the manager let the police in. If there had been, the cops would've taken my concerns more seriously."

"Or they snatched her from this apartment and cleaned up after themselves." He dropped a heavy hand on her shoulder. "I'm sorry about that bloodstains comment. I forget sometimes I'm talking to Leanna's sister. I'm not used to working with...civilians."

"Who are you used to working with?" She looked up and locked eyes with him.

His hand tightened on her shoulder when the dead bolt clicked from the living room. He leaned toward her, his warm breath stirring her hair as he whispered in her ear, "It's someone with a key. Into the closet."

She froze, and Alexei had to grab her arm and pull her off the bed. He hustled her in front of him to the closet and propelled her inside. He closed the door, drawing a gun from his jacket pocket.

He always had it with him—and right now she couldn't be happier.

He gave her a gentle push to the back of the closet and arranged Leanna's clothes around her. As Britt inhaled her sister's signature musky perfume, she almost doubled over from the pain in her gut.

She must've emitted some scared-animal sound because Alexei put his finger to his lips. Then he crouched among the folds of Leanna's clothing and widened the space between two of the slats with his thumb and forefinger.

The front door slammed, and she jerked. She nestled in closer to Alexei's body, his warmth shoring her up. Her new position also gave her a view of Leanna's bedroom.

She took shallow breaths as she listened to shuffling noises from the other room. Could it be the apartment manager checking on something?

Heavy footsteps trudged down the short hallway, and a man burst into the bedroom.

Britt's fingers bit into the leather of Alexei's jacket when she recognized Jerome.

He flung himself across the bed and heaved out one terrible sob. "Lee, I'm so sorry."

ALEXEI DRILLED A knuckle into Britt's hip as he watched the bartender from last night thrash and moan on the bed. Just because Britt knew Jerome, there was no reason for her to reveal herself to him—and no reason at all for her to out Alexei.

But Britt kept as still as one of those shoes on the closet floor.

Jerome dragged a pillow over his face, wrapping his arms around it. His body convulsed with his sobs, and then, apparently spent, he knocked the pillow aside and stared at the ceiling.

Alexei's jaw ached from clenching his teeth, so he widened his mouth, shifting his lower jaw from side to side. He'd better relax. Who knew how long Jerome would gaze at the popcorn on the ceiling. He might even dissolve into another crying jag.

When Alexei realized he was still poking his knuckle into the curve of Britt's hip, he stretched out his fingers and smoothed them over the spot. He had to be more careful with Britt. He wasn't with his sniper teammates on this assignment. He kept making insensitive comments about Leanna and then would feel twenty shades of guilt as he watched the color drain from her face.

If he had to be stuck in a closet cheek to cheek with someone for hours, he preferred Britt to any one of his sniper teammates—even Slade, who smelled damned good most of the time.

After another five minutes of contemplation, Jerome

rolled off the bed. He wiped his face with the hem of his T-shirt. Then he smoothed out the covers and plumped up the pillow before placing it back at the head of the bed.

He took a look around the room, and Britt pressed against Alexei's shoulder when Jerome's gaze lit on the closet.

Alexei coiled his already-tense muscles. If Jerome approached their hiding place, Alexei would have to take him down before he could identify him or Britt. He had no clue what Jerome's little performance meant, but Alexei wasn't going to take any chances—not with Britt's safety.

Jerome patted the sides of his short Afro and exited the room. A minute later the front door opened and closed, and the key scraped in the lock.

Still, Britt didn't move a muscle.

Alexei shifted his position. "He's gone."

Britt collapsed against the clothes. "What the hell was that all about? Do you think Jerome killed Leanna? Is that what he's sorry for?"

Pushing open the closet doors, Alexei took a deep breath. Even the stale air of the apartment trumped the cloying scent of perfume that overwhelmed him in the closet.

"I don't know." He waved a hand at the made-up bed. "Do you get the feeling this isn't his first trip to this apartment?"

"Oh, yeah. This is some kind of ritual for him. The act seemed to calm him, as if it satisfied his need to expunge his guilt."

Alexei's eyebrows shot up. "Looked like he was crying on the bed to me."

She shrugged as she ran her hands along her sister's clothing, as if straightening out the folds for her return. "I'm a psychologist in the real world, a marriage-family-child counselor."

"Which is why you were able to take off however much time you needed to do your sleuthing. And where do you practice? You never told me where you lived, although I'd assumed it wasn't LA."

"Charlotte, North Carolina—and you never told me a lot of things about yourself." She snapped the closet door closed.

He moved away from her and his desire to run his fingers through the soft strands of her hair. "Do you think the guilt Jerome was...expunging is a result of murder?"

"I don't know. Would a murderer want to be caught rolling around on his victim's bed, spreading his DNA? And what would his motive be? Leanna mentioned a bartender once or twice as being a nice guy—nothing more."

"Maybe that's your motive." Alexei moved into the living room and lifted the edge of the blind to survey the walkway in front of Leanna's front door. "All clear."

"You mean, he was hoping for something more than friendship and Leanna wanted to keep it platonic?"

"It happens." *Must happen to Britt all the time.*

"Then Leanna's disappearance didn't have anything to do with Sergei's family, the Tattle-Tale or Tatyana."

"You sound...disappointed."

"Disappointed that my sister was murdered by a love-struck bartender instead of Russian sex traffickers? I just want her home safe. I want to hear from her. I want to know she's okay." Britt's voice hitched on the last word, and she covered her face with both hands, her blond hair spilling over her wrists.

"I know. I say stupid things sometimes. I have no tact. The typical blunt Russian." Alexei rubbed a circle on her back. "But whatever happened to your sister, I'm going to help you figure it out."

She peeked at him through her fingers. "Even if it has nothing to do with your investigation?"

"Even then. What's Jerome's last name? I can start by checking him out."

"It's Carter. Jerome Carter." She swirled her finger in the air. "Are you going to look him up on your magic phone that will immediately spit out his name, rank and serial number?"

"Maybe." He took a turn around the room. "Let's get out of here before any more surprise visitors show up. Did we leave everything as we found it?"

"We didn't disturb anything, but I don't know if we can say the same about Jerome. What was he doing in here before he came into the bedroom? I heard some rustling noises like paper being shuffled around."

"Paper." His gaze darted around the room and stumbled over Leanna's easel. The dark, tumultuous painting now had a white corner. "Looks like he disturbed the painting on the easel."

In three steps he crossed the room to the window and lifted the corner of the heavy paper. "There's another painting beneath this one."

As he held the corners of the top painting, Britt reached over him and squeezed open the clips holding it to the easel. Alexei tugged the paper, and it peeled away from the easel, revealing another, much different piece of art beneath it.

A young woman from the waist up, nude, her arms crossed over her breasts, stared back at him with dark, fathomless eyes. Alexei's eye twitched, and his left hand curled into a fist.

"Oh, that's different from her usual."

"Do you see that?" He traced his finger along a tattoo on the underside of the woman's forearm. "A snake curled around the letter *B*."

"Not your typical hearts and butterflies."

"I know that tattoo."

"You do? What is it?"

"It's the sign of the Belkin crime family, and this woman is their slave. This is Tatyana."

Chapter Four

Britt ducked closer to the painting, her hand to her throat. "A tattoo? They tattoo the women who work for them?"

Alexei almost stopped himself from correcting Britt. Why did he always have to drag her onto the dark side where he resided? Then he shook his head. She never once asked him for protection, and if they were going to find out what happened to Leanna, she had to know the whole ugly truth.

"Maybe I wasn't clear before, Britt. Tatyana doesn't work for the Belkins. She's part of their sex network. They pay her in room and board and drugs."

"And those women at the Tattle-Tale?"

"The waitresses and dancers work and get paid just like you, but it wouldn't surprise me if Sergei was using the Tattle-Tale as a feeder system for the sex ring."

She released the clip at the top of the easel and tugged at the corner of the portrait. "I'm taking this with me. Tatyana and Leanna must've been friends. She probably told my sister about the trafficking."

"Putting Leanna's life in danger." Alexei refused to discuss whether or not he believed Britt's sister was already dead. He had no doubt the Belkins would murder

Leanna for her knowledge, but she may have been able to slip away before they got their chance.

As to why Leanna hadn't contacted her older half sister and told her everything? Britt seemed to have romanticized her relationship with Leanna into something it clearly wasn't. If he wanted to give Leanna the benefit of the doubt, which he gave anyone, maybe she was protecting Britt. But disappearing without a trace was not the way to do it.

Britt knelt on the floor and rolled up the painting. "If Belkin's people did search Leanna's apartment, or… packed her things to make it look like she'd gone of her own free will, they missed this painting. There's no way they would've left this here for the police or anyone else to find, would they?"

"No, especially with that tattoo prominently displayed, but that means Jerome knows something, as well. He definitely looked at this painting before he came into the bedroom for his breakdown." He put out his hand to help her up.

"Thanks." She tucked the rolled paper under her arm. "I'm going to get to know Jerome better tonight."

"Is that a good idea?" Alexei scratched his jaw. "We don't know anything about him."

"Yet. You were going to use your resources to investigate him, right?"

"Yes."

"And while I'm at it, I'm going to get to know you better, too, Alexei Ivanov. I know you're not an artist or a boxer."

Of course Britt had checked him out. She wasn't stupid, or particularly trusting…despite her angelic looks and her halo of blond hair.

"You should know by now you can trust me, or Sergei would've fired you before your shift tonight."

"Oh, I'm pretty sure I can trust you, but can you trust me?"

He narrowed his eyes, noticing for the first time that Britt's pretty face included a stubborn chin. "What does that mean?"

"I offered to help you, too, but I have to know who you are and why you're investigating the Belkins if it's not the sex trafficking. And if you don't tell me—" she dragged Leanna's keychain from the front pocket of her jeans and dangled it in front of his face "—I'm going to have to complain to Sergei about a suspicious man who comes to the club by himself and doesn't even watch the dancers."

He raised an eyebrow as humor and annoyance battled in his face. "You're kidding."

"I'm not kidding. You know everything about me and what I'm doing here, and you just keep tossing out these tantalizing hints. If we're gonna be a team, I don't want to be kept in the dark."

"You do realize that if you mention me to Sergei, I'll have to out you, too."

She snorted, her delicate nostrils flaring. "You wouldn't do that and put me in danger."

Alexei studied her face, his gaze moving from her dark green eyes to her resolute jawline. He'd prided himself on playing it close to the vest, but his protective instincts must've been on full display. "Pretty sure of yourself, huh?"

"Oh, yeah. I work with people every day, their deepest, darkest feelings all out there in the room between us."

"What if I told you you'd be compromising national security if you told Sergei about me?"

"I'd tell you that you'd better start talking."

As BRITT SAT across the dinner table from Alexei, she ripped a roll in half and dredged one piece in the small plate of olive oil between them.

She wouldn't really have exposed him to Sergei, and he probably knew that—at least she hoped he did. If Alexei had decided to tell her his secrets, he was doing so because he wanted to. The man across from her wouldn't allow himself to be forced into anything.

She held up the bread, dripping oil, and asked, "Why'd you choose this place for dinner?"

"Long Beach is far enough away from Hollywood to ensure we won't run into anyone from the club, close enough to get you into work on time, and I heard the Italian food was good here."

"You seem to be in a talkative mood, so I'd better strike while the iron is hot. Is Alexei Ivanov your real name?"

"Guilty." He held up one hand.

"Are you FBI, CIA, DEA?" She ticked off each acronym on her fingers. "I've run out."

"None of the above. I'm a US Navy SEAL sniper."

She widened her eyes. "That's not what I expected to hear."

"If it makes you feel better, I'm here under the auspices of all those other agencies and more. The work I'm doing here is for a task force on terrorism."

Britt wiped her mouth on the napkin and took a gulp of water. This was heavier than she'd expected. "The Belkins are terrorists?"

"Not exactly." He flicked the side of his water glass with his fingernail and the ice tinkled. "We have reason to believe they're working with terrorists—it wouldn't be the first time."

"They're working with terrorists *and* they're sex traffickers. Anything else?"

"I'm sure there's more. The Belkins are a crime family. Back in Russia, criminals and terrorists are usually natural enemies. The majority of crime families are Russian, and the majority of terrorists in Russia are Chechen—no love lost there. But here?" He spread his hands.

"Anything goes if it's profitable?"

"Exactly." He tapped his head. "You're a smart woman, Britt. It's going to get you in trouble."

"Don't worry about me." She brushed some crumbs from her fingertips. "How do you hope to prove this link between the Belkin family and terrorists?"

"We have to catch them in the act—meetings, payments, exchanges. If the Belkins are smuggling women into the US to work in their clubs and then trafficking them, they might also be helping the terrorists get their people into the country. If the Belkins are dealing in arms, they might be supplying those weapons to the terrorists. We only have our suspicions at this point, no proof."

The waiter delivered their lasagna. "Anything else?"

They both declined, and when the waiter left, Britt pushed her plate aside and crossed her arms on the table. "And I suppose you can't just call the LAPD or the sheriff's department to raid the clubs."

"They keep everything legal on the surface. Those women at the clubs? They're just topless dancers, nothing illegal about that. If someone is paying them for sex, the police can bust them on pandering charges, but Sergei, or rather his father, is too smart to let that happen. The women they get over here from Russia are too afraid to come forward, or they're drugged. In a lot of cases, their families are at risk back home in Russia."

"Tatyana must've trusted Leanna enough to tell her what was going on."

"And put her in danger."

"Leanna probably encouraged Tatyana without realizing how serious it all was."

He aimed his fork at her food. "Are you going to eat that?"

"I ate too much bread." She hunched forward over her crossed arms. "If I can find some proof of the trafficking in the club, that'll help you, right?"

"You're not going to find proof of that. Don't even try, but if you can find out who Tatyana is and where she is now, that would help." He reached out and grabbed her wrist as she pulled her plate toward her. "Discreetly."

"I'm a therapist. I'm the definition of discretion."

He released her wrist. "I'm going to be at the club tonight."

"Do you think that's a good idea?" She jabbed at the thick layer of cheese smothering her lasagna, hoping that wasn't jealousy that just flared in her chest. "A single guy at a club like that—two nights in a row?"

"I have to start making contacts." He plunged his fork into his lasagna. "Don't tell me you don't have any lonely male clients. Going to strip clubs is not exactly a social event for some men."

"Yeah, I guess I have a few clients who frequent nudie clubs and hookers." *But none of them look like you.*

"Men in town for business. Newly divorced men. All types, I'm sure."

Her gaze darted to the third finger of his left hand and nothing had changed. He didn't even have a tan line there. "Has that ever been you?"

"Going to strip clubs by myself?"

"Newly divorced."

"Never married."

Nodding, she pressed her lips together to squash out her smile.

"Never wanted to get married—not with the job I have."

Now she didn't need to try. Her happiness at his first declaration evaporated after his second. "I'm pretty sure tons of military guys are married, even navy SEALs who are deployed. I know that for a fact since I volunteer to work with PTSD survivors."

"That's admirable." The customary tightness of his jaw relaxed, and his blue eyes almost sparkled. "I have a teammate, a friend, Miguel, who went through the wringer when he was captured by enemy forces. He's dealing with a lot of the ramifications of his imprisonment."

"Is he married?"

"Yeah, just got married. Has a son."

"I rest my case."

"You had a case? I know a lot of military men are married, but it's not for me."

If she had any appetite for her meal, she'd just lost it completely. "We'd better head back up north. I don't want to be late for my shift."

Ten minutes later, Britt stepped outside the restaurant and lifted her face to the sea-scented fog that had rolled in from the Pacific. She and Alexei had arrived separately again, and now she knew why as she watched him straddle a motorcycle.

After adjusting his helmet, he lifted his hand in goodbye and roared out of the parking lot. As she watched the taillight of his bike get sucked into the fog, she straightened her spine and marched to her car.

Whether Alexei Ivanov was marriage material or not was no concern of hers. She'd never met a man yet who wanted to stay. Why would Alexei be any different?

BRITT SMILED AT Jerome and then dropped her eyelashes, trying to hide the pity in her eyes. She didn't believe for a minute that Jerome had anything to do with Leanna's disappearance.

Apparently, Alexei didn't either since he'd revealed at dinner that Jerome had been honorably discharged from the army and had never been in trouble with the law. They had no reason to suspect him…but Britt still wanted to know what the scene in Leanna's apartment meant.

Jerome swiped the bar with a cloth for about the tenth time since she'd been standing there and glanced over his shoulder at the back of the club. "Have you seen Sergei tonight?"

"No. Why?"

Jerome licked his lips. "Ah, just wanted to confirm some supply orders with him."

Britt shrugged. "I'm sure he'll come in later. Doesn't he usually?"

"Onto the floor of the club later, but he's typically

in his office before the club opens." On his final swipe, Jerome knocked the condiment tray, and two maraschino cherries jumped from their container and rolled on the counter.

Plucking them up by their stems, Britt dangled them close to her lips. "Can't use these in the drinks now, right?"

"Knock yourself out."

She pulled the cherries off their stems with her teeth and then spun around to continue setting up the tables.

Jerome had better lose those jitters before he talked to Sergei and aroused his suspicions. She wished she could assure Jerome that his after-hours foray into the club last night had been wiped clean from the video footage, but she couldn't do that without giving up Alexei.

Jessie was the first one in again, and she helped Britt with the setup.

As Britt handed Jessie a candle, she asked, "Have you gotten up the courage to ask Sergei for an audition yet?"

"As a matter of fact, I asked him last night since he seemed to be in such a good mood."

"And?"

"And I'm going to shake my stuff for him after closing time tonight."

Britt touched Jessie's arm. "Be careful."

"Really?" Jessie snorted. "I can handle a guy like Sergei. Besides, Irina's sticking around, too."

"That's good." Although she didn't trust Irina either, Britt squeezed Jessie's arm. Was she one of the Belkins? She'd forgotten to ask Alexei.

"What was the name of the dancer who quit, anyway?" Britt held her breath, expecting the worst. She hadn't wanted to ask before because she was afraid Leanna had lied to her once again about not stripping anymore.

"The dancer who quit? They come and go." Jessie flicked her long fingernails in the air. "I think the last one who left was Tatyana or something Russian like that. Maybe Natalya. Is that Russian? I can't keep them straight."

Britt clenched her jaw to keep it from falling open. "I think it's Russian. Why did Tatyana quit?"

"Who knows? Left over four months ago. Scared little mouse who didn't belong on the stage." Jessie smoothed her skirt over her curvy hips. "You ready to have your socks knocked off, Sergei?"

Britt froze. She didn't have to turn around to know Sergei was right behind her. His spicy cologne invaded her nostrils, invaded her space.

How much of their conversation had he heard?

"I'm ready for socks to be knocked off, Jessie." He put his hand on Britt's shoulder and she jumped. "You ready to knock socks off, too?"

Britt plastered a smile on her face and twisted her head over her shoulder. "I think I already told you—I'm no dancer. I prefer to be on this side of the stage."

"Maybe you're right. Russians—" he snapped his fingers above his head and stomped his feet "—are natural dancers. Most of our dancers here, Russian."

"The Tattle-Tale Club is hardly the Bolshoi." Britt placed her last candle on the table and felt Sergei's stillness behind her.

She turned to face him and a cold dread seeped into

her flesh as she met his flat, dark eyes. Sergei didn't like to be mocked.

"I—I'm just kidding. The women I saw last night are quite good, and the guys loved them."

Sergei's thin lips stretched into a smile that didn't reach his fathomless eyes. "Tattle-Tale has only the best. Maybe not Bolshoi, but Bolshoi of topless dancers, eh?"

Jessie poked him in the chest. "And I'm gonna show you this American girl can outdance any Russian chick. C'mon, Sergei. You've had a few Russian women in here who had absolutely no stage presence."

Britt's face ached from the fake smile and now a pain lanced her gut as she waited for Jessie to drop the other shoe.

"Ha! Who is that? All Tattle-Tale dancers beautiful girls."

"Sergei." Jerome broke into their circle, waving some receipts. "I need to talk to you about a couple of orders."

"Jerome is all business. That's what I like. You two—" he wagged his finger between Britt and Jessie "—back to work."

Britt didn't breathe until she'd slammed the ladies' room door behind her. Hunching over the sink, she stared into the mirror. Had Sergei known she and Jessie had been talking about Tatyana? Had Jerome interrupted the conversation to stop it?

Jerome must know something about Tatyana. He'd seen Leanna's painting of the woman.

Maybe she and Jerome could pool their resources and help each other. He'd definitely interrupted that conversation just when Jessie was going to mention Tatyana, revealing that the two of them had been discussing her.

She did not want to get on Sergei's radar as someone interested in Tatyana. Look where it had gotten Leanna.

The customers rolled into the club, repeat clientele and groups of men and some couples and some loners—including Alexei.

Jessie had his table again, but Britt would have to manage at least one visit before the night was over.

During a particularly dead set, Britt parked herself next to the bar on Jerome's end. She watched him retrieve a couple of bottles of beer from the fridge and then put her hand over his when he set them on her tray.

"Jerome, do you know where that dancer Tatyana went?"

He didn't even meet her eyes as he poured vodka into two shot glasses. "Leave it."

Ducking her head close to his, she whispered, "You do know something, don't you?"

He cinched her wrist, his fingers damp from the vodka bottle. "Are you looking for your sister?"

She jerked her hand away, knocking over a shot glass. "How did you know?"

"Lee showed me your picture." He whipped a towel from his waistband and mopped up the vodka on the tray. "You'd better hope she didn't show anyone else."

"Can you help me? We can help each other."

"Not here." His gaze darted to the left and right. "When the club closes, meet me in front of Rage. You know it? It's on Sunset."

"I'll find it."

Jerome replaced the vodka. "Keep moving."

Britt hoisted her tray and delivered the drinks. She'd have to get word to Alexei before he left.

He couldn't come with her. He wouldn't want Jerome to ID him as anything other than a devoted fan of topless dancers.

A short while later, Britt tapped Jessie on the shoulder. "You look busy, and I'm a little slow. Do you want me to take a couple of tables at the stage for you?"

"That would be great. I don't want to wear myself out before my big audition tonight." Jessie pointed to the other side of the stage from where Alexei was sitting. "You can take those few on that side."

"Will do." Britt headed to the opposite side. Let Jessie think she misunderstood her.

She waited on the table next to Alexei's and then sidled up next to his. She smiled and batted her lashes. "I'm meeting Jerome at some bar or club on Sunset after closing time."

He nodded. "No, you're not."

"He already knows who I am." She scribbled something on her notepad. "He knew right from the start. Leanna showed him my picture."

He swore under his breath. "You need to get out of here. Quit."

"That's not going to happen. He knows something, and he's willing to tell me." She tipped her head toward the stage. "Someone wants your attention."

He couldn't stop her without making a scene, so he hunched over the table and tipped the dancer.

Did he have to try to fit in so convincingly?

She hadn't even taken his drink order, but she'd seen the empty shot glasses on his table and the glass of water. She suspected that he dumped some of his vodka in the water glass to keep his head clear.

When she returned to the bar, Jerome waved her on

to the other bartender. Was he afraid she'd start asking him more questions?

The next time she returned to Alexei's table, she included a note with *Rage* written on his cocktail napkin.

She placed the shot glass brimming with vodka on the napkin and smiled. "But don't show yourself. We're meeting in front, but I don't know if we're going inside. Do you know the place?"

"I don't, but I'll be there before you. Don't go anywhere with him."

"I won't." She took the cash he held out. "Enjoy the show—but not too much."

She hurried away from his table. Why had she said that? He was going to get the wrong impression of her, which was that she found him devastatingly attractive, and the only topless woman she wanted him ogling was her.

Nope, that was the right impression, all right.

The next time she turned around from the bar, Alexei was gone. Just as well. Maybe she'd see him at Rage.

She and Jerome avoided each other, too. In fact, this whole club was becoming a minefield.

Closing time couldn't come soon enough.

As the club emptied out, Sergei emerged from his office and smacked the bar. "Jerome, you take off early tonight. Irina and I stay for audition, and we'll close up."

"Are you sure?" Jerome's eyebrows collided over his nose. "I don't have a problem closing."

"I know you don't. We got this one."

Jerome shrugged but the crease remained across his forehead. He finished what he was doing and left the rest for Sergei.

As Britt brought up the last of the candles to the bar,

Sergei smoothed his finger on a lock of her hair and then wrapped it around his finger.

"You want to stay and watch audition, Barbie Doll? Maybe you learn something."

Her breath hitched in her throat, but she managed to turn her lips into a smile. "No, thanks. I'll leave the dancing to Jessie."

She inclined her head to escape.

His grip tightened on her hair for a split second, and then he released it. "Serve yourself."

"It's 'suit yourself.'" She smacked her pad of paper on top of the bar and wiggled her fingers at Jessie. "Good luck."

"Thanks, sweetie."

Britt slipped through the back door and leaned against it for a few seconds, taking deep breaths of gar-bage-scented air. She preferred it to the air in the club.

Something moved to her right, and she jumped.

The homeless guy from the day before held out his hand. "Any spare change?"

She dug a couple of bucks of her tip money from her purse and thrust them at him. "Here you go."

"Thank you, ma'am. I'm Calvin."

"Nice to meet you, Calvin. I'm Barbie. Take it easy out here."

"You, too."

She loped down the alleyway and hopped into her car. Maybe Jerome had information that Alexei could use, information he didn't know what to do with on his own.

Britt looked up the directions to Rage on her phone and joined a line of cars in the late-night traffic. From what she knew about this city, parking wouldn't be easy to find on the Strip even at this hour.

She drove around the block and then headed down a side street, finally parallel parking in front of an apartment building. She squinted at the sign proclaiming permit parking only and shrugged. If she got a citation, she'd put it down to the price for Jerome's information.

Tugging at her short skirt, she strode down the sidewalk toward the lights and hubbub of Sunset Boulevard, her tennis shoes a welcome relief from the heels she wore on the job. She turned left at the corner and then ran to make the light to cross the street.

Halfway into the crosswalk, she spied Jerome leaning against Rage's exterior. A steady flow of pedestrians crisscrossed in front of him, most heading home after a night of partying but some still looking for action.

Was Rage still open? Did Jerome believe they could talk under cover of the noise and crowd inside? Alexei didn't want her going anywhere with Jerome, but they couldn't very well stand out on the sidewalk and discuss a Russian crime family—if Jerome even knew that was what he was dealing with.

She reached the other side of the street and walked toward Jerome, who'd shoved off the building. They made eye contact.

A bunch of people staggered out of the bar behind Jerome, hanging on each other and laughing. The surge of humanity moved toward him and engulfed him, one of the party even grabbing Jerome's hand to drag him along for the hilarity.

Jerome broke away from her and stumbled against a man coming up behind him. Jerome turned and jerked, as if exchanging words with the man.

Britt picked up her pace, the group from the bar now impeding her progress. Somebody screamed, and Britt pushed past the last woman in the group, her heart pounding out of her chest.

When she had a clear view of Jerome again, he was on his knees, clutching his midsection. A rush of adrenaline shot through Britt, and she careered forward on wobbly legs.

Someone else screamed, and by the time Britt reached Jerome, he had fallen on his side, blood soaking the front of his shirt.

Britt dropped to her knees, pressing her hands against Jerome's tattered, bloody shirt. "Call 911. Somebody call 911."

She leaned forward, her nose almost touching Jerome's. "Who stabbed you?"

He parted his lips, and a trickle of blood and foam ran into his ear. "I loved her. I loved Lee. They killed her."

Chapter Five

"Walk past him, walk past him, walk past him." Alexei murmured the words like an incantation, but his spell failed.

He watched through narrowed eyes as Britt rushed to the fallen man and crouched beside him. The crowd around the victim ebbed and flowed—some scrambling away from the mayhem, and others circling in morbid fascination. A siren wailed somewhere in the distance, but too close for comfort or, at least, Britt's safety.

Alexei righted his bike and kicked up the stand with his boot. Traffic on the Strip had slowed to a crawl—a combination of the bars closing and the commotion on the sidewalk outside of Rage.

He edged his motorcycle into the traffic and then pulled an illegal U-turn in the middle of the street. He rolled to a stop in front of the red curb and yelled, "Britt! Britt!"

She whipped her head around, her face a pale oval, her arms elbow-deep in Jerome's blood.

"Get away from him now. Get on the bike."

Britt was no longer the only person kneeling beside Jerome. A man had ripped off his shirt and had it bunched against Jerome's stomach. A woman stood on the curb waving her arms. The sirens' blare sounded closer.

Alexei got ready to park his bike and haul Britt away from the scene if necessary, but she staggered to her feet. She spun around, wiping her hands on her skirt. With jerky movements, she made her way to the curb just as the first emergency vehicle pulled to a stop behind his bike.

"Climb on the back and hold on. I'll give you my helmet in a minute." He dipped the bike to one side, and as soon as he felt Britt's arms around his waist, he gunned it.

He turned right off Sunset and headed for the hills—literally. The Hollywood Hills climbed up above the noise and madness of the street, and Alexei kept going until he reached an unpaved road that circled around the property of one of the big houses.

He cut the engine and pulled off his helmet. "Are you okay? You looked ready to faint back there."

"I—I'm fine. There was so much blood from his chest to his abdomen."

"Stabbed." Alexei climbed off the bike and held out his arm to support Britt. "Did they kill him?"

"He was still alive when I reached him. Then he lost consciousness. I don't know if he died or not." She covered her face with one bloodstained hand.

"Hop off. There's a place to sit on the log here. I don't think the homeowners will mind too much…as long as they don't see or hear us." He placed the helmet on the ground and took her arm.

She slid from the back of the bike and collapsed on the log, a sparkling view of LA below wasted on them. "It was horrible. I didn't even see who did it."

"It was a man who came up behind him. He used the partygoers as a cover. He probably stole Jerome's wallet for good measure to make it look like a robbery." He sat beside her on the log.

She choked. "Did he walk past me?"

"No. He ran into the street after he stabbed Jerome, dodging cars and ducking between them. I lost sight of him, and I think he may have gotten into a car that was part of the line of traffic on the street." He rubbed her back, feeling the ripples of fear still coursing through her body. "That's a good thing. He didn't know Jerome was meeting you. Didn't see you."

"How did they know he was there at that particular time?"

"Sergei probably had him followed from the Tattle-Tale. I'm sorry they attacked Jerome, but I'm glad you weren't with him."

"Do you think we can find out where the ambulance took him and check up on him?"

"We probably won't need to do that. A stabbing in the middle of the Sunset Strip? Even if it goes down as a street mugging, that's going to be news." He tucked a lock of hair behind Britt's ear. *Solnishka.*

"God, the blood." She rubbed her palms against her skirt. "I don't know how he could've survived that."

"I'm sorry you had to see it. It's the stuff of nightmares."

"He loved her, you know." A tear dropped from her lashes and rolled down her face.

"Your sister? Jerome spoke to you before he passed out?"

She dipped her head and more tears dripped off the

end of her jaw. "Yes. He told me he loved Lee. He told me something else, as well."

Alexei wedged a knuckle beneath her chin and tilted her head. "What did he say?"

"He told me they killed...Tatyana. That's why Leanna was so scared. She knew what they'd done."

Not a surprise, but why kill a woman about to make some money for you?

"I suppose he didn't say why Tatyana was murdered, did he? You weren't by his side that long before that man joined you, the one who took off his shirt." He cupped Britt's face with one hand, his fingers nestling in her hair.

"He didn't say. He told me he loved Lee and that they killed her. I thought he meant they killed Lee, but when I asked him, he said it was Tatyana they killed. I asked him if he knew what happened to Lee, but he lost consciousness at that point."

"Maybe he'll make it." Alexei didn't have much confidence Jerome would survive that attack. Sergei's guy would've made sure of that.

Britt pinned her hands between her bouncing knees. "Why do you think Sergei had Jerome killed? Do you think he knew about him and Lee?"

"If he did, he would've made a move on Jerome earlier. You said your sister's been missing a month?"

"Over a month." She hunched her shoulders. "Do you think Sergei heard me and Jerome or maybe saw us talking on camera?"

"Sergei would've had his guy wait for you, too. It must be something else Jerome did to set off Sergei's suspicions. I wonder what Jerome was doing in the club last night after hours."

"I think Jerome was worried that Sergei may have seen him on the footage from the night before because he seemed nervous when Sergei told him to leave early."

"Turns out Jerome had good reason to be nervous." He put his arm around Britt and drew her close. "I'll get you back to your car."

She grabbed his jacket in her fist. "Alexei, I'm… scared. I don't want to go back to my place tonight, not alone, anyway. Can you follow me home?"

"What if someone's watching your place?" He held up a hand when she gasped. "I'm not saying you're under their surveillance, but they just attacked Jerome, and you were ten feet down the sidewalk from him."

"I hope his attacker didn't recognize me." She folded her arms across her stomach.

He didn't want to send Britt back to her apartment by herself, but he didn't want to risk being seen with her if someone was watching her place. He had a solution that made perfect sense.

"Why don't you come to my hotel with me tonight? Nobody's going to be watching me, and nobody followed us up here."

"Wh-where are you staying?"

"Beverly Hills."

"Must be nice."

"Let's just say I'm setting up a certain persona—in order to make contact with the Belkins."

"Like some wealthy Russian businessman or something?"

"Something like that."

Her shoulders slumped forward as if she'd been holding her breath. "I appreciate the invitation, if it's not too much trouble for you to put me up in your hotel room."

"Not at all."

The only trouble for him would be keeping his hands to himself.

ALEXEI PUSHED OPEN the door of his room, and Britt tripped across the threshold with her mouth open. "This isn't a room. It's a suite."

"Yeah, I think all the rooms on this floor are suites. Feel free to make yourself at home."

He let the door slam behind him, and Britt jumped.

"I'm sorry. You're still on edge."

She shrugged out of his leather jacket, once more inhaling the scent that had made her feel safe as she clung to him on his motorcycle, and hung it on the back of a white upholstered chair.

Spreading her arms, she said, "I suppose it doesn't help that I look and feel like a wreck. It's a good thing you have a bike that you were able to park close to a side door. I don't think the doorman would've let me in looking like this."

"You look like that—" he sketched lines in the air with his finger "—because you came to a man's aid. Having said that, you do have blood on your skirt, blood smears on your blouse, and that helmet didn't do your hair any favors."

She put a hand to her head. "I'm almost afraid to look in the mirror."

"This hotel supplies plenty of big fluffy towels and so many toiletries in there I don't even know what they are." He waved his hand toward the other room. "I pretty much limit myself to the shampoo and the soap, so knock yourself out."

"What about clothes?" She plucked her white blouse,

stiff with Jerome's blood, out of the waistband of her skirt. "I can't exactly put these back on."

"In addition to those big fluffy towels, the hotel provides his and her bathrobes. I'm not a bathrobe kinda guy, so take your pick. That'll suffice for tonight at least."

She pointed to the door leading to the bedroom. "Through there?"

"Yeah, robe's in the closet." Alexei crossed the room to the writing table by the window. "While you're doing that, I'm going to try to find out some info on Jerome."

"I pray he makes it."

"Me, too."

Britt snapped the bedroom door behind her. Sagging against the wall, she covered her face with her hands. What if Sergei had the same man go after Leanna? When Jerome had said that they'd killed *her*, Britt had almost collapsed on top of him. Then he'd clarified that he meant Tatyana. Was that any better? Leanna had somehow become embroiled with Tatyana's problems and put her own life in danger.

That was so Leanna.

Buffeted by life's inconsistencies and cruelties, Leanna had a soft heart and always reached out to others in trouble. If she'd had half the compassion Leanna did, she'd have come to her sister's rescue a lot sooner.

Britt turned toward the mirrored closet and stumbled to a halt. She gagged at the blood smearing her clothes and even stuck in her hair, the night's terror crashing all around her again.

She toed off her shoes and yanked the skirt off over her hips. She practically ripped the buttons from her blouse in her haste to peel it from her body. She dropped it on top of the skirt and slid open the closet door.

Alexei's clothes rustled with the movement, and although she wanted nothing more than to run her hands through his things and press her face against the soft materials, she hung back. She'd wiped off most of Jerome's blood on her skirt, but the remains still stained her hands pink. She'd probably already gotten blood on his jacket when she'd climbed onto the back of his bike as the cops arrived.

Alexei had been right to get her out of there. She'd have a hard time explaining to Sergei why she'd been with Jerome after hours.

She yanked one of the terry-cloth robes from its hanger and trailed it on the floor behind her as she walked to the bathroom. She stood at the entrance to the bathroom, drinking in the black-and-white tiled floor, the step-down oval tub with Jacuzzi jets and the open shower with two showerheads facing each other. The whole setup gave her sinful ideas about the man in the other room, but she was here to heal and recover—not seduce.

She shimmied out of her underwear and snagged a towel neatly folded on a shelf beneath the vanity. As she draped it over the rack closest to the shower, she realized she had the option to heat the towel while she was showering. She flipped the switch on the warmer. She could get used to this.

She cranked on both showerheads for the hell of it and stepped between the dueling sprays.

Thank God the blood on her hands hadn't stained her flesh. It did leave a pink cast on the washcloth until she rinsed it out over and over.

She made generous use of the high-end products Alexei had dismissed, massaging the fragrant shampoo into her scalp. By the time she finished her shower, the knots between her shoulder blades had loosened and she'd stopped grinding her back teeth.

The towel rack worked, and she buried her face in the warm terry cloth, wishing she could melt away and forget the feel of Jerome's slick blood between her fingers. She finished drying her body and then wrapped her hair in the towel.

The lotion the hotel stocked was good enough for a face moisturizer, and she slathered it on her cheeks and down her throat. She ran the hair dryer over her hair, snuggled into the robe and faced the mirror—almost a new woman. Her eyes still looked like they'd seen a ghost—several ghosts.

She huffed out a breath and picked up her damp towel from the floor. When she returned to the bedroom, she kept her eyes averted from the big bed in the center of the room and swept up her soiled clothing, wrapping the skirt and blouse in the towel and tossing the bundle in a corner of the bathroom.

When she strolled into the other room, she almost turned right around when she saw the midnight blue of Alexei's eyes turn black.

"I have some bad news, Britt."

"Is it Jerome?"

"He didn't make it."

She sank to the edge of the sofa, the rosy flush of her shower turning ice-cold. "Are you sure?"

He tapped his laptop. "An online news website is reporting it as a murder. Man knifed to death for his wallet."

"Oh my God. Why? Why did they have to kill him?"

"He knew too much, like your sister." He held up one finger. "Not that I'm suggesting your sister met the same fate."

"If she didn't, where is she? Why did the Belkins kill Tatyana? They had her over here, had her working at one of their clubs. They had her exactly where they wanted her, right? She even had the tattoo. Why would they go through all that trouble to groom her only to murder her?"

Alexei clasped the back of his neck with one hand and stared out the window. "I've been asking myself those same questions. Tatyana must've threatened to escape, or maybe they just pegged her as a risk when she started communicating with Leanna. She represented some kind of threat to them."

"Poor Jerome. He lost the woman he loved, and then he lost his life. What do you think he had to be sorry about? Why that scene at Leanna's?"

"He probably regretted not being able to protect Leanna, especially if she came to him for help." His profile at the window seemed carved in stone.

And then it hit her. A man like Alexei would move heaven and earth to protect someone he loved. To be loved with that kind of intensity would be overwhelming, but then, Alexei had proclaimed himself immune to any kind of lasting love.

It must be love of country that motivated him. The navy had taken him off military duty for this assignment. They tagged him as the man for the job for some reason.

"I'm not sure where we go from here. Where I go from here."

He turned from the window and perched on the edge of the sofa next to her, his knee banging against hers. "Back to Charlotte. Back to your clients, who need you. Back to safety."

"Leanna needs me. I was never there for her. I abandoned her when Mom died. I was her big sister, and I should've stayed with her."

"You can't blame yourself for that. It wasn't up to you. How old were you when your mother died?"

"Ten. Leanna was seven."

"At ten, you weren't going to be the one making the decision where you or your sister wound up. Your father's people made their choice."

"It was a bad choice."

"It was cruel." He traced the tip of his finger along the curve of her ear. "But it's not your fault. Is that what you're doing in LA? You're trying to make it all up to Leanna?"

"I'm trying to find her. Who else but me?"

He shifted his hand to the back of her neck beneath her damp hair. "I'll do it. I'll try to find Leanna."

"You're here to find terrorists."

"One may lead me to the other."

She tipped back her head and studied the ceiling. "If I leave now, I'll feel like I'm giving up on my sister all over again."

"Don't make any decisions tonight. You've had a rough time."

"What did the news story say about Jerome?" She nodded toward his laptop, still open on the desk.

"The authorities don't know he's Jerome Carter yet. His killer took his wallet, I guess to make it look like a common street robbery. The story I read didn't give out much information—just that a man was knifed for his wallet and died of his injuries on the way to the hospital."

Britt curled her legs beneath her on the sofa. "Did the article mention any witnesses?"

"It didn't mention a mysterious blonde who was the first at the man's side and then disappeared, if that's what you're wondering. Did you get a good look at the guy? You could always phone in an anonymous tip."

"I didn't really see him. He came along at the tail end of a bunch of people coming out of Rage, but I don't think he was in the bar himself. Those people surged toward me, and I lost sight of Jerome for several seconds. When the people parted, I saw Jerome turn to face a man wearing a gray hoodie. Is that what others are saying to the police?"

"I didn't read any witness accounts. You can bet Sergei's guy is not going to be ID'd by anyone. The police aren't going to make any connection between Jerome and his place of work." Alexei stretched his arms over his head. "It's late. You should get some sleep. Take the bed in the other room."

"I don't want to kick you out of bed." She couldn't imagine any scenario where she'd kick Alexei out of bed. "I mean, kick you out of *your* bed...*the* bed."

He rescued her with a smile and patted the sofa. "This is fine for me. You're the one who had the traumatic night."

"Yeah." She splayed her hands in her lap, palms up. "I just washed the stains of a dead man's blood from these hands."

He traced the lines on her palm with his fingertip. "I wish I could read your palm and tell you everything was going to be okay, that you'll find Leanna and make amends."

"You've done a lot already." When he removed his finger from her palm, she rubbed her hands together, feeling the tingle of his touch. "I guess there's nothing left to do tonight but sleep."

He shot off the couch, all business. "I'll grab a pillow or two from the bed and a blanket from the closet. If you want something a little less bulky to sleep in, you can borrow one of my T-shirts."

"Okay, I might take you up on that." She uncurled her legs and walked to the bedroom. Pausing awkwardly at the door, she asked, "Do you need to get into the bathroom first?"

"I won't be long." He shut down his computer and breezed past her into the bedroom.

She sat on the edge of the bed as he grabbed a pillow and blanket and took them into the other room. Then he disappeared into the bathroom.

Once she heard the water running, she shed the robe and grabbed one of his T-shirts from the closet. She slipped it over her head and hugged the soft cotton around her nakedness. Even this small connection to Alexei made her feel safe.

Maybe he was right. She should quit the job at the Tattle-Tale and leave it to the US government to take down the Belkins—not that some nameless, faceless bureaucrat would give a damn about Leanna or Tatyana. But Alexei did. He cared.

She snuggled between the sheets of the king-size bed and flicked on the TV for company—it would have to do.

Alexei emerged from the bathroom, the edges of his

short dark hair flipping up with the dampness. He still had on his jeans and T-shirt, but he carried his motorcycle boots in one hand.

"You all set in here?"

"I'm going to fall asleep to the TV."

"I do the same thing. What are you watching?"

"An old comedy." She pointed the remote at the TV screen.

"I like that one, too." He hovered at the door. "Try to get a good night's sleep, Britt."

"You, too."

He pulled the door closed behind him, and she slumped against the pillows. Everything from his T-shirt to the bedsheets was freshly laundered, so she couldn't even revel in his masculine scent for company.

She traced over the lines of her palm as he had done, and her hand tingled in remembrance of his touch. If she left now, not only would she be giving up on Leanna but she'd also have to leave Alexei Ivanov forever.

And she wasn't ready to do that.

Chapter Six

The following morning, Britt peeked out of the bedroom door to find Alexei on his computer again. She tiptoed up behind him and peered over his shoulder. "Ariel? Is that your girlfriend?"

He jumped and slammed down the lid of his laptop. "Whoa. Sneaking up behind people like that is a good way to get your lights knocked out."

She blinked. "You mean you were ready to punch me in the face?"

"Instinct."

"Whew." She wiped her brow with the flick of her fingers. "Is that what they teach you in navy SEAL school?"

"Yeah, instinct."

He clearly had no intention of answering her question about Ariel. "Anything else in the news about Jerome?"

"His murder made the morning shows, and they identified him. Maybe he still had his phone, and they ID'd him that way or took his fingerprints, which would be on file with the army."

Britt snapped up the remote and turned on the TV. "Maybe Leanna will hear the news wherever she is, and it'll bring her out."

"Or drive her further underground."

She surfed the channels but had missed the local morning news shows, and a murder on the Sunset Strip hadn't made national news—yet.

Alexei opened his laptop again and presumably continued his communication with Ariel. "I'm going to order us some room service for breakfast, and then we'll take a car to your car. I don't want either of us riding on the bike without a helmet and risk getting pulled over. But first you need to get some clothes. You can't wear that skirt and blouse in the light of day."

"How am I going to go shopping?"

"If you didn't notice last night, this hotel has everything. There are a couple of clothing stores on the first level. Give me your size, and I'll pick up a dress for you—something simple so it won't matter if it's not a perfect fit."

"All right, but I'm going to have to go out this afternoon and buy another black skirt and white blouse to wear at the Tattle-Tale."

He twisted his head around. "So you decided to go back?"

"I sort of have to, at least for tonight's shift. How would it look if I quit or disappeared right after Jerome's murder?"

"What does it matter if you're on your way back to North Carolina?"

"That remains to be seen."

He lifted his shoulders. "I'm not going to tell you what to do, except to look at the breakfast menu so we can eat and get out of here."

And they did just that. Alexei showered while she

waited for the food to arrive. Then they ate, and she showered while he went downstairs to buy her a dress.

He came back with a casual loose-fitting blue dress that hit her right above the knee.

She twirled in front of the mirror on the toes of her sneakers. "Not bad."

"Looks good on you. Ready?"

Alexei ordered a car from his cell phone, and a driver picked them up in front of the hotel.

Britt didn't know the name of the street where she'd left her car, so she gave the driver the address of Rage.

The driver adjusted his rearview mirror. "A guy was killed over there last night."

Alexei squeezed her thigh. "We know. Terrible."

"Took the guy's wallet." The driver shook his head. "So not worth it, man. If someone wants my wallet, they can have it."

When they reached Sunset, Britt hunched forward in the back seat. "I think it's…that street. You can just drop us at the corner."

He let them out, and Britt started walking down the block, her heart pounding. "I don't see my car."

"Are you sure this is the street? Maybe it was the next one over."

"I know it's this street because of the signal at the intersection. The two blocks on either side of this one don't have a signal at Sunset."

Alexei cleared his throat and grabbed a pole with a street sign on it. "This street is permit parking only."

"Yeah, I know that. I didn't think I'd be leaving my car overnight. Where the hell is it, then?"

"You'll have to call the LA sheriff's department. They'll tell you where your car is, and you can pick it up." Crossing his arms, Alexei wedged his shoulder against the pole. "I'll get you another car to take you to the tow yard, and I'll get myself back to the hotel. Do you need money to get it out?"

"No." She kicked the pole. "I completely forgot I was parked illegally. You can't come with me?"

"Don't think it's a great idea for us to be seen together."

"I feel like I'm the other woman." She should be so lucky.

He tugged on a strand of her hair. "I'll wait with you while you call the police, and I'll call another car."

Fifteen minutes later as the share car pulled up to the curb, Britt clutched her cell phone, where she'd entered the name and address of the tow yard she'd gotten from the sheriff's department.

Alexei opened the back door of the car for her, and she placed her hand on his arm. "Will you be at the club tonight?"

"Yeah. I talked to a few guys last night, and I want to continue my progress with them. Besides, I don't want to leave you on your own there."

She curled her fingers into his flesh. "First Leanna, now Jerome. I'm not going to let them get away with this. Someone is going to have to pay."

She expected him to shrug off her fierce declaration, but he wedged his knuckle beneath her chin and tilted back her head, his dark blue eyes smoldering.

"Someone *is* going to pay if I have anything to say about it."

As she watched him from the back window of the car, she had the distinct feeling that Alexei had his own agenda.

STANDING BEFORE THE mirror in the dressing room for the dancers, Britt flattened her hands against her new black skirt and smoothed it against her thighs. Her gaze flicked away from her own reflection to the scene behind her—some of the dancers sniffling about Jerome's death, others hugging each other, and some of the women over it already and slipping into their barely there costumes.

Sergei had given a rousing give-'em-hell speech after announcing the murder of Jerome, telling the waitresses and dancers to get out on the floor and do their best because that was what Jerome would've wanted. Britt curled her lip at her image. She sincerely doubted that.

She turned away from the mirror, hands on her hips, and surveyed the chaotic scene before her. Still no sign of Jessie. Had she heard about the murder earlier and called in sick? Or had something happened at the rehearsal last night?

Britt's stomach rolled. When she took this job, she figured she'd poke around, maybe overhear a few choice conversations and collect enough evidence to either find Leanna or go to the police. She never imagined she'd land right in the middle of a human-trafficking ring with a Russian crime family working with terrorists.

She never imagined she'd meet a man like Alexei Ivanov either.

She tucked her purse between two others on the bench next to the dressing room door. Another waitress squeezed in beside her and wedged her bag among the line of purses.

Britt put her hand on the waitress's arm. "Amy, have you seen Jessie tonight?"

"She called in sick. Shannon is subbing for her shift."

"Because of Jerome?"

Shrugging her shoulders, Amy pushed out of the dressing room.

Britt followed Amy out to the bar, where Sergei had set up a tip jar with Jerome's picture taped to the rim. Nice of him to take up a collection for the family of the man he had murdered.

She grabbed a notepad from the stack next to the collection jar and nodded at the new bartender. "Hi, I'm Barbie."

He studied her from beneath a pair of bushy eyebrows and hesitated so long she thought he hadn't heard her. Then he held out his hand. "Stepan. You dancer?"

"No."

He immediately released her hand.

"I'm a waitress. Are you new, Stepan, or from one of the other clubs?"

His curious brows turned into suspicious ones as they created a V over his nose. "I work here and there. Wherever they need me."

Ah, a loyal Belkin follower. Stepan wouldn't be sneaking back into the club after hours or crying on a missing waitress's bed. Sergei had learned his lesson.

Alexei still hadn't been able to tell her why the Belkins had killed Jerome. They couldn't have known that he was in the club that night, because Alexei had cleaned that video. Had Jerome been up to other suspicious activity? Had they known about his connection with Leanna?

A chill raced down her arms. If having a connection to Leanna could get you murdered, what would Sergei do to Leanna's sister?

The doors had opened, and patrons began filling

the tables that bordered the stage. Britt's heart jumped every time she caught sight of a tall man with dark hair, but Alexei hadn't appeared with the first wave of customers.

At the bar on a drink run, Britt stationed herself next to Shannon, the waitress filling in for Jessie. "Did you talk to Jessie? Is she sick?"

"I didn't talk to her." Shannon rapped her knuckles on the mahogany of the bar. "Hey, Stepan. This margarita is supposed to be blended, not on the rocks. Redo."

Without a word, Stepan snatched the drink from the tray.

Shannon rolled her eyes. "He's no Jerome, is he?"

"That was so terrible. I still can't believe he was killed in that awful way." Britt busied herself by arranging the drinks on her tray. "D-do you think that's why Jessie took the night off?"

"I didn't think they were that close. Jerome kind of kept to himself."

Snapping fingers appeared between their faces, and Britt jerked back, almost stumbling against Sergei right behind her.

"No talking about Jerome. Didn't you hear me? We take up collection, but this is happy place for happy people."

"We weren't talking in front of the customers. Chill." Shannon hoisted her tray of drinks and pushed past Sergei.

Sergei glanced at Stepan, pointed to his own eye and then made his fingers into a gun, pointing it at Shannon's back.

When he caught Britt looking at him, Sergei raised

one shoulder. "She's a pain, that one. Don't ever be a pain, Barbie Doll."

"Hey, I'm just here to do my job." She grabbed her own drink tray. "By the way, how did Jessie do at her audition last night?"

Sergei splayed his fingers in the air and tipped his hand back and forth. "My socks still on."

Britt allowed herself a tight smile before escaping from his presence. Maybe Sergei told Jessie she wasn't good enough to be a dancer and Jessie left in a snit.

When Britt dropped her first order, she glanced toward the door and locked eyes with Alexei. She let out a breath. He was still alone. Was he hoping to make more contacts tonight? Did those contacts include Sergei?

Of course, Alexei didn't take a seat in her section. It made it that much harder to talk to him casually. Maybe he wanted her to stay away.

She needed to tell him about Sergei's response to Jerome's murder and that Jessie hadn't shown up for work, but maybe he didn't want to hear about all that. He hadn't come out here to investigate the Belkins' sex-trafficking operation. Her drama must be keeping him from his true purpose. Maybe Alexei was right and she should just go back to Charlotte.

If in the course of doing his job Alexei found Leanna, he'd tell her. He might even go out of his way a little to discover Leanna's whereabouts. She needed to let him do his job.

Alexei had sat at a table close enough to her own station that she had an excuse to make contact. Squeezing past his table, she knocked over his drink.

"I'm so sorry." She crouched next to the table, mopping the spill with some cocktail napkins. "Did you see the tip jar for Jerome on the bar?"

"No. That's big of him."

"Sergei doesn't want us talking about Jerome in this happiest of places on earth."

"I'll bet he doesn't. Anything else unusual tonight?"

"Jessie, one of the waitresses, auditioned for a place on the stage last night and she didn't come into work today."

"Was she close to Jerome?"

"I don't think so." She dropped a wad of soggy napkins on her tray. "One of the other women said Jerome hadn't been close to anyone...except Leanna, although nobody seemed aware of their relationship. How do you think Sergei knew about it?"

"We don't know if that's why he offed Jerome. It could be something else, like why Jerome was sneaking around here after hours. I cleaned one tape, but what if there were others and Sergei got an eyeful of Jerome on one of his nighttime visits to the club? We don't know what Jerome was doing here."

"I'd better get moving or the others are going to wonder why I'm polishing this table."

"I don't want you leaving here alone tonight. Tell me where you're parked, and I'll follow you home on my bike."

"I'm in the alley, but two businesses down from this one."

"Any trouble getting your car today?"

"Nope. I paid the tow yard, and they released my car."

"Okay. Be careful tonight, but I'm right here if you need me."

Britt finished the remainder of her shift with her heart in a warm bubble. She owed it to Alexei to get out of his way. He'd become preoccupied with protecting her, and although she had no complaints, he had his own job to do. He'd joined a couple of other men at their table, so she hoped he was making headway in his own investigation.

At the end of the night without even looking at Alexei's table, she knew he'd left. The room almost felt colder, her protective shell a flimsy thing.

Sergei and Irina had called it quits almost an hour ago and Stepan was shouting orders and ogling the dancers at the same time.

To escape the tyrant, Britt joined the dancers as they streamed into the changing room. She deserved to duck out early. What could they do, fire her? She would quit before that happened.

The purses crammed on the bench inside the dressing room must've reached critical mass, as several of them had fallen onto the floor, including hers.

Britt dropped to her knees and started shoveling items back into her purse—wallet, phone. Her breath hitched when she realized anyone could've gone through her things, but she kept her driver's license under the seat in her car, and she'd password-protected her phone, even though Alexei had been worried about the pictures on it.

Opening her purse wide, she bounced it a few times to redistribute the items. She bit her bottom lip, plunged her hand into her purse and rooted to the bottom of it. The receipt from the tow yard must've fallen out.

She tilted her head sideways and peered under the bench. She pinched one receipt between her fingertips, but it was too small to be the tow receipt, and it belonged to someone else.

She sat back on her heels, scanning the floor for the receipt. Then it hit her.

The receipt indicated the address where her car was parked when it had been towed. If the wrong person saw that, he'd know she'd been in the area where Jerome had been murdered.

She flattened her body against the carpeted floor for a better look under the bench.

"What are you doing down there?"

Britt twisted her head to the side, meeting one of the dancers' heavily lined eyes. "My purse fell off the bench, and I'm missing something."

"Money?"

"A receipt."

She shrugged and waved her fingers at the bags shoved against each other helter-skelter. "Maybe in someone else's purse. You should look."

Britt didn't want to bring any more attention to the receipt than she already had with the dancer, Gypsy, so she poked around in a few purses but didn't see her receipt in any of them.

"Find it?" Gypsy hitched her own purse over her shoulder.

"No. Maybe someone threw it away."

"Was it important?"

"Not really."

Gypsy swept out of the room and knocked the purse on the end of the bench to the floor. Britt sighed. Management needed to find a better place for purses, or maybe they did it on purpose to search their employees' bags.

She gathered the spilled contents of the purse and started shoveling the items back inside. A drawing on the back of a business card caught her eye, and she dragged it close with her finger for a better look.

She caught her breath and shot a quick glance over her shoulder at the two dancers talking in front of the mirror. She traced her finger over the snake wrapped around the letter *B*—the tattoo Tatyana had on her forearm—the sign of the Belkins.

She flipped the card over. The name and address of a tattoo parlor in Hollywood occupied the other side. Britt slipped the card in the pocket of her skirt.

If someone had taken her receipt, she could play the same game.

She placed the purse back on the bench. She'd find something else to do in the changing room and wait for the owner. She pulled out her phone and pretended to scroll through texts, but she didn't have to wait long.

One of the women chatting by the mirror pulled her blouse over her head. "I see you tomorrow night, Tracy."

She snagged the purse on the end and exited the dressing room with a wave to Britt.

Britt tucked her phone back into her purse. "Pretty girl. What's her name, Tracy? I still don't have everyone's name down."

"That's Mila. She's from some little village in the Ukraine. They come out here with stars in their eyes, hoping to make it in Hollywood, and they wind up in joints like this." Tracy dragged a tissue across her mouth to wipe off the bright red lipstick. "Or worse."

"Worse?"

Tracy put a finger to her pale pink lips. "How about

you? Do you have aspirations to be a dancer, or are you happy slinging drinks?"

"I'm a waitress, and that's okay with me. I just stumbled on this place because the club was hiring, and Irina told me there was an opportunity to make a little extra money working parties for Sergei's family."

"The Tattle-Tale always has openings—high turnover. I'm leaving myself pretty soon."

"Why?"

"Moving to Vegas with my boyfriend. He's a dealer, and as soon as he gets a job at one of the casinos out there, I'm gone."

"Seems to be an epidemic of that."

"What?" Tracy brushed past Britt to claim her own purse.

Britt lowered her voice. "Women leaving the Tattle-Tale to take off with their boyfriends. Jessie told me another waitress left to go off with her boyfriend."

Tracy dipped her head and dug through her bag, pulling out her keychain. She swung it around her finger. "I didn't hear that. Gotta go."

Britt looked around the empty dressing room. How many people suspected something was off at the Tattle-Tale? Tracy seemed anxious to be on her way once she'd mentioned the other waitress leaving with her boyfriend. Or had she imagined that?

Another bunch of women bustled into the room, chattering. Stepan must've corralled them into cleaning up, and Britt didn't want to be caught by Stepan.

She exchanged a few words with some of the women, who were complaining about Stepan, and then slipped into the hallway and out the back door. She'd kept Alexei waiting long enough.

"Hello, Barbie."

Britt jumped, hugging her purse to her chest. She let out a breath when she saw Calvin pushing his cart. "How are you doing, Calvin?"

"Brilliant."

"You need a few bucks?"

Calvin muttered to himself and shuffled past her.

Britt dug a couple of bills out of her tip money and tucked them into the pocket of Calvin's tattered jacket as she walked by. "Just in case."

She strode to her car, holding the remote in front of her to unlock it. Several of the bars on this stretch of the boulevard had back doors, and most of the parking in the alley was reserved for the employees of these businesses, so Britt had more company than just Calvin. And Alexei had to be watching from somewhere on his bike.

When she slipped onto the front seat and started her engine, she detected a single headlight at a distance behind her. She wanted to let him know about her missing receipt and about the tattoo-parlor card, but he hadn't given her his cell number. Hadn't wanted his number on her phone, but they had to have a better way of contacting each other than fevered conversations at the Tattle-Tale.

She turned out of the alley onto the street and joined the light traffic. Although there were quite a few bars in this area, all closing at 2:00 a.m., this stretch of road in Hollywood didn't compare to the glut of clubs and bars on that piece of real estate on the Sunset Strip where Jerome had been murdered. Still, she felt safe with Alexei on her tail.

She figured he knew her address, but she signaled

at every turn anyway until she turned onto her street lined with apartment buildings.

She parked at the curb a few buildings down from her own. At least she had the right permit to park on this street.

To her surprise, Alexei pulled up on his bike behind her.

As she got out of the car, he cut his engine. Putting her hand on her hip, she said, "Aren't you afraid to be seen here?"

He lifted the helmet from his head. "There's nobody around. Nobody followed you. Everything okay?"

"Not exactly."

"What happened?"

"I—I lost the receipt for my car."

He swung his leg over his bike. "The tow yard?"

"Yeah, the receipt that shows where I was parked last night—right in the vicinity where Jerome was attacked."

"You lost it at the club?" He ran a hand through his hair, making it stand up on end even more than the helmet did.

"I don't know if *lost* is the right word. The purses in the dressing room had fallen over. I noticed the receipt was gone when I was putting my stuff back in my bag."

He kicked the toe of his boot against the curb. "That's not good. What about your name? Is your real name on the receipt?"

"I am Barbie Jones here in LA. I have a driver's license, car registration and apartment lease to prove that. The receipt is for Barbie Jones."

His eyebrows shot up. "How'd you manage that?"

"Don't ask."

"Okay, so the name on the receipt will check out, but the address where your car was parked is a problem— if someone didn't just throw it away or one of the other women accidentally put it in her purse."

"I hope that's the case, but there's more."

"That new bartender?"

"A piece of work, but it's not him." She drew the card from her pocket and handed it to Alexei.

He held it up to the streetlight a few feet away. "What is it? It's too dark out here—no moon."

"It's a business card for a tattoo parlor." She took her phone from her purse and flicked on the flashlight, holding it over the card pinched between his fingers. "Turn it over."

He whistled. "Who had this?"

"One of the dancers—a girl named Mila."

"Russian?"

"Ukrainian."

"I wonder if they're sending her in for a tattoo."

"We need to stop her. She can't know that's the next step to joining their sex ring."

"Maybe she does, maybe she doesn't. I'm keeping this." The card disappeared into the pocket of his jacket. "I'm going to walk you up. This isn't a great area."

"It's the best I could do." She crooked her finger. "This way."

She led Alexei up to the second floor via a set of stairs on the outside of the '50s-style apartment building, a coat of stucco slapped on its sides, not too different from Leanna's place, except these individual apartments created a horseshoe around a sad little courtyard with some droopy palm trees stationed in the four corners.

Britt slid her key home in the dead bolt and then twisted it in the door-handle lock. She'd left a lamp on in the furnished living room, just like she always did.

When she stepped over the threshold, she tripped to a stop and covered her mouth. The lamp was the only thing the same as she'd left it.

Chapter Seven

Alexei widened his eyes. Britt Jansen was either a slob or someone had tossed her place, and by the way her shoulders were stiffening, Britt was no slob.

He pulled his gun out of his pocket and touched her back with his other hand. She jumped.

"Sorry." Grabbing her sleeve, he dragged her back, behind him. "How many rooms?"

"It's an old-style bachelor. This room and a bathroom over there." She pointed an unsteady finger at a door to the right.

"I'm assuming you didn't leave your place like this."

Her gaze darted to the weapon in his hand as she shook her head.

"Stay here while I check out the bathroom. When I tell you it's clear, close and lock the front door."

"And if it's not clear?" She eyed the bathroom door.

"Run like hell."

He crept toward the bathroom, although if the intruder were hiding in the shower, he would've heard them by now. No need for stealth—just firepower. Leading with his gun, Alexei kicked open the bathroom door. It shuddered and swung open on an empty room.

He yelled over his shoulder. "Clear. Lock that door."

The front door slammed, and seconds later Britt joined him at the entrance to the bathroom, hovering over his shoulder, pinching his sleeve. "They know."

"Check to see if anything's missing." His pulse jumped and he jerked, banging his shoulder with hers. "The painting of Tatyana."

The color drained from her face. "I hid it."

"Where?"

She took his hand, pulling him out of the bathroom behind her. "When I moved in, the landlady pointed out some loose floorboards by the window. Of course, she hasn't fixed them yet and probably won't."

She dropped to her knees in front of the window that looked out on the courtyard. She flicked back a worn area rug, and using her key, she jimmied the edge of one of the slats of wood.

"Hang on." He slid a knife from his pocket and flicked the blade. He inserted it along the crack between two of the floorboards and jiggled it. He pried up one of the boards and flipped it up, exposing a dark cavity beneath the floor. "Can you tell if it's there without pulling up the whole floor?"

She lay on her belly and aimed her phone into the space. "I see it. It's still there."

She rolled over onto her back, flinging one arm across her face. "Thank God they didn't find it, but they suspect me. It must be the tow-yard receipt. Do you think that's it?"

"Unless Sergei makes a habit out of searching new waitress's apartments, he must've had his goons come here for a reason."

He rose from his crouch and extended his hand to her. "It's a good thing you had the brilliant idea to hide the painting. If the intruder had seen that, there would've been no suspicion left in Sergei's mind that you were going to pose a problem."

She grasped his hand, and he pulled her to her feet.

Brushing off the front of her clothes, she asked, "And the tow-yard receipt? What does that tell him?"

"Tells him you were in the area when Jerome was murdered. Lots of people go to that part of town at that time of night. The killer didn't see Jerome with you or anyone else."

"I have an idea." She slumped into one of the two chairs in the room. "I can confess to a couple of the girls that I was supposed to meet Jerome for a drink that night, had trouble parking, and by the time I got to Rage, Jerome had been killed. I was too afraid to talk to the cops."

Alexei took the other chair and hunched forward, his elbows digging into his knees. "Why do you need a story when you're leaving?"

Britt's chin formed a hard line that he was beginning to recognize.

"Who said I was leaving? Mila is at risk. Jessie is missing. We can't let the Belkins continue to use young women and destroy them and their dreams."

He clasped his hands and rested his chin on his interlocked knuckles. Britt not only wanted to save her sister, but she also wanted to rescue every woman in that club.

"Britt, what I'm working on will bring down the Belkins and all of their operations in LA, including their sex-trafficking ring. I made some contacts, and I'm hoping to get invited to one of their parties at the banquet hall."

"What if it's too late for Mila?"

"It's not your job to save Mila, not if it compromises your own safety." He pushed out of the chair and wandered to the window. "Are you trying to compensate for not being here to save your sister?"

As soon as the words left his mouth, before he even heard Britt's breath hiss between her teeth, he knew he'd made another boorish blunder.

The chair squeaked behind him, and she joined him at the window, her face tight. "Are you trying to psychoanalyze me?"

He turned toward her and rubbed his hands up and down her stiff arms. "I'm sorry. It's none of my business why you want to help Mila, and I'm not implying that the only reason is that you see her as some kind of substitute for Leanna."

She lifted her shoulders. "That's okay. As a therapist, I'm self-aware enough to know my motivations. Doesn't make them any less compelling."

"I just don't want to see you put yourself in danger anymore, although I guess that's not any of my business either."

Her eyelashes fluttered, and his pulse quickened. Did she want her safety to be his business?

He swept his arm behind him, encompassing the room. "We know whoever broke in didn't get the painting of Tatyana, but what did he get? You haven't checked to see if anything else was missing. Laptop?"

"My laptop's in the car." She drove the heel of her hand against her forehead. "I left it there, under the seat."

"We'll get it in a minute. It's a good thing you had it there. Do you make a habit of taking it with you to the club?"

"I don't have Wi-Fi here. I stopped at a coffeehouse on the way to the Tattle-Tale tonight so I could check emails and catch up on a little work. I do still have clients who need me."

Who didn't need Britt?

"Anything else?" He spread his arms. "No notes from Leanna or pictures tying her to you? Those bills?"

"Look at this place." She ducked around him and opened and closed the door of the microwave, which was the extent of her kitchen in here. "Bare bones, and I paid her bills and tossed them."

"So, all they have on you is a receipt from a tow yard, indicating you were in the vicinity when they murdered Jerome—unless they don't have the receipt at all and you've given them some other reason to suspect you."

"There's nothing, and I'm going to alleviate Sergei's suspicions about the tow-yard receipt."

"By spreading it around that you were in the area that night?"

"I'm going to admit that I was supposed to meet Jerome—for a date."

"Is that a good idea considering they'd pegged Jerome as public enemy number one? They must've had something on him to eliminate him like that."

"He knew something about Tatyana or about Leanna's disappearance."

"Or both."

"Doesn't mean he told me."

He dropped into a chair and drummed his finger against the arm of it. "I wonder what Jerome was doing at the Tattle-Tale that night he returned when we were there and if it had anything to do with his murder."

"But Sergei never saw him come back because you

did that voodoo on the tape and erased Jerome's late-night visit."

"Maybe that wasn't Jerome's first late-night visit back to the club. Maybe he'd done that before and Sergei *did* see him on the surveillance video."

"Did you even pay attention to what he was doing when he came back? I didn't. I was too freaked out."

"He went behind the bar, but I don't recall what part of it or what he did back there, but—" he snapped his fingers "—we can replay it. I have that video on my laptop."

"That might help. I have a better idea now what's what behind the bar and may be able to make some educated guesses about what Jerome was doing there, but that means I am going back to the Tattle-Tale, and I'm going to drop the word about me and Jerome. Sergei can believe what he wants." Britt wedged her hands on her hips as if expecting to do battle.

"All right, but you're not going to be there on your own. I met a guy tonight, another Russian, and he's going to introduce me to Sergei tomorrow night, or I guess I met him last night, and he's introducing me to Sergei tonight."

"You're not introducing yourself as Alexei Ivanov, are you?"

Alexei's lips curled into a smile. As much as he'd like to see the look on Sergei's face when he heard the name Alexei Ivanov, he wasn't ready for that yet. "I'm Mikhail Orloff—Mickey."

Britt winked. "Barbie and Mickey—I like it."

He liked it, too, liked her and everything about her.

"Better than Barbie and Ken." He jerked a thumb

over his shoulder. "Get your things, and let's go, Barbie."

She wrinkled her nose. "Go where?"

"My hotel in Beverly Hills. Do you think I'm going to let you stay in this dump after it's already been compromised?"

"What happened to not being seen together?" Her cheeks flushed a pretty pink.

"Nobody connected to the Belkins or the Tattle-Tale is going to see us in Beverly Hills, especially not at that hotel. You can't stay here, Britt. It's not safe. It never was."

"All right. Give me a few minutes to pack my stuff." She walked to the window and kicked aside the carpet. "Why don't you get the painting?"

As he crouched down to lift the floorboards, she threw open a set of accordion closet doors.

"I take that back. My little jewelry case is missing."

He looked up from trying to squeeze his arm into the cavity. "Anything of value?"

"No, just some costume pieces. Maybe Sergei told whoever broke in to make it look like a random burglary." She turned, holding a dress to her chest. "Do you think it could've been?"

"Doubt it. It's just too coincidental. How would a random thief know you were out tonight? Why would he chance it? I'm sorry but why would a burglar even hit a bachelor like this? You don't even have a TV."

"Don't worry. You're not offending me." She hauled a suitcase from the closet onto the daybed, which must double as her bed.

He returned to the project of removing the painting, and Britt stopped shoveling clothes into her bag. "I don't think you're ever going to get your arm in there without removing the next floorboard. Hang on. I'll get it."

She knelt beside him, and the ends of her hair tickled his arm as she bent over the gap in the floor. "Let me."

Her slim arm disappeared into the floor, and she retrieved the rolled-up paper and dropped it. "I think I need to find a better place than this."

"There's a safe at the hotel. We'll stash it there." He tipped his head toward her bag. "Do you have everything you need?"

"In case they come back, I don't want it to look like I moved out, so I'll leave a few things."

Britt finished packing and locked up the apartment.

Before Alexei got on his bike, he said, "Pull up to the valet parking attendant, and leave your car with him. Meet me at the room."

About thirty minutes later, Alexei sprang for the door after a soft knock. "What took you so long?"

Britt patted his arm as she breezed past him, wheeling her bag behind her. "He's gotta get to my car, give me my ticket, I gotta give him a tip. These things take time." She collapsed on the couch. "I'm exhausted."

"No kidding." He held up the painting. "I'm going to put this in the closet for now and see about getting it locked up tomorrow. You can have the bathroom first, and the bed's all yours."

"Mmm." She fell onto her side and curled up her legs.

When he went into the bedroom, he ran his hand along the freshly made bed and then turned down the covers. The maid had hung the shirt Britt had worn the night before on the back of a chair, and Alexei plucked it up and pressed it against his face. He inhaled Britt's scent from the folds of the cotton.

Was he crazy inviting her back here? What else could he do to keep her safe, other than send her home to North Carolina? Britt was no puppet to be jerked this way and that. She wanted to stay at the Tattle-Tale, and he wasn't just making excuses for himself. He couldn't order her about.

He dropped the T-shirt on the chair and ducked into the closet. He propped up the painting in the corner in the back.

When he returned to the sitting room of the suite, Britt's cheek rested on her hand, and her hair trailed off the edge of the sofa.

He nudged her shoulder once, and she murmured in her sleep.

If he carried her to the bed, she might wake up, and she looked so peaceful, the little crease of worry between her brows finally smoothed out. If he carried her to the bed, he might be tempted to crawl in beside her.

He shook out the blanket the maid had folded at the bottom of the sofa and tucked it around Britt. With one finger, he smoothed the hair from her face and whispered, "Good night, *moya solnishka.*"

BRITT ORDERED ANOTHER iced tea from the poolside waitress and stretched her arms over her head, reaching for the sun. She tipped her glasses on top of her head and squinted at a boisterous group at the other end of the pool deck. Was that a celebrity with his entourage?

Sighing, she curled her toes. She could get used to lounging at a rooftop pool overlooking the palm-lined streets of Beverly Hills. The only improvement would be having Alexei beside her, but he'd headed out this afternoon for some secret meetings in an effort to solidify his fake identity and get invited to the party at the Belkins' banquet hall.

When the waitress returned with her tea, Britt held it over her body, letting the cold drops from the sweating glass hit the warm skin of her belly. The sun had finally broken through the marine layer, and it was baking all the pretty people at the pool—not that her mission included fun in the sun, but after the few days she'd had since meeting Alexei, she needed some downtime.

Her immediate goal tonight included offering an excuse for being in the area when Jerome was murdered... and getting close to Mila to see if she'd gotten the tattoo yet.

"Don't get burned."

Shading her eyes, she glanced up at Alexei, towering over her. The crisp suit he wore fit him like a glove, and her mouth watered. She cleared her throat. "Sharp-dressed man."

"Playing the part." He sat down on the edge of the chaise lounge next to hers and hunched forward, the material of his jacket stretching across his muscled shoulders.

She blinked and adjusted her sunglasses. "Did you get your invitation to the party?"

"Almost have it nailed down. I'm meeting an FOS at the Tattle-Tale tonight."

"An FOS?"

"Friend of Sergei. Turns out Sergei has a lot of friends that I'm sure his father doesn't even know about. Makes my job of infiltrating the inner circle easier, but Sergei had better hope Olav never finds out how fast and loose he's been with his favors."

"Olav is Sergei's father?"

"Yes."

Alexei almost spit out the word, and it hung between them as Britt waited for the rest of the story on Belkin the elder. Several awkward seconds later, she realized she wasn't going to get it.

The chaise lounge creaked as Alexei rose. "Dinner in the room before you head out for your shift?"

She nodded. Through narrowed eyes she watched Alexei's back as he walked toward the elevator. He had something going on with the Belkin family he wasn't sharing with her. It probably wasn't any of her business, but she wished he'd trust her enough to tell her the whole truth behind his mission.

Of course, once that mission came to its successful conclusion, she'd never see Alexei Ivanov again. She closed her eyes and pressed the cold glass against her cheek.

And she wasn't ready for that.

LATER THAT NIGHT, Britt scanned the Tattle-Tale as she grabbed a pad of paper from the top of the bar. She tapped Stepan on the arm with a pen. "Do you know if Jessie is working tonight?"

He lifted and dropped one shoulder. "Jessie, Jessie, I don't know Jessie. All girls the same here."

She rolled her eyes. "Yeah, you mean none of them will go out with you."

Stepan's hand shot out, and he grabbed her wrist, cinching his fingers around it. "Not like the other guy, eh? I hear you supposed to go out with other guy. Didn't work out."

She jerked her arm away from his grasp. "At least Jerome had some class."

"Had."

Britt spun away from Stepan with her heart pounding. So her story had gotten around already. She'd told a couple of the other waitresses about her ill-fated date with Jerome. Hopefully that would answer any lingering suspicions Sergei had about her presence on Sunset the night he'd had Jerome murdered.

A tap on her shoulder had Britt clenching her fist and jerking around.

Irina's penciled-in brows shot up. "Are you okay, Barbie?"

"Sorry." Britt blew out a sigh. "I thought you were Stepan."

"That man—" Irina slid a sideways glance at the bar "—doesn't belong here. We will get someone new soon. Let me know if he is bothering you. Can you come to the office with me for a minute?"

"Of course." Britt pressed a hand against her belly, where nervous knots twisted. Had they found out she was Lee's sister? Was she going to be fired for dating Jerome? Had they noticed her talking to Alexei?

Irina led her to Sergei's office, where Britt had last been with Alexei, and waved her into the chair across from Sergei's desk.

"I hear from a few other girls that you were going to meet Jerome the night he was killed."

"Yes, that's right." Britt twisted her fingers in her lap. "I'm sorry if that's not allowed. That's why I didn't tell anyone and then when…" She covered her eyes with one hand.

"It's not against rules, but we don't encourage it. Jerome should've known better." Irina reached up and twirled one of the studs in her ear. "Did you see anything that night? Should you talk to police? I don't think they've found the man who killed Jerome."

Britt's head shot up, and she widened her eyes. "I don't want to talk to the police. I didn't see anything. I was late, so I parked illegally. When I came around the corner of Sunset, the police were already there, and when I saw it was Jerome lying on the sidewalk, I ran away. I ducked into a bar down the street, and I…got drunk. I'm ashamed to say it, but I was freaked out. I-it was a robbery, right? That's what I heard."

"It was robbery. His wallet and watch were stolen."

"I hope this isn't going to get me fired. I really need this job right now. On top of everything, my car was towed that night, and I had to pay to get it out of the tow yard, and to add insult to injury, someone broke into my apartment last night and stole my jewelry." She ended the last syllable on a whine for maximum effect.

The door swung open, and Sergei stepped inside the small office, immediately overwhelming it with the scent of his cologne.

Had he been listening at the door? She hoped so.

"Nobody getting fired, Barbie Doll. You need extra cash? We need one more waitress."

"I'm already working tonight." Britt half rose from her chair. "In fact, I'd better get out there now since the club already opened."

"I'm talking about another gig. We throw big party tomorrow night. One of the waitresses not going, so you take her place." He reached over and patted her cheek. "Just no more dating bartenders, eh?"

Britt licked her lips. She'd be at the same party as Alexei, at the banquet hall. She might even get an opportunity to meet Olav Belkin, the head of the crime family.

"Thank you. Yes, I'd like to work." She scooted past Sergei and paused at the office door. "Which of the waitresses backed out of the party?"

"Jessie." Sergei snapped his fingers in dismissal. "Worthless girl. Quit when she didn't get dancing job."

Britt nodded and gritted her back teeth through her smile as she backed out of the office. What had happened to Jessie?

The next hour, she worked her tables in a fog. Nobody seemed to know anything about Jessie, and Britt was afraid to show too much interest in the other waitress's whereabouts.

When she spotted Alexei seated at a table with two other men, she snapped out of her fog. She had no way to communicate with him tonight, but then she'd be seeing him back at the hotel after her shift.

He'd warned her to make absolutely sure nobody followed her from the club. He'd be keeping a safe distance on his bike to run interference in case he noticed something.

Alexei and his party had a table of honor, front and center, courtesy of Sergei—and as the newest waitress, she didn't rate those tables.

At the end of the night, Britt made a point of crowding into the changing room with the dancers so she could talk to Mila, who was primping at the mirror.

Britt spied a tube of lipstick on the floor and kicked it toward the mirror. She followed the silver cylinder and bent forward, sweeping it up in one movement. "Did you drop this?"

Mila turned from the mirror, her hand still raised in mid-mascara stroke. "No, that is not mine. Vera?"

"Not mine."

Britt dropped her gaze to Mila's slender arms, unblemished by any tattoos, and let out a long breath. The dancer hadn't made it to the tattoo parlor yet. And when she did?

Britt's gaze darted around the room at the other dancers. None of them sported tattoos—at least not the *B* with the snake on the underside of their forearms.

What happened to the women once they got the tattoo? Was dancing in one of the Belkins' clubs the first step to working in their stable?

Had Leanna discovered all of this? Surely, more than a few of the women must have some clue about that side of the Belkins' operation. It didn't have to be a death sentence.

Then why get rid of Tatyana? Leanna? Jerome? Was she next? Britt shivered. She wouldn't be next with Alexei on her side.

She grabbed her purse from the bench. "Night, all."

She slipped out the back door of the club and hitched her bag over her shoulder as she trudged to her car. None of the shadows or noises in the alley scared her because she knew Alexei was close by.

A rattling sound came barreling up behind her, and she jumped to the side. Calvin rolled past her, his feet on the edge of his shopping cart.

"You in a hurry, Calvin?"

"No, just enjoying summer. No overcast skies today."

"It was beautiful." Britt dug into her pocket and pulled out a handful of her tip money. She called after Calvin. "I got something for you."

Calvin dragged his foot on the ground to slow down his basket and made a U-turn. He pushed his gray hair out of his eyes before holding out his hand.

Britt crumpled the bills into his palm, and he closed his hand around her fingers, his grip stronger than she'd expected. When she tried to pull away, he tightened his hold, leaning in close, the alcohol on his breath fierce against her face.

His faded eyes glittered, and he whispered, "You're like her, like Lee-Low."

Chapter Eight

Britt sucked in a breath and grabbed the grimy sleeve of his shirt. "What do you know about Lee-Low?"

"Barbie? You okay?" Irina charged toward them down the alley. "Go away, you filthy man."

Calvin yanked away from Britt and skated away on his basket.

"You all right, Barbie?" Irina circled her finger at her temple. "He is crazy person."

"I'm okay. I was just giving him a little money, and he got excited."

Irina wrinkled her nose. "Don't encourage him. He hangs around here all the time. I call police once."

"He's harmless."

"I walk you to car anyway."

"Then who's going to walk you to your car?"

Irina winked and opened her purse wide enough for Britt to see the gun tucked inside. "As Americans say, Misters Smith and Wesson walk me to car."

Swallowing, Britt gave Irina a weak smile.

Once she was safely in the driver's seat with the engine running and she saw Irina getting into her own car, Britt hugged the steering column and rested her forehead on top of the steering wheel.

What had just happened? How did Calvin know Leanna and what made him say she was like her?

Britt grabbed the edge of the rearview mirror and searched behind her for Calvin, but Irina had scared him off. Had Irina been trying to send her a message by showing her that weapon?

She rolled the car forward with her eyes still glued to the mirror. No single headlight lit up in the distance. Maybe Alexei had gotten tired of waiting for her. She pulled onto the boulevard, and like magic the solitary light appeared in the distance behind her like a comforting beacon. She made a few turns like Alexei had instructed her to do earlier, all the while watching her mirrors for any suspicious cars making the same turns. The only one following her was Alexei on his motorcycle.

It made her feel safe, although she'd had nothing but trouble in her life since the moment she ran into Alexei in Sergei's office. But if Alexei hadn't been there that night, Sergei would've seen her on the surveillance video and she might be dead…like Jerome. Like Jessie? Like Tatyana? Like…? No, she wouldn't go there. She had to talk to Calvin to find out what he knew about Leanna.

The manicured streets of Beverly Hills began to replace the grittier streets of Hollywood, and Britt breathed a little easier. Nobody but Alexei had followed her.

She dumped her car with the valet and nodded at the doorman as he jumped to open the door for her. She beat Alexei to the room and was waiting for him by the window when he walked in.

"Success." He pumped his fist in the air. "I got an invitation to the Belkins' party tomorrow night."

"So did I."

His eyebrows shot up to his messy hair. "You?"

"Sergei asked me to work."

"No!"

It was her turn to raise her eyebrows. "Excuse me?"

"Not a good idea." He shrugged off his jacket. "Do you know what goes on at those parties?"

"I'm thinking the exchange of a lot of information. Maybe I can even get a better look into the Belkin family organization."

"That's the Belkin family *crime* organization. How do you think those women with the tattoos get started?" He smacked a fist into his palm. "Parties like these."

"That's even better. If Leanna knew something about the sex trafficking, maybe I can find out what happened to her there."

"Doubt it." He raised a finger as if to shake it in her face and then thought better of it, collapsing in a chair and stretching his legs in front of him. "I suppose it's not going to do me any good to tell you not to go."

"Nope." She walked toward him and stepped over his long legs in her path. "I've got more to tell you."

"You always do. Were you able to convince everyone you had a date with Jerome the night he was killed?"

"I think so, but there's more." She sat on the edge of the sofa, crossing one leg over the other and kicking it back and forth to release her nervous energy. "Have you seen the homeless guy who hangs out in the alley behind the club?"

"I think so. Older guy with a basket?"

"Yeah—Calvin. I've talked to him a few times, given

him some money, and tonight he told me I was like Lee-Low."

"He knew your sister?"

"Yeah. I was going to start grilling him, but Irina saw us and yelled at him, scared him off."

"She'd scare anyone off. Did she hear what you two were talking about?"

"She was too far away to hear anything, and then she showed me her gun in her purse."

"Doesn't surprise me."

"That she has a gun or that she showed it to me?"

"That she has one. She's at that club, working late—not the most upstanding clientele in that place."

"There was something else." Britt stopped kicking her leg and tucked her hands beneath her thighs. "The reason I'm working the gig tomorrow night is because Jessie canceled."

"Jessie?"

"I told you about her. She's a waitress, and she stayed late at the club the night that Jerome was murdered, and I haven't seen her since. She called in sick the next night, wasn't there tonight, and Sergei asked me to fill in for her at the party."

"Another disappearing woman." He held up three fingers and ticked them off. "Tatyana, Lee and now Jessie. I don't want there to be a fourth."

"There's not going to be a fourth."

"She says with confidence." He rose from the chair and joined her on the sofa. "How can you be so sure?"

Turning toward him, she cupped his stubbled jaw. "Because I have you."

Alexei's blue eyes darkened and kindled, as if a flame burned in their depths. He took her hand gently and turned it over, drilling a finger in the center of her palm. "You do have me…for now."

Britt snatched her hand away and jumped up from the couch. Did he have to be so brutally honest? Was she asking for forever?

Although she wouldn't mind forever. She pressed a hand to her warm cheek. He'd seen it in her face.

She had a careful mask that she wore in sessions with her clients, but she dropped it as soon as she left her office. If her clients could see her real face, the emotions playing across it as they unveiled their anxieties and fears and scary thoughts, they'd fire her. She made up for that stoicism on her off time—with a vengeance.

Alexei appeared next to her, resting one hand on her hip. "I mean, I'm here for as long as you need me."

She cracked a smile. "Be careful making promises you can't keep, Russki."

His hand slid to her waist, and the kiss he pressed against her lips tasted of vodka and expensive cigars and an aching truth.

She didn't mind truth. She accepted his kiss, on his terms…for now. It was all she had.

He whispered against her mouth, "I can't promise you anything more than tonight."

After she untangled her tongue from his, she whispered back, "I'm good with tonight."

He'd lifted her in his arms before she even knew what he was doing. When he carried her into the opulent suite's bedroom, she clung to him tighter, wanting to commit every detail to memory for future daydreams.

He poured her boneless form from his arms to the bed and pointed to his feet. "Need to get these motorcycle boots off first."

"Take your time." She toed off her sneakers and rubbed her tight calves. "I wouldn't mind trying out that shower in there with the two heads."

"Would be nice to scrub off the filth of that club from both of our bodies."

"I'll do yours if you do mine." She yanked her white blouse from the waistband of her skirt and unbuttoned the top two buttons. "There's even a towel-warming rack in there. I used it earlier."

"If you say so. I can't figure out half the things in that bathroom."

"I'll start warming up a couple of towels." She floated to the bathroom like she was walking on air, her feet barely touching the carpet.

She draped two fluffy towels over the warming rack and cranked on both showerheads. She shimmied out of her skirt and peeled off her blouse. She kicked both into the corner just as Alexei appeared at the door naked and so fine she didn't know where to look first.

She choked. "That was fast."

"Any complaints?"

"Does this look like complaining?" She pointed to the big smile on her face.

"And you—" he approached her like a panther assessing his prey "—are very, very slow."

He wrapped his arms around her and unhooked her bra. Then he slipped both of his hands into her underwear and cupped her bottom. Pulling her close, he speared her with his erection.

She sucked in a breath. "I thought we were going to shower first."

"We are, but I'm good at multitasking." And then he

proved it by caressing her flesh and kissing her mouth, all while making her insides quake and quiver.

When he let her up for air, she held up her hand. "Hang on. I need to put my hair up."

While he tested the water spraying from the shower-heads, Britt twisted her hair into a bun and shed her panties. She ran a hand down his back and muscled buttocks. "How's the water?"

"Perfect." Turning toward her, he encircled her waist with both hands. "Like everything else in here."

The cavernous shower had no door, no curtain, not even a border step into the wet tiles, and she and Alexei moved seamlessly into the warm jets.

The water hit the backs of his shoulders and trick-led onto his chest, clinging to the black hair scattered there. She laid a hand between his pectoral muscles, spreading her fingers and curling them into his flesh. "My skin is so pale next to yours."

He cupped her breasts and then smoothed his hands down her sides and clamped them on her hips. "Your skin is so soft next to mine."

The huge shower suddenly seemed tiny and close, the spray beating down between her shoulder blades sud-denly scorching hot. She leaned into him, her tongue darting along his collarbone, flicking at the droplets of water.

"You forgot washcloths, so I guess I'm going to have to use my hands to wash your body." He reached past her and cradled the bar of soap in his palm before lath-ering it between his hands.

"Oh well," she managed weakly.

He started just beneath her chin, his soapy hands skimming down her neck and shoulders, where he stopped to caress the knots that had been building there for days.

Circling his palms on her breasts, he said, "You have the most perfect breasts."

"Mmm." She closed her eyes as her nipples peaked and crinkled beneath his touch. "What makes a breast perfect?"

"The fact that they seem at home right here." He cradled her breasts with both hands, sluicing his thumbs across her nipples.

The electrifying sensation shot to her belly, and she grabbed his biceps. "You're turning me to jelly, and I need to do some exploring of my own before I'm too weak to lift one finger."

She soaped up her own hands and traced the muscles and hard edges of his body. She explored his body like a woman devoid of sight, her fingertips registering every dip and hard plane. The feel of him beneath her touch satisfied some deep urge within her that she couldn't name.

He shivered. "It feels like you're painting on my skin, making your mark."

She chewed on her lower lip. This was supposed to be a quickie hookup designed to slake their crazy thirst for each other, get it out of the way so that they could return to serious business without distraction.

She curled up one corner of her lip and ran her soapy hands along the length of his erection. "I'm just teasing you before the main event."

He growled and lunged forward. "Let's get to the main event on the bed. I don't want either one of us slipping in here and cracking our heads on this expensive tile."

They both stepped back under their showerheads and rinsed off, and the space between them gave Britt a shiver.

Alexei reached for the rack and yanked one towel free. "It worked. This is warm."

He pressed the towel against her, and she melted against the heated terry cloth. "That's nice. I'm going to have to consider one of those for my bathroom at home."

"Me, too." He grabbed the other towel.

He'd never even told her where home was.

Britt left the shower first, and the two small steps between her and Alexei yawned between them like a gulf. They'd shared a deep connection in that shower, one that she'd broken, one that Alexei had never wanted.

Her cell phone rang from the other room, and it acted like a prod, just like it had ever since the day her sister had gone missing.

"I have to get that." She tucked the towel around her body and scurried into the sitting room. The light from her phone glowed on the sofa where she'd left it.

She lunged for the cell and glanced at the unknown number as she answered. "Hello?"

A husky, harsh whisper replied. "The baby, find the baby."

Britt frowned at Alexei, who'd followed her out from the bedroom, wrapping his towel around his waist.

"I think you have the wrong number."

"You're Lee's sister."

Britt caught her breath. "Do you know where she is? Do you know where my sister is?"

A man's laughter from the background came over the line, and the caller's voice dropped even lower, her

Russian accent more pronounced. "Find baby. Find baby and bring them all down."

"What baby? Whose baby?"

"Tatyana's baby."

Chapter Nine

Britt shouted into the phone. "Tatyana has a baby?"

Alexei's pulse jumped, and he mimicked pressing a button with his thumb to get Britt to put her phone on speaker.

"She's gone." Britt stared at the phone cupped in her trembling hand.

"Tatyana?" His gut churned. "Your sister?"

"No, no. The caller. She hung up."

"Who was she? What did she say? Tatyana has a baby?"

"I don't know who she was." Britt lifted her bare shoulders. "The caller had a Russian accent, and she knew I was Lee's sister. She said something about finding Tatyana's baby."

"What's that supposed to mean?" Alexei drilled two fingertips into his temple where a sharp pain lanced him. "How'd she get your number?"

"Leanna must've given it to her." She tipped the phone back and forth. "I can call her back."

"No!" The force of his exclamation startled Britt, causing her to drop the phone.

"Why not? She knows me, she knows Leanna and

she knows Tatyana has a baby somewhere. I'd say she's a good place to start."

"You don't know who that was or whose phone she was using. What did she sound like, other than the Russian accent?"

"She was whispering. She sounded scared, nervous. I heard a man in the background."

"Exactly." Alexei bent forward and swept up the phone from the carpet. "Maybe she wasn't using her own phone. Do you really want to call back someone else's phone? Tip him off?"

"Whoever that is already has my number in his phone."

"If he notices the number and calls you back, you can play dumb. If it really is this woman's phone and she wants you to find Tatyana's baby, she'll call you back."

Britt crossed her arms, her balled fists digging into her sides. "What does it mean? She said find Tatyana's baby and bring them all down."

"Bring them down? If Tatyana was pregnant, she wouldn't be much use to the Belkins." Alexei tapped the phone against his forehead. "Maybe that's why they got rid of her."

Britt's face blanched, and she plopped down on the edge of the sofa. "We couldn't figure out before why the Belkins would harm one of their women if she could turn a profit for them. Maybe that's what happened. Tatyana got pregnant, and the Belkins had no more use for her, but I still can't figure out where my sister fit in."

"Tatyana made the mistake of confiding in Leanna, and the Belkins found out."

She slumped against the sofa back. "Do you think there's a chance Leanna knew they were onto her and got away? When she sent me that text, she was worried about something. Leanna never worried about anything."

He knelt in front of her and tucked the towel more firmly around her body. "Let's keep that hope alive. Now, get some pajamas on and crawl between the sheets. It's late."

She jerked her head up, and the bun loosened, her blond hair falling around her shoulders like a cloud. "Y-you're joining me?"

"Britt." He took her hand and pressed a kiss in the middle of her palm. "That's probably not a good idea right now."

A smile trembled on her lips. "We've already sort of seen everything there is to see of each other. You can at least share the bed with me."

He folded her hand against his heart. "Believe me, it's a sight I won't soon forget, but if I'm lying next to you in that big bed, I don't think I could resist you."

She blinked at him.

"And I need to resist you."

She snatched her hand back and bounced up from the sofa. "Yeah, that's a good line. I'm sure you use it often. We'll discuss strategy tomorrow."

Brushing past him, she nearly toppled him over. She shut the bedroom door with a sharp click, which was way worse than a slam.

He fell face-first into the sofa and pounded his fists on the cushion. What the hell had he been thinking? If that phone call hadn't interrupted them, he'd be making love to Britt right now in that bedroom. That sounded great, better than great, at the moment, but what would happen when he left? When he got his next assignment? He didn't want anyone waiting for him.

His pregnant mother had waited for his father...and his father had never come home.

THE NEXT MORNING, Alexei woke up and pulled the tangled blanket to his chin, exposing his feet to the chilly air-conditioned room. He'd slept naked since he didn't dare go into the bedroom last night after Britt flounced out of here.

The bedroom door cracked open, and she stuck her head out. "Are you decent?"

He was about to remind her that she'd already seen his indecent side but thought better of it. Neither of them needed any reminders of last night.

He sat up on the sofa, pulling the blanket around his waist, eyeing her long legs extending from her shorts. "Yeah. Whoa—you're already dressed and ready to go. Where?"

"I have to buy a dress for tonight. Sergei doesn't want the waitresses wearing our usual uniforms." She walked farther into the room, swinging a pair of sandals from her fingers.

"Yeah, I'll bet he doesn't. You need to be careful tonight, Britt. This is a party for the Belkins' associates to meet young, accommodating ladies working for the Belkins."

"Well, I'm not accommodating." She tripped to a stop and dropped one of her sandals, red flags flying in her cheeks. "I mean, I won't be accommodating to any of Sergei's friends."

He cleared his throat. "I hope you have a choice. I'm

going to be doing my own thing there and might not have a chance to look out for you."

She snatched the sandal up from the carpet. "I can handle myself."

He had no doubt Britt could handle herself under normal circumstances, but the Belkins were anything but normal. He didn't want her slipping away from him.

"Can we meet for lunch and discuss that…strategy?"

Steadying herself with one hand on the credenza, she shoved a sandal onto her right foot and, like a stork, switched to her other leg to put on the left. "All right. I'll be in the area since I'm going to take advantage of shopping in Beverly Hills while I'm here." She dropped her cell phone in her purse. "Should we pick a time and place now since you don't want me calling your phone?"

She made that security measure sound…bad. Maybe it was best he'd raised her prickly side and she'd decided to keep him at arm's length. It would make leaving her so much easier. "Patio of The Ivy at noon."

"See you there." She left the room with a flourish and a cloud of floral perfume.

Alexei blew out a breath and dropped the blanket to the floor. Teaming up with a woman was a lot different from working with his SEAL team members. He sneezed. None of them wore perfume, for one thing— at least not that he knew of.

He yanked his phone off its charger and thumbed through the messages. What he wouldn't give to have one of his buddies here. He'd even take Slade Gallagher.

He strode into the bedroom and glanced at the tumbled bedclothes. Had she had a restless night, too? He fell across the bed, dragging a pillow over his face. He inhaled the same scent that was floating around the sitting room right now—sweet, feminine, desirable. Closing his eyes, he pictured Britt in the shower, water beading on her soft skin, her lips parted as he skimmed his hands across her body.

The vision gave him an instant erection, and he shoved off the bed and headed toward the shower. He needed a cold one if he hoped to maintain his resistance to Britt Jansen's considerable charms.

LATER THAT DAY, Alexei sat across the table from Britt as she toyed with her salad. "I ended up spending too much money, but at least I can wear the dress again."

"It's not too—" Alexei waved his fork in the air "—sexy, is it?"

She wrinkled her nose and stabbed at a tomato. "It's a little black dress, elegant."

"I'm sure that's not what Sergei had in mind, but good for you. You don't want to be mistaken for anything other than a waitress."

"I don't plan on it. Do you know the layout of the banquet hall?"

Alexei tapped his phone on the table next to his plate. "There's a Russian restaurant in the front. The restaurant is separated from the banquet hall by a foyer or anteroom with restrooms. There's a stage in the hall, tables and chairs and private rooms off the main area, down a hallway."

"Are those actual pictures?" She jabbed at his phone with her finger. "Have you been there?"

"I found some pictures of it online and downloaded them, although maybe it will be set up differently for this event." He took a sip of ice water. "I'll be assessing the guests, but mostly I'm going to ingratiate myself with one guest in particular—a supposed arms dealer. I'll also be getting on Sergei's good side."

"Is Sergei really involved in the—" she ducked her head and looked both ways "—terrorist activities? Somehow I just can't picture him hobnobbing with committed terrorists."

"You're probably right. I can't imagine old Olav Belkin would trust his son with operations of that magnitude. That's what makes Sergei ripe fruit for plucking. He's a fool."

"You don't think the FBI has already tried plucking that particular fruit?" She hunched forward, burying her chin in her hand. "It *is* the FBI that would handle a crime family like the Belkins, isn't it? Or are you already working with the FBI? You never really told me how a navy SEAL sniper wound up in LA."

And he wasn't planning on it now. He didn't want to scare her off at this point—or maybe he did. If she knew the truth, she might back off, go home.

He shrugged and picked up the second half of his burger. "I can't tell you that."

"Not sure why." She narrowed her green eyes. "It's not like I'm going to reveal secrets to the press or anything. I'm assuming you haven't told the agencies involved in this about me."

Chewing slowly, he placed his burger back on the plate. He slid the napkin from his lap and wiped his mouth and then his hands, folded it over and positioned it next to his plate.

Britt's gaze tracked his every movement. "Well, have you?"

"I have not."

"I didn't think so." She flipped her hair back from

her face. "You'd be in a world of trouble if they found out, wouldn't you?"

A muscle ticked at the corner of his mouth. "I'm going to be in a world of trouble anyway."

"What do you mean? I'm not going to rat you out." She ran her fingertip across the seam of her lips. "If you help me find out what happened to Leanna, even if you don't, nobody will ever hear a peep out of me. W-we can pretend we never met."

He toyed with the edge of the napkin. "It's not about you, Britt."

"I don't get it. Why are you going to be in trouble?" She tilted her head to the side, and her golden hair slid over one shoulder.

"Because I'm not working with an agency. I don't have much of a plan, and I don't have any backup… except you."

He closed one eye, formed his fingers into a gun and aimed it over Britt's shoulder. "I just want to kill Olav Belkin."

ALEXEI'S WHISPERED WORDS sent a chill racing up Britt's spine, and she gripped the edge of the table. Oh God, she was sitting across from a maniac.

"I… You… Who are you?" She half rose out of her chair and then thumped back down.

He covered one of her hands with his, and if she'd given in to her first instinct, she would've snatched it away. But Alexei's hand felt warm, secure. He'd protected her, kept her safe…and lied to her.

"I'm Alexei Ivanov, US Navy SEAL sniper. That's all still true, but I'm also the son of Aleksandr Ivanov, who was murdered by Olav Belkin, and I'm here to avenge that murder."

She licked her dry lips and sucked down some iced tea through her straw. "So, there's no connection between the Belkins and terrorists? You're just trying to get close enough to Belkin to…kill him?"

"There is a connection. The Belkins have worked with terrorists before, in Russia. It's not new territory for them. If I can take down Olav Belkin, his terrorist connections will run scared." He spread his hands. "It's a win-win."

"Except what you're doing is illegal. If you're caught, it will end your career, regardless of the favor you're doing the world." She grabbed his hand, digging her nails into his skin. "Is your vengeance worth that? Everything you worked so hard to achieve?"

His gaze dropped to his hand in her possession. "You know, I never even met my father. My mother was pregnant when my father was murdered, and I was born in New York after relatives got her out of Russia."

"How did it happen?" Maybe if she could get him to talk about it matter-of-factly, putting his Russian passion aside… "How did your father know Belkin, or was it random?"

His head jerked when the waitress showed up to take their plates. "Anything else?"

"Coffee for both of us." Britt wagged her finger between herself and Alexei.

He shoved his dark hair back from his face with one hand. "It wasn't random. My father was a shopkeeper in Saint Petersburg. Belkin was a member of the *Vory v Zakone.*"

Britt raised her eyebrows. "The what?"

"*Vory v Zakone*. The Russian mob in the old Soviet Union. It literally means 'thieves in law.' They were involved in all criminal activities—drugs, girls, extortion. And my father—" he lifted one shoulder in that very Russian manner of his "—objected to those activities. The *Vory* answered his objections by slitting his throat one night in his shop."

Britt covered her mouth with both hands. No wonder Alexei wanted revenge. She'd been ready to do violence against Sergei for lying about her sister, and she didn't even know if he was involved in Leanna's disappearance yet.

"That's awful. I mean, I have no words, really." She pressed her lips together when the waitress returned with their coffee.

Alexei dumped some sugar in his coffee with a shaky hand, his jaw tight.

So much for tamping down that Russian temper.

"Alexei." Britt stirred some cream into her cup. "What did your father want for you?"

"Are you going to psychoanalyze me?" His lips twisted. "No need."

"Would your father want you to avenge his death at the risk of your own future? What about your mother? She left the Soviet Union, raised you here away from all that, away from the old grudges."

"I had my chance once." Alexei held his coffee cup aloft and stared over the rim into the distance, into some other time and place. "I had an opportunity to take out Belkin, had him in my sights."

"What stopped you?"

"Duty and country. I had a different assignment at the time. I completed the assignment, and shooting Belkin at that point would've compromised everything, compromised the safety of my teammates."

"And now?"

"I'm on my own."

"What is your official reason for being in LA?"

"I don't have an official reason. I'm on leave between deployments."

"Your…unit…" She waved her hand in the air. "The navy doesn't know where you are?"

"They know I'm vacationing in LA."

She drove the heel of her hand against her forehead. "You can't do this, Alexei. I won't let you. You'll destroy everything you've worked for."

"On the contrary, this is everything I've been working for. The terrorist group Belkin is courting is one controlled by someone my team has been after for a very long time. Someone who captured and tortured one of my teammates." He snapped his fingers. "Like I said, a win-win for everyone."

"Except you." She ran her finger along the rim of her cup. "Is your mother still around?"

He threw her a sharp glance. "She lives in Florida with her second husband."

"And how do you think she'd feel if you were arrested for murder? Court-martialed? She must be extremely proud of her navy SEAL son."

"You—" he leveled a finger at her "—don't play fair. Is this how you beat your clients into submission?"

She folded both of her hands around one of his. "Think about it. Think about her. Do you really believe she wants you to revisit those old hurts from the old country?"

"It's not right." The corner of his eye twitched, and

his hand in her possession clenched into a fist. "My father tried to do the right thing, and not only was he murdered for it, the police did nothing to bring his killers to justice."

"Paid off?"

"Paid off and scared. The *Vory v Zakone* controlled that whole area. That's why my mom had to get out."

"I understand that thirst for revenge. Why do you think I basically gave up my life in Charlotte to come out here? I want to find out what happened to my sister, I want the people who threatened her, the people who killed Jerome, to be punished, but there are ways—legal ways."

Alexei snorted and disentangled his hand from hers. "Legal means are useless against people like this. Didn't you discover that already with your sister?"

"What you and your team of snipers do is legal. You don't run off and go rogue...do you?"

"We can't. It would get us a court-martial."

She smacked the table. "Exactly. Don't do this, Alexei. Your sense of satisfaction will be short-lived, and if the authorities figure out who killed Belkin, your career will be over. You'd be hurting so many people—your mother, your teammates...me."

His gaze jumped to her face. "I never want to hurt you, Britt."

The heat sparking from his eyes melted her insides. Even if she couldn't have this man, she wanted to know he was free and doing the job he was supposed to do.

She spread her hands on the table, her two thumbs meeting. "It would hurt me to know that you were in some military prison serving time for killing that dirtbag Belkin. There has to be another way."

Alexei pinged his fingernail against his coffee cup. "Maybe if I can get some serious evidence that Belkin is working with Vlad, the task force will give me the go-ahead to pursue the investigation."

"Wait. What?" She tucked her hair behind one ear. "Who's Vlad and what task force?"

"Vlad is an enemy sniper. We don't know what nationality he is, but he uses a Russian sniper rifle—just like mine. We've been tracking his activities for a few years. He graduated from his sniper-for-hire activities to forming his own terrorist network. So far, we've been able to thwart his plans in the US."

"He's plotting attacks here? And this is the person the Belkins are dealing with?"

"We think so. He tried hooking up with a Colombian cartel, but we were able to quash that. This is obviously his next effort to expand his operations in the US."

"There's a task force to bring him down?"

"Exclusively dedicated to the goal. Some of my teammates were assigned to the task force at various times in the past several months." He shrugged. "The Belkin crime family connection is just chatter at this point."

"But if you can prove it, you might get the go-ahead from this task force to investigate?"

"That's what I'm thinking. It's not—" He drummed his fingers on the table. "This task force is not a typical one. Navy SEALs were called back to the States to perform operations under the radar. Much of what they did was out of the bounds of law enforcement or military justice."

She swirled the coffee in her cup, a smile creeping to her lips. "Sounds right up your alley. What do you need to do to make this happen?"

His brows collided over his nose. "Even if I find the proof of the Belkin-Vlad connection, I might not be the task force's first choice to lead the charge. They know my background."

"Would make perfect sense to me. Who better to infiltrate the Belkin operation than a Russian American who speaks the language?"

"There is something to that. It seems like my teammates were chosen for their specific assignments because of their connections to the people involved. The task force leader, Ariel, is not your typical CIA policy wonk."

"Ariel?" Britt sucked in her bottom lip. "That's who you were emailing before. I thought she might be your girlfriend."

"Honestly, I'm not even sure she's a girl, and I never sent that email."

"Aha!" She wriggled in her chair. "So, you had already thought about contacting the task force."

"It had crossed my mind."

Britt pulled her phone closer and checked the time. "Then we both know what we have to do tonight—you need to find evidence of Vlad, and I need to find clues about Leanna."

"Just be careful. I think you have an idea of whom you're dealing with now."

"I pretty much knew that from the beginning."

The real surprise had been the confession of Alexei Ivanov—a story worthy of a Russian novel with betrayal, vengeance and redemption.

She just had to make sure this story didn't feature a doomed love affair.

Chapter Ten

Britt studied Alexei as he faced the full-length mirror in the hotel room, picking an imaginary speck of lint from his impeccably tailored jacket.

"I do have one question for you." She smoothed the skirt of her black dress over her thighs. "If the government is not sponsoring and paying for your so-called vacation in LA, where is all the cash coming from for the fancy crib and threads?"

"Crib and threads?" He cracked a rare smile and then patted the pocket of his jacket. "Self-funded."

She leaned into the mirror next to him, dabbing at her lipstick. "I didn't realize the navy paid so well—even for hotshots like you."

"After my mother moved to the States and had me, she met a very wealthy Russian businessman. The man, my stepfather, treated me like a son and gave me everything I wanted—still does. I have a half sister, and they treat her like a princess. I think she even pretends she's a Russian princess." He rolled his eyes.

"Does your stepfather know what you're doing out here?"

"No. He'd tell my mother. This—" he swept his hand

across the suite "—is all from my trust fund, which I rarely touch."

"Would your stepfather approve of what you're doing? Or what you were *going* to do?"

"Approve? No, because it would upset my mother, but he'd understand. He comes from that same world, and that's why he left. All business was controlled by the *Vory*, and after the fall of the Soviet Union, the oligarchs moved in to claim the spoils. Maks chafed under the restrictions and the graft and became a self-made billionaire here."

"After tonight, it won't come to that." She bumped him with her hip. "Move it, Russki. You're primping more than I am."

"You don't need to primp." He pinched the hem of her dress between two fingers, rubbing them together. "You look beautiful."

Alexei's compliments were simple, straightforward and gave her a warm glow inside because she knew they were sincere.

"You look beautiful, too." She spun away from the mirror to face him and smoothed her hands against the lapels of his jacket. A pulse throbbed deep in her belly, and she kissed his mouth. He couldn't possibly blame her for that, as his lips were inches from hers and she never did have much self-control.

His eyes flickered but he didn't back away from her. "Remember our signal if you're in trouble?"

"I'm going to twist my hair around one hand. Don't worry. I'm going to be fine. This is a party in a banquet hall behind a restaurant. I'm going to be serving drinks and Russian caviar."

"Just don't forget what this party is all about." He

touched a finger to her nose. "Despite what Sergei may have told you or even the other waitresses, this is a gathering of wealthy men and the desperate young women who are bound to serve them."

Britt shivered. "It makes me sick. Leanna must've been livid when she found out what was going on."

"Don't make the same mistake she did. Don't show your hand."

"You either, Mikhail Orloff." She tugged on his lapels. "How are you getting to the party? You're not riding the motorcycle in this getup, are you?"

"Town car."

"Fancy. I have to drive over in my old clunker."

"Just be careful."

"You said that already."

"Can't be said enough."

She held up a hand. "Okay, I'm leaving. I'll see you over there, and I *will* be careful."

She slung her bag over her shoulder, and as she reached the door, Alexei's stride ate up the space between them.

He grabbed her shoulders and planted a kiss on her that totally messed up her makeup—and damn, she didn't even care.

Forty minutes later, Britt pulled up in front of Eastern Nights, the Belkins' flagship restaurant. A valet parking attendant rushed to her window.

She flashed him a smile. "I'm the help. Where do we park?"

"Pull around the corner, and park in the lot behind the restaurant." He waved his arm behind him.

She parked her car and then stood beside it to wait

for two of the other waitresses as they pulled into a parking space.

One of the women, Theanessa, rubbed her hands as she approached Britt. "Get ready for some great tips tonight."

Britt nodded. The only tip she wanted was the one that would lead her to Leanna.

As they all pushed through the back door of the restaurant, Britt asked, "Are the dancers going to be putting on a show tonight?"

Theanessa smirked. "Hell no. This party's supposed to be a little higher class than that. There's a band, some dancing—not the topless kind—and it's mix and mingle for Sergei's friends and some special ladies."

The other waitress nudged Britt with her elbow and whispered in her ear. "High-class escorts."

"Oh." She put a hand to her throat. "But we're just serving drinks and appetizers, right?"

"You're not a guest, girl." Theanessa shed her sweater to reveal a low-cut red dress. "We get our minimum wage plus tips. Those escorts are making the big bucks."

Britt bit her bottom lip. She doubted the escorts, as Theanessa called them, were getting paid at all if they were part of the Belkins' stable.

She blew out a breath. "Well, I'm just here to be a waitress because Jessie pulled out. Do either of you know what happened to Jessie? I haven't seen her for a few days."

"Nope." Theanessa gave the other waitress a little push from behind. "The Tattle-Tale has a high turnover."

Britt slid a glance to the other woman, whose name she couldn't remember. Had she been about to spill the beans on Jessie? Britt would have to get her alone tonight for a few discreet questions.

That was all she was here for—discreet questions.

When all the waitresses had arrived, they gathered around Irina for instructions.

Irina, still wearing her yoga pants and oversize blouse, clapped her hands. "All right. Guests begin arriving in about ten minutes. Pick up trays of vodka and wine and work crowd with those. If someone wants mixed drink, they go to bar unless you want to get it for them. You pick up trays of appetizers in the restaurant's kitchen. Any questions?"

One of the waitresses raised her hand. "H-how will the guests know we're not…guests since there's no uniform for tonight?"

Britt laced her fingers in front of her and studied Irina's face. Everyone seemed to know what this party was all about. Would Irina acknowledge that now?

The older woman crooked her finger, and one of the busboys approached the group holding a plastic bin in his arms.

Irina pointed to the floor, and the busboy dropped the bin. She then leaned over and grabbed something from it. A white apron dangled from her fingertips. "You wear these. Then you don't get pretty dresses all dirty."

Britt eased out a sigh. She'd rather wear a frilly white apron than be mistaken for an escort.

Irina tossed out the apron, and Britt caught it with one hand. As she tied it around her waist, Theanessa nudged her back.

"Kinda ruins the effect of our sexy dresses, doesn't it? Why didn't Sergei just have us wear our regular black skirts and white blouses?" She flounced off, dragging the apron behind her on the floor.

The young waitress Britt had met in the parking lot sidled up next to her. "I'm glad we're wearing something that's gonna say we're waitresses and not…hookers."

Britt lodged her tongue in the corner of her mouth as she smoothed the apron over her dress. "Well, they're not exactly hookers, are they? I mean, they're like escorts."

The woman rolled her eyes. "Call it what you want. They're gonna get paid for sex."

"I'm just here to serve drinks and food." Britt lifted her shoulders. "Do you know what happened to Jessie? Sergei said she quit."

"I'm just here to serve drinks and food." The waitress yanked the ties on her apron and turned her back on Britt.

Britt wandered around the room, taking in the orchestra tuning up on the stage and the two bartenders setting up on either side of the large hall. Stepan, Jerome's replacement at the Tattle-Tale, lifted his hand in a wave, and Britt waved back. She just wanted to fit in tonight and not cause any waves.

Maybe once Alexei got his proof of the ties between Belkin and Vlad, she'd go home and leave it up to that task force to find Leanna…or at least tell her what had happened to her sister.

Britt blinked back the tears that tingled in her nose and trailed her hand along the textured paper on the walls. Her hand dropped off at the gap created by a small hallway tucked off the main room.

She poked her head around the corner, noting several closed doors. She'd already seen the bathrooms between the restaurant and the banquet hall, so these couldn't be restrooms. She glanced over her shoulder and took a step into the hallway.

One of the doors swung open, and Britt jumped back.

Irina emerged, pursing her lips when she noticed Britt. Irina bore down on her and grabbed her upper arm, the Russian woman's bony fingers digging into Britt's flesh.

"Nothing here, Barbie. Guests will be arriving soon. Get tray of drinks and get busy."

"Sorry." Britt shook her off. "Just exploring."

"No exploring. Just working."

As Britt walked away, she placed a hand against her pounding heart. Irina had an iron grip—and she was completely loyal to the Belkins...and armed.

Drawing in a deep breath, she squared her shoulders and strode toward Stepan's bar. "Do you have any trays ready yet?"

"Just getting started. You help me?"

"Sure. What do you need?"

He handed her an expensive bottle of vodka, icy cold, and pointed to a tray of shot glasses on the table behind her. "Fill those about three-quarters."

"You got it." She tipped the vodka into glass after glass until they all shimmered with the clear liquid. "Do you want me to do another?"

He gestured toward the entrance, where several people had begun to gather. "Time for one more, and then we get busy."

He set up another tray of glasses for her and lined up two more chilled bottles of vodka.

As she watched a stream of liquid pour into the first

shot glass, she asked, "You've worked these parties before?"

"Once."

"Do they get pretty crazy?"

"Crazy?" He laughed. "Not crazy with these boring old men."

She finished off the tray with a flourish. "Well, I hope these boring old men tip well."

"They will." Stepan's gaze tracked down her body.

Britt folded her arms across her chest. "That's what I'm talkin' about. You're on your own now, Stepan. I'm going to start mingling with the vodka."

She hoisted one of the trays and couldn't get out of Stepan's slimy presence fast enough. Since she'd filled that first tray, more guests had arrived and were fanning out across the room to park at tables and wander to the back of the banquet hall to check out the long table, groaning with Russian delicacies.

Britt kept watch for one tall, dark, good-looking Russian with blue eyes, but Alexei hadn't arrived yet. Instead a squat, silver-haired man in the middle of the room held sway over a group of people hanging on to his every word.

She had a visceral reaction to the man, like a punch to the gut, and had no doubt she was watching Olav Belkin in action.

Stretching her lips into a smile, she approached a cluster of men. "Vodka?"

Two of the group relieved her of two glasses, and she dived into the growing crowd to dispense with the rest. She circled back around to Stepan's station, dropped off the empty tray and picked up one crowded with flutes of champagne.

This cargo gave her a better opportunity to get up close and personal with more of the women guests. She glided up to three men and two women, the women perfectly made up and exquisitely dressed.

"Champagne?" She proffered the tray and almost dropped the whole thing when one of the women reached for a glass, exposing the small, fresh tattoo on the underside of her forearm.

Britt's eyes bounced to the woman's face, and this time the tray wobbled in her hand so much a couple of the flutes tipped over.

Britt grabbed a bunch of napkins from the stack on her tray and blotted the puddle of liquid. "I am so sorry."

"No problems." Mila took another glass and smiled. Then she ducked her head. "You coming to party tomorrow night at Rage, Barbie? Last night for me as dancer."

"Oh, I'll try."

With her pulse racing a mile a minute, Britt scurried back to the bar—not Stepan's—and placed the tray on the table next to it. Wedging her hands on either side of the tray, she leaned forward. Mila had gone through with it. She'd gotten the Belkin tattoo, and now she was here at this party as a commodity. She was moving from dancer to escort.

She squeezed her eyes shut. Mila didn't seem to be here under duress. She'd smiled, taken a glass of champagne, looked beautiful.

"Hey, Barbie, right?"

Britt looked up and met Theanessa's eyes over a tray of food. "Yes."

"If you're between deliveries, can you take this food out there?" She winked. "I have to make a little detour."

Britt shifted her gaze over Theanessa's shoulder, and it collided with an older man's beady black eyes.

His stare hardened, and Britt looked away. Did Theanessa know what she was getting into? Did any of these women?

Reaching out her arms, Britt said, "Sure, sure. I'll take it."

"Thanks."

As Theanessa handed off the tray, Britt grabbed her wrist. "Be careful."

Theanessa's laughter trilled in her throat as she spun away toward her new friend, leaving Britt gripping the heavy tray with two hands, the edges cutting into her palms.

She waded back into the crowd, which had thinned out a bit once the orchestra had struck up its first tune. Several couples claimed the dance floor, the women like colorful butterflies floating closer and closer to the spiders' webs.

Britt spotted Alexei with two other men, heads together. Did he realize Olav Belkin was in the room? Of course he did. He probably had him on his radar at all times.

She zigzagged through the mass of people to reach him and ducked into their circle. "Appetizers?"

"Thanks." Alexei selected blini with smoked salmon from the tray.

One of his companions touched her hip. "I don't know. What's on the menu?"

Britt's smile tightened and she raised the tray close to his face. "Only what's on the tray."

The man guffawed and elbowed the third member of the group in the ribs. "She's feisty. I like feisty."

"Boris." Alexei stepped in front of the man, breaking his contact with Britt. "I want to continue our discussion about that proposition."

"Ah, for a young man, you're too interested in business. You let go a little."

Alexei clapped Boris on the shoulder. "There's plenty of time for pleasure."

Britt took the opportunity to slip away from the group. She brushed past another waitress and snatched a shot glass of vodka from her tray. Without looking one way or the other, Britt downed the vodka in one gulp.

She coughed and dropped the glass onto her own tray, but at least the booze steadied her jangling nerves and shaky hands. She had to get a grip. She couldn't fall apart every time one of these guys made a pass at her. She could always complain to Sergei. From what she understood from the other women, Sergei didn't want any of the waitresses getting any side action. Theanessa was taking her chances.

The night went on in much the same way—fending off a few advances and delivering food and drink, and then mostly drink, to the partygoers. She'd wanted to snatch a few minutes with Alexei but didn't want to raise suspicions.

Apparently Alexei didn't either as Britt hadn't seen him with Olav once. It must be killing him to be so close to the man who'd murdered his father.

As the action picked up on the dance floor and the waitressing consisted more of collecting empty glasses and plates than delivering anything to the guests, Britt began scoping out the different areas of the banquet hall. While the women were attentive to the male guests, she hadn't witnessed any groping or manhandling. Did they all just go quietly away to hotel rooms?

The hallway at the back of the room where Irina had shooed her away commanded Britt's attention more than once throughout the evening. The movement in that spot was discreet but noticeable.

Her gaze swept the room of preoccupied people, and she meandered toward the hallway, keeping a tray in her hand for appearances' sake. She turned the corner into the hallway quickly and flattened her body against the wall. A door opened, and she placed her tray on the floor and crouched forward as if fixing her shoe.

Through the veil of her hair, she watched as a man exited the room and strolled back to the banquet hall, adjusting his shirt collar.

She wanted to be ready the next time a door opened, so she continued down the hallway and positioned herself between two of the doors, facing two other doors. Again, she pretended to be fussing with her shoe and left the tray on the floor—just a waitress collecting herself.

Five minutes later, her patience was rewarded as the door across the hall opened, the glow from the room creating a rectangle of light on the carpet. She shifted away from the light.

The man at the door spit out something in Russian, clearly angry. A woman responded, and Britt recognized Irina's voice. She jerked her head up to peer into the room and clapped a hand over her mouth.

Irina sat on the edge of a bed where Jessie, wearing lacy lingerie, was sprawled out. She looked dead— no, drugged—her head rolling to one side and her arm sweeping the floor where it hung off the bed.

Britt braced her hand against the wall to push to her feet. She began to careen toward the open door. She had to save Jessie. She had to protect Leanna.

Before she could take one more step, a rough hand clamped over her mouth from behind, jerking her back, lifting her off her feet and dragging her toward the exit.

She clawed at the fingers restricting her air and arched her body, but her actions were futile.

Maybe she'd find Leanna after all.

Chapter Eleven

The man's words came at him in a fog, and Alexei dragged his gaze away from the hallway where Britt had disappeared several minutes ago with an empty tray.

He had an idea what went on back there, and she had no business in that vicinity.

Holding up a hand to his companion, he said, "Excuse me, David. A girl I've had my eye on all night is finally alone. I'm going to try my luck."

"Go, go, man. Enjoy yourself."

Alexei cut through the crowd, making a beeline for the dark hallway. As he took the corner, a door slammed, but another opened in the back. From studying the layout beforehand, Alexei knew that door led to the parking lot behind the banquet.

The darkness obscured his vision, but he could make out two figures going through that door—and one was struggling.

Alexei jogged down the hallway, his adrenaline spiking when he saw the empty tray on the floor.

He burst through the exit door, and the weak light affixed to the back of the building shed a yellow glow over a man choking Britt.

Ice-cold rage ran through his body, and he launched

forward, grabbing the man by the back of the neck. Alexei yanked him off Britt and shook him like a rag doll, the toes of the man's shoes scuffing the asphalt.

Alexei squeezed the man's carotid artery, and he went limp in his grasp.

Britt had scrambled to her feet and grabbed Alexei's arm. "He's out. Let him go."

He dropped the man and he fell in a heap. Then he stepped over the man's prone form and pulled Britt into his arms. "Are you all right? Did he hurt you?"

"He choked me." She stroked her throat. "If you hadn't come out here, I don't know what he would've done. How did you know? What were you doing in that hallway?"

"I've had my eye on you all night, *moya solnishka*." He smoothed her hair from her flushed face. "When you didn't emerge from that hallway, I knew something had gone wrong."

"I'm glad you did. I guess that secret sign we discussed doesn't work if you're out of sight." She drove her forehead against his chest. "I—I saw Jessie in one of those rooms. You know, the waitress who auditioned for Sergei. Alexei, she looked drugged. Completely out of it."

He wrapped his arms around her tighter, wanting to protect her from all the ugliness in that place. "You know what those rooms are used for?"

"I didn't think the couples would be hooking up right here. I figured they'd leave for a hotel room or something."

"If the men want a taste before they buy, that's where they do it."

She pushed away from him and staggered backward. "I think I'm going to be sick. Why Jessie?"

"Maybe Sergei thought she understood what it meant to be a dancer, and when she balked, he took other measures." He crouched next to the fallen man and shoved up one of his eyelids. "We need to get out of here before this guy comes to."

"What are we going to do? Where are we going to go?"

"Who else was in the room with Jessie?"

"Some Russian man and Irina."

"Did they see you?"

"I don't know. I don't think so. The door was swinging closed again right when I saw Jessie on the bed and that—" she aimed a toe at the unconscious man "—goon came up behind me."

"So, right now only the three of us know you were in that hallway and saw Jessie. This guy—" he went further than Britt and kicked the man in the side "—doesn't even know what you saw."

"What does that mean?"

"It means we're going back inside and pretending nothing happened." He took her by the shoulders and turned her to face the building. "You go first. Grab your tray, and get back to work. If you see Irina, act normal."

"That's going to be hard to do." Turning to face him, she circled her throat with her fingers.

"You can do it, Britt. Put that poker face you use with your clients into action."

"What are you going to do? We have to save Jessie. I think the man in the room was angry because she was nonresponsive. We have to get her out of there."

"Right now, I'm going around the front, and I'm

going to bum a cigarette from someone, as if I went out there for a smoke." He pinched her chin. "I'll think of some way to get Jessie out."

"And Mila. The dancer who had the tattoo artist's card. She's here tonight—with the Belkin family tattoo on her arm."

"We can't save them all, Britt, at least not until the entire operation is brought down."

"Tatyana's baby. The woman who called me said finding that baby would bring them all down."

"So will linking the Belkins to Vlad's terrorist network."

She gathered the front of his shirt in her hands. "Are you any closer? Did you find something?"

"I might have."

"You saw Olav Belkin tonight, didn't you?"

"I did. How did you know him?"

"He was easy to spot."

Alexei clenched his teeth. It had taken all his self-control not to haul off and punch the old man in the face. And if he'd had a gun with him...? But he'd never planned to take Belkin out in public like this. Just a well-placed bullet from a great, great distance.

He shook his head. Britt had been right. What would that achieve except for slaking his thirst for revenge?

Taking her hand, he said, "Let's see the rest of this night out. The man who attacked you might not be so willing to tell anyone what happened. The Belkins are unforgiving bosses. The fact that this SOB landed out in the parking lot facedown would not bode well for him with the Belkins."

"Okay." Britt pulled in a deep breath and straightened her frilly apron.

He squeezed her hand before letting her go. "Do not stop by that room or any of those rooms. Get your tray and go."

She turned at the door and mouthed the words *thank you*.

Brushing off his jacket, Alexei took off for the front of the restaurant. He stepped over a row of bushes to change his direction and make it look like he was coming from the restaurant's front door.

He joined a group of men smoking and chatting. "Does someone have a cigarette? I'm trying to quit, but you know how that goes."

"I'm gonna quit at the end of the summer. I promised my wife." The man shoved a half-empty pack of smokes and a matchbook into Alexei's hand. "Keep 'em."

"Thanks." Alexei put a cigarette between his lips and struck a match from the Eastern Nights matchbook and lit it. He tucked the matches into the front pocket of his jacket, an idea forming in his head.

The group broke apart, and some of the men left and others wandered back into the party. Alexei followed them, tossing his unsmoked cigarette to the ground and crushing it beneath the toe of his shoe.

Once inside, he scanned the room and let out a breath when he spotted Britt carrying a tray of empty glasses to the kitchen. His contact had already left for the evening, more interested in business than pleasure, so Alexei didn't know many of the people left—except the Belkins, including Sergei. He'd been able to get the measure of the man...and the man had been lacking.

Olav still held court in a corner of the room, relaxing on a deep sofa, two young, gorgeous women on either side of him. If Alexei had his rifle with him, it would be so easy to take Belkin out right now. Then it would be lifted—this burden he carried. Of course, he'd probably be dead before his bullet hit Belkin. And Britt would be on her own.

There was another way, but Alexei didn't want Belkin to get off again by agreeing to work with the FBI to nail Vlad. Alexei wouldn't allow that to happen—not this time.

He moved into the anteroom between the restaurant and the banquet hall and nodded at a couple of women walking arm in arm to the restrooms.

He stood in front of a painting of the Black Sea and then reached into his pocket for the book of matches. He struck one, and pinching it between his thumb and forefinger, he held it up to the sprinkler head.

A small curl of smoke kissed the edge of the sprinkler, and it sputtered to life. Water splattered against the painting and, in a chain reaction, set off the other sprinkler heads in the foyer.

Then Alexei poked his head into the kitchen, where several busboys were washing and stacking dishes. He yelled, "Fire! Get out!"

The busboys looked at each other, and Alexei shouted, *"Fuego!"*

They dropped the dishes and crowded out of the kitchen.

When they'd all left, Alexei held a match to another sprinkler head and pulled the fire alarm by the stoves. As the alarm wailed, he smiled to himself. "That should do it."

By the time he returned to the banquet hall, chaos reigned. The sprinklers had gone off in the hall, also. Women screamed and held their hands over their heads to protect their hair and makeup from the relentless streams of water.

Sergei charged through the room, waving his hands and yelling, "No fire department. No police."

Sergei's words just caused more panic as the men with hookers on their arms either disengaged themselves or ran for the doors, dragging their newfound companions along with them.

Alexei's gaze darted among the pandemonium until it rested on Britt at the entrance to the hallway. Their eyes met, and he shook his head.

He threaded his way through the agitated guests to reach Britt. "Leave now. Check in with Irina, if you want. I'll knock on those doors and sound the alarm."

Just then, the bartender who wasn't Stepan rushed past them and saved Alexei the trouble. He banged on each door and shouted in Russian, "Get out. Get the girls out now. Police coming."

Alexei nudged Britt. "There you go. It's over."

"I'd kiss you right now, but I don't want to raise any eyebrows." She kissed her fingers instead and pressed them to his throat. Then she joined the herd of people making their way to the exits.

Alexei edged along the walls of the room until he came up behind the sitting area where Olav had stationed himself throughout the party with his inner circle.

Someone had left a jacket draped across one of the chairs. Alexei grabbed it and felt the pockets. Bingo. He slipped the cell phone from the jacket's pocket and dropped it into his own. He was starting his own collection.

He tented the abandoned jacket over his head and

made for the nearest exit just as the first set of fire
trucks rolled onto the scene. The firefighters wouldn't
find a fire or even a faulty sprinkler system, and they
sure as hell wouldn't find any evidence of a party for
rich men and a bevy of beautiful escorts.

Alexei had made out a lot better. He'd found a couple
of cell phones, had made contact with a weapons dealer
and had gained Sergei Belkin's trust.

But more important than any of that? He'd saved
Britt from a thug's attack.

An hour later, Alexei joined Britt in the hotel room,
stretched out on the sofa, watching TV with her laptop beside her.

He shrugged out of his jacket and sat in the chair
across from her, hunching forward on his knees. "Nobody approached you tonight about the attack in the
hallway?"

"No. Sergei's minion must've been too embarrassed
to tell his boss someone had gotten the better of him."

"But he's going to tell him you saw Jessie in that
room. Somehow, he'll get word to Sergei that he saw
you in the hallway and you ran away—something to
protect himself but implicate you. He's most likely a
loyal drone."

Britt drew her knees to her chest and wrapped her
arms around her legs. "I can talk my way out of it, just
like I did with the towing receipt."

He launched out of the chair and knelt beside the
sofa. "No, you can't. You saw Jessie in a room, drugged,
noncompliant. Are you going to convince Sergei you
don't care about that?"

"I can pretend I didn't see anything. How best to
prove that by coming into work like nothing happened?

If I bail now, Sergei's going to know for sure I saw something." She rested a hand on the back of his neck. "It would be my word against the man's who attacked me."

"Exactly. Why would Sergei believe some waitress he just hired over a loyal foot soldier? And about that foot soldier, he's going to find it strange that you didn't report the assault. Why wouldn't you, unless you knew you'd seen something you shouldn't have seen."

"What's the guy going to do? Approach me and ask why I didn't tell on him?" Her fingers wiggled into his hair. "I've never seen him before anyway. There were lots of waitresses there that night, many of them in black dresses. It was dark in the hallway, and he came at me from behind. He probably never even saw my face."

He closed his eyes, trying not to be swayed by the gentle fingers massaging his scalp. "You have a hundred and one reasons not to go back to the Tattle-Tale."

"I'm not going back tomorrow, anyway. I finally have a day off."

"Good."

"And you? Do you think you have enough information for the Vlad task force to get put on this assignment officially?"

"I think I do. I met a man at the party who's an arms dealer. If Belkin is partnering with terrorists, it will involve weapons, most likely in exchange for drugs—pure opium from Afghanistan. It's another inroad, and I'm going to contact Ariel about it."

"I'm glad." She dragged her fingers through his hair and brushed his cheek with her knuckles. "That was a crazy idea you had."

Grabbing her wrist, he snorted. "My idea was crazy?

And your idea about infiltrating the Russian mob to find your sister was perfectly sane."

"I didn't know Leanna was involved with the Russian mob until you told me. I just thought it was something straightforward, like an affair with her boss." Britt let loose with a long sigh. "I wish it had been so simple. Ever since I saw Jessie in that room, I've had a cold fear in my belly about Leanna."

He pressed his lips against the inside of her wrist. "You're afraid she might've wound up like Jessie."

"Do you think it's possible?" She slid her legs off the sofa and dug her elbows into her thighs. "I thought the Belkins only wanted young women from Russia, women cut off from their families, alone, desperate. That's not Jessie. She must've done something, said something during that audition that set Sergei off."

"The Belkins are capable of anything." Alexei rose to his feet and stretched. "It's been another long night. Get to bed, and we'll debrief tomorrow."

"I don't think I ever thanked you." She stood up beside him and curled her arms around his waist. "You saved me from that man and then you saved Jessie and probably a few other women by setting off the sprinklers."

"I didn't save those other women, Britt. They won't be saved until the Belkin crime family is stopped."

"Bring them all down." She tapped her lower lip. "Find Tatyana's baby."

"I'll leave that to you. I'm going to track down these weapons and see if I can discover the link between the Belkins and Vlad." He gripped her shoulders and took a step back, away from her aura that seemed to swirl around him. "Get some sleep."

She dropped her hands, releasing him. "What are you afraid of, Alexei?"

"I'm afraid of leaving you."

She blinked. "People have been leaving me all my life—my father, my mother, my sister. You're the surest thing I've had in a long time."

Her words made his heart hurt, and he reached for her again. "Your father's family took you in."

"Oh, yeah." She gave him a little wobbly smile. "Took me away from my baby sister, whom I'd been protecting since she was born, plopped me into the middle of some perfect family that always regarded me as the junkie's kid. My uncle Jason took me in because he thought it was his duty, but he never loved me. And his wife?"

"I'm sorry. I didn't realize that's how it was for you."

"Don't get me wrong." She placed her palms on his chest. "I was grateful for what they did. They were generous with their money, put me through school and wanted to pay for graduate school, but I refused that. They just weren't so generous with their love."

She unbuttoned the top buttons of his shirt and slid her hands inside, splaying her fingers against his bare skin. Her touch scorched him, and he ached with wanting her.

She leaned in, her voice low and husky. "We have a connection. If we explore that connection for one night or two or eight and then you have to leave me, I'll consider myself blessed, not abandoned."

"Anything can happen, *moya solnishka*."

"I know." She grabbed the hem of her dress and pulled it up and over her head. She dropped it in a heap at her feet. "And I've been meaning to ask you, what does *moya solnishka* mean?"

He ran a hand through the blond strands of her hair. "'My sunshine.'"

Her luscious lips curved into a smile. "Then let me be your sunshine—even if it's for one night."

Chapter Twelve

Britt hung on to the heavy arm draped around her waist from behind. For being a reluctant lover, Alexei had taken to the task like a champ.

Stretching her legs, she wiggled her toes against his feet. She'd lied to Alexei. This one night or two or eight with him would never be enough, but she'd never tell him that.

If he believed he could be a better navy SEAL if he had nobody waiting for him, counting on him, loving him, she had to let him have that—even if he was wrong.

His father had been taken from his pregnant mother for doing the right thing, but fate didn't always twist that way.

His breath warmed the back of her neck as he sighed.

She wriggled around to face him and watched him wake up. Would he recoil in regret once it sank in that he'd succumbed to his desires? Their desires?

He peeled open one eye and ran the pad of his thumb over a lock of her hair across her breast. *"Moya solnishka."*

That answered that.

Cuddling into his chest, she said, "That's not fair. I want a cool Russian nickname for you."

"I like Russki, especially when you say it with that bad Russian accent."

She laughed and then felt guilty as hell. What right did she have to be lying in this sumptuous bed with this sumptuous man when Leanna was God knew where? The same feeling had poked her each time she'd scored a goal in soccer or had gone on vacation or attended the prom. What right did she have to be happy when her sister had been stuck with some foster family?

Alexei stroked her back from her neck to her derriere, resting his hand on the curve of her bottom. "What's wrong?"

"Here I am, living it up in a swanky Beverly Hills hotel with a hot guy in my bed, and my sister's still missing."

"And you should be doing what exactly that you aren't already doing? You've put your life in danger countless times to find her." He pulled her closer, hooking one leg over hers. "You're doing enough, Britt. It's not your fault your father's people didn't want to take in Leanna."

How many times had her own therapist told her that? But when Alexei told her the same thing with his arms tightly wrapped around her, his breath hot in her hair, his hands caressing her flesh—she almost believed it.

She sniffled and rubbed her nose against his shoulder. "Speaking of taking on unrealistic burdens, are you going to contact the task force this morning with your findings and proposition?"

"Yeah." He rolled onto his back and crossed his arms behind his head. "I'm almost afraid to."

"Because you think they'll tell you to stand down and they'll send someone else out here to finish the task?"

"That about sums it up."

"Then you have to let it go and trust others to do the job."

Twisting his head to the side, he said, "Even if those others aren't going to look into the sex trafficking and find out what happened to Leanna?"

She swallowed hard. Alexei had nailed it. If the people in charge told him to back away from the Belkins, she might never be able to track down Leanna. She had no illusions that she could go up against the Belkins herself, even if she found evidence that they'd...harmed Leanna. Even if she found that baby. Tatyana's baby.

He nudged her head with his elbow. "Even then?"

"Even then. Maybe you could put in a word about the trafficking, about the baby."

"Back to the baby." He kissed the top of her head and then rolled out of the bed.

"You didn't hear this woman on the phone. She sounded so sure of herself."

"We don't even know who called you. Did anyone give you any hints last night? Wink at you? Try to get you alone?"

"Only Stepan."

Alexei stopped in midstretch. "What does that mean?"

"Don't worry. It's not just me. He's interested in all the ladies."

"I wonder how much he knows about what's going on."

"You planning on finding out?"

"Could be a good resource. A lot of times these low-level disgruntled drones are ripe for turning on their bosses."

"Not sure I'd call Stepan one of those, but do you know who else I want to talk to?"

"I'm afraid to ask."

"Calvin, the homeless guy who hangs out near the Tattle-Tale. He obviously knows Leanna. Maybe he saw something. Maybe she told him something."

"You'd better not be caught talking to him near the club. Irina already saw you two together. She might get suspicious."

"Maybe I can lure him away with the promise of lunch."

"Just be careful."

"Can I lure you out with the promise of breakfast?" Stretching out her arms for him, she scooted to the edge of the bed.

Grabbing her hands, he pulled her to her feet and against his body. "Only if I can lure you into the shower first."

She bared her teeth against his collarbone. "This hard body is the only lure I need."

And just like that, Alexei made her forget everything for several blissful moments—but not before she said a silent apology to Leanna and a prayer.

After breakfast, Britt watched Alexei zoom off on his motorcycle while she finished her coffee at the outdoor café on Sunset.

The baby in the stroller at the table next to hers gurgled and waved his sticky hand in her direction. She wiggled her fingers in response, and he rewarded her with a toothless smile. She melted just a little bit inside.

"He likes you." Mom dabbed a trail of drool from

the baby's chin. "Do you and your husband have any children?"

Britt raised her eyebrows. "My husband?"

"Oh." The woman glanced at the chair Alexei had vacated. "Sorry."

"He's my…" Britt waved her hand in the general direction of the empty chair. "…boyfriend."

A rush of heat swept from her chest to her hairline. Why had she lied? She *had* slept with Alexei. That had to qualify as boyfriend status—if just for the day.

"That makes sense since the two of you still seem like you're in that goo-goo-eyed stage."

The warmth of Britt's face deepened. If a stranger could figure out the way she felt toward Alexei, the man himself must be wondering what he could do to extricate himself from her…goo-goo eyes.

The woman's friend returned to the table to save Britt any further embarrassment.

As the women gathered their things, Britt studied the baby. She needed to find a baby of her own. She waved at the little guy again as his mother pushed the stroller onto the sidewalk.

Why had the mysterious caller told Britt to find Tatyana's baby? How did one lose a baby in the first place? The woman hadn't mentioned finding Tatyana, just the baby. That seemed to indicate mom and baby weren't together.

How could a mother be separated from her newborn baby? Britt's hand tightened around her coffee cup. Death would separate a mother and baby. What would happen to a baby with a dead mother?

Britt had worked with clients who'd lost their children due to drug addiction, and Child Protective Services had always stepped in to take charge of those kids until mom and dad got clean and sober.

She tapped her fingernail against her cup. Maybe she could start there. LA was a big city, but how many Russian mothers had given birth in the past two months?

She glanced at the time on her phone. Before she got back to the hotel to do some research on her laptop, she had a stop to make at the Tattle-Tale—or at least the alley behind the Tattle-Tale.

Did Calvin hang out there all day or just at night? She'd seen him only at night, but then, she'd been at the Tattle-Tale only at night.

Alexei had already paid the bill and left the tip, so Britt scooted her chair back from the table and hiked up the street to her car. She drove to the club and parked around the corner.

Daylight didn't do much to improve the alley, although more businesses had their doors open, and the midday sun expelled the lurking shadows and hidden corners.

She strode down the middle of the asphalt, veering to the right as a car rolled past her. As she approached the back of the Tattle-Tale, she peered around the corner of the Dumpster where Calvin usually parked his basket.

He'd found another location today, or maybe he had a different hangout during the day.

The back door of the Tattle-Tale burst open and Britt jumped, her hand to her heart.

"Hey, Barbie. You come to see me?" Stepan grinned as he hoisted a plastic garbage bag into the Dumpster.

"N-no." *Damn, what timing.* "I was hoping someone would be here though. I wanted to check my time card. I think I forgot to clock out the other night."

He stepped back and shoved the door wider. "What luck."

She took a few tentative steps toward the open door, but Stepan didn't budge. Instead, he swept his arm forward, ushering her inside the building.

Stepan wasn't a big man, but he hadn't left her much room, so she had to squeeze past him, getting a whiff of stale coffee and cigarettes from his breath.

"How about that mess last night, eh?" He let the door slam behind them, and Britt jumped again—this time internally.

"That was pretty crazy. Do you know if there was even a fire?"

"Just sprinklers. Faulty system maybe, but all those fine people ruined their fine clothes."

His lips twisted into a sneer, and Britt thought about Alexei's comment about disgruntled employees—not that she'd trust Stepan here and now. If Alexei wanted to feel him out, she'd leave that up to him.

"What are you doing here so early?"

"Little cleaning, little inventory." His dull eyes narrowed as she made a beeline for the rack of time cards. "You can't check your time card tonight?"

"I'm off tonight." She flicked her time card out of the rack and squinted at it. "Oh, good. I did clock out."

"Now that I have you here." He stepped into the hallway, blocking her access to the back door. "You want to help a little behind bar? Just polishing glasses. I'll tell Irina and you get some extra pay."

She opened her mouth as every fiber in her body screamed *No*, but then the memory of Jerome sneaking behind the bar that first night she'd met Alexei flashed into her brain. She'd never been able to get behind the bar since that night without arousing suspicions.

"You know, I could use a few extra bucks." She brushed her hands together. "What do you need?"

"The glasses get spots. Sergei don't like spots." He whipped a towel from his waistband and pressed it into her hands. "You go behind bar and check all shot glasses. Spots? You wipe clean."

"I can do that. Didn't have anything planned anyway."

"Pretty girl like you, no boyfriend? No hot date?"

Oh, I have a hot Russian boyfriend, but only in my mind.

"I just moved to this area. I don't know a lot of people."

He gave her a sidelong glance. "You knew Jerome."

She sucked in a breath and held the towel to her face. "Don't remind me. That was terrifying."

"Not a good date." He shook his head as if Jerome had planned to get murdered on their date.

"It wasn't a date, really. He knew I was new to town." She hunched her shoulders. "It was awful."

"You saw it happen?"

He'd shuffled closer, and she couldn't breathe. She'd been crazy to stay here with him.

"No." She took a few steps back. "I couldn't find parking. It was all over by the time I got out of my car and walked to Sunset. Not a great invitation to the city or to dating."

"Better luck next time."

She spun around and called over her shoulder. "I'll get going on those glasses. What are you going to be doing?"

"Checking inventory in supply room." He held up a clipboard.

Her pulse didn't steady until she was behind the bar and she could hear Stepan banging around in the back. Aware of the camera watching her every move, Britt parked in front of a plastic dish rack of shot glasses and plucked out the first one.

She held it up to the light over the bar and rubbed it with the cloth Stepan had given her. She and Alexei had reviewed the footage from that night, and Jerome had been able to avoid the camera by ducking behind the bar near the sink. She'd do the same. Whatever Jerome had done that night, it hadn't taken him long.

She worked her way through the rows of glasses in the first rack and then shuffled to the next one—one step closer to the sink. She finished that set and stationed herself in front of the third, right next to the sink and above the area where Jerome had been crouching that night.

With one row of glasses polished, Britt shook out the cloth and peered at it. She dropped it on the bar and squatted down on her haunches.

Stacks of cocktail napkins, pads of paper for orders, matchbooks and pencil stubs littered the shelves beneath the bar.

She hunched forward and reached past a stack of coasters. Her fingertips brushed cold hard metal. She traced an oblong box with her hands and pulled it off the shelf, knocking several coasters onto the floor.

She set the strong box on the floor and flicked up the latch with trembling fingers. She lifted the lid and stirred the contents with her index finger. Old receipts and a few pictures of women in various stages of undress rustled and shifted in the box.

Could these pictures be important? Had Jerome taken them? She picked up a few and shuffled through them.

A broken plastic band fell on the floor, and Britt picked it up. She smoothed out the slightly curled bracelet against her knee, and her heart jumped as she saw the name Tatyana printed on the plastic.

Britt leaned back to get the band in the light, and as she read the words printed there, her blood ran cold. In her hands, she held Tatyana Porizkova's hospital bracelet, dated about a month ago.

How had it gotten here? Was this hospital stay related to the birth of Tatyana's baby? She snatched one of the receipts from the box and scribbled down the information from the bracelet.

"How's it going?" Stepan called from the hallway.

Britt shoved the receipt and wristband into her pocket and closed the lid on the metal box. She replaced it on the shelf, arranging the other items in front of it, and popped up from behind the bar just as Stepan rounded the corner.

"I'm almost done with this third set of shot glasses."

"Barbie, you're slow. Can you do that whole row?"

"Sure I can." She finished polishing the rest of the glasses with her mind racing. Jerome knew the bracelet was there but hadn't wanted to take it in case someone noticed it was missing. Either that or he found it and put it there himself. But he wouldn't have hidden something like that at the club. Was that what he'd planned on telling her the night he died? Was he going to tell her about Tatyana's baby and the significance of that baby?

She could understand why the Belkins wouldn't want one of their women to get pregnant, but why would they go to such great lengths to hide that pregnancy or even harm the pregnant woman and anyone who knew about the pregnancy? How could a little baby bring down a criminal organization like the Belkins'?

The caller had been right. She had to find Tatyana's baby. That baby seemed to hold the key to everything.

She fingered the hospital band in the front pocket of her jeans. And now she knew exactly where to start—Cedars-Sinai Medical Center.

Stepan joined her behind the bar and elbowed her in the ribs. "You do good job, Barbie."

"Thanks." She laced her fingers together and stretched them in front of her. "I'm going to take off now. Are you going to Mila's party at Rage tonight?"

"In my dreams." He rolled his eyes to the ceiling. "Girls only, just dancers and waitresses. You going?"

"No, I'm going to get to bed early. Have a good night."

"Enjoy hot date, Barbie."

She snorted and slid out from behind the bar. Grabbing her purse from a chair, she waved.

Outside the club, she rested her back against the door and scooped in a deep breath of garbage-scented air. What was that bracelet doing there?

She pushed off the door and tripped as a man emerged from behind the Dumpster, her nerves still raw. Calvin had appeared after all.

As the raggedy man shuffled forward, her heart dipped. A different transient had taken Calvin's spot, a younger man.

"Sorry, I thought you were someone else." She held up her hands to the homeless man planted in front of her.

"You lookin' for Calvin?"

She glanced over her shoulder at the back door of the Tattle-Tale. "Well, sort of. Do you know where he is today?"

"He don't come here in daytime." The man tugged at the dirty cap on his head. "Do you wanna know where he crashes during the day?"

Britt eyed the rough hand thrust at her, palm up. She dug into her purse and pulled out a ten-dollar bill. She waved it at him. "Will this tell me?"

"Uh-huh."

She tucked the money into his hand, and it disappeared into the capacious folds of his coat, draped over his slouched form in the seventy-five-degree heat.

"He's in the park down on the corner." He jerked his thumb to the right.

"There's a park on this street?"

"That patch of grass and trees near the freeway on-ramp." He tapped his temple with one finger. "You know Calvin ain't quite right in the head."

"Are you saying he's dangerous?" Britt took a step back from the cloud of alcohol fumes emanating from the man's pores. This guy seemed a lot sketchier than Calvin.

"Nah, just don't know what business you'd have with him."

"Business? I wouldn't call it business." She pointed to the end of the alley. "That way and then left toward the freeway?"

"That's it. Can't miss it."

Britt heard a click behind her and spun around. She

stared at the metal door leading to the club. "Was that door open?"

Her homeless guide hunched into his coat. "Nope."

"All right, then. Thanks for the tip."

She exited the alley on the other side and got into her car. She drove up the street to the so-called park with its scrappy patches of dried grass and bushes that dotted a trail to the area beneath the on-ramp.

She parked the car and gripped the steering wheel, puffing out short breaths as she watched a man duck under the canopy of trees by the on-ramp. Calling this a park was generous. It looked like there could be a homeless camp beneath the freeway, away from prying eyes.

Maybe if she just stood on the sidewalk and yelled for Calvin, he'd come out to meet her. She didn't think she wanted to see what inhabited this particular urban gathering place.

After debating the wisdom of visiting a homeless camp, Britt grabbed her cell phone from the cup holder and opened the car door. She could get 911 on speed dial if she had to.

Putting one foot in front of the other, she marched toward the edge of the sidewalk. She cupped her hand over her mouth to make her voice heard above the roar of the freeway. "Calvin? Calvin, are you in there?"

She held her breath, listening for an answer. Several seconds later, she stepped onto a patch of grass, rough with pebbles scattered through it. "Calvin? It's Barbie. I—I have something for you."

Britt jerked as something crashed through the bushes, and a man stumbled into the clearing from beneath the pillars of cement. Calvin, his jacket ripped and bloody, staggered toward her and keeled forward.

Her heart rattling her rib cage, Britt launched forward and dropped to the ground beside him. "Calvin? What happened?"

He sucked in a wet breath, and a line of blood trickled from the corner of his mouth. Up close, she could see his battered face and split lip. She put her hands on his thin body to feel if he had any other injuries or if any blood was seeping through his clothing.

Calvin coughed and strangled out one word.

"What?" She put her ear close to his lips. "What did you say?"

He rasped, "Nothing. I know nothing about Lee-Low."

Britt caught her breath. Childlike, Calvin had just admitted he *did* know something about Leanna.

She whispered, "What don't you know about Lee-Low, Calvin? I won't tell anyone."

His cloudy eyes shifted over her shoulder and widened for a split second—right before a boot landed against her ribs.

Chapter Thirteen

Back from the warehouse and ensconced in the luxury
of his hotel suite, Alexei tapped Send on his phone and
blew out a breath. He'd just secured proof positive that
the Belkin crime family had taken delivery of a ship-
ment of weapons—none that they needed to run their
little empire here in LA. These weapons could start a
war or two, and as much as the Belkins destroyed any
area they inhabited, they counted on the niceties of
society to keep selling their drugs and women to any
wealthy takers.

Those arms were meant for someone else, most likely
in exchange for the raw opium Vlad could provide the
Belkins from the fields of Afghanistan. Ariel had to
see the sense in pursuing this connection—and had to
see the sense in keeping him on the assignment. He'd
already infiltrated the Belkins at the innermost levels.

He watched his phone, but if he expected Ariel to respond immediately, it looked like he'd be disappointed.

His eyebrows shot up when he noticed the time on
his cell. He'd been surprised that he'd made it back to
the hotel before Britt. Wasn't she going to poke around
the baby angle? She couldn't do that over the phone?

He'd declined to give her his cell phone number because he didn't want it in her cell phone contacts, but he should've bought a temp phone so she could contact him.

What he *had* done, without her knowledge, was install a tracking device on her cell phone, and after the attack on her last night, he felt justified. Now he felt worried.

He called up the locator on his phone and cursed in Russian when he saw the pin in Hollywood, right near the Tattle-Tale. Why had she gone to the club? She didn't even have a shift tonight.

His pulse picked up speed. Unless she didn't go to the club willingly. Who knew what that thug who'd had her around the throat told his bosses?

He swept the keys to his bike from the TV stand and rushed downstairs. He secured his phone on the handlebars of the motorcycle so he could watch the locator app.

When he rolled past the entrance to the Tattle-Tale, still closed, he drew his brows over his nose. The pin on the app had shifted, no longer located at the Tattle-Tale but still in the area.

He gunned his bike and made a U-turn, following the GPS on the phone. When he saw Britt's car parked on the street near the freeway on-ramp, he swallowed hard. Had she broken down in that old rattletrap she drove?

As he rolled up behind the empty car, an icy fear dragged a finger down his back. Where had she gone?

He parked his bike on the street and pulled his helmet off his head. The muffled cries he heard had him sprinting toward the noises coming from the area below the on-ramp.

He couldn't see anything until he got to the sidewalk that bordered the grassy strip. And then what he saw fueled a burning rage in his gut, and he flew at the man pummeling Britt, who was flailing her arms at her attacker and bicycling her legs from her position on the ground.

Alexei tackled the man, gagging on the sour stench rising from his body. Alexei slammed his fist into the man's face and had the satisfaction of hearing a distinct crack.

Blood poured from the guy's nose, and he spit out a stream of foul expletives as he swung at Alexei. Alexei stepped back from the punch and then kneed the man in the gut, bringing him to the ground.

Britt tugged on his sleeve. "Let's go. I don't want to be here when the cops arrive. I just called 911. Calvin's hurt."

"Calvin?" Alexei stomped on the man's hand, the same hand he'd been using to beat Britt. He crushed it beneath his boot until the man screamed in agony.

Alexei looked up to see Britt crouched beside another homeless man, his face bloody and broken.

She whispered something to Calvin and then launched herself at Alexei. "Please, we need to get out of here to avoid questions."

The sound of a siren in the distance uprooted Alexei's feet from the ground. "Meet me at the diner where we went the first night we met."

Britt nodded and jogged to her car.

Alexei followed her the three blocks to the diner. She parked first and sat in the car. When he got off his bike, he approached the driver's-side window, which she powered down.

"Do you want to tell me what just happened back there?"

"How did you find me?"

"We'll discuss this inside. You need some ice for your eye. Head to the restroom as soon as you get inside to clean up." He reached inside the car and flicked some weed stems from her hair. "Are you all right?"

She dabbed her fingertips across her face and gazed at the smears of blood on her fingers. "I'm okay."

They entered the diner, and Alexei grabbed a table in the back, next to a window on the parking lot, while Britt scurried to the restroom, head down, hair creating a veil on either side of her face.

He asked for a couple of waters and kept one eye on the plastic menu and the other on the parking lot. He didn't know what to expect right now. Why had two homeless men been fighting with Britt?

She emerged from the bathroom with a puffy bottom lip and a red mark at the corner of her eye, but she'd cleaned up the blood and looked better than he'd expected.

She slid into the booth across from him and sucked down half the water with a straw. Then she closed her eyes and rested the back of her head against the red vinyl banquette.

"Do you want to start at the beginning?"

She opened an eye—the one not rimmed in red. "How'd you find me?"

"I put a tracker on your phone, but that's not important. Tell me what happened."

"I went to the Tattle-Tale to find Calvin to see if he could tell me any more about Leanna. I didn't expect anyone to be there."

"Who was there?"

"Stepan the bartender."

"That's just great. What story did you tell him for being there?"

"I told him I wanted to check my time card. He believed me."

"As far as you know."

"I really don't think Stepan is involved too much in the criminal activities."

"Did you check it and leave?" Alexei looked up and smiled at the waitress. "I'll have a cup of coffee and a piece of lemon meringue pie."

"I'll have a diet soda, whatever you have, and the grilled cheese sandwich." She shrugged at Alexei. "I missed lunch."

When the waitress took their menus and left, Alexei stuck his fingers in his water, fished out a couple of ice cubes and wrapped them in a napkin. "Put this on your right eye, and maybe you can avoid a shiner."

Britt pressed the makeshift ice pack to her face. "I was at the club for more than a few minutes. Stepan corralled me into helping him."

"You stayed there with him? Alone?"

"He was okay after a few of his clumsy attempts at flirtation. I think he just does it because it's expected. He really doesn't try that hard."

"Go on." Alexei circled his finger in the air. "How did you get from helping Stepan in the Tattle-Tale to being some transient's punching bag?"

"Remember that first night when we saw Jerome return to the club and duck behind the bar, out of the camera's eye?"

He'd never forget that night when he'd met Britt. "Yeah, of course I remember."

"I thought it would be a good opportunity for me

to get down there and see what was so important. I haven't been able to get behind the bar yet during one of my shifts." Her knees, bouncing beneath the table, knocked his. She must've found something, and she was dying to tell him.

"And?" He hunched forward.

She rose up slightly from her seat and pulled something from her pocket. She tossed it on the table between them.

He ran the pad of his thumb over the curled-up piece of plastic, reading the words printed there. "It's Tatyana's hospital bracelet from Cedars-Sinai. So, she had that mystery baby in the hospital. You found this beneath the bar?"

"It was in one of those metal lock boxes, but it wasn't even locked. It was just in there with other junk, but Jerome must've known it was there. Maybe he found it at the club, but what would it be doing there?"

"I doubt Jerome found it." Alexei scuffed his knuckles against the stubble on his chin. "He wouldn't keep it at the club. He might've discovered it in that box. He wouldn't want to take it to tip anyone off, so maybe he went back to take a picture of it."

Britt bounced in her seat. "I never thought of that. Of course, he took a picture. During the staged mugging, his attacker stole his phone. But that doesn't explain why the wristband was there in the first place."

"I think it's obvious." Alexei steepled his fingers and peered at Britt over the tips. "Tatyana must've been at the Tattle-Tale wearing her hospital ID."

She crossed her arms, hugging her body. "Why would they have her there after she'd just given birth? What did they do with her?"

"I don't know, but now we know where that baby was born."

"I hope…" She pressed her fingertips against her lips. "I mean, they wouldn't kill a baby, would they?"

"Your female caller told you to find the baby. It sounds like she knew what she was talking about, and she wouldn't have you looking for a dead baby, would she?" He grabbed Britt's hand and chafed it between his. "Finding that bracelet was great, but that doesn't explain the attack on Calvin and you."

Britt paused as the waitress delivered their food.

As she cut her sandwich in half, she said, "I finished up my work with Stepan and left out the back. I saw a transient, and I thought he was Calvin at first and said his name. He wasn't Calvin but said he'd tell me where he was—for a price. So I handed him a ten, and he directed me to that area by the on-ramp."

Alexei rolled his eyes. "You thought it was a good idea to pay a homeless man for information and then head to an obvious homeless camp under the freeway?"

She brushed her fingertips together, sending a shower of crumbs onto her plate. "I was going to stand away from those bushes and call Calvin out to me."

"Didn't work out that way, huh?"

"Calvin did come out of the bushes, beaten and bloodied, and fell to the ground. I went to him, and out of the blue he said he didn't know anything about Lee-Low." She took a big bite of her sandwich, and after she swallowed she dabbed a napkin against her mouth. "Which of course means he *does* know something about her."

"Maybe, maybe not. He knew that's what you were going to ask him about. Maybe he had a moment of clarity and was telling you the truth. He knew Lee-Low from the club, she was nice to him, you were nice to him and you reminded him of Lee-Low." Alexei flicked a dab of meringue from his pie and sucked it off his finger. "How'd the other guy get involved?"

"While I was trying to help Calvin, the other guy attacked me. Kicked me in the gut for starters."

"Was he with Calvin? Did he try to rob you?"

She dropped her sandwich on her plate. "The Belkins sent him, Alexei. He was the same guy I had talked to in the alley."

The dread that had been building in his gut reached up and grabbed him by the throat.

He'd suspected Britt's run-in with the transient had something to do with the club, but he'd been hoping it was random. No such luck.

He shoved his plate away, the tart lemon now sour on his tongue. "How did they arrange that? The Belkins must've paid the other transient to beat up Calvin, or they had one of their henchmen do it, and then they had him lure you to that spot by the freeway."

"That's what I thought as soon as I realized who was attacking me."

"It was Stepan."

"Wait. What? How do you figure? Irina was the one who saw me with Calvin."

"But Stepan is the only one who saw you today. When you got there, he probably called Irina or Sergei and put out the word. They beat up Calvin as a warning and ordered the other transient to attack you. Do you think Calvin's going to make it?"

"I think so. I didn't see any mortal wounds, and he was talking to me. The beating I took, while not—" she dabbed her fingers high on her cheekbone beneath her eye "—pleasant, wasn't life-threatening either. What was the reason behind that?"

"It was a warning. They have no idea what you know or why you're talking to Calvin. They do know Calvin hangs out behind the Tattle-Tale. He may have seen things, even if he doesn't understand what those things mean. They don't want you or anyone else talking to Calvin and getting any ideas. Of course..." He smooshed a piece of piecrust with the tines of his fork.

"Of course what?"

He flicked Tatyana's hospital band with his finger. "You did take this."

"I wasn't thinking. I had it in my hand, and Stepan was coming. Maybe I should put it back."

"Not now."

"Maybe they won't be looking for it. It seems like someone tossed it in that box as an afterthought. Jerome just ran across it because that's his domain. They wouldn't think it would mean anything to anybody."

"And yet it *did* mean something to Jerome—and it got him killed."

Britt licked her lips and took a gulp of her soda. "We don't know that. Due to your mad video skills, Sergei never saw Jerome return to the club that night and crouch below the bar."

"They could've seen him before. Maybe that's not the first time he looked at that wristband. Are you working tomorrow night?"

"Yes."

"I don't think it's a good idea for you to go in."

"I could put the bracelet back."

He shook his head. "An even worse idea."

"What about you?" She slumped in her seat and ripped a piece of crust from her sandwich. "Any luck?"

"As a matter of fact." He held up his index finger. "Wait—I haven't checked my messages."

"You communicated with Ariel? You found something?"

As he pulled his phone from his pocket, he said, "My new friend introduced me to a cache of weapons he has on the market, but only in limited quantities because he already has a big order."

"The Belkins?"

He glanced down at his phone and smacked the table. "Yes!"

"You have the okay from Ariel?"

He huddled closer to Britt over the table and read from the text. "'Sounds promising. Proceed.'"

"That's it?"

"There's an attachment with more info. I'll read it when we get back to the hotel." That knot he'd had between his shoulder blades melted away, and he took a big bite of pie.

"That's great, Alexei. You're official now."

"That'll mean a lot when it comes to resources. I'll have the whole CIA and FBI behind me now—or at least the parts that Ariel can tap into."

"I gather the Vlad task force itself is pretty hush-hush within these agencies?"

"Need to know, which is why you know just about everything. You're in this up to your neck." He picked up Tatyana's wristband by one jagged edge. "We're going to start using my newfound legitimacy with this."

"How?"

"We have hackers who can search a hospital's database. We're going to find out exactly why Tatyana was in the hospital, when and what happened to her baby."

"If my informant was right, finding the baby could cause havoc for the Belkins, and then they won't be in any position to negotiate with Vlad or anyone else."

Alexei drummed his fingers on the table. "I don't know how one baby could impact the Belkin crime family. If the baby belongs to some john, I don't know how we prove that, and even if we do, hookers and escorts have babies every day. It's not going to hurt the Belkins."

"I don't know. Maybe my source will call back. Maybe she works at the Tattle-Tale. That's why I have to keep going back there." Britt picked up her phone from the table. "I'm going to call the hospital to see if I can find out anything about Calvin. Which one do you think he's at?"

"Cedars-Sinai—same hospital as Tatyana."

Britt widened her eyes. "That's perfect. I think we need to pay Calvin a visit."

"Are you up for that?" He shoved the pie plate at her. "At least finish my pie. You deserve pie for getting kicked in the ribs."

She wolfed down the last three bites and ended up with meringue on her chin.

He dabbed his finger on her face and sucked the sweetness into his mouth. "I'm gonna put that down to you not being able to feel your face after getting punched."

She smiled and grabbed his hand. "I'm glad you're legit now, Russki…and not just because of the perks."

"I am, too, but it doesn't mean I'm not taking Olav Belkin down—for good."

"I know that." She squeezed his hand. "But now it's sanctioned."

Sanctioned or not, Belkin was a dead man, but the fire that had roared in his chest every time he thought about Belkin had died down to a kindling. He still wanted to avenge his father's murder at Belkin's hands, but over the past week his passion had burned for a different cause—keeping this woman safe from harm.

As ALEXEI DROVE her car to the hospital, Britt's jaw ached, and she had one arm wrapped around her midsection, pressing against her sore ribs. Maybe she should be checking in herself.

If Alexei hadn't found her, how far would that homeless guy have gone? What marching orders had Sergei or Irina given him?

The strikes against her had been piling up. The Belkins knew she'd been in the vicinity when they'd murdered Jerome. Someone had seen her in that hallway where she witnessed Jessie, drugged and compromised. Irina had caught her talking to Calvin, and now she and Calvin had both paid in blood for that conversation.

What next? Would they finger her as the person who'd taken Tatyana's hospital wristband? Did Sergei even know the wristband was in that metal box? It seemed like a foolish place to hide evidence that could destroy an entire criminal operation.

Or maybe that phone call from the Russian woman had been a hoax just to play her.

She slid a glance at Alexei, hunched over the steering wheel to maneuver through LA traffic. Had he thought of that already? Probably. He didn't miss much, including her insane attraction to him.

Now she had to make good on her promise that she could have a fling with him and then let him go. The sigh escaped her lips before she could stop it.

"I know. Traffic is bad, but we're almost there."

"Emergency room, right?"

"We'll start there."

After parking the car on the rooftop of the parking structure, they made their way into the crowded emergency room and walked to the reception desk.

Britt folded her hands on the counter. "Excuse me. I saw...two men at the corner of Gower and the 101 off-ramp badly beaten and unconscious. I called 911 from my car but couldn't stop. I was wondering if they were okay. Can you tell me anything?"

The nurse at the desk didn't look up from her computer. "Are you a relative?"

"No, just a concerned citizen."

The nurse lifted one shoulder in a half-hearted attempt at sympathy. "We can't give out any information on patients. You can try calling the police. That would be LAPD's Hollywood Division."

Britt bit her bottom lip. "Can you at least tell me what floor Maternity is on?"

That got her attention. The nurse glanced up. "Ninth."

"Thanks."

Alexei put his hand on the small of her back and steered her out of the waiting room. When they reached the hallway, he stabbed the elevator button with his knuckle. "That was a waste of time."

She huffed out a breath as she stepped into the elevator car. "Try to do a good deed."

"Do you expect to have any better luck up there?"

He jabbed his thumbs upward. "If anything, Maternity is going to be even more cautious."

"I just want to look around as long as we're here."

"I can get the info on Tatyana faster through my sources."

"We drove, we parked, we failed. Now we're here, so let's have a look."

Alexei saluted. "Right, chief."

"I like that other name better."

The elevator bumped and then settled on the ninth floor. They stepped out of the car, and the cheerful vibe lifted Britt's spirits. She bumped Alexei's shoulder with her own. "This sure beats the emergency room."

"Babies." He pointed down the hallway to a glassed-in room.

Britt approached the window and placed both hands on the glass. "Just look at them all. Getting ready to face the world."

"Everything ahead of them."

Britt began dragging her finger across the smooth pane of glass. "Rodriguez, Miller, Schwartz, Gomez, Rousseau."

Not all the babies were currently occupying their bassinets. Must be with their moms. She continued reading the names on the labels until she stumbled across a familiar one. She grabbed Alexei's arm. "The baby. Tatyana's baby."

"Where?" His body stiffened beside her.

"In the back row." She tapped on the window. "It's empty, but it says Baby Porizkova."

"You're kidding."

"I'm not. Do you see it? The label is pink. She had a girl."

"Could Tatyana still be here?" Alexei glanced over his shoulder, as if expecting to see her in the hallway behind them.

"I don't know. Do you think Jerome was wrong about her death? We can't very well poke our heads into all these rooms."

A nurse with a clipboard under her arm came up to the nursery door and entered a code on the keypad.

"Excuse me?"

Alexei had nudged her in the back, but it was too late. The nurse turned at the door. "Yes?"

The nudge turned to a pinch, but Britt carried on anyway. "Where is the Porizkova baby?"

The nurse's eyes grew big, and Britt's stomach sank. At least Alexei had stopped jabbing her.

"Are you a relative?"

There it was again, that magical hospital word that opened doors and got you private information. Alexei spoke Russian. Maybe he could pose as a relative.

She took a breath, and Alexei's knuckle drove into her back, just below her sore ribs. He must've read her mind.

"N-no, but the name is familiar. My sister has a Russian friend, and I thought it might be the same person."

As wide as the nurse's eyes were a minute ago, she'd turned them into slits. "Was this friend pregnant?"

Alexei stepped beside her, his body vibrating with tension. "No. She wasn't pregnant. I don't even think that's the same name. You know those Russian names—always sound the same."

The nurse cocked her head. "What are you doing here?"

"We went to check on a friend in Emergency, and I

thought it would be fun to look at the newborns." Britt giggled and patted her aching belly. "The old biological clock is ticking, I guess."

The nurse cracked a tight smile. "I'm sure you understand why we don't want strangers wandering around the nursery."

"Of course."

Alexei took Britt's arm. "Let's go see if Bob is ready to go yet."

He marched her down the hallway to the elevator with an iron grip on her wrist, as if he were afraid she'd run back to the nursery.

They stood shoulder to shoulder at the elevator, but Britt didn't dare say a word.

An older woman joined them, a canvas bag over her shoulder. "So sad for that little one."

Britt's gaze took in the woman head to toe. Not a nurse. She had a volunteer badge pinned to her sweater.

Britt gave her an encouraging smile, the kind she used to get her clients to divulge their deepest, darkest secrets. "The little Porizkova baby?"

"Yes. I heard you asking about her." She shook her gray curls. "Poor little mite doesn't have a mother."

"D-did her mother die in childbirth?"

"Worse." The volunteer pursed her lips.

What could be worse than death? Britt gave Alexei a quick glance. "What happened to her?"

"She up and walked out of the hospital after her little girl was born. Didn't say a word to anyone. Just up and disappeared."

"Oh." Britt put a hand to her thundering heart. "That's terrible. Maybe she didn't have a choice. At least she didn't abandon the baby later."

The woman sniffed. "Could've gone through the regular channels for adoption."

"Her baby's still here?"

"She was a preemie." The woman patted her bag. "I ought to know. I knit a cap for her. I knit all sizes, and that little one took the smallest size. I also cuddle the newborns, and that one's a sweetie."

Britt noticed Alexei wasn't poking her in the back during *this* conversation. "How long has the baby been here?"

The elevator doors opened, and Alexei held them open for the old woman.

"About a month. She's almost ready to leave, but where will she go without a mother?"

"I'm sure she'll be adopted by a loving family."

The woman spent the rest of the elevator ride talking about her knitting and the other newborns. When they parted ways in the parking structure, Britt turned to Alexei.

"What do you think happened?"

He put a finger to his lips. "Wait until we get to the car."

When they reached the nearly empty top level of the structure, Britt finally took a breath. They walked to the car, and Alexei opened the door for her. She slid inside, her knees bouncing as she waited for him to come around the other side.

When he shut the door, she rounded on him. "We did it. We found Tatyana's baby."

He ran his hands over the steering wheel but didn't start the car. "I don't think she left that baby on her own."

"Do you think the Belkins took her out of the hospital?"

"I'm sure of it. They probably would've taken the baby, too, if they could've made it past the dragon nurses."

Britt shivered. "Thank God for the dragon nurses. Do you think they've tried to take the baby?"

"Maybe that's why the nurse went on high alert when you expressed interest in the Porizkova baby. That or she was going to call the police to question you." He smoothed a hand down her thigh. "Sorry for poking at you. That's what I was trying to avoid—questioning by the police."

"Yeah, that would've been a disaster." She yanked at her seat belt. "I think my sister knew something about this baby. Like you said before, if it were the trafficking and escort business, the Belkins could've gotten around that. There's something about that baby. Could the baby be addicted to drugs? Would the Belkins worry about that?"

Alexei's nostrils flared and his eyebrows collided over his nose. He yanked the keys from the ignition.

"Britt, get out of the car!"

"What?" Already on edge, she'd grabbed the handle.

"Out of the car! It's gonna blow."

The force of his voice pumped a flood of adrenaline into her system, and she pushed against the door. It swung open. She tumbled out.

Alexei was still shouting, so she sprinted away from the car and waved at two people heading her way. She panted, "Stay back."

She didn't even hear her second word above the deafening explosion behind her. As the blast propelled her several feet forward and she hit the cement, she had just one thought. *Alexei.*

Chapter Fourteen

Britt's ears were ringing, but she could still hear the woman several feet away screaming. She raised her head, propping her chin on the cement floor of the parking structure, her head swimming. The two people who'd been walking toward her were still on their feet, but their white faces were a study in shock.

Groaning, Britt rolled over, her sore ribs making it hard to breathe—or maybe that was the acrid black smoke drifting toward her. Had Alexei made it out alive?

As she blinked her eyes, Alexei's face floated above her, and she sobbed out his name.

"Britt!" He dropped beside her. "Are you all right?"

She sat up, clutching her midsection. "I am now. Was anyone hurt?"

"There weren't that many cars up on this level. Nobody on my side." He tipped his head toward the two people by the elevator, hugging. "They got lucky. You saved their lives."

"You saved my life." She held up her purse, still hanging over her shoulder. "I'll call 911."

"Let them do it. Let's get out of here."

"My car."

"Destroyed. You don't want to explain to the police why the car of a waitress at the Tattle-Tale was sabotaged. We don't want the police nosing around and revealing your true identity…or mine, until we can get what we need from the Belkins."

"Won't the police track the car to me anyway? Or at least to Barbie Jones?"

"Not if I, or the task force, have anything to say about it." He wrapped his arms around her gently. "Can you stand up?"

"Yes." She leaned on Alexei, and he rose to his feet, pulling her up with him. Her legs wobbled like cooked spaghetti, but she grabbed his arm and the world steadied.

As they passed the couple, still clinging to each other, Alexei held up his phone. "You okay? We're going to call 911."

They both nodded, still in shock.

They weren't the only ones. Britt hung on to Alexei as he bypassed the elevator. On their way down the stairs, they met a few people rushing up to the rooftop parking level.

One man asked them, "What happened?"

"Some couple's car exploded. They're okay though. Nobody hurt." He brushed past the man, towing Britt along with him.

When they reached the street level, Britt finally felt like she could breathe, and she scooped in a big breath even though her ribs protested.

She grabbed Alexei's hands. "Do I look as messed up as you do?"

"Just a little smudged. Do I look like I've been

through hell?" The sirens wailing down the street propelled Alexei into motion again. "Let's keep walking."

Britt tripped and looked down at her sandal. "My sandal's broken."

Alexei glanced up and down the street. "Let's go to that fast-food restaurant and clean up in the bathroom before we go back to the hotel."

By the time Britt washed the soot and dirt from her face, arms and legs, ran her hands through her tangled, smoky hair and returned to the restaurant, Alexei was seated at a plastic table with two drinks in front of him.

He looked up from his phone, where he was texting. "I got you a diet soda, but it's self-serve, so you can dump that and get what you want."

"This is fine." She collapsed into the hard chair across from him and sucked down the soda, the cold drink soothing to her scratchy throat. She tipped her drink toward his phone, as he placed it on the table. "Texting Ariel?"

"Yeah. That's the downside to being official—I have to report everything, especially if I want the task force to take action."

"Like covering up the owner of an exploding car?"

"Exactly."

Britt toyed with her straw, almost afraid to ask the next logical question. She cleared her throat. "How'd they know I was at the hospital?"

"We weren't followed. I know that for a fact. I kept watch and took a few evasive moves on our way from the diner to the hospital. There's no way someone followed us."

"That means...?"

"It means they put a tracker on your car."

She squeezed her cup so hard, she popped the lid. "When and why did they do that?"

"You're kidding, right? The Belkins have several reasons to suspect you—your so-called date with Jerome the night they offed him, your presence outside the room where they were holding a drugged waitress and your conversations with a transient who probably knows more about the Tattle-Tale than he realizes. When you showed up at the club and you didn't even have a shift, they figured enough was enough."

"Do you think Stepan told Sergei I was there, and they put the bug on my car then?"

"Probably. I hope so."

"Really?" She shook the ice in her cup. "Why is that?"

"Because if they put the tracker on your car last night during the party, they know you went to a hotel in Beverly Hills instead of back to your hovel in Hollywood."

"As it is, they know I left the club, stopped by the homeless hangout under the freeway, went to a diner down the street and then went to the hospital. That's not incriminating."

"The same hospital where Tatyana's baby is currently taking up a bassinet in the nursery?"

"The same hospital where the ambulance took Calvin after his beating. Wouldn't it make sense I'd check up on him?"

"Maybe." Alexei shrugged and winced. "Until they realize Tatyana's hospital band is missing. They just tried to kill you, Britt. I don't think Belkin is buying that you were at Cedars-Sinai to check on Calvin—or at least he's not taking any chances."

Britt propped her forehead in her hand, and one tear

leaked from the corner of her eye. "If they tried to kill me for my suspicious behavior, they must've killed Leanna—only she didn't have a navy SEAL protecting her. As usual, I lead the charmed life, and she gets the short end of the stick."

The tear rolled down her cheek and trembled on the edge of her jaw until Alexei dabbed at it with his rough fingertip. He whispered, "I would've helped Leanna if I could have, too."

Tilting her head, she rested her cheek in the palm of his hand. "I know you would have, but you were here for me, not her."

"I'm sorry I wasn't here for Leanna, but I thank God I was here for you." He traced the shell of her ear. "Let's get back to the hotel so I can put some queries into motion—we're going to find out everything we can about Tatyana and the birth of that baby."

When they got back to the hotel, Britt collapsed on the sofa and closed her eyes. "I suppose this means I can't return to work at the Tattle-Tale."

The cushion next to hers sank as Alexei sat next to her, and her body tilted toward his, her shoulder bumping his. He felt solid, and she didn't move, resting against him.

"Now that they've determined you're public enemy number one, they could do anything to you there—drug you, arrange for an accident, kidnap you. No, you're not going back." He held out his phone, cupped in his hand. "My sources are already expunging your name from that car, and Ariel has someone hacking the records at Cedars-Sinai to get information on Tatyana and her baby, although that's not where she wants my focus."

Britt opened one eye and rolled her head to the side. "She wants you back on the arms dealer."

"That's what's going to bring down Belkin." He kissed the top of her head. "You must be starving. It's late for dinner."

"My stomach is still in knots. I don't know if I could eat anything."

"You managed to wolf down a grilled cheese sandwich after that transient kicked the stuffing out of you."

"Yeah, then things escalated a hundredfold from getting punched a few times to getting my car blown up." Her cell phone buzzed from her purse on the floor, and she leaned over to grab it.

Alexei put his hand on her arm and asked, "Who is it?"

"It's—" she peered at the display and bolted upright "—it's that number from before—the woman who told me about Tatyana's baby. Maybe she knows we were at the hospital."

Before he could stop her, she answered the call and put it on speaker for Alexei to hear. "Hello?"

"Don't hello me, you Russian whore."

Britt jerked her head to the side to stare at Alexei, whose mouth had dropped open.

"Excuse me?" She tried to put on her best Russian accent.

"I've been trying to catch my husband, Gary, for months now, and I finally found your number on his phone."

"Gary?"

"Don't play dumb. I know he's been sneaking around behind my back to see you. I even know your name— *Mila.*"

Britt covered her mouth with her hand. "I—I…"

"You'd better find some other sugar daddy. I'm warning you. Stay away from my husband."

The outraged wife ended the call, and Britt dropped the phone. "It was Mila. She called me from her boyfriend's phone to tell me about Tatyana's baby."

"We can't be absolutely sure it was Mila. It could've been any of the women. Maybe this Gary was at a party with several of the dancers from the club. It could've been any one of them."

"Maybe, but there's one sure way to find out."

"How are you going to get in touch with Mila? You're not going back to the club."

"I know she's working tonight. It's her last night, and the other women are having a party for her at Rage."

"Rage? Why would they pick that place?"

"I don't know, but I plan to be there."

"Absolutely not. What if the Belkins are there?"

"The Belkins aren't going to be there. This is for the women only. Stepan told me."

"You asked Stepan about the party?" He drove two fingers against his temple and massaged.

"I just wanted to confirm it was Mila's last night. Why would he be suspicious about that? I told him I wasn't going."

"Sergei is obviously suspicious about everything you say and do, and Stepan seems to be a loyal lackey."

"I'm going, and…I want you there, too."

"Nothing could keep me away." He cupped her face in his hands, and his blue eyes blazed in the same way they did when he talked about avenging his father's death.

An answering flame leaped in her heart along with the hope that this time that passion burned for her.

BRITT'S TAXI PULLED up in front of the Rage nightclub at two thirty in the morning, and she didn't even look at the spot where Jerome had been felled. Instead, she straightened her tight skirt and strutted to the door.

After 2:00 a.m., Rage turned into a private club, but that just meant an increase in the cover charge and a more exclusive clientele as the club turned away potential patrons. The bouncer didn't turn her away, and Britt sashayed into the dark, crowded room.

High-pitched giggling led her to the corner where the women from the Tattle-Tale clustered around two or three sofas and several bottles of expensive champagne.

Britt waved to a few of the women and tried to catch Mila's eye, but the dancer didn't even look up when Britt joined the group. Maybe Alexei had been right and some other woman had called her from Gary's phone.

Theanessa bumped Britt's arm. "You didn't work tonight, Barbie?"

"I had the night off, but I didn't want to miss the party."

Mila's gaze shifted to Britt over the edge of her champagne glass and bounced away as quickly.

Britt grabbed a flute of the bubbly from the table and downed half of it. The warmth of the booze immediately seeped into her muscles.

Several men approached their group and pulled some of the women onto the dance floor. Shaking off an invitation from one of them, Britt scanned the crowd for Alexei. She thought she saw him a couple of times, but couldn't be sure.

Would any of the women from the Tattle-Tale recognize him?

The spot on the sofa next to Mila finally cleared, and Britt parked next to her. "How was your last night?"

Mila tossed back her champagne and grabbed another glass. "Like every other night."

"You're going to work for the Belkins in…another capacity?"

Mila's fingers tightened on the delicate stem of the glass. "What are you doing here, Barbie? You should go home."

Britt took a long, shaky breath. "I spoke to your lover's wife tonight."

The glass jerked in Mila's hand and the golden liquid sloshed over the edge. Mila licked her fingers. "My lover?"

"Gary. The man whose phone you used to call me." Britt pinned her gaze on Mila and didn't move a muscle. Had she gone too far?

"I've told you all I'm going to tell you…Britt."

"I need more. There's someone who can help us, help Tatyana."

"Tatyana dead."

Britt gulped. "Help her baby, then. Her baby is still at the hospital. The Belkins already know I was there. They planted an explosive device on my car."

"Baby in danger." Mila's hands were shaking too much to hold the glass. "You have police? Someone to help?"

"Yes."

The dancer's wide eyes darted around the club. "Not here. They watch." She tapped her arm near the tattoo. "They follow with tracker."

"The ladies' room?" Britt grabbed Mila's hand. "Come with me."

They ducked into the back hallway with three single-use bathrooms and found one empty. Once inside, Britt locked the door behind them.

"Tell me what you know about Tatyana's baby, about my sister."

Mila rotated her arm at the elbow to display her tattoo with a red mark next to it. "Your sister like me—tattooed for Belkins and tracker implanted under skin. Ready for trafficking."

Britt sagged against the wall. "Where? Where is she? Where's Jessie?"

"Warehouse in Van Nuys."

"And the baby? What's so important about Tatyana's baby that the Belkins would kill to keep quiet?"

"The baby is old man's—Olav Belkin. Old *Vory v Zakone*." Mila ran a finger across her throat. "Very bad. Very dangerous."

Britt's stomach churned. "I still don't understand. We both know the Belkins can work their way out of that."

"Not this time. Tatyana seventeen. Tatyana only seventeen." Mila grabbed Britt's hands. "Do you understand? This underage, no agreeing—it bring Belkin down. Do you understand?"

"Even if the sex is consensual, it's not legal."

"Yes, not consensual. They take baby tonight. They kill baby. They destroy the evidence."

"No! We won't let them hurt that baby. They won't hurt any more people."

A zinging noise came from outside the bathroom, and the hair on the back of Britt's neck stood up as she twisted toward the door.

Two seconds later, the door exploded inward as someone put his boot through it. In another second, the barrel of a gun followed, and Mila's body jerked.

Mila's hand clenched Britt's for a moment until another shot hit her in the chest and she dropped to the floor.

Chapter Fifteen

Alexei's pulse picked up speed when he saw Britt and the Ukrainian dancer slip into the back of the club. His pulse went into overdrive when he saw the goon at the bar push away from his beer and lumber after them.

Shoving his hand into the inside pocket of his jacket and closing his fingers around the grip of his gun, Alexei followed them. If he'd gotten his gun into this club, that other guy probably hadn't had any difficulty either.

Alexei sidled around the corner to the dark hallway, dotted with a few restrooms and leading to the back alley. The man turned once, and Alexei dived behind a machine dispensing condoms.

As he straightened up, Alexei heard the crash of splintering wood and the distinct whizzing sound of a silencer. The blood roared in his ears as he raced down the hallway, his weapon raised and ready.

When he reached the open door, the scene before him clicked as if in a single picture—Mila dead on the floor, Britt hovering above her, the man's gun tracking toward the back of Britt's head.

Alexei squeezed the trigger, and the man keeled over—on top of Britt in the small space.

He took a step inside the bathroom and cranked his head over his shoulder at a woman coming their way. "Not this one. Someone's really sick in here."

"Ugh." She made a U-turn and disappeared inside another restroom.

By the time he turned around, Britt had wriggled from beneath the dead man. "We have to leave—now."

"No kidding." Alexei stepped over the shooter and grabbed Britt's arm, pulling her up. "Back door."

She squeezed past him into the hallway, and Alexei shoved the man's body farther into the bathroom, locked the door from the inside and slammed it.

When they hit the alleyway, Britt grabbed his jacket. "We have to go to the hospital and get the baby. Belkin's going to kill her tonight."

Alexei called up a car on his phone while he took Britt by the hand and hustled her out of the alley. "What did Mila tell you?"

"The baby is Olav Belkin's—and Tatyana was only seventeen. It's statutory rape, and the DNA from the baby can prove it."

Alexei didn't think his fury at Belkin could get any more heated—but he was wrong. "That bastard. He's gonna pay—for everything."

The car Alexei had called up from an online service pulled up to the curb several doors down from Rage and flashed its lights.

Alexei crowded Britt into the back seat and told the driver to take them to Cedars-Sinai. "And hurry."

The driver joked, "She's not pregnant, is she?"

Britt hunched forward in her seat. "No, but this is about a baby, so step on it."

In a low voice, Britt told Alexei the rest of Mila's

story about the warehouse of women waiting to be groomed and trafficked. Alexei knew this story—if the women weren't already addicted to drugs, they would be by the time they left that warehouse.

He hoped to God Britt's sister was still alive by the time the place was raided. If they could get their hands on that baby, Belkin's associates and maybe even his own son would be singing like canaries...and Vlad wouldn't be able to do business with the Belkins under so much scrutiny.

Dragging his phone from his pocket, Alexei whispered to Britt. "I'm contacting Ariel now. She'll make it easy to get protection for that baby."

"Can she do it now? Mila seemed to think the Belkins were coming for the baby tonight."

"We'll be there until Ariel can get reinforcements. We'll protect that little baby."

The driver squealed to a stop in front of the hospital. "Record time."

"Thanks." Alexei waved his phone. "I'll add a big tip for you."

With his hand on Britt's back, Alexei hustled them both into the quiet lobby of the hospital. They took the elevator up to the maternity floor, but as soon as they stepped out of the car, his senses went on high alert.

The hallway and front desk were completely dark, and the nurses were murmuring among themselves.

One of them called out from the darkness. "Get Maintenance to get our backup generator going and do a check on all the patients."

"It's go time." Alexei squeezed Britt's shoulder. "They're here."

Her body jerked. "The baby."

Somebody screamed at the other end of the hallway, and Alexei tensed his muscles. "Maybe they already took her. Wait here."

Alexei spun around, following the noises through the hallway, glowing with auxiliary lights. A group of people were crowded around something on the floor, and Alexei's gut lurched.

He shouldered his way through and let out a puff of air when he saw an orderly slumped on the floor, groaning.

"What happened?"

A nurse turned her pale face toward him, her eyes dark and wide. "We don't know. The lights went out suddenly, and then we found Noah unconscious on the floor. Something's not right."

"Someone call 911. Get security up here."

Another scream caused a cold fear to clinch the back of his neck. He ran back to the elevator where he'd left Britt, but she was gone. He lurched toward the nursery and stumbled to a stop.

Various hospital employees, including an unarmed security guard, stood in a semicircle around Britt, cradling a baby against her shoulder.

A man stood beside her, a gun to her head.

"Anyone make a move, this woman dies. Let us by, and I take woman out and let her go."

Alexei's nostrils flared. *Yeah, right.*

Alexei shoved his hand in his jacket pocket and caressed his gun as he moved silently toward the reception desk. He didn't want the man to see him with a weapon. If he did, he'd shoot Britt and take the baby. He might even do that now, but he probably didn't want to cause panic among the hospital workers.

Better to walk Britt out of here with the baby, kill her later and take Tatyana's baby—and then kill the baby to destroy all evidence of Olav Belkin's disgusting crime.

As Alexei edged around the reception desk, he met Britt's eyes.

She immediately removed one hand from the baby's back and twirled her hair around her finger. The signal they'd established earlier.

Little late for that. He knew she was in trouble.

When she released her hair, she flicked her hand out to her left side. Then she tipped her head in the same direction.

Alexei's gaze tracked to her left. He swept past a doctor, an orderly and a new mother still in her hospital gown. Then he backtracked to the old orderly and his heart slammed against his chest.

Olav Belkin himself, making sure his baby daughter wouldn't incriminate him.

Alexei had him.

If he took the shot now, who could blame him? Alexei could say he saw Belkin's weapon. He must have one on him. He figured him as a risk to the hospital workers and the baby. DNA tests would soon determine he was the father of Tatyana's baby. Alexei would be exonerated for killing Belkin.

Alexei shuffled behind the reception desk. His eye twitched. A muscle at the corner of his mouth jumped. He pulled out his gun.

Then his gaze shifted back to Britt, snuggling that baby against her chest.

If he took the shot and killed Belkin, the man holding Britt would take his shot and kill Britt...or the baby.

If he didn't take the shot, he'd allow Olav Belkin

to defy death again. His crime family would cease to exist—for a while. He'd wind up incarcerated with three hots and a cot and the ability to run his empire from a prison cell.

Alexei raised his weapon and took the shot.

Britt screamed again as the man holding her at gunpoint crumpled beside her.

Epilogue

Britt tucked Summer into her bassinet and smoothed back a soft lock of blond hair from the baby's forehead. "Sweet dreams, *moya solnishka*."

She curled up in a chair next to the bassinet, tucking one leg beneath her, and grabbed a book.

"Don't you have that baby book memorized by now?" Leanna sauntered from the kitchen, a glass of wine in each hand. "Take this. You need it."

"I'm not the one who was held in a warehouse for over a month getting drugged up."

"I'm not the new mother."

"I'm not either—yet. I'm just the foster mom, and they might not even let me bring her back to North Carolina with me."

"Well, her mother and father are dead, and I doubt they're going to hand her over to the father's family." Leanna snorted.

Britt sucked in a breath. "You know that Olav Belkin had a heart attack in prison?"

"Of course. Why try to keep it from me?"

"I thought it might…upset you. I mean, remind you."

"I'm not going to forget anytime soon, Britt, but that was the best news I've had in a while. That, and my friend Calvin's going to be okay—back on the street, but okay."

"When are you going to get that tattoo removed?"

Leanna shrugged. "What's one more? Maybe I can have my guy turn it into something cool."

"I wish Tatyana had never confided in you."

"Well, she did, and I confided in Jerome." Leanna sniffed and held the back of her hand to her nose. "How were we supposed to know?"

"I'm sorry about Jerome…and Mila. All that for a little baby."

Leanna reached into the bassinet and traced her fingertip around the edge of Summer's ear. "What did you call her? Something Russian? I think I've heard enough of that language to last me a lifetime."

"It means…" A knock at Leanna's apartment door stopped Britt, and she pressed a hand to her heart.

"It's over, Britt." Leanna patted her knee. "Thanks to you. See what I mean about those nerves? Drink up."

Leanna crossed the room to the front door and peered out the peephole. "Someone to see you."

"Me?" Britt half rose from the chair.

Leanna swung open the door and said, "Hey, navy SEAL guy. Took you long enough."

Britt fell back in the chair. "Alexei."

He stepped inside the small apartment, filling the room with his presence. Filling her heart.

"How's…the baby?"

"She's great." Britt took a gulp of wine.

"Did you two hear the news about Belkin?"

Leanna raised her wineglass. "That's why we're celebrating. Want some?"

"No, thanks."

Sighing, Leanna grabbed the wine bottle by the neck. "If you two don't mind, I'm gonna polish this off in the privacy of my own room."

Alexei leaned over the bassinet and wiggled his finger beneath Summer's chin. "She's a cutie."

"D-did you get all debriefed and everything?"

"I did."

"Was Ariel upset you never made the Vlad connection?"

He lifted a shoulder. "No. I did stop the deal. Vlad will never get his hands on those weapons. After Belkin's arrest, his associates scattered far and wide, and Stepan is cooperating with the authorities for immunity. And the FBI was able to free those women, including your sister and Jessie. That's a win for everyone."

"You didn't get to kill Belkin."

"But I got to save you instead." He perched on the arm of her chair. "A much better deal."

"Did you come here to tell me about Belkin? Are you leaving soon?"

"Yes, yes and yes."

She held up her hand, counting off three fingers. "That's three answers to two questions."

"I answered the third question you didn't ask."

"Who said I had a third question, Russki?"

"Do you want me to ask it for you?" He slid his fingers through her hair.

She rested her head against his arm. "Enlighten me."

"Or maybe I should ask you."

"By all means." Her pulse had started throbbing in her throat, and her body tingled in anticipation.

"Do you want to wait for me? I promise I'll come back to you—every time."

She swallowed hard. "You're not just talking about this one deployment?"

Alexei slid into the chair, pulling her into his lap. "I'm talking about forever because I can't live without my sunshine."

When he kissed her mouth and ran his hands through her hair, she believed him.

She broke away from the kiss and cupped his jaw with one hand. "You want me to wait for you even though I'll have Summer, the daughter of your enemy?"

"It's not Summer's fault, and that may be just what I need."

"To help me take care of Belkin's daughter?"

Alexei turned his head to press his lips against her palm. "To replace hate with love…because I've discovered that's the best revenge of all."

* * * * *

RANGER DEFENDER

ANGI MORGAN

For Shizue, Tamami, Kazuomi and Tosh.
Friends whom we miss and love dearly.
Thanks for the characters and
your years of support!

Prologue

From the journal of Dr. Kym Roberts
Case 63047 Evidence Tag 63047-2

Subject Nineteen has been fascinated with death since the patient was thirteen. The subject has not killed squirrels or other small animals. Far from it. The curiosity has led the subject to research what happens at the time of death.

As with many of the subjects in this study, Nineteen is a near perfectionist, becoming more debilitated at every juncture. The patient is so obsessed with the "perfect death," they can't move forward. In some ways this will keep them from the implementation of this fantasy.

The subject is fascinated and refers to "the perfect death" as if something supernatural will occur when it's found. Subject Nineteen stated that begging from the murder victim for their life would not be a necessary part of the "perfect death." Subject Nineteen stated the actual killing would need to be swift and not detract from the scientific approach. The Subject also stated that the death would need to be respectful so dignity is always involved. The planning, the hunt, the capture are all unnecessary details to the perfect kill in their opinion.

Subject Nineteen has described the moment of death to be like a symphony. Each phase building upon itself until there is a crescendo…a wonderful moment of song-ful bliss. But for the most part, Subject Nineteen can't get past the rehearsal stage. Taking this metaphor one more step, they would not only need the orchestra to perform perfectly, the surroundings would also need to be perfected at the same time.

Only the limits of their perfectionism hold them in check. Wavering from the idea of flawless keeps them from attempting murder. So in Subject Nineteen's case, we hope the obsessive compulsion disorder and need for perfection will prevent the attempt.

Leaving no room for error, the obsessive compulsive need that Subject Nineteen maintains will lead to disap-pointment and a further downward spiral. This very well may be the source of the night terrors.

Treating one disorder will not resolve the other and pos-sibly will make each worse. And although Subject Nine-teen hides it well, the attachment disorder is deeply seated and may be the basis of all the other disorders.

Time is not on our side since eventually, the patient will determine the flaws and overcome. Therefore, Subject Nineteen is a danger to society and should be committed to a facility for a strict psychiatric evaluation and treatment.

EVIDENCE NOTATION

Other entries in this handwritten journal end with a summary of each subject's treatment—if any—along with instructions for other staff members. The treatment sum-mary portion of Subject Nineteen's entry is missing. As in not written or torn from the journal.

Blood spatter pattern indicates the journal was open to Subject Nineteen's page and the deceased was seated at her desk, even though the body was moved to and posed in the chair normally occupied by patients.

A slash from right to left, indicates a left-handed upward movement, which severed the right jugular. Force is consistent with a person standing behind the victim.

Chapter One

"How can a little research and a few interviews get you in trouble?" Wade Hamilton asked. "Besides, I've done all the hard work."

Slate Thompson wasn't on as thin ice as his fellow Texas Ranger. But the entire team knew that one wrong step would shake up Company B—and not in a good way. Wade's hunches about cases were putting more than one of them in the hot seat. So Slate had a right to be wary.

"Then do it yourself," Slate countered.

"You know I'm out of a job if I break ranks again. Come on, you can do this in your sleep, Slate. You're one of the best investigators I know."

"That's beside the point, and if you're attempting to schmooze someone, stating that they *are* the best is better. Especially if it's the truth."

"You read the journal about Subject Nineteen?"

"You stood over my shoulder while I did." Slate stretched backward in his wheeled chair, balancing himself with a booted toe under his desk. He tossed a ball of rubber bands over to Wade. "Moron."

"Just verifying you can read."

Slate popped forward, clicking off the screen as Major Clements walked through the office. Recently, he managed to stop by and check on Wade's progress through the "punishment" boxes—files that were either a last check on cases coming up for trial or completely cold.

"How you doing, Wade? Slate, you aren't busy? Need something to help that along?"

"No, sir. I'm about to head out the door. I…uh…have a lunch date, sir."

Major Clements clapped Wade on the shoulder, then tapped the multiple file folders at the corner of the desk. "Power through, son. We're a little shorthanded out there." Then he continued to his office.

Clements was about fifteen or maybe even twenty years older than either Wade or Slate. But he looked ancient, like a cowboy who had spent one too many years in the saddle. He walked straight, but his belly hung over his belt buckle, a serious silver piece of artwork with the Texas Ranger emblem over the Texas flag. He was one of the few men, in Wade's humble opinion, who wore the uniform's white hat exceptionally well. Like it fit.

Slate, on the other hand, always felt better wearing a ball cap.

"You going to look at that case for me?" Wade whispered. "Victor Watts confessed so it looks like a slam dunk. But my gut's telling me that something's not right. I'd do it myself but…"

Slate waved for him to pass over the file. "You're damn lucky I'm not reporting you to the old man."

"Now, why would you do that, Slate? We get along so well. If I was gone, you'd have to break in another ranger and you know how fun that is." Wade locked his fingers behind his neck and leaned back in his chair.

The bruising had faded, but he was still squinting through a severely beaten eye. The man had spent days in the hospital and come back to work with a cloud hanging around him so thick, everyone was pretending they couldn't see him.

Everyone except Wade's partner, Jack MacKinnon, Heath Murray and himself. They were a team. They'd come into Company B at the same time and had a special bond. Didn't seem like anything could break it.

Even Wade being assigned the punishment boxes.

Most of the reasons Wade had been desked weren't public knowledge. Jack knew more than anyone in the Company and he wasn't talking. But over beers, both Jack and Wade had considered themselves very lucky to have a job.

Jack's temporary assignment to help the Dallas PD hadn't gone without speculation. It also coincided with his new roommate—of the feminine persuasion. Heath, Wade and himself included hadn't spent any serious time with the lady… Megan Harper.

Yet.

Everyone in Company B had seen the results of "the Harper case," as it was referenced. However Wade and Jack had gotten involved, it was Wade's fault for playing a hunch. His saving grace was that whatever he'd done had saved Megan Harper's life and captured a man whose mental health was still waiting to be evaluated.

Saying yes to one of Wade's hunches was usually easy. Hell, this particular ranger had a long line of successful hunches that had played out with many a bad man behind bars. Slate opened the file. He had to admit that he wanted to help.

"You'd be on your own most of the time, buddy," Wade said from the next desk. "Of course, if I'm wrong, then there's nothing to do anyway."

Slate nodded, contemplating. Breaking the rules really wasn't his thing. Then again, he'd wanted to be in law en-

forcement to help people…not knowingly send an innocent man to jail.

Yeah, there was a chance that Wade was wrong. But
when the man went with his gut, he just rarely was.

"I'll do it."

"Why does your intonation hold a giant *but* at the end?"

"Maybe because there is one. I want the story of why
you're sitting at this desk instead of on current cases."

"You interview Vivian Watts—Victor's sister—and
you'll get it."

"That was easy." But there had to be a catch. The smile
on his friend's face was mixed with sadness. Totally not
like him.

"Not as easy as you think. Watts's sister moved to Dallas and has been proclaiming his innocence ever since."

"This is a problem because…"

"The trial starts next week. She's going to want to go
public if the Texas Rangers are reopening the case. You're
going to have to keep her totally quiet. Still interested?"

"If I say no, you're going straight to Heath with this,
aren't you?"

"Yeah." Wade laughed, leaning back in his chair and
tossing a pen next to the stack of files.

"He's better with a computer. I'm the best investigator you've ever worked with. Remember?" Slate stood,
grabbed the jacket from the back of his chair, shoved his
arms through and stuffed his hat on his head for emphasis.

"I think we're remembering that conversation differently. But I'll let you have your exit, Mr. Best Investigator."

Slate left the offices, with Wade's laughter echoing
down the hall. He tossed the folder onto the seat of his
truck, questioning what he'd just committed himself to.
The page of the doctor's notes with the evidence notations
he'd read earlier stuck out in his memory:

Other entries in this handwritten journal end with a summary of each subject's treatment—if any—along with instructions for other staff members. The treatment summary portion of Subject Nineteen's entry is missing. As in not written or torn from the journal.

Blood spatter pattern indicates the journal was open to Subject Nineteen's page and the deceased was seated at her desk, even though the body was moved to and posed in the chair normally occupied for sessions.

A slash from right to left, indicates a left-handed upward movement, which severed the right jugular. Force is consistent with a person standing behind the victim.

One case could ruin a ranger's career or come close to it. Just like Wade. Was he willing to risk it? Was he willing to break the rules for someone he didn't know?

Yes.

Hell, did his career actually compare with the lifetime he'd wanted to protect the innocent?

No.

His adrenaline was pumping for once, ready to help someone in need.

Chapter Two

Planning the perfect death wasn't easy, but she wanted one. It was the only way. Abby read the doctor's diagnosis and recommendations every morning. It was in her bedside table drawer, tucked away from the world but in exactly the same place for her daily routine.

She awoke, showered, dressed for her day and read the report as her tea brewed. She might be groggy from a poor night's sleep, but she still put in her contacts and read the torn sheet of notepaper from the journal.

It took her the same number of minutes to read the other papers she'd collected. Three diagnoses over three years from three different cities. Her tea would be ready for a dash of lemon to help her concentrate.

Holistic remedies suited her much better than the prescriptions she'd used since her twenties. Stopping the input of chemicals into her body was the best thing she'd ever done.

It was so freeing.

Her mind could think on multiple levels like it hadn't for the past several years. She sipped the last bit of her tea with her blueberry tea biscuit. More brain energy and antioxidants. She'd need to be on her toes this morning for the next phase of her experiment.

Killing Dr. Roberts had been eye-opening. An epiphany

of sorts. Abby no longer was held back by perfectionism. Her death demonstrated it was no longer necessary. The good doctor's analysis had allowed her to move forward last year. Finding the perfect form of death would take practice, yes. But the doctor's death had provided enlightenment—of a sort.

If she couldn't perfect the act of death herself, she'd enlist others to help in her research. Simple enough.

She covered her lips and giggled, ready for her day of research to begin. She couldn't say that she loved this day each week. As Dr. Roberts pointed out, the unfortunate attachment disorder kept her from loving anything. But this day gave her a bit of excitement to look forward to. Moving toward the completion of a project should give a normal person a sense of accomplishment.

And she was so close.

The alarm went off on her phone. She gathered her things from the hall table. Purse, lunch and then the clean surgical gloves and mask from their dispensers. She walked to the door and stood there waiting for it to open, then reminded herself that she had the right to open it when she wanted.

Four years away from the prison they called a hospital and she still had moments where she forgot she was free to move as she wished. It was less than a minute of her life every now and again, but she resented every wasted second it took to force herself to reach out and turn the doorknob.

Thinking about her habits, she crossed the parking lot and climbed the steps to wait under the awning. Dwelling on the idea that her quirks were odd was a waste of time. That's what had sent her to Dr. Roberts to begin with.

A mistake. But a corrected mistake. Using Victor Watts had been an uncontrollable moment of fury. Talking to him before his test had always been nice. Pity because he seemed perfect for the ultimate experiment.

Taking a job at the Veterans Affairs Hospital eighteen months ago had been a moment of brilliance. Her father's attorney had used very little energy to convince the owner of a pathetic little box of a house on Denley Drive to sell. She would have preferred to continue living in the five-star hotel. Her parents could afford it. Instead, her parents insisted things would be better if she didn't.

At least the new house had a specific and organized place designed to meet her more than rational needs. And if she wasn't allowed to drive, walking across the parking lot to the Dallas Area Rapid Transit station was at least convenient. The last time she'd met with her father's attorney, he joked how fitting it was that the two stores nearby were a pharmacy and second-hand shop. He'd laughed at her.

The light rail arrived to take her down Lancaster Road. The job was mundane, her social life nonexistent, but it was all worth it for her research.

The Veterans Affairs Hospital gave her the subjects she needed. Broken, easily manipulated men who had the strength and the wherewithal to perform the necessary duties. *Ha. Duties.* They had the strength to fulfill the experiment Dr. Roberts wrote would never come to fruition.

The doctors were wrong. Everyone was wrong.

Perfection in death was possible.

So close. So so close.

Moving from this venue would be difficult. But working with this group of men and women was coming to an end.

Changing a variable in last week's test would be interesting today. The small amount of excitement she could feel recharged her with purpose.

"Hi, Abby," Dalia said from reception. "Looks like we have a full day of appointments. You're going to be busy."

"Wonderful." She'd practiced the good-morning smile and mimicked the intonation most used when they were excited for their day. The smile that continued on Dalia's face indicated that Abby had managed to keep her voice free of sarcasm.

She picked up the charts as she did every morning and took them to their small, efficient office. There were tapes ready to be transcribed and yes, a full day of veterans checking in for their sleep studies. The private at eight o'clock would be perfect. According to the notes in Simon Evans's chart, he didn't have a history of violence, but she could change that.

She could definitely change that.

Simon arrived right on time. Abby prepped him for his EEG and then the technician applied the nodes to begin the procedure. No one could connect her to the actual study, which was in a sleep lab, on a different floor, on different days. No one at the shorthanded Veterans Hospital ever questioned her competent help.

The electroencephalogram monitored brain waves while a patient slept. It set up a baseline and then monitored the volunteers throughout the sleep studies. Perfect for her needs since each participant needed a session per month.

Two of her experiments had succeeded recently.

It wouldn't be long. Not long at all.

Simon was snoring. She checked the monitor. He seemed to be in full REM. She locked the outside door so they wouldn't be disturbed, cautiously placed earphones over Simon's head and turned on her carefully recorded message.

For the next hour, her softly spoken words about injustice, violence and murder repeated. Keywords that helped the subject draw the logical conclusion that death was the only possible solution for their problems.

The tape ended. Three hours of sleep was all the patient was allowed. The timer dinged, she awoke Simon and alerted the technician it was time to finish. Once he cleaned up, she brought the questionnaire to be completed along with the second page for her own study.

Simon passed the next appointment on the way out—Private Second Class Rashad Parker with debilitating night terrors. He'd already tried to choke his girlfriend in his sleep. Abby went through all the steps, waited until he entered rapid eye movement and introduced her tape.

Curiosity was the closest she got to elation. She thought Rashad would have succumbed to her mind-manipulation last week. With her new keywords, culmination was probable within the next couple of days.

Wouldn't Dr. Roberts be surprised if she was still around?

She covered her lips and giggled.

Chapter Three

Wiping down yet another table, Vivian Watts stepped back to let a man slide into the booth. "I'll be right back with a menu."

The lunch rush was over and in another hour she'd be off until she came back for the double tomorrow. And then she'd be done and never wanted to see another chicken wing as long as she lived. When she told the manager she'd need off next week for the trial, he agreed and promptly fired her.

Nothing personal, he'd said. Of course it was, she'd replied. And that was the end of the conversation. One more day to feel greasy. At least she'd be clean while standing on the precipice of bankruptcy.

Was it really bankruptcy if you didn't own anything to be lost? Probably not. So technically, she'd be homeless without two shiny dimes to her name. Technically.

If all else failed, she could reenlist in the army. Who knows, this time she might be a commissioned officer since she'd earned her degree. She really didn't want to go back into uniform. Of course, it would be better than wearing this little chicken wing thing.

She dropped the dirty stuff behind the bar, stuffed her last tip into her apron, grabbed a water and snatched a menu on her way back to the new table. It would be another single instead of the four-top that just filled up.

"Here you go. Can I get you something else to drink?" The nice hands taking the menu drew her to take a closer look at her latest customer.

Beautiful blue eyes shone bright in a tanned face. Very clean-shaven cheeks and chin, which was unusual with the beard fad for the twentysomething crowd. Crisp, overly starched shirt. There was a cowboy hat resting on the table to go along with the open badge of a... Texas Ranger.

Open in the way they identified themselves. "I have nothing to say to you."

"I get it, Miss Watts, and I'm sorry to bug you at work. I'm not here in an official capacity."

"The badge looks pretty official to me."

"Yeah, I get that. I wanted you to know who I am and that I'm legit." He pushed the badge back into his pocket. "I know now's not a good time, but I'd like to ask you a few follow-up questions at your earliest convenience."

"That also sounds very official." She glanced around at the emptying tables. "If you aren't going to order anything, I'd appreciate you leaving. The manager is particular about wait staff fraternizing with the customers. He particularly hates it."

"Oh, I'm ordering. I'm starved. I'd like a basket of ranch habanero wings, side salad, fries and sweet tea."

"This is a real order. You're not expecting it on the house or anything? If you want the cop discount, I have to get the manager or it comes out of my check."

"Real order. Real tip. Especially if the tea glass never runs dry." He handed her the menu. "I'm Slate, by the way."

"I'll be right back with your tea."

A week before Victor's trial and a Texas Ranger shows up saying it's unofficial business? Hope. A slim chance of it bubbled into her heart. Just as quickly, her rational mind took out a needle and popped it.

It had been over a year with no hope. A year of visiting her brother and faking a positive attitude so he didn't lose all hope. She wouldn't allow this one man who was here in an unofficial capacity to rattle her heart.

All the emotional strength she had left was reserved for her brother. Period.

Tea and salad to the table. Menus to another. Sneak a look at the ranger who's watching something on his phone. Clear and wipe down a booth. Salt shakers filled for the next shift. Order up. Wings for the ranger.

"Need anything else?" she asked, sliding the basket in front of him.

He performed an ordinary shake of his head just like many customers had before him.

"Why should I talk to you without Victor's lawyer present? Not like he'd know what to do if I wrote it all out for him. Why should I listen to you?"

"I just have a question."

"For me?" She stuck her thumb in her chest, realizing too late that it drew his eyes to the bulging cleavage her waitress outfit emphasized. "Not Victor?"

The ranger dropped his hands in his lap and looked at her. Really looked at her, like very few people had in the past year.

"I can't make any promises, Vivian. I just picked up your brother's file this morning, but I have a question that I hope you can answer. Maybe it'll lead to another question. That's all I've got at the moment."

Honesty. Clarity.

And a trickle of hope.

"I…uh… I get off at two." She was about to cry because of that one snippet of misplaced emotion.

"Can I meet you—"

"I no longer own a car, officer."

"Slate's fine. There's a coffee shop three doors down. That okay?"

"Sure. I'll get your check."

She turned quickly and used the corner of the bar towel to wipe the moisture from her face. Maybe he hadn't seen it. Who was she trying to fool? Looking at her—really looking and connecting with her eyes—that's *why* she was crying.

He'd seen it.

She punched in his ticket number and waited for the printout. No one else noticed her shaking hands or her racing heart. No one noticed anything except her hurrying through the rest of her shift.

Slate finished his wings with half a pitcher of tea still on his table. She'd dropped it off so he wouldn't run out. He paid and was gone forty-five minutes before she finished up.

She grabbed her jacket and wished she'd brought a change of clothes. Having a serious, even unofficial conversation in the short, revealing T-shirt would be hard. She could keep her jacket on.

Sure. Coffee. That's all this was. One Frappuccino and one question.

With the stupid hope that it would be another…and then another…

And then the reopening of her brother's investigation and surely proving that he was innocent. No trial. They could go home.

Oh, my gosh. That was why she hadn't let herself hope during the past year. One small peek at the possibility and she was back to leading a normal life in Florida. She couldn't do this to herself and certainly couldn't do it to her brother.

She hated…hope.

Chapter Four

Meeting Vivian Watts at work seemed like a smart thing to do, until Slate remembered the waitress uniforms at the restaurant. But that was after he'd walked through the door and asked for her section. Immediately noticing how smoking hot she was stopped coherent thought.

And then she'd cried.

Mercy. He was just like any man wanting to do the right thing. He wanted her to stop crying.

He knew he could help make that happen. All he had to do was find a murderer.

Choosing a table in the far back corner of the coffee shop, he opened a file no one in the room should see. The chicken wings sat like a lump in his gut. Maybe the acid from the strong brew would help with the digestion. Good thing he didn't have a weak stomach or he'd be losing it all by studying the murder scene pictures.

He wanted to help Vivian and Victor Watts. But it did all boil down to one question that no one had ever asked her brother.

"Officer."

He flipped the file shut and stood, pushing back his chair. "You want something?"

"No. I'm fine." Vivian sat and pulled her coat tighter. It was sweltering hot inside the shop despite the November chill that hung outside. Well, she was wearing hot pants and half a T-shirt.

"It's Slate. Lieutenant if this was official, but again, I can't make any promises."

"I stopped believing in promises about the time my brother was arrested for murder. Every promise that was made to us by the Dallas police was broken. And then there's been the three court-appointed attorneys who *promised* they'd find the real murderer."

"I'm sorry you've had to go through this experience. It doesn't feel fair, but the evidence does point to your brother."

"Spare me, Lieutenant. Until you've lost everything you've had and are about to see your only family convicted of murder in a state that has the death penalty... Please, just ask your question so I can go home."

"Sure." He opened the file to a copy of the murder victim's journal entry. "Can you tell me if your brother ever participated in a study performed by Dr. Roberts?"

"The answer is already in your file. He was seeing her for a sleep disorder. Night terrors. Yes, he knew the victim. Yes, he had an appointment with her the day she was murdered. No, he'd never mentioned that he had a problem to me. No, he never mentioned wanting to kill anyone. No, he hasn't been the same since he was discharged from the army." She pushed away from the table. "Thank you for taking a look at Victor's case. But I really have to get home—"

"Subject Nineteen. Was that your brother's number?"

"What are you talking about?" She sank back onto the metal chair.

"No one's ever mentioned how your brother was linked to the murder before?"

"All I know is that my brother was participating in a

VA-approved sleep study sponsored by Dr. Kym Roberts. She was one of the doctors conducting the study where she was murdered."

"That's all in the file."

"So what does this subject number mean?" It was actually the answer he wanted to hear.

Watts was a part of the study. The police had verified that much. But there was nothing in the file verifying he was Subject Nineteen. What if it was a different person? They'd have another suspect. But he couldn't share something like that. It would wreck the prosecution's case. Slate wouldn't get "box" duty like Wade. He'd be looking not only for a different job, but a different profession.

No one would hire him if he shared that type of information.

"I can't show you the evidence."

"You mean whatever made you question Victor's innocence?"

"Yes. So you've never heard of his status in the study as a subject number?"

"As far as I can tell, it wasn't a blind study if that's what you're referring to. I have a copy of it at home. It doesn't include the names of the participants but it has information specifically for Victor. Do you need it? Could I bring it to your office tomorrow?" Vivian scrunched her nose, sort of grimacing.

"You said you don't have a car. Perhaps I could give you a lift home."

"There's an office supply store around the corner from my apartment if you need copies."

"That'll work."

"Lieutenant, I know you said you weren't reopening Victor's case. It does sort of sound like you've found something new." She bit her lip, pulling her jacket even tighter around her.

"Why don't you show me the copy of the report you have? That's the first step."

The sky broke open in a severe thunderstorm that had been threatening all day. Slate stuck his hat on tight, tucked the file into his shirt and gestured for Vivian to stay at the door. "No sense in the both of us getting soaked. I'll be right back."

Slate ran the two blocks to his truck, dumped his hat in the back seat, locked the file in the middle compartment and drove back to the coffee shop. A little over ten minutes. But when he pulled up outside, Vivian wasn't standing near the door. He waited a couple more minutes. Then he pushed on the flashers and ran inside to see.

"Hey." He got the attention of the barista. "Where's the woman I was with a few minutes ago?"

"You left. She left. I don't know where."

"Well, if that don't beat all."

Cranking the heat once inside the truck, he dialed Wade. "So?" his friend asked first thing.

"I met with her. How 'bout you look at the list of things in the evidence file?" Slate paused, slapping the file against his thigh waiting while Wade pulled up the rest of the information.

Information he'd deliberately left out to entice Slate to look further into the case.

"Got it."

"Is there a follow-up report from a sleep study that the victim was conducting?"

"Nothing."

"So if I thought the list was necessary to answer the questions that we had…"

"I knew it!" Wade said with force, then repeated himself in a lower voice. "You'd need to sweet-talk a copy, not request it through a warrant. Seriously, Slate, if you have those kinds of doubts, take it to the district attorney's office."

"I need a couple more things clarified and then I'll head there."

Yeah. A couple more questions like…why didn't Vivian wait at the coffee shop? He opened the incomplete file Wade had given to him to pique his interest, then added Vivian's address to his GPS. Traffic was pretty bad in the downpour. He wasn't surprised that someone who didn't own a vehicle lived right on the bus route, but he was surprised that Vivian wasn't home.

He was already soaked but standing on an apartment doorstep would only draw attention to himself. And it was getting colder by the minute. So he waited in the truck. He had a perfect view of the door, but several minutes later, there was a knock on his window, followed with a gesture to roll it down.

"Get in!" he shouted.

Vivian ran around to the opposite side and jumped in the front seat. Soaked to the skin, still dressed in the short shorts and T-shirt.

"I thought we agreed I'd give you a ride."

"I appreciate it, Lieutenant, but I didn't want there to be any misunderstandings." She dripped on the papers she had in a folder. "The top copy is the original. You can see that the cover letter is a diagnosis and the results of the study."

"They mailed this to you?"

It didn't look identical to the other report even though it began the same.

"To my brother. This is where he lived prior to his arrest." She opened the door. "I'll be heading inside now. Thanks for looking at Victor's case…even unofficially."

"But I'm not."

Too late. The door was shut and she ran up the sidewalk. So he took the time to compare the two papers.

This report was in the same tone as the journal page. Formal, doctorly, professional. And dated recently. It was also signed by an assistant who had been interviewed just after the doctor's murder. The statement, along with numerous others from hospital staff, was in the file. The recent report…was not.

Nothing new.

Except there were names. Summaries of group sessions. No one was referred to as a subject and there sure as hell wasn't a Subject Nineteen.

"Damn. They have the wrong guy."

Chapter Five

"Your brother's innocent."

"I know."

Vivian opened the door wider, no longer embarrassed that the one-room furnished apartment had a pullout couch and a kitchenette with half a refrigerator. She'd passed that stigma three months ago when she calculated she'd be out of money by the beginning of the month.

One more week before the trial and two more days with a roof over her head.

She gestured for the Texas Ranger to enter and wait on the cracked linoleum by the door. "Let me get you a towel."

On the way to the bathroom, she shoved the bed into its couch position and tossed the cushions back on it. But another glance at the ranger confirmed that he was soaked to the skin...just like she'd been a couple of minutes earlier.

"There's a fold-up chair behind you."

"That's okay, I don't mind standing. And dripping." He laughed.

Lieutenant Slate had a good laugh. Deep and sincere that crinkled the skin near the corner of his eyes. She pulled a clean towel from the shelf and caught herself checking what she looked like in the mirror. And then picking up the hand towel and wiping the nonwaterproof mascara from under her eyes.

She tossed the towel across the small area into the ranger's hands. He took off his hat, looking for a place to set it, then carefully flipped it upside down into her—thankfully—empty sink.

Briskly, he brushed the worn cotton across his short hair, then used his hand to slick it back down again. "Sorry about the puddle."

"No problem." She sat on the couch, tucking her cold feet under her, seriously glad that she'd put on lounge pants instead of jumping into the shower.

"You're very patient," he said, shifting his boots into a wider stance. "If someone told me my brother was innocent after he'd confessed to a murder, I'd be chomping at the bit for an explanation."

"I'm tired, Lieutenant Slate. That's all. And you'll have to forgive me for not being excited about your announcement that you are not reopening his case. I've known my brother was innocent from day one."

"It's just Slate, ma'am. Slate Thompson. And I get it."

"And I'm Vivian. Definitely not a ma'am." She gestured to the end of the couch. "Please sit. A little water isn't the worst thing that's been on that cushion."

"If you're sure?" he asked, but he was already shrugging out of his jacket and hanging it over hers on the back of the door.

When he turned around, she saw the file folder with the sleep-study report stuffed into the back of his jeans.

"That was one way to keep it dry."

"Yeah." He pulled it around front and tapped his palm with it several times. "So, this report sheds a new light on your brother."

"I'm not a silly, inexperienced sister, Lieutenant Thompson." By using his formal name, she wanted to keep things a little more professional than they looked in her shabby studio apartment. "Honestly, I turned over the original report to Victor's attorney the day after it arrived here. He said there was nothing he could do with it. That it didn't prove anything since the prosecution had already submitted the study as proof of his guilt."

The momentary elation she'd felt in the coffee shop had long passed.

"I disagree." He leaned forward, resting an elbow on his thigh in order to look at her and handle the copy at the same time. "This isn't the report that's in the file."

Had she heard him correctly? "I'm not following."

"This report was written by Dr. Roberts's assistant and sent to the participants nine months after Victor's arrest."

"So it couldn't be a major part of the prosecutor's case, right? I'm so stupid."

"I wouldn't say that."

"How could I have missed something that evident?"

"Look, Vivian, don't beat yourself up. You don't have access to the evidence. I wouldn't either if it hadn't been a ranger who made the arrest."

She sat forward, close enough on the small couch that Slate's heat rose like steam around him. There was no use trying to keep the relationship professional. He'd be a family friend for life when they got her brother out of jail.

"So what happens now? Do you need Victor's lawyer or do you have all that information in the file? I should get dressed. I want to be there when you tell him." She stood and realized he hadn't moved.

He dropped his head and tapped the papers onto his palm again.

"What? I thought you said this would clear him?" She crossed her arms and wanted to look angry, but was afraid she looked a little ridiculous in her silky lounge pants and sweatshirt. Tapping her bare toe on the old carpet didn't present too much power either.

His hesitation only made her angrier and more anxious.

"Mr. Thompson, please." She let her arms drop to her sides, afraid the tears would return and she'd totally lose it this time. "Just tell me."

"I'm not supposed to be here." He finally made eye contact with her. "I work for the other side. You get that, right?"

"And you'd want to sentence my brother to death even knowing he's innocent?"

"No. That's not it." He jumped to his feet.

The small room had never seemed as small as at that very moment. It wasn't that Slate towered over her. She wasn't a short woman, but the panic she'd been warding off consumed her. It covered her like a suffocating blanket and she had a hard time breathing.

The more air she took in, the less she could breathe.

"Vivian, look at me. I'm not going to hurt you."

His hand covered her mouth. She dug her fingernails into the side of his hand attempting to remove it. It wouldn't budge. She felt the panic of not being able to breathe but forced a small amount of air through her nose.

"Listen to my voice. You're hyperventilating, Vivian. I'm going to help you slow down your respirations. Try to count backward from ten in your head."

He tugged her one direction and went the other. Ending the move so they faced each other. "That's it. Deeply through your nose."

She shook her head, feeling the panic again with the lack of oxygen. *Ten.*

"In."

She sniffed as best as she could.

"Now let it out."

The sound of her breath hitting his fingers was weird. "In."

It was broken, but she managed, catching the hint of coffee on him. *Nine.*

"Deeper," he whispered closer to her ear. "Let it out slowly."

She obeyed. *Eight.*

"You got this. Now I'm going to take my hand away. Just keep breathing in and out."

Freedom washed over her as he dropped his hand and took a step away.

"In. Out. Just think calm."

Seven. She covered her face, unable to look into his obviously concerned eyes.

"You okay now?"

"I think I can… That's…that's never happened to me before."

"I apologize for the up close and personal, but I didn't have a paper bag in my pocket."

She swayed and his hands darted out to steady her. "Whoa. I think I'm a little light-headed."

"No surprise. Why don't you sit again? I'll get you a bottle of water." He helped until the back of her knees bent against the couch and she sat.

"Tap. Glasses…" She pointed above the sink. The dishes were on an open shelf. He wouldn't have trouble finding them. "That was…so embarrassing."

Slate moved his hat out of the sink and filled a glass, then handed her the water. "Do the panic attacks happen often?"

"Never."

He looked at her like that was hard to believe, but he didn't say the words. "I figure this is a lot to take in. You're gonna have to trust me."

"Does that slow-talkin' cowboy act work on a lot of the girls?" She watched his puzzled reaction. Had she miscalculated him? Was he for real? "Look. I don't trust anyone anymore. Victor and I have been screwed over by the best of them. Just tell me what's wrong with this report and why aren't we on our way to the attorney's office?"

"Yeah, about that." He grimaced slightly while sucking air through his teeth. Then he arched his hand down the back of his head and scratched his neck. Then he put his hands in the air like he was stopping her from moving. "You're not going to have another attack, are you?"

She crossed her arms and legs in answer.

"My buddy was checking the file to make sure everything on our end is ready to go next week. Heath might have arrested your brother, but no one in my Company had anything to do with the investigation."

"So?"

"I don't actually have permission to be working the case."

"Oh. I understand. You'd rather not be involved so you're going to let my brother hang."

"No, that's not exactly what I meant." He pulled his phone from his back pocket.

"Mr. Thompson, it's time for you to leave." She stood and pointed to the door.

He held a finger up in the air with one hand, bringing his phone up with the other. "One second. Just give me— Wade. Look, your hunch was right. Yeah, I've got a good lead, but I'm going to need some time. No." He brought his light blue eyes up from looking at the carpet to meet hers. "I did not get food poisoning. I'll put in for the time off. I just wanted to be sure you'd be around for tech support. Yeah, man. *One* of the best." He disconnected, shaking his head then rubbing his forehead right between his brows.

"What was that about?" she asked, trying not to feel pleased or excited or both.

"I'm going to help you." He took off his badge hooked on his shirt pocket and tucked it away with his ID. "I just can't be a Texas Ranger while I do."

"You're really going to help me? Help Victor?" That bubble was back, ready to pop with his next words.

"I didn't sign up for this job just to step aside and see an innocent man go to prison." He stepped back toward the kitchen and picked up his hat, now on the two-burner stove. "Now that you know the logistics on my end, let's go see Victor's attorney. I'll be in the truck while you dress. It's still raining out there. You might want to bring an umbrella."

Was that a wink while he secured that Stetson on his head?

It didn't matter. She felt years older than Slate Thompson. And her heart was a little short on...

Well, everything. It was depleted. Empty. Desperate for any human kindness.

The tears came as soon as Slate pulled the door shut behind him. Just a short, easily controlled attack while she gathered clothes.

Who knew what they'd be doing later. And she meant *they*. There wasn't any way in the world she was letting that cowboy get out of her sight until she found out everything he knew about Victor's case.

Slate had only met the poor, pitiful, chicken wing waitress in dire need of help. He had no idea what she became when she put on her business suit. It might be her last one, but she looked and felt like she was in control.

Normal.

Chapter Six

Half an hour passed. Then another ten minutes. Slate was stepping out of the truck to see what was keeping Vivian when her apartment door opened.

It was one of those jaw-dropping moments that didn't happen very often in his life. He'd kept it together and hadn't cracked a smile in his Department of Public Safety days when a girl took off her top trying to get out of a speeding ticket. The man who thought his clothes were on fire and spit a bottle of water all over his uniform—he'd handled it all with a straight face and no disgust.

But seeing Vivian Watts step onto the wet sidewalk in a blue suit made him take a second look. And maybe a third. Her wild dark brown hair was neatly tucked at the back of her head. He noticed because he ran to her side of the truck and grabbed the umbrella she'd brought with her.

Helping her onto the front seat, he politely waited for her to put down a towel. It gave him plenty of time to admire the line of her calf and the height of the matching blue heels. Not to mention a close-up view of the shapely behind in her tight-fitting skirt.

The wolf in him came out. His lips were all puckered to let loose a howling whistle when he caught himself and kind of sucked air through his teeth. She noticed. Yep, she smiled, knowing what was blowing through his mind.

He ran to his side of the truck, chucking the umbrella in the back seat. His tie had been off since he'd left for lunch, but the way she was dressed almost made him feel guilty enough to put it back on.

Almost.

"I'm assuming we need to go to your place for you to get dry clothes. I'm fine with that by the way."

"I live west of the metroplex on a ranch. It's sort of out of the way."

"So the cowboy thing isn't a thing? It's genuine?"

"That'd be me."

"You don't mind being wet?"

"Well, I've been worse. Beer once. Now that's sticky when it dries." Slate had already looked up the address of the attorney in Uptown.

"As much as I'd like to hear about you covered in beer… I think you take a left here."

"Not around this time of day. It really is a funny story."

"I gather."

Slate tapped on the radio, immediately turning it down. "You don't have to worry. I looked at directions and traffic before you got in the truck."

"Do you think we should talk about what happens now? How do we get the report if Victor's attorney didn't keep the copy I gave him? Are you sure you know how to get to his office? I think you missed another turn."

Lots of questions he wasn't prepared to answer. "Let's just take it one thing at a time. First step is to get there and ask for a copy of the study. We compare. We might get lucky."

"Lucky? How long have you been a ranger?"

"Almost two years. I was fortunate to be stationed here in Garland. That's close enough to help out my family.

How about you? What did you do before you came to Dallas or have you been here awhile?"

"I studied international business and had an internship at one of the top companies in Miami."

"You gave all that up to come help your brother."

"That didn't sound like a question."

Slate stated fact. He admired her for it. She didn't know there was a personal financial report in the file. One reflecting she and her brother were broke. He'd read her statement to the police, an interview that confirmed most of the information obtained through the VA.

"Are you going to tell Victor's attorney that you're reopening his case?"

"One step at a time, remember?" Slate didn't have permission to do anything. Unfortunately, the attorney would know that. "Why don't you tell me about your brother?"

"As in…?"

"What problem was he having? Something like he couldn't sleep, right?"

"Night terrors. He's had them since returning from the Middle East. He's never really talked to me about his time in the army. The most common question from you guys is do I think he's capable of killing someone." She paused, taking a look out the window. "The answer is I don't know. I haven't spent a lot of time with him after he left the military. He came to Dallas because of Dr. Roberts and her study. He wanted to be a part of it and live a normal life."

"Look, Vivian." He was about to cover her hand but he redirected his hand to the steering wheel. "I'm on your side. Honestly, I don't know if they'll reopen the investigation. I'm pretty sure the prosecutor will fight it since he thinks his case is pretty solid."

"Then what are we doing?"

The windshield wipers banged out a rhythm, adding

a slow swish as the rain turned to a sprinkle. "Not giving up."

"I never did."

He turned to face her, seat belt stretched tight across his
chest. "If your brother is truly innocent…neither will I."

Where the hell had that come from? That whole fight-
ing-for-justice thought earlier? Maybe. More than likely.
It couldn't have anything to do with the wolf whistle he'd
swallowed along with the urgent need to puff up his chest
and rescue the fair maiden. Naw…nothing like that.

Or exactly that.

He'd wanted to help Vivian and her brother since meeting her in that ridiculous waitress outfit. The suit, however,
fit her to perfection. It was much sexier than the skimpy
shorts. Even though he'd enjoyed looking at her legs.

Someone behind him honked a horn. The light was
green and he continued to the law office. He parked and
Vivian didn't open her door.

"Look, Slate. As much as I appreciate your promise,
I'm not holding you to it. You seem like a nice guy. I have
no idea why this is happening to my brother, but it's not
your responsibility."

"Let's talk to your lawyer and compare the reports. See
what he thinks is going on. Throw around some ideas.
Then maybe we can grab dinner and talk."

VIVIAN WAS RELUCTANT to walk down the street with Slate
to one of his favorite restaurants. The visit with Victor's
lawyer had been a bust. Even her favorite suit couldn't
make her feel better about the cavalier attitude he'd shown
by not keeping the appointment.

It began to sprinkle again. Slate grabbed her hand and
hurried through the dinner crowd on Maple Avenue and
crossed the street.

"Here we go. I'm starved." He released her hand and shot both of his through his hair, slicking the longer portion on top straight back like he had in her apartment.

"You just ate three hours ago." She swiped droplets of water from her sleeves, then pulled a curl back under control, tucking it behind her ear. "Slate, I…um… I can't eat here."

Sam and Nick's was the third most expensive steak house in Dallas. She knew only because she listened to customers talk about the amazing places they'd been to—other than her chicken restaurant. She had agreed to come with him to dinner, but she wasn't going to order anything. She couldn't. The money in her wallet was bus fare to get her back and forth to court.

"Sorry, I should have asked if you're a vegetarian or vegan. Look, there's a place every fifty feet around here. I'm sure we can find one for non-meat eaters." He grabbed her hand again.

The doorman stared at them.

"I'm not a vegetarian," she whispered. Then she leaned in closer to him. "This place is too fancy for me."

"Well, shoot. My mouth is salivating for a good sirloin." He took a step away from the door, letting another couple pass through. "Wait. This is my idea. My treat. Can we eat here now?"

As much as she'd lowered her voice to avoid embarrassing looks, Slate spoke loudly, not seeming to catch a hint of her embarrassment—at all. He tugged gently on her hand, backing up to and through the open doorway.

The maître d' recognized Slate as he turned around to face her. "We can seat you right away, Lieutenant Thompson."

The couple that was before them had just been told it was a forty-five minute wait. Vivian looked at the ranger and he promptly winked at her. He also still had hold of her hand. Firm grip.

"They do have really good sirloin here."

"So this really is one of your favorite places. They know you on sight."

He bent close to her ear, his warm breath cascading over the sensitive lobe. "I sort of stopped a robbery one night. They won't let me forget it." He jerked his chin to a framed article hanging on the wall.

Well, how about that. He was a real-life hero. She got closer, along with the couple now behind them in line, and read all about the armed robber who hadn't made it out the door because a Texas Ranger had been dining here.

"Thank God. That's the first gun we've seen out in the open like this," the woman in line said. "I didn't know what to think. Do you wear your weapon when you're on a date?"

"Actually, ma'am—" Slate's accent turned super slow and drawn out "—I'm required to have it with me at all times. Unless I've been drinking, of course."

The maître d' returned and Slate's heavily countrified accent disappeared as he spoke with Candace—he knew the young woman by name—and asked her how her son was getting along at his new daycare.

Seated at a table for two near the corner, Slate held out Vivian's chair and seated himself against the wall. He waved off the menus.

"Mind if I order for you?"

"Not at all." She might as well let him. If he was buying, she wouldn't have to look at the prices and wonder how she'd ever repay him.

"Double the usual, Mikey. And how's your kid brother? He going to pass chemistry?"

"Yes, sir, Senor Slate. We got him the tutor and it was

free. Just like you think." The waiter raised his brows and looked at her. "You want a drink, Miss? And house salad dressing like Senor Slate?"

"That would be great, and water's fine. Thanks."

"He's a good kid," Slate said as Mikey walked away. "When his father was killed, he had to quit high school to support his family, but he got his GED."

She was almost speechless. Almost. "Are you for real? I mean, I thought there was some reason you were offering to help me. Some gimmick. Or something that you're hiding from the police. But it seems like you genuinely care. Do you?"

Slate Thompson looked surprised. No, he actually looked terrified.

"I hadn't... I..."

"Don't worry, Slate. Your secret's safe with me."

There weren't too many people in the world who truly cared about others anymore.

"I'm sorry we didn't have a chance to discuss the case with your— I need to take this." He withdrew his phone and answered. "What's up? No, I'm in Uptown. Yeah, twenty minutes with sirens. You're certain? I'll check it out."

"Don't worry about me," Vivian said, "I'll take the bus home."

"There's been a murder-suicide at the VA Hospital. One of the men in the same study as your brother." He scanned his phone. "If you don't mind waiting in the truck, I can take you home after. Easier than trying to find the buses in the rain. Come on."

He asked the waiter to make it a to-go order, paid the bill and left her to go get his truck.

"He's such a nice man," the maître d' said after the door shut behind him. "He saved my life during that robbery.

The guy held a gun under my chin and said he was going to blow my head off. After the whole terrifying thing was over, Slate brought a counselor by to talk with me before my shift a couple of days later. There's no way I'll ever be able to repay him."

"He seems very kind." *Amazing is more like it.*

"Here's your order," the waiter said, handing her the bag of food.

Right on cue, Slate pulled up under the awning.

She climbed into the passenger side. "I don't want to be a bother, Slate. You could drop me at the Rapid Transit station and I can get home from there."

"You'd ruin your shoes waiting in the rain. I promise, I won't be long. Wade, one of the guys in my Company, gave me the heads-up."

"Do you believe it's related to my brother?"

"Another ranger *thinks* it's one of the guys in the study."

"Right. No promises."

Get a grip. Slate Thompson had a job. He was doing it, and a side benefit was helping Victor. There was no reason to think any part of it was personal.

No matter how often he held her hand.

Chapter Seven

There is more than one way to kill. There is more than one way to kill. There is more than one way to kill.

Abby wrote in her journal, but scratched each sentence out quickly. She covered it with her hand so no one could see it. Even if she was alone and in a private office.

That didn't matter. The government spied on everyone through all sorts of devices, and the police were everywhere.

Cell phones had cameras. Stoplights had cameras. Cars had back-up cameras. They were everywhere. She couldn't get away from them.

Spies were spies and had to be dealt with. But there was no one around. No one to deal with for the moment.

The doctor had said journals were important. Dr. Roberts had a journal and had written about her as a patient, had written about them all. Abby had taken care of her in the best way she could. Not a perfect way, though. Abby hadn't found that yet.

Dr. Roberts had been right about that particular problem. Abby needed to find it soon. The day was getting close when she'd need to move and start over in another city at another hospital.

"I am not crazy. Dr. Roberts told me I wasn't. I can believe her," she whispered.

Abby needed another pencil. She'd scratched out her last journal sentence so hard, she'd broken the tip. She looked around, but there wasn't another near her to continue. She rolled the chair closer to the small window facing the front of the building.

It was two hours past time to go home. Catching her normal train wouldn't be possible. She was familiar with the alternative, taking a cab, but that wasn't possible either. And she was hungry.

Her subconscious suggestions with Rashad Parker had been so successful that he hadn't waited. He'd gone to the cafeteria, secured a knife and stabbed two people, then slit his throat. Now the hospital was on lockdown.

If she'd known it would work so well, she would have followed him. Now she had been ordered to stay in her office until the hospital was cleared, until the police were certain no one else was at risk.

It was four minutes past dinner.

She moved away from the distracting police lights and arranged the patient binders by date. Then numeric order. She checked the contents to verify that she'd organized them correctly. She'd already finished transcribing the dictation. She listened again. There were no corrections to be made.

She couldn't allow herself to panic just because her schedule was off. She needed to journal more. That would calm the rising nervousness.

A knock on the outer door relieved the moment of panic. She tucked her journal into her handbag with the microtapes she'd used on the sleep-study patients today. She practiced the concerned look she should have in the glass of the only picture hanging on the wall.

The knock persisted. She grabbed her handbag and twisted the lock.

"Come in." She stepped away from the door and waited for the person on the other side to open it.

"Ms. Norman?" The man wasn't dressed like a policeman. He wore a suit and tie.

"Yes. May I go now?"

"Sorry, it's taken a while to clear the offices on each floor. We understand that you had a Rashad Parker here today."

"Yes. He's one of the sleep-study patients. Is he okay? Did something happen?"

"You seem concerned. Was he acting strangely? Make any threats toward anyone?"

"No, of course not." She added a breathiness that indicated worry. She'd studied an emotional thesaurus and practiced at eight o'clock each evening for half an hour. Even so, unable to pursue her normal routine was making her a bit anxious. "May I leave now? I've missed my train and the second train, too."

"I apologize. I forgot to introduce myself. Detective Arnold. Here's my card. I'll have one of the officers escort you out of the building. Mind if I have a look around?"

"I do. I'm not the doctor or the technician. I just set things up for them. There are patient files in here and records. I believe you'll need a court order to proceed with the hospital." She gripped the knob and pulled the door closed behind her. "Which officer will see me safely outside?"

"Burnsy. Will you take Ms. Norman out?"

An officer in full uniform with an automatic weapon took her to the stairs. "Sorry, ma'am, but the elevators are off-limits."

"I prefer the stairs."

On the ground floor, she waited and allowed the officer to open the door—having to remind him that it was the polite thing to do for a lady. She slipped on her surgical gloves and mask for the ride home. She might be forced to take public transportation, but she would not succumb to the germs. She had important work to finish.

Finally out of the building, she took a deep, satisfying breath. There were so many things to add to her study journal. She wished illustrations were possible but her drawings were elementary. She'd never be able to include the images she had in her mind of Dr. Roberts as she died. A shame she hadn't taken actual pictures.

The walk through the sprinkling rain to Lancaster Road let her observe the television reporters, the police and the bystanders. The streets were empty except for those types of vehicles. She sat on her bench next to the Veterans Affairs building at the corner of Avenue of Flags and Liberty Loop, taking a moment to reevaluate.

How would she get to her apartment? Not by sitting here. The light rail train home arrived every fifteen minutes. Police blocked the street and rail entrance but as people came down, they showed their hospital badges and were let by. That's all she had to tell them. She needed by to get home. She had seven more minutes to get on the platform.

A man spoke to both the officers who monitored the road. He showed them a badge. She could hear him offer to help with the situation. But more startled to hear him asking specific questions about Rashid Parker.

"This guy was on my radar and I want to ask the detective in charge to keep me informed. You can understand that, guys, right?"

Abby quickly took out her phone and snapped a picture of the officer. She tried to zoom in on the license plate of the truck he'd gotten out of, but the dimming light and mist made it impossible.

Why is he asking about Rashid?

"Walk past," she whispered behind her mask. "You've missed the train home. You have five minutes and twenty seconds before the next one scheduled. You can control the obsessive-compulsive disorder. You control you. You are not a compulsion." She channeled the last words, repeating them again and again until her feet moved.

Before she allowed herself to think, she showed the police officers her hospital identification. She was even able to pull down the mask so they could verify. She walked through to the next corner, passing the truck, pretending to be absorbed in her phone, but taking pictures of the truck and its occupant.

The woman inside looked familiar. Someone in the study? No. Maybe one of their relatives? She'd look it up when she returned home. She had a file on everyone participating in her study. Knowing everything about them was crucial, including anyone who might care for them and be an outside influence.

But why was a relative at the hospital? And why was she with a police officer? The dark-haired woman was the wrong race to be waiting on news of Rashid.

Her research would give her answers. Reminding herself that today had been excellent, with excellent results. The murder-suicide was the fastest response she'd ever accomplished.

If Abby experienced joy, there would be elation when writing the details of this event. Such a success.

She was one step closer to discovering the perfect death and implementing it on herself.

Chapter Eight

Slate opened the truck door and Vivian jumped from her skin. He climbed inside and chose not to mention that the doors should have been locked even if he was on the outskirts of the taped-off area.

"I couldn't find out much more than what Wade told us. Does the name Rashid Parker mean anything to you?"

"No. Should it?"

"So your brother never mentioned him or anything?"

"My brother barely speaks to me and never about his doctor's murder. It's always events from our childhood, before he joined the army. Does it mean more if he knew Mr. Parker?"

The obvious reason might just be that her brother was guilty. But something told Slate he wasn't. More than Wade's hunch. Something bugged him about Subject Nineteen and the fact that Victor wasn't part of the blind study described in Dr. Roberts's journal.

That had to mean something.

"I look at it this way. I don't like coincidences in any case I work." He was thinking aloud, but being honest with Vivian was essential. "This case has way too many for my comfort level. I'd never hand it over to a prosecutor. I'm surprised the Dallas DA accepted it."

"This feeling of yours—it has something to do with the sleep study?"

"It's sort of a rule of mine. The first itch makes me scratch my head. An investigator might accept one. But then when the second coincidence hits, you're getting into territory that needs another verification. When the third pops up? Well, three coincidences mean something's hinky and your case is about to go to hell."

"Did you discover three?" she asked. "Are you worried about sharing something that might clear my brother? I'll be contacting his attorney whether you do or not."

"That's not a problem. I'll contact him tomorrow." The officer waved them through the intersection and a waft of his sirloin made his stomach growl. "You have steak knives at your place?"

"If not, I give you permission to eat with your fingers."

"Like a wild man. Cool."

"But you still have to explain. What does Rashid Parker have to do with my brother?"

"One. Wade didn't obtain the complete list but he confirmed Parker was at the hospital for the study. Don't ask me how, I'm not asking him. But Parker is definitely a part of the same sleep study that your brother was involved in. Two. None of those men and women are listed as *subject* anything. And three…"

"Yes?"

"Three is that it feels off, too convenient. Why did your brother confess and why has he never been able to recall the details about that day? Everything else, yes, but not that day?" His stomach growled again. "Can you dig me a roll out of the sack?"

"There's a fourth thing." She handed him two fluffy yeast rolls.

"Yeah?"

"The incidents both happened at the VA Hospital."

"Damn, you're right." He inhaled a buttery roll and swallowed. "That's one too many."

"Rolls?"

He laughed. "No. The number of coincidences."

"So do you think they'll let you reopen the case?"

"Hold on a sec." Slate called Wade through his hands-free set, leaving it on speaker so Vivian could hear. "You still at the office, man?"

"Where else am I going to be until these files are done?"

"Forget I asked. Give Heath the necessary info and he'll run his magic on that sleep-study list."

"So my hunch was right?"

"You can lord it over me later." He quickly looked at Vivian. "Call Heath. I need that info before I hit Watts's lawyer's office in the morning."

"I'll get him started. We looking for anything in particular?"

"If I'm right, you'll know." He disconnected as he pulled in front of Vivian's apartment. He could see the hesitation in her body language before she pulled the door handle. "Look, Vivian, I should probably get home."

She visibly relaxed. "Thank you for everything, Slate. I should head inside. I'm working a double tomorrow, so would you leave me a message if you find anything?"

He nodded and pushed the dinner sack at her when she set it in her vacated seat. "You take it. I'll pick up a burger on the way home."

"I can't possibly."

"It's the least I can do for dragging you around in the rain."

Her head shook from side to side. "You aren't going to take no for an answer, are you?"

"I'll stop by the wing place if I find anything."

"Thank you for your help."

"I haven't done anything yet."

Vivian's expression filled with sadness and regret. With that, she shut the truck door. He could read people pretty well and she was silently screaming that she didn't expect anyone—especially a lawman—to help. He waited for her to go inside her apartment, then called Wade again.

"Miss me already?" Wade answered.

"Check with the OIG for the VA. See if they have any weird reports or complaints."

"That would be the Office of Inspector General for Veterans Affairs that won't be open until tomorrow. And what will you be doing?"

"I'm going home and repairing a barn stall like I told my dad I would. I'm also about to beg my mother to fix me dinner. Totally starved."

"Bring the leftovers tomorrow. Payback for me doing all your legwork."

"You're the one sitting behind a desk, man. I'm the one sitting on wet denim from doing your legwork on this hunch of yours."

"And it's paying off."

"Tomorrow, man."

It was probably better that Vivian Watts had to work a double tomorrow. Probably better since he needed to wrap up his current caseload before he could take vacation days and help her. He couldn't flash around his badge, but mentioning that he was a ranger might open some doors that had been slammed for her.

Statistics weren't in their favor. He wouldn't be just another man who got her hopes up and left her hanging.

Chapter Nine

"I could never have assumed that Rashid would react to the suggestion before he left the hospital." Abby pulled at her cuticles with tweezers. She spoke to the only person completely familiar with her work, herself.

Several doctors, including Roberts, had ordered her to stop, stating it was unhealthy to pick at her nails. They were wrong.

Her skin was raw, but there were still pieces. She picked more furiously before looking up into her red, freshly scrubbed face. Certain there was another layer of dirt on her epidermis, she obtained another washcloth, rubbing and scrubbing as hard as she could.

Setting the cloth onto the counter, she switched back to the tweezers, picking until the bright red of her clean blood seeped around the nail. She went to the cabinet to remove the last washcloth from the sealed bag. She would begin the cleansing process again until she was positive the germs from walking on an unfamiliar street were no longer present.

"Enough!" her reflection yelled.

"I can never get clean enough," she answered behind the cloth.

"You must control yourself, Abby. Break from your routine. There is work to be done. Check the list you made while waiting for the train. It's thorough."

"Yes. I need to identify the woman in the truck." The tweezers caught her eye. She dropped the newer white cloth on top of the metal but immediately had to place them in the sterilizing jar.

"My darling Abby. You are so smart and will find my answers. The perfect death will be ours. I've always had faith in you."

Her encouraging voice from the mirror echoed in her mind as she found her pocket notebook. Flipping the pages, she saw the step-by-step lists of exactly what to do next with her study.

The doctors had all told her that conversing in the mirror wasn't mentally healthy either. They were wrong, too. After talking with the mirror woman, everything was always much clearer.

The goal to merge with her through a perfect death was even more necessary.

She connected her laptop to the external memory, careful to remain free from the internet. Her research on each of the sleep-study veterans confirmed her suspicion. The woman in the truck was the sister of Victor Watts. She'd almost forgotten about the young man.

What was the sister doing with an officer at Rashid's death? What about another veteran's death would pique the curiosity of a family member from the sleep study?

The voice in the mirror, both perfect and sterile, was right again. Follow the steps, follow the lists she'd already written. She could concentrate on the list and avoid the problems culminating from her disrupted day.

Even though her schedule had changed, it was deeply satisfying news that Rashid had reacted so quickly. A very hopeful sign that her experiments were working even better.

So what if family were curious. She had a plan already in place to take care of anything or anyone who might upset her goals. One phone call would activate him to perform whatever deed needed. He'd taken care of problems before and never remembered. He could take care of this, too.

Many times she'd been to doctors, trying to overcome the debilitating obsessive compulsions that sidetracked her from completing her work. They'd all failed, concentrating instead on the one thing that made her focus, gave her clarity. Attempting to take away the voice in the mirror wasn't right. The perfect voice that brought precision to her thoughts.

The voice was serenity. The voice was excellence.

The voice was necessary.

Vivian Watts…was not.

Chapter Ten

Vivian savored every bite of half a steak. She carefully wrapped the other portion in foil and stuck it in the freezer. Then she packed her laptop and caught a bus for the nearest free Wi-Fi.

She hadn't given Slate the only copy of the study. He might not have vocalized all his thoughts, but she caught on pretty quick. The other thing she could do was research.

She didn't trust that Slate or the others would get the complete list of participants, but it couldn't be that difficult to find them. There had to be some way to narrow down the sleep-study list. It was easier than anticipated since it was specifically focused on veterans. Then it became apparent that nothing had happened to the females in the study, but the guys were a different story.

The study was in two parts, one prior to Dr. Roberts's death and another after. The results had been published in recent medical journals so Roberts's coworkers could continue the research. There were sixty participants—thirty of each gender. But no names.

The search she conducted was the first that came to her mind…murders by veterans limited to the previous year. Some had been seen at the VA Hospital, including her brother. Without much specific information, she couldn't be certain, but it looked as if the number of incidents involving local veterans had dramatically increased.

"Why hasn't anyone looked into this?" she mumbled in total shock. Rashid Parker was the fourteenth man she'd found in the surrounding area.

She dug through her purse, looking for Slate's card. The announcement that the library would close in a few minutes had already been made. She saved all the pages of research as screenshots, printed and put them in a folder to work with at home.

The phone call to Slate would have to wait until her break the next day. The card gave his office and cell numbers but she didn't really have any information for him. What could she pass along? She'd wait for the half-hour break she'd get between her shifts at the restaurant.

Once home, she packed her suitcase just in case the landlord decided to act on the last day of the month instead of the morning of the first. She retrieved a second suitcase from the closet with the few possessions her brother had. Laptop and valuables were in a smaller bag that she'd take with her and store under the counter—whether the chicken manager liked it or not.

She'd sold her car, sold her possessions in Florida and felt like she'd hit rock bottom. But each time she thought about herself, she remembered the eleven months her brother had been in jail. Eleven months of suffering, of defending himself, of thinking he'd killed the doctor that he'd spoken so highly of.

According to Victor, Dr. Roberts was going to "fix" him, "cure" him. The plan was that he'd participate in her study and she'd know exactly how his brain ticked. And if they knew that…the night terrors would stop.

Vivian had never understood why he'd harm the only person who had given him hope. The one doctor who could take his nightmares away. She'd mentioned that to his lawyer with every visit. After a month, she no longer had access to discuss her brother's case. The lawyer wouldn't see her. She had no legal recourse. No access to any discovery or evidence the prosecutor had obtained.

In the dark. No legal recourse to fight for her brother. The second and current attorneys had refused to discuss the case with her at all.

There it was again. The flicker of hope shone like a bright star in the sky, twinkling just out of her reach. Slate didn't seem like a person who would flicker out. He was more the type who provided secure warmth like the sun.

She fell sleep. Her dreams of being a young child playing with her brother in a warm field quickly changed to the sun burning her skin. The feeling that she was lying on the ground had her twisting. Somehow she knew it was the padding that tried to pass for a mattress. She was asleep, but then she wasn't.

Police cars. Firefighters. Loud sirens and lights. She was dreaming. It felt like a war documentary. Something from World War I. Loud cracking, explosions, gas masks, shouting. She wanted to wake up.

"Don't struggle. We got you!" The voice came through a fog.

Stuck between dreams and waking, she struggled to understand the man's words through his gas mask. She didn't like the dream and struggled more. She twisted round and round in the sheets, tangling them around her legs until she was paralyzed. She couldn't move. Couldn't breathe.

She needed to wake up before she died.

"Miss. Miss!" A hand on her shoulder shook her awake.

Vivian opened her eyes, an oxygen mask on her face. She coughed, wanting to sit, but she was strapped to a gurney and couldn't move.

She shook her head. "Let me up," she said under the plastic.

"Sure. Are you injured? Do you know where you are?"

The men around her looked like paramedics. Each unbuckled a strap and she was free.

"What happened?" She pushed up to a sitting position, coughing the entire way.

"The whole apartment building is in flames," someone cried behind her. "They're still getting people out."

"Do they…do they know how it started?"

"Not yet."

She swung her feet to the side until they hit the ground. The paramedic handed her the oxygen and didn't take no for an answer, pushing it to cover her nose and mouth.

The dream made sense now. She hadn't been in World War I with rescuers and masks hiding their faces. She'd been in a fire. The major portion of the blaze was at her apartment. She watched the men battling inside and out of the tiny place that had been her home.

Oh, my God. It couldn't have started with her. Nothing had been on, not even the heater. So what had happened?

The paramedic draped the blanket over her shoulders. She gripped it around her neck like a protective cloak. *Pajamas. Thank God she'd been wearing them.*

She watched, helpless. There was no going back to her brother's apartment. Her living space. Gone. Everything she owned was inside. Gone.

"You're so lucky you faced the street. They knocked down your door first. I watched them pull you out. I thought you were dead." A woman stood next to her dressed in a long robe and slippers.

Dressed as she was, Vivian assumed she was one of the neighbors who'd had to abandon their home, too. "Are you okay? Need to sit down?"

"No. I was out walking my dog." She opened a flap of her robe and flashed the face of a small Chihuahua. "Me and Bohemian are just fine. We live on the other side of the block." She pointed down the street as she clasped the dog and covered him with the thick robe.

"Do you have a phone?"

"Sure. Call anyone you like, honey. I sure hope someone can come get you since you ain't getting back into that apartment." She pointed to the burned-out hollow where she'd been sleeping. "You are really lucky to be alive."

"I think so, too."

She tapped for Information. "Do you have a number for a local Texas Ranger's office? I think he said it was in Garland."

Chapter Eleven

"You brought her here? Home?" Heath Murray asked from his bedroom doorway. "Doesn't this break a ton of rules or something?"

Slate had been awakened by the emergency phone call from his office. It took him over an hour to find Vivian, who'd been taken to a local emergency room. "Where else do you suggest I take her? She refused to go to a hotel and insisted on a women's shelter."

"It's better than hiding the truth from the major." Slate's roommate stood in his boxers, squinting from the lack of contacts, hair standing straight out from his head. "What's wrong with the women's shelter?"

"She'd be eaten alive there." He lowered his voice and took a step closer to his friend. "She's got nothing, man. Every penny she had, her phone, her laptop…all gone."

"I can hear you," Vivian said, standing between the kitchen and the living room. "And I did tell him to take me to a shelter. He's the one who's being stubborn about this."

Slate turned back to her. "Honestly, it's not a big deal. I don't know why Heath's so bent out of shape. You're staying here tonight and that's the end of it."

"Well, since I'm sort of stranded, I have no choice. But I'm definitely the one sleeping on the couch." Her fingers clung to the blanket the EMTs had provided. Her feet were barely protected with hospital or crime scene paper boo-ties. She was probably in shock, and yet she stood straight and undefeated.

"Please take his room," Heath said, throwing up his hands. "If you don't, I'm never getting back to sleep."

Slate slapped him on his bare shoulder. "Since you're up…"

"I'm not." Heath took his skinny legs and bare feet back down the hall. "I'm not up. Figment of your imagination walking here."

Slate didn't watch him go. He just waited for the door to slam. It did.

"I'm taking the couch and you're staying in my room. It also has a private bath so you can get cleaned up. You breathing okay? They told me to watch out for wheezing."

"I should never have called you. I only did in case you tried to find me with news about Victor's case and the per-son answering the phone insisted I give a reason."

"I'm glad you called."

"I think someone deliberately set that fire."

He was taken off guard that Vivian had said it. Not that the thought hadn't already been in his head since the mo-ment she got a hold of him.

"Yeah, one too many coincidences. But why now? They've had months to do something like this. Why wait until I poked my nose into it?"

"I went to the library after you dropped me off and began my own research."

"And?" He leaned against the wall, growing conscious of the dirty ranch clothes he'd thrown on to go find her.

"I didn't have anything definitive. Nothing except a rise in violent behavior from veterans. Out of the fourteen news articles I read, at least half the relatives mentioned they thought the accused had been getting better since seeking treatment at the hospital."

"Parker would make fifteen and your brother would be another. Sixteen men? All veterans? What time frame are we looking at?"

"I went back a year before I ran out of time. I don't think you can call it a coincidence, Slate."

"You went back to your apartment after the library. Was anyone acting suspicious or seem to be following you?"

"No. It was another hour or so before I got ready for bed. I wanted everything packed and ready to leave with me." She pursed her lips together, a classic tell that she thought she'd said too much to him.

"Leave?"

"Oh, my gosh, I might as well tell you since you're going to find out anyway." She sat on the couch, resting her elbow on the arm and rubbing her temple with her fingers. "Victor's lease is up and I couldn't sign a new one. The manager increased the rent three times and told me he didn't want me staying. So you might as well take me to the shelter. I'm going to be living there anyway."

"You couldn't afford to find another place?"

"I spent everything I had on cheap private detectives who didn't connect any dots. You've gotten further in one day just looking at a sleep-study report."

"I have special resources."

"I plan on returning to Miami after the trial next week. I'll try to get a job with the firm I worked for before all this began. I'm not sure if they'll take me back, but they at least said to contact them."

How much more bad luck could this woman take?

"And what do you plan on doing until then?" Slate could assume what the answer was. The thoughts running through his head went against everything he'd worked for, trained for. "You can't be serious about staying in the shelter?"

"It's conveniently located near the courthouse and jail." She dropped her head to the back of the couch. "Don't worry about me. I'll be fine."

"What about your job? That's a long way by bus and DART."

"Tomorrow—I mean, today was my last day. The manager wouldn't give me time off for Victor's trial. Do you think anything survived the fire?"

She was on the verge of tears and collapse. Did she even realize she'd almost died? There was a high probability that someone had tried to kill her.

"We'll take a look as soon as they give the go-ahead to get back in," Slate promised.

"Oh, for the love of Pete, man. Ask her already," Heath yelled from his room.

Slate turned to Vivian and covered her hand resting on the sofa. "Please take my room. You do *not* want to face him walking around in the morning. He's a jackass before coffee."

"Ask me what?"

"Good grief, I'll say it." Heath stuck his head out between the door and wall. "She can stay here and I'll keep my mouth shut about it. No one from the Company will know. But I need sleep. Please go to bed."

"I can't possibly stay here. You know nothing about me and can't open your home like this."

"Look, this is easier than it seems. You can stay in the guest bunkhouse. My family runs a sort of dude ranch and gives riding lessons. We'll get you set up tomorrow. But for now, Heath's right. You need sleep. Come on."

He gently tugged her hand and the rest of her body followed.

"I don't like giving in."

"Consider it a compromise. Both of us win."

"Even me if I can get some sleep," Heath said sarcastically as they passed his door.

"I'm truly sorry. I didn't mean to be a bother."

Slate closed his bedroom door behind them so his roommate could get back to sleep. Vivian's voice shook like she was close to being hysterical or she was heading into shock. She also smelled like the fire. Smoke clung to her clothes and even her hair, which was loose and curly around her shoulders.

"Through there. Clean towels in the cabinet." He pointed. He went to the bathroom door and opened it, gesturing for her to go through.

Vivian didn't move. At least her feet didn't. Her hands covered her face and the dam of tears broke. She cried silently into her palms. He watched her shoulders shake and her upper body begin to fold downward to her knees.

He did the only thing a good ol' country boy could... caught her to him.

Holding her, it didn't matter how late it was or that she smelled like smoke. All there was right then was defending Vivian from anything else crappy happening to her. She was right that he barely knew her. But she'd given up everything for her brother.

Everything.

That type of loyalty was worth staying up all night to help save.

"It'll be okay, Vivian. Go ahead and cry. Get it out. You'll be okay."

THE STRONG ARMS wrapped around her gave Vivian a sense of belonging she hadn't had since Victor left for his tour overseas. But this wasn't her brother.

It was a stranger who had quickly become her lifeline. Her only lifeline that was keeping her from fending for herself on the street. It had been a while since someone showed her so much kindness.

The more she thought about it, the more she cried. The more she cried, the tighter Slate held her. She pushed at his chest trying to back away… He cupped the back of her head and encouraged her cheek to rest on his chest.

She didn't care. If he'd hold her longer, she'd let him. Everything was just so… She didn't have the energy to think how desperate her situation had become. The tears tapered off and she could finally get herself under control. Her body was aware of the strong muscles under her hands and against her torso. Naturally muscled from hard work and sweat.

Slate smelled of smoke, hay and clean dirt. His skin had a natural muskiness that completely matched the nice-cowboy image he portrayed.

The smoke, she soon realized, was totally her. Remnants of a building burning around her. *Oh, my gosh.*

"If someone wanted to kill me, they didn't have to follow me home. They already knew where I stayed because that's where Victor lived when Dr. Roberts was murdered."

"That makes sense." He leaned back, looking at her and swallowing hard like he was confused. "You ready for that shower now? I don't have any flowery soap, but you'll get clean."

"Yeah, I probably should." She stepped back and then turned around, catching a huge whiff of smoke into her lungs.

The visceral reminder of how she'd narrowly escaped hit her. In fact, she hadn't really escaped at all. Whoever called 911 for help—and the sheer luck that her door faced the street—had brought the firefighters to her rescue first.

"I'll be fast." She had to get the smoke off her. Now.

She marched to the bathroom, shut and locked the door, then turned only the hot water on. Steam began building up immediately. She coughed and coughed, clearing her lungs until she could breathe easier. Then washed her hair until she lost count of the number of rinses it took to get the smell out of it.

Afterward, she dried with a fluffy yellow towel that matched the bath decor and wrapped it tightly around herself.

It was a small bath of soft yellows and blue and the steam seemed to turn to smoke. It was just her imagination. She'd been unconscious for the entire incident. She didn't have any memories of the actual fire. It didn't make sense that she could know it wasn't real and still panic.

That didn't matter.

The fear of being trapped in a burning building surrounded her, taking over any logic she'd ever maintained. She burst out of the small room, unable to catch her breath.

"Oh, my... God. I..." she huffed. She cupped her hands over her mouth like Slate had that afternoon but couldn't keep them there.

The closed bedroom door opened, banging against some western gear. Slate took one look at her and pulled her to him. His calloused hand, stuck between his shirt and her lips, didn't let any air to her lungs, forcing her to slow her rapid intake through her nose.

He held her tightly but managed to tilt her eyes to look at him. Holding her gaze, he counted in a whisper.

"Fourteen, fifteen, sixteen, ninety-two, ninety-three. Count with me, Vivian."

"Ninety-four, ninety-five," she mumbled under his fingers.

"That's right. Six, seven, eight," he began.

"Nine, ten, eleven." She stopped, breathing easier if not completely normal.

"You're good, now?" He hugged her tight, then shifted his hands to cup her shoulders. "Two in one day. You said you've never had this happen before? Back up a bit, darlin'. Yeah, just like that." He guided her elbows. "Okay. There. Sit. You're right by the bed."

"I'm okay," she managed in spite of the heavy wheezing. "I don't know what's wrong."

"Now's not the time to think about it. You should squeeze between these covers and try to get some rest. Your body will feel better in the morning."

"I... I can't." She self-consciously tucked the towel tighter, unsure what she could ever think about that would make her close her eyes again.

"Is a T-shirt okay? I'll wash your stuff in a minute." He patted her clumsily on the back.

The man hadn't hesitated when he'd flattened her to his body to stop the hyperventilating. Now his awkward hesitation brought a smile to her lips. He took out a clean—almost starched—white T-shirt and placed it in her hands. Did a double take, then switched it out for a dark navy.

"I'll see you in the morning."

The door shut and she was alone. She dressed, hung the towel over the shower bar and dropped her head onto a pillow that reminded her of comfort and safety.

It smelled just like Slate.

Chapter Twelve

"Your problem's having another nightmare, man." Heath kicked Slate's foot that had fallen off the end of the couch. "Time to get up anyway."

No daylight came through the windows. Just the light above the coffee maker had been flipped on. In the moment it took Slate to register why he was on the couch, he heard Vivian's cries.

"My problem?"

Heath was dressed for ranch duties. "I still can't believe you let Wade talk you into helping him. You know what happened when Jack helped."

Slate sat up, scratching his head. "Hell, Heath. Jack got a commendation from the state."

"I mean Wade's on desk duty. If he's caught working on this…he's done."

Vivian cried out again. Slate headed her direction.

"Just think hard before you dig yourself—and Wade—into a deeper hole."

Slate knocked softly on the door, waiting to see if Vivian would settle down or wake up. There was no reason for her to wake up as early as him and the other ranch hands. He'd rather have a plan of action in place, too. But it didn't matter.

Vivian alternated between a whimper and a cry. It was

obvious she was having a nightmare. He peeked inside the door and saw that the sheets were caught around her legs. Her hair was tangled around her neck. Her face was damp with sweat.

He left her momentarily and retrieved a damp rag, a bottle of water and a robe that his mother had given to him three Christmases ago. Rarely worn and long enough to cover her better than the T-shirt.

God, he was glad he'd switched the color. As he approached the bed, he could see only the outline of her breasts through the dark blue instead of embarrassing her with see-through white.

"Vivian." He touched her foot a little more gently than Heath had kicked his. "Hey, Miss Watts. Time to wake up. Everything's okay."

"What?" Her eyes popped open wide and she immediately began to cough.

He twisted off the water bottle top and stuck the bottle out in front of her. She nodded her head, dripping with sweat like she'd actually been in a fire. He moved to the side of the bed and knelt to her eye level.

"You okay?"

"Where—oh, right, the fire. What time is it?" She tugged at the sheets, then the T-shirt. "I'd get dressed, but pajamas aren't going to get me very far."

"I'll throw them in the dryer in a minute. I do have this robe." He patted the end of the bed, then handed her the damp cloth. "And this."

"Thanks. Slate, you're being far too kind. Maybe you can take me to the shelter. I'm sure they have clothes but I might need to borrow something to get there."

Grateful and definitely independent.

"Sure…on the clothes. No to the women's shelter." He checked his phone. "We don't need to go over this again.

Okay? It'll be easier on everyone if you're close by. I need to call Wade and the office. Be right back."

Dialing the number, he left the room before she could object again.

"This better be good," Wade said, sounding asleep.

"I thought you'd be up and on your way to the office. In fact, get your butt up. I need some answers."

"Answers for what exactly?"

"I need to know if arson is suspected in a fire."

"I'll need more details than that. Like where and why do you suspect arson?"

"I believe someone tried to kill Vivian Watts last night. Her apartment building caught fire around midnight. Fortunately, no one was injured."

"If you were trying to get me out of bed the same ungodly hour that you do, you've done it. Now stop kidding around."

"No joke, man. She lost everything. I picked her up from the hospital—"

"What do you mean, *you* picked her up?"

"She didn't have anybody else. Look, I'm taking a few days off to check this out. But you've got to do some legwork with the police, fire, et cetera."

"So the hunch was right?"

"No time to gloat, man. Get me some answers. I gotta go feed the horses."

He cut off the call during Wade's next word. "I need coffee," he muttered to himself. "I think I'll even drink Heath's strong stuff this morning."

The smoke-scented clothes he'd slept in would be good enough for barn work. He filled his travel mug, yanked on his boots and headed outside. First light, and Heath was already saddled and working his mare in the paddock.

Slate climbed to the top of the fence and watched, sipping coffee that he normally watered down. A lack of sleep and the need to think a bit faster this morning got him used to the thick-as-mud mixture pretty quickly.

"Stardust is looking pretty good there, Heath. You taking her this weekend?" Slate's dad asked his roommate, then turned to greet him. "Morning, son."

"Morning, Dad."

Heath eased up the mare and sauntered her to the fence where Slate's dad was leaning.

"Naw. Probably withdrawing this weekend, sir. I think my caseload just got heavier."

Heath cut him an I-can't-believe-you're-pulling-this look.

His dad turned to him. "You pulling out, too, son? That mean your mother and me can take off to the casino?"

"Yeah, I'll be around to take care of things."

"If you can't, your sister will be around to give her lessons. Hot diggity." His sixty-year-old father did his version of an Irish jig with muddy boots and his jeans tucked inside them. Then a quick look back to Heath. "Sorry you won't be competing, guys. But we have this free weekend stay and upgrade at the casino in Oklahoma."

"Don't worry about things here, Dad." Slate jumped from the top rung. "I better get started. Hey, is Mom up?"

"Is that a real question?" His dad slapped the wood rail. "You boys want breakfast?"

"Early morning for me, sir." Heath took Stardust around the paddock again. "Thanks anyway."

Slate nodded. "Let me feed the horses and I'll be right up."

"Mind getting the gate?" Heath asked.

Slate walked the same direction as his roommate while his dad headed back to the house. "Before you say a damn word. Yes, I'm going to tell him I've got a guest. There's no reason to keep it a secret."

"I was just going to remind you that it's very possible someone attempted to kill your *guest* last night and you might warn your dad to sleep with his gun loaded while she's here."

Slate laughed. "No need to tell him to do something he's already doing. But I'll mention it." He closed the gate behind his partner, watching him ride into the field.

Finishing his chores, he texted Wade for an update as he scrapped his boots outside the back door of his mom's kitchen.

One word came back: ARSON.

Had he brought danger into his parents' lives? Stupid question. Of course he had, by bringing an unknown back to his home. He'd never once thought that his law-enforcement career would put anyone at risk other than himself. He was helping, bringing justice to the innocent.

Did that trump safety? *Dammit.*

Not only did Vivian's brother need him to find the real murderer, he now needed to protect his family. Solving this case fast benefited everyone.

He'd need more background on Vivian, her brother, the victim and who benefited from the doctor's death. All things Wade could look up. He texted him to ask. Wade responded with another one-word answer: DUH.

The smells of bacon, fresh biscuits and eggs drifted through the screen door. The smell alone made his stomach long for food.

"Morning, Slate. Dad said you might want breakfast." His mom opened her arms for a hug.

"Yes, ma'am. Got extra?"

"You been smoking cigars again, son? You smell all

smoky." She turned back to her skillet of scrambled eggs. "I thought Heath didn't want anything."

"Actually, I have a houseguest."

"Oh." His mother's voice singsonged a variety of notes, which was a signal that she approved. "This is almost done."

"It's not like that. I was checking out a hunch about this murder case and the accused's sister was in a fire last night. She didn't have anywhere else to go."

"So you brought her here. That's admirable."

"Well, I thought so. Until I found out someone's probably trying to kill her."

His mom faced him with both hands on her hips. "You're worried about me and your dad? Or do you need our help?"

"Yes and no. I think it's a good idea that you're leaving for a long weekend. I'm sure I'll have all this cleared up by the time you get back Sunday night."

He better. The trial began Monday morning. That was less than a week.

"I'm sure your dad will take whatever precautions you think are necessary. We'll leave first thing in the morning. That'll give you four days. In the meantime, I'll let you take breakfast home so she won't have to deal with meeting us today." She set out plastic containers with enough breakfast to feed four people.

Mainly because she knew Heath would eat no matter how many times he told her it wasn't necessary to give him food. She enjoyed cooking…so why not let her? But she also included Slate's guest without him asking.

"You're a great mom. You know that, right?" He kissed her upturned cheek.

"And you're a good son. Now, what else do you need?"

Slate grabbed a slice of crisp bacon, shoving it in his

mouth quickly before his mom snatched it back. "Clothes. Any of Sophia's laundry still here?"

"I'll get it along with some clean towels. I'm sure you boys are running low." She wiped her hands on her apron, heading to the laundry. "There's an extra jacket hanging by the door. It should fit unless your guest is as tall as you."

"Vivian." He opened his containers, put bacon and eggs on a biscuit and took three bites between words. "Her name's Vivian Watts. And she's not tall. Barely reaches my shoulders."

"Well, I look forward to meeting her. Will you be in for supper?"

"Don't count on it, Mom. This isn't a social stay."

"There's no reason to be rude, kiddo. I'll make sure your fridge is stocked with girl food. You know, something that's fresh and not frozen." She set the food containers on top of the laundry basket and placed it in his hands.

"I'm serious, Mom. She'll probably want her privacy. She's going through a rough time right now."

"She was in a fire, sweetie. I figured out the rough time on my own." She held the screen door open and waved him through. "I'm a phone call or text away. All I'm doing is cleaning my sewing room today so if you need me… I'm here."

"Thanks. And thanks for breakfast."

"Don't eat it all before you share it." She let the screen close and he heard her mumble, "I swear it's like I never taught him any manners at all."

"THE NEWS SAID no one was injured in the fire. My building isn't habitable any longer. All those people are homeless because of me."

"Not your fault," Slate said with his full mouth, doing his best not to be rude.

"I had already packed the few things Victor and I had left. Do you think they were destroyed?"

"We'll check." He kicked the door closed and went to the kitchen.

"Where's your roommate? The one who thinks I'm a problem."

"He didn't mean that." Slate unloaded the basket he'd returned with. "You hungry? Mom made breakfast."

"I didn't realize your parents live here. Look, if someone tried to kill me, then I should leave for the shelter. You can't argue with me about this any longer."

"You're staying. My parents are aware."

"You have to stop being so kind," she whispered.

She would have left an hour ago if she'd had money to pay a cab. Or shoes. Or even pants. Instead, she'd stayed with no phone. No laptop. Nothing to do except become more paranoid and aware of the burden she would become if she stayed.

Taking advantage of Slate's generosity was problematic. Nothing good could become of it.

"Mom sent some of Sophia's things. My sister has a habit of starting her laundry and not hanging around until it's finished. To tell you the truth—" he took a bite of a biscuit "—I think my mom secretly enjoys folding it all up for her. Sure beats cleaning horse stalls."

Slate faced her with jeans, T-shirts and a jacket. "I figured we could stop by a store later to get you a couple of pairs of shoes and other stuff you need."

Vivian didn't need a mirror to tell her what he was thinking. She concentrated on slowing her breath so she wouldn't lose it. No more hyperventilating. There wasn't a reason to react to kindness with a panic attack. She drew a deep breath through her nose and let it out through her mouth.

"You want to eat or get dressed first?"

"It's the unknown." She couldn't ignore the fact that she was fighting to maintain control. "I'm so sorry. I don't want to be a charity case. I don't know when I'll ever be able to repay you."

Slate took plates out of the cabinet, added food and gestured for her to sit at the small round dining table. He handed her a fork before getting salt and pepper. Then he poured two cups of coffee before he joined her.

Vivian tugged her robe's belt tighter and made certain there weren't any gaps. She was starved and the food smelled delicious. Slate didn't wait for her to take a bite. He seasoned his eggs, buttered his biscuits and ate.

"You okay?"

She nodded.

"I'm not sure what's the best way to get out of this situation. I kept thinking that a better job would come through. I was handling things paycheck to paycheck until the landlord decided he wanted me out."

"Let's just take a day at a time. After I shower, we'll check out your apartment, talk with the fire marshal, see what's what. Then we decide what comes next." He set his elbows on either side of his plate. "It'll be easier for me and my team if you stay with me. If you insist on the shelter, that means I'll be cranky from the crick in my neck."

"I don't understand."

"You staying at the shelter means I'm awake most of the night watching the place from my truck. Then Heath's even moodier, since I'm sure to twist his arm into helping me. It's better on all of us if you can stay here. See? It's really a very selfish plan."

She doubted that.

"Is your roommate in law enforcement, too? I thought he was a ranch hand or something. Didn't he go riding?"

"Heath works and trains his mares every morning before being a Texas Ranger. He pays Mom and Dad a lower boarding fee by living here and helping out on the ranch. Every other weekend, he rodeos. He more than earns his keep and even helps out with giving riding lessons."

"He seemed upset that you brought me here."

"He'll get over it. Mind putting that away while I get cleaned up?" He pointed to the food.

"Not at all."

While Slate got ready for the day, she tidied up, then hurried into the borrowed clothes. There was a laptop sitting on the coffee table, but she couldn't bring herself to invade the privacy of whoever owned it. She'd be patient.

Time may be running out. But after waiting eleven months for someone to help—or even care—she could wait another hour.

Chapter Thirteen

Arson. The thought had crossed her mind. Even though she'd brought up the possibility, she still didn't want to believe it. Slate was speaking with the Dallas fire marshal and an arson investigator while she waited in his truck.

On the bright side, Slate's sister seemed to be taller, but was basically the same size. Heath had delivered a variety of clothing when he returned from his ride. He'd apologized for being rude or wary of her arrival, as he'd put it. At least she didn't have to find free clothes.

Or shoes. Slate had taken her to a store and wouldn't let her go inside alone. Each time she picked one thing out, he put three in the cart. He'd spent way too much money, but she'd stashed the receipt in the small purse he'd chosen while she was in the dressing room.

Her emotions were still bouncing everywhere. Hard to control—harder still to predict. The urge to feel sorry for herself was overwhelming. She really wanted to give in by binge-watching a series and eating a bag of chips and salsa.

Adding to that self-pity was the fact that she didn't have a couch or bed to crawl under the covers and watch anything. But she wasn't a poor-poor-pitiful-me girl. She and her brother had faced hardships before. They could overcome this situation, too.

Slate walked around her apartment building with his

hands in his pockets. He'd taken his Texas Ranger star with him, showed it to the two men he was speaking with and then dropped it inside his shirt pocket. He'd mentioned during the drive that his involvement would need to be low-key. She wanted to join him, to look at everything, hear the words of the inspectors and see if anything had survived.

The desire to walk the seventy or so feet to her former apartment and pull her suitcases from the fire remains was significant. So much so that she had her seat belt off and the door slightly ajar. She could overhear Slate coaxing the officials. Promising to give them any information he and she discovered. Assuring them that if she were the intended target, she was safer in his custody than anywhere else.

The contents of her apartment had been cleared, since the fire had definitely been set on the outside of the building. She had her doubts about whether the laptop or phone would work again. Everything she or her brother owned would reek of smoke, but at least they'd have something.

A head nod from one of the guys, and Slate walked directly to her two suitcases. He jerked them up like they were empty. Straight out of the mud and muck that now covered everything. She shut her door as he tossed them into the back of the truck.

"They don't have any idea who set the fire. It's not unusual that no one sees anything or wants to get involved. Whoever it was…complete amateur. They had no experience, according to the investigator. Didn't try to make the flames big or anything."

"From here, it just looked like one corner was burned." She stretched to see if either suitcase was black. Neither was; they were just very dirty from the firefighters putting out the flames.

"That's right. They poured gasoline on the ground

around the natural gas line, left the can and drove away. It's only about ten feet from the parking lot."

"And at that time of night and in the rain, no one would think to be watching out their window."

"Right. But at least we have a place to start," he said and lifted the corner of his mouth in a teasing grin.

"No one saw anything. I don't understand."

"Whatever we did yesterday caught someone's attention."

"I know this isn't in my wheelhouse like yours, but I still don't see where that gets us."

"Trust me."

"Where are we going now?"

"I made an appointment this time with your brother's lawyer, told him it was about payment. That should get him in the office. Then we'll head to the VA Hospital." He turned the wheel, heading in the same direction as the day before.

At least he'd gotten an appointment. The attorney had refused to see her several times, always stating that Victor didn't want her involved. When had she lost her tenacity? Her determination?

When had she allowed herself to be so defeated?

"Don't you have work?"

"I took a few days off."

She was in a far bigger debt to Slate Thompson than he could ever know or that she could ever repay. He was helping a stranger, giving her hope and courage. She was about to tell him exactly that when his hand covered hers.

"This has got to be hard on you. I have a feeling you've been doing everything yourself. For the record, do you and your brother have any other family?"

She shook her head. "This part of our story always seems to convince the police or lawyers that Victor is guilty. We're a product of the system. I was raised by a normal foster-care family. My brother is five years younger and was placed in a different home. I managed to see him about once every three months or so. It got to where his foster family wouldn't allow us much time on the phone or especially together."

"So everyone thinks he's a bad product of a bad system."

"That's the nice way to say it." Vivian nervously rubbed the tops of her thighs. "Without anything—family, friends, a support system or money—our only option for a college degree was the army. By the time Victor turned eighteen, he'd had enough of school. He took his GED and left for boot camp."

"Wait." He looked at her like he was confused. "You were in the army? You can shoot a gun?"

"Can't you?" she asked.

"Yeah, but I'm better with a shotgun. I almost had to bribe someone during the last qualification."

He had to be kidding.

He chuckled. "Aw, yes. I've seen your level of confusion before. A Texan, raised on a ranch, who can't shoot? Okay, so I'm pulling your leg a bit. It's not far from the truth. Continue."

"I'd been saving money and had no intention of letting him enlist, but he did it while I was overseas. We didn't see each other for about six years. Oh, we wrote more often in the beginning. But the emails got fewer and took longer to send. Part of that time, I was in school at Florida State. Other times, I didn't know what part of Afghanistan Victor had been assigned to. He mustered out in San Antonio, opting to stay in Texas to work with Dr. Roberts and her sleep study."

"The file said he had night terrors. That's from the army?"

"Yes. Pretty bad ones, from what I understand. But that doesn't mean he's a murderer."

"Agreed. It doesn't."

The sun left his tanned face as he pulled the truck into a parking garage. She'd been so engrossed in the telling of her and Victor's story that they'd arrived at the attorney's office building without her realizing.

"Let's go see if we can find a place to start."

It didn't take long to walk from the parking garage into the sleek glass building. The Public Defender's Office was located at the county courthouse, but Victor's lawyer was assigned by the court and in Uptown. The door to the office was locked and no one was inside. It wasn't unusual.

"Does he have a receptionist?"

"The building might be nice, but in the past several months, I've never seen anyone working with or for attorney Ned Stevens," she explained to Slate.

He knelt at the door. At first she thought he was tying his shoe or something, but remembered he wore boots. Then he pulled out a small pocket-size case. "I am certain that breaking and entering is illegal in all fifty states, Slate. Some places in the world they even cut off your hands. You're an officer of the law. You should know that."

"I'm tired of this guy never being in his office when he says he will be." He twisted pick tools in the lock.

"Why do you even have those tools?" she whispered.

"Funny story. I was a resident assistant in college and—"

"Someone's coming. Your funny story will have to wait."

Slate slid his tools back in his jacket and they stood with

their backs against the door, waiting for the footsteps to advance from around the corner.

"Anyway, these two freshman football players got it in their head to change the locks on my floor," Slate continued.

"As in the doorknobs?" Vivian asked.

A nicely dressed woman, carrying a briefcase, came into view and passed them.

Slate acknowledged the passerby with a nod of his head. "Crazy, right?"

"It doesn't make sense. No one could do that."

"They could if they had a master key to the building." He knelt down, pulling out his two picks.

"You are not going to continue with this? Slate!" she whisper-shouted. "People are returning from court or lunch or wherever. Let's just wait for Mr. Stevens."

"No time. Keep your ears open."

"We have..." she bent next to him "...no other pressing appointments."

"We only have five days." He stuck picks back into the lock. "I imagine there are a lot of names on that list to check. We need to see what's in your brother's file. Today."

She cupped his shoulder. "Slate. This isn't the way."

They stood. His eyes darted around her face. Hers probably did the same since she caught all the small crinkle lines near his eyes and the corner of his mouth. A tiny lift began on the left side of his mouth, then stopped. His lips parted slightly and she caught a whiff of coffee.

She didn't mind. He smelled good.

Wait a minute! How did they get so close? He was practically a head taller than she was and yet somehow his eyes were now at her level. That meant so was his mouth. Their position shifted as subtly as his smile.

One step forward, and his hands were planted on either

side of her shoulders. He tilted his head and gently pressed his lips against hers. She did what any sane woman in her place would do…she kissed him back.

Her arms were at her sides, but that didn't stop them from reaching out and sliding around his waist to his back. Her fingers didn't meet anything soft. Muscles were rock hard across his sides and under his jacket. His freshly pressed shirt was crisp under her fingertips.

One of his hands dropped to her shoulder as her lips parted and he swirled his tongue next to hers. Was she still thinking? Or just absorbing every tantalizing feeling coursing through her body.

"Miss Watts?"

She jerked her head to the right where the voice had spoken. "Mr. Stevens. Sorry, you caught us…off…off…"

"You caught us." Slate winked and made a clicking noise like he might be telling a horse to move. She stared at him while pushing at his chest with her left hand. He moved in slow motion, one hand dropping to her hip instead of pulling away completely. Did he want—

He did. The sincere look, the kiss, the touches…it was all to…to what? Catch her off guard or Ned Stevens?

"Slate Hansom." He finally moved his body and stuck his hand out to shake Ned's.

"For real? Oh, sorry. Of course you're real. I'm…" Keys out, Victor's attorney pointed to the door. "I need…let me just open this." Ned squeezed between them. "Oh, my. I was sure I locked it."

"Would you look at that. We didn't even think to try the knob while we were waiting," Slate said with a heavy, drawn-out Texas inflection.

Ned passed through the door and they followed. She gripped Slate's bicep, stopping before he took a step inside.

Giving him a stern look, letting him know she knew what he'd done, she half mouthed, half whispered, "Hansom?"

He shrugged. "It's all that came to mind."

"Please, please. Have a seat." Ned pointed to the one chair in the room that looked like it was office furniture from the fifties. "My apologies for being late. And Mr. Hansom, there's a folding chair for you right behind the door."

"Great. Just let me scoot behind you, hon."

What game was Slate playing? Why go to such efforts to make Victor's attorney think they were a couple?

He placed the chair directly next to hers and took her hand between his, continually patting it as if comforting her. As much as she enjoyed being touched, his constant tapping reminded her of all that he had at stake. Why would he risk everything for her and Victor?

"Now that we're all settled, what can I do for you?"

"We've come about the study my—"

"Mr. Stevens, I sure hope you don't mind my being here," Slate interrupted. "Our Vivian here needed to let you know about how to contact her now. You see, her apartment caught fire last night and she lost everything she owned."

"I'm so sorry to hear that." Ned handed them a note-pad and pen. "Just write your phone number down and I'll put it in your brother's file. But really, you could have just phoned. Your message mentioned something regarding a payment?"

Slate wrote two numbers and handed it back to the attorney. Ned shuffled through several files on the corner of his desk and tugged Victor's out of the stack. He slipped the paper inside and left the folder on top.

"I thought it would be better to come down and meet you personally and let you know Vivian's not in this alone any longer. She's staying with me now."

"That's all well and good, Mr. Hansom. But I can only share details of Victor's case with Victor. I've been over this with Miss Watts several times. Her brother has been very clear about his wishes."

"He's my only family and we think we have a new le—"

"Honey, I'm sure Mr. Stevens is doing his best."

Vivian was about to let Slate *Hansom* have every pent-up frustration she'd been keeping to herself. But he smiled—a terrible fake attempt that made her want to cry.

"Look," Ned began. "There's really nothing new. You can look up the arraignment information since it's a matter of public record. The prosecutor hasn't contacted me since the first offer of a plea bargain. You know that your brother confessed but decided to go to trial. Nothing's different. If you'll excuse me, I have a very busy afternoon."

Ned Stevens, attorney at law, was only interested if more money was involved. That was very clear as he dismissed them.

"There is just one more thing, Mr. Stevens." Slate leaned forward slightly, lowering his voice. "Vivian mentioned that you've been recommending private investigators for her to work with. I hope that my humble investigation isn't going to turn up anything untoward between you and them. Is that a possibility?"

The attorney's face contorted. "Out. I'm not going to stand for you insulting me in my own office."

"You're right, Stevens." Slate's voice was back to his normal, commanding self. "Time to go, Viv."

Her stare went from man to man. Slate hadn't mentioned any of that to her. Nothing. Stevens continued to point toward his door as Hansom put the folding chair away. She managed to hold her peace until they rounded the corner by the elevators.

"I have no idea what that was all about or what it accomplished. But a heads-up would have been nice."

"Oh, man, I think I dropped my keys in the office. Be right back." He pivoted and ran back the way they'd come.

She waited at the elevator, literally tapping her foot with her arms crossed hugging her body. Right until another person walked up and pushed the down button. Vivian stepped to the other side of the hallway, concentrating on not acting annoyed. She wasn't. She was worried.

Helping her was one thing. Risking his career was quite another. What was Slate's motivation? Why would he do something like that?

"Let's go." Slate jangled his keys in the air just as the doors opened.

"Why did you keep interrupting me before I could tell him anything?"

He ignored her. He took her hand in his, holding onto her through the parking garage until he opened the door, waiting to help her into his ginormous truck. Once in her seat, he winked at her and made his clicking sound again.

"I got it."

"I know. You showed me your keys on the fifth floor."

He took several folded pieces of paper from behind his back. "No. I got your brother's file."

Chapter Fourteen

"You stole that?" Vivian's voice echoed throughout the parking garage, followed by a cough.

No one was around on their floor of the parking garage, but Slate didn't want to take any chances. He closed the passenger door then rushed inside the extended truck cab and closed his door to let her shout if she wanted.

"You okay?" He shoved a bottle of water into her hands to help with the coughing left over from the smoke inhalation.

She nodded slowly as she sipped from the bottle.

"Keep your voice down. And no, I didn't steal it." Slate scratched just above his ear, deciding he should be totally truthful. "I did sort of coerce it. If you want to get technical."

"Why?"

He'd expected her to ask how. Not why.

"Why keep your voice down? It's sort of obvious." Her look of puzzlement threw him for a loop. "Wait, why what?"

"I can't believe you'd do something so stupid." She shook her head and rubbed her hands together the way he'd observed loved ones who worried about men he was tracking for arrest. "Why would you do something like that?"

Her anger was baffling. He'd obtained the information

they both needed to continue the investigation, so why wasn't she happy?

"You're angry."

"Yes."

"At me? I'm trying to help."

"By blackmailing my brother's attorney?" Vivian's voice first raised, then dropped off to a whisper.

"That guy is definite appeals grounds for incompetency."

"You're serious? You blackmailed him."

That tone was…astonished? Was she as surprised by his actions as he was by her reaction? He hadn't explained his actions in a very long time, probably not since high school. But he could…if it would clear the air and get them out of a parking garage.

"Blackmail is too strong a word."

"It won't help Victor if you break the law and end up in jail, too."

"Wait a minute. I just sort of twisted Stevens's arm a little. I got a heads-up from Wade this morning that your lawyer friend might not be a hundred percent on the up-and-up. So I fast-forwarded the process a little by suggesting you might not press charges."

"Another decision that you made unilaterally instead of saying two words of warning to me?" She swished her curling hair from her face and behind her ear. "What if I want to sue him for the money he's taken?"

"I didn't say anything about my office not pressing charges." He grinned, hoping it would put her at ease. "Bottom line, Vivian. I'm a trained investigator. I want to investigate, to find justice for the innocent. Your brother's case reminded me of that. I just want to help."

"You really believe he's innocent? Even after the police got a full confession?"

"Things don't add up. One glance at the file and I'm wondering why no one checked out who Subject Nineteen is. I agree that person is the likely murderer. I just don't think it's your brother."

"That's your true motivation for helping us?"

"A long time ago, I decided that being a part of putting the bad guys behind bars was important. At the time, it seemed like one of the most significant things a man could do. I don't know where I got that idea. It doesn't matter. But it stuck."

"You can't become one of those men while trying to help me."

"You mean picking the lock." He cringed inside and out. "Okay, I might have been showing off a little. What if I agree to rein it in, do everything by the book? You okay with using this information?"

He lifted the papers from the seat between them. She nodded.

"Where do we start?" she asked.

"We'll need to go back to the VA Hospital. But I think checking out the information you uncovered yesterday might help us narrow down our search."

"Because someone tried to kill me?"

He put the truck in gear. "After you discovered something. Must be important."

"I'm not certain I found anything at all."

"That's where having this list is vital. We begin a search of violent crimes like you did and then compare it to the people on this list. I'll also get an appointment with the person in charge of any studies at the VA that Dr. Roberts was involved with."

At a red light, he snapped a picture of the list with his phone, stared at the image to make certain it was readable, then texted it to Heath. He turned south toward the VA Hospital on Lamar.

Vivian looked at the list. "There are at least seventy names here. It'll take quite a while to get through them."

"Not for a computer geek who knows what he's doing."

His phone rang. "Right on cue." Knowing how his partner was going to react, he lifted it to his ear instead of leaving it on speaker. "Thompson."

"No," Heath answered as predicted. "You aren't involving me in this off-books investigation that Wade instigated. I have Skylar Dawn on Saturday and told Sophie I'd cover the kid's riding lessons this weekend."

"Mom and Dad appreciate that. Since you can't help me, could you just explain how to run one of the cross searches you do?" He watched the confused looks pass across Vivian's lovely face.

"Have you asked one of the techs at headquarters?"

"Not really, but I thought I could put it together. If you walk me through it." As soon as he admitted that, he knew Hearth would know he'd been right to assume it was about Victor's case.

"Weak strategy. It won't work on me."

"What? I have a strategy? I just want your advice," Slate said, knowing his friend would see straight through his helpless act.

"No way. I'm not getting involved." Heath cut the connection.

Slate wasn't worried. Heath was reluctant…a lot. He dropped the phone in the cup holder.

"What now?" Vivian asked.

"We wait. He's going to change his mind."

"Slate, we can go to the library and look up the information ourselves. Most of it is public."

"It'll take too long. Be too public."

"But we won't be asking your friend to do something he feels uncomfortable—"

The phone rang. This time, Slate put it on speaker for her to hear.

"Fax me the originals. I'm not wasting my time typing in all these names."

"Thanks, man."

"Slate, take me off speaker."

Vivian faced the window, giving him as much privacy as a person could in the cab of a truck.

"Yeah?"

"You sure you want to do this?" Heath asked. "I'm assuming you don't want anyone around here to know what you're up to."

Slate heard office sounds in the background. "Officially, you're right. I'm not on a case. But I have less than a week to prove this theory. Their lawyer's a joke, man. He's getting kickbacks from investigators that have taken every penny she has."

"So this is charity."

"Not on your life. It's doing the right thing. Victor Watts is innocent."

"You think. I'm staring at a copy of his signed confession."

"Something's off with this one, Heath. Wade got a feeling and the same day I start looking into things, Vivian's apartment is set on fire. There may be other victims here. We gotta get to the bottom of this."

"Yeah, I know. We can only keep this under wraps so long. Somebody's going to find out what you're doing."

"I'll owe you, Heath."

There was a long pause. Long enough for Slate to drive half a block. "I'm the one who owes you, man. We both know that you're losing money boarding my horses and me until I get on my feet."

"We can get into who owes who later. I'm finding someplace to fax you this list. We need to know if anyone has been involved in a criminal outburst or worse."

"You got it."

They disconnected and Slate passed the phone to Vivian. "Can you look up a store that sends faxes?"

She did. She brought up the map so he could follow them. And then she rested her elbow on the armrest, covering her mouth with her slender hand.

Having someone be angry because he helped was new to Slate. Most of the time, he didn't care if he got credit for a win or not. Team effort and all that. But in this situation, he thought Vivian would at least be appreciative of his innovation to get Heath to help them. It was going to save tons of time.

He pressed his lips together, staring at her during the red lights. She stayed in the car when he sent the fax. He didn't get it. Shouldn't she be happy he was helping her, getting things moving along?

"What's the matter now?" he asked.

"I'm just…sort of overwhelmed. Why are you…? Whatever we do to clear my brother's name, I don't want you or your friends to get in trouble. You don't even know us."

"Vivian. Maybe I didn't explain this well before. As a Texas Ranger, I help people all the time that I don't know. You've reminded me why I got into law enforcement. To protect the innocent. I believe your brother is one of those innocents. Something happened and he needs help. I'm willing to give it."

Slate put the truck in gear and pointed it toward the VA. They'd nose around, ask if anyone had noticed anything about the man who attacked people in the cafeteria. There were lots of things they could do before getting Heath's search results.

"I can never repay you for this." Vivian used the bottom edge of her shirt to dab at tears.

"Who said I was charging?"

Chapter Fifteen

They were back.

What are they doing here? Abby had broken her routine this morning to watch the news. She knew no one had been injured in the fire. She was disappointed, but the plan wasn't perfect. It should have scared Vivian Watts or at least deterred her.

And yet, here she was, walking next to the man with a badge. They weren't on the fifth floor, where the EEG lab was located. She passed them by Admissions when she delivered paperwork to the billing office. There was no recognition on their part. They seemed to have no idea who she was.

The impulse to tear off her gloves was so overwhelming it forced her to stop in a restroom. Her cuticles needed to be cleaned but she didn't have her supplies. She picked at the edges until the perfect version of herself calmly told her to stop.

"There is no reason to panic, Abby. They don't know who you are. If they connect Rashid to you, it will only be through the EEG lab, so there's no reason to panic."

Perfectly stated and logical. They didn't know her. If the opportunity presented itself, she could pretend, or why not initiate the introduction? She dried her hands, thinking of possibilities. Who was on her list of afternoon appointments?

"I know it will be hard, Abby, but check if the next sleep patient is here. Begin early. You can allow yourself to be ahead of schedule and let that patient follow Vivian Watts and her law enforcement officer," the voice in the mirror said.

Drawing on her protective gloves, Abby mentally prepared herself for the rigors of deviating from her routine. She needed a name for the man accompanying Victor's sister.

She could do anything if it kept her studies on track. By eliminating all the other possibilities, she'd be left with the right choice. They would obtain the perfect death. Nothing would detour them.

Abby headed to the cafeteria looking for her adversaries, for the only two people who could cause her problems. The man was easy to find. His badge was prominently displayed as he spoke to employees who worked in the cafeteria.

Vivian stood at his side. She may have looked uninterested to people who had no stake in the questioning. But Abby could see her taking notes on her smartphone. The woman was very astute.

Abby stood in line with no intention of consuming anything she bought, but she had to look inconspicuous. She had to appear to accidentally overhear the questions the man was asking. She had to obtain the introduction.

Looking on her phone, she took pictures of Victor's sister and her accomplice. *Texas Ranger Slate Thompson.*

"Excuse me," she said after a few minutes near them. "I couldn't help but overhear that you're asking about Rashid Parker. I can't believe what happened yesterday. And to think he was in the EEG lab. I just can't believe it."

Abby imitated the worry, stress and astonishment that many of the people who'd seen Rashid the previous day had demonstrated. She concentrated on the expressions the others had shown or she covered her mouth with her hand to hide her lack of emotion.

"Slate Thompson and this is Vivian Watts."

"Abby Norman. I assist the EEG lab technician." She pulled her hands back to her sides before the ranger reached out to touch her. "He was such a nice man."

"Can you tell us what an EEG lab is and what you do there?" Vivian asked.

"An electroencephalogram is a test that detects electrical activity in your brain. I help set it up for the technician, type up notes, get the patients settled. I have no idea why any of them need monitoring. You'd have to ask their doctors."

"Thanks. You've been very helpful," Slate said, then turned back to Vivian.

How dare he be so dismissive!

"Walk away," said the voice from the mirror. "You know who they are. Now you can eliminate them both."

Chapter Sixteen

After getting a handle on Rashid Parker's day, they hadn't discovered anything that would have set off a rampage. Vivian didn't feel any closer to discovering why her brother had been accused of murder. Heath had narrowed down the list of names from the sleep study. Names, numbers and addresses were now being compared to crime reports.

"You look discouraged," Slate said.

"Four hours in that hospital and, yes, I feel useless. Are we making any headway?"

"We have a list of names to check out. We also know that Parker just seemed to lose it over nothing. The guy was eating lasagna and salad one minute and stabbing someone the next. Other than that, no one can remember anything unusual about him. We know he wasn't angry, wasn't complaining, wasn't talking to himself, wasn't unusual in any outward way."

"What does any of that tell us?"

"It sort of fits the description of your brother. No outward signs of distress. Parker seems to have just snapped."

"You said several names on this list had committed violent crimes?"

"Yes."

"Another reason to interview their family and friends."

Vivian walked closely at Slate's side. She was skimming

the list on his phone, trying to find the names she'd discovered last night. They had parked in the hospital's farthest southern lot, one of the newest overflow areas that still had construction machinery in the corner. It was away from the main buildings and garage cameras.

They were almost back to the truck when she heard a loud wail. A different type of dread took over her body. Fright of the unknown, but with the feeling of an attack.

Slate pushed her aside. She fell on her knees onto a median of newly planted grass. She heard running footsteps as the scream of attack got closer. Out of the corner of her eye, she saw a large man hit Slate across his shoulders with something.

She rolled to her back, looking for the phone. Getting help was all she could think of to do. Their attacker lifted a piece of wood to hit Slate again.

"Hey!"

He had a wild, crazy look in his dark eyes. Longish hair, a green jacket with patches. She didn't know how she focused on so much of him, but she took it all in. Army boots like her brother wore.

The shout came from her. She crab-walked backward on the grass to get away when the man faced her. But before he took two steps, Slate was on his feet, jerking the man's arm to spin him around.

Slate looked like a man who was used to dealing with attackers. Each move seemed automatic, ready for the anticipated blow. Maybe in a normal fight, the other man wouldn't have stood a chance. But the attacker looked like he was on drugs.

Wild-eyed and crazed. Slow but hard, deliberate movements. A car pulled through the drive, distracting the attacker. Spinning, Slate lifted his leg and let the force of his boot knock the crazy man's piece of wood behind a backhoe.

Slate shoved a shoulder into the man's middle. They both went down into a pile of construction rubble.

Their attacker grabbed a piece of loose rebar and charged. Slate blocked the crazy man's swing, keeping the rebar inches away from his skull. They went down a second time.

Rolling over. Then back. Slate punched the man's side until he cringed, giving Slate the split second he needed to throw him off and roll to a crouch. This time, the man shook his head, looked around, turned and ran.

By the time Slate was on his feet and running, a car sped out of the parking garage. Vivian couldn't catch any of the license plate. Her eyes locked with the surprised look on the man's face as he drove away.

This man might have answers to their questions. She ran after the car, but he turned the corner and was gone. Slate caught up with her and pulled her to a stop, swinging her around into his arms.

"You okay?"

She nodded and looked at the crowd gathering at the doctor's entrance. Men were approaching, others pointing.

"Get in the truck," Slate ordered. "Quick."

"We're not waiting on the police? Do you think we can catch him ourselves?"

"No. He's gone. I'd prefer to go home and not hang around to talk with the VA or DPD."

"Aren't we going to check out these names?"

"We're going home."

"But what if—"

"Dammit, Vivian. You may not need to regroup, but I just took a two-by-four across my shoulders. My jaw hurts like a slab of concrete hit it. Oh, wait—it did. I need an ice pack, aspirin and a shower."

BACK AT HIS HOUSE, Slate didn't waste any time before putting three aspirin into his palm, swallowing them and jumping into the shower. He was sore but with no permanent damage. The forty-minute ride back from the hospital had been pretty quiet. Vivian plugged in his phone for power and searched through the list.

He didn't mind. His head was full of questions. Had their attacker been hypnotized? Drugged?

The first thing that was clear to him was that he'd never seen the man who'd attacked them before. The second thing was that the man had been intent on doing serious damage, not robbing them.

Coincidence?

How many times had he hated that word? When he was working a case, it just didn't feel right as an explanation. There was only one logical answer. Someone in the hospital was related to the murder of Dr. Roberts and the suicide of Rashid Parker.

But how?

What did one have to do with the other?

The quick shower he took did nothing for the soreness between his shoulder blades. And nothing to answer the many questions he'd racked up on the drive home.

The steam of the shower in the small bathroom didn't cover the smell of his mother's fajitas from the other room. Spicy chicken and beef, fresh salsa and warm tortillas… His stomach growled while he dressed and listened to laughter in the kitchen.

"Okay, I hear Slate. I better skedaddle." His father gave him a thumbs-up before he pulled the front door shut behind him.

"Feel better?" Vivian asked.

"Cleaner at least." Slate gestured to the closed plastic containers. "You eat?"

"I was waiting on you. It smells delicious."

"Mom's a great cook. She still hasn't passed on her special marinating recipe. Hungry?"

"Starved. I think we skipped lunch."

"My stomach doesn't have to think about that. It knows the answer."

Vivian was dressed the same but seemed more relaxed. Had his dad accomplished something in the last ten minutes that Slate hadn't been able to do by being with her all day?

He passed her a plate and pulled lids off the containers. His mother had gone all out. He recognized the homemade guacamole and knew how good it would be. What he didn't know was if his parents really understood that Vivian wasn't a girlfriend.

They dug into the food.

"This is really delicious." She took another bite, then another. "So what do we do next? I have some names and—"

"Eat. We eat. I'll grab my laptop after and see what Heath recommends."

"Oh," she said, swallowing a bite. "I didn't mean to read the texts, but you gave me your phone to work on and they kept popping up."

He finished off his first fajita and made a second while he waited on Vivian to barely touch hers. He stretched his arms, then rolled his neck trying to relieve the tenseness.

"You have a road rash." She set her plate aside and retrieved his cold pack from the freezer, wrapping it in a dish towel before holding it against the side of his face.

He winced, pulling away. She gently cupped his chin to keep him from moving.

"It didn't look as bad as that makes it feel," he mumbled out of the corner of his mouth that he could move.

"Thanks, by the way."

He replaced her hand with his to hold the cold pack against the scrape. "I'm the one who should be thanking you. One word and you turned that guy's attention away from splitting my head in two."

"Then you kept him away from me. I don't understand the why of it all. Do you think he was the one who set the apartment fire last night?" She sat and picked up her fajita.

"I don't know. I was too slow to catch any of the plate number."

"Me either. Do you think he's on this list?"

"I don't know what's connecting all this together. It just keeps getting stranger. Eat up. It's better hot."

They ate and each downed a bottle of water. He wiped his lips and rolled his neck again, making a note that a chiropractor visit may be in his future.

"Do you need to see a doctor?" Vivian asked.

"Not yet. Hey, what did Heath say in that text?"

"That he was called to a scene and not to expect him home."

He snapped the plastic lids back onto their containers. Before he could stand, she already had them stacked and in the refrigerator.

"Do you think it would hurt you if I rubbed your neck a little? I don't want to make it worse," she said while washing up their dishes.

"Go for it."

She rubbed her hands together to warm them. He didn't care when they were still cool against his skin. She kneaded around the neck of his T-shirt, then across to the top of his shoulders.

"That feel okay? Nothing seems out of place."

"No. Just sore. I feel stupid that I let someone run up behind us with a two-by-four."

"We've had a long day. There's nothing to feel bad about."

"I am running on a couple of hours of sleep. I haven't done that in a while now. Most of my job lately has been eight to six."

"That explains it then."

He felt some of the stiffness melting away. It was a little sensitive where the board had hit, maybe bruised, but with each squeeze and knead of the muscle, it relaxed.

"It's a lot better. Thanks."

"Would you mind if I used your laptop? I could sign on as a guest if you have anything I shouldn't see."

"Sure, and it's totally my personal files. Mainly ranch inventory, stuff like that. I don't bring office files home for my laptop." They moved the short distance to the living room, giving him time to realize she *was* the work-related file that he'd brought home. "I'll go get it."

He grabbed the laptop from his dresser and hobbled back to Vivian just in time to catch her rubbing her own neck.

"Did you get hurt when you fell?"

"No. It's just normal stiffness from sleeping on a couch and working as a waitress."

He set the laptop on the coffee table and walked behind the couch, which sat in the middle of the room, separating it from the kitchen. He could easily reach Vivian's shoulders from there.

"Sit back. Let me return the favor. I got this."

At least, he thought he did. Right up to the moment he touched her curly hair and dropped it to her left shoulder. Right up to the time he touched the tense tendons across

her back. Maybe right up to the moment he saw his fingertips dip under the edge of her shirt.

Or it might have been the exact moment he realized
Heath wouldn't be coming home.

Chapter Seventeen

Slate's right fingertips skimmed the supersensitive part of her neck that curved into her shoulder. His left fingers joined in on the opposite side before all ten gently but firmly massaged.

For the first minute, Vivian couldn't really think. It had been so long since she'd had the muscles in her neck artfully manipulated. Strong fingers hit a knot and immediately began to untangle it.

"How's that? Too much?"

"No," she said, keeping it simple. If she didn't, she'd be blathering about how absolutely wonderful it felt.

He pushed his hands under the loose neck of the T-shirt and kneaded the tops of her shoulders. He never broke contact with her skin, just kept kneading and stroking.

"You're really good. Have you had lessons about how... to do this?" Her eyes had closed somewhere after the first minute or two.

"Nothing professional."

"Should you be doing this?"

"I'll stop if you want me to." His hands paused. She shrugged and he began kneading her shoulder blade.

Why have him stop? This was innocent enough. Just a shoulder rub. Nothing unprofessional. No. Wait. Everything about it was unprofessional, but was there anything about their relationship that should remain segregated? Hadn't they already crossed a line since she was staying at his house?

If she were honest, she'd wanted to cross a line when she'd first seen him sitting in her booth at the wings restaurant. The desire grew with everything they did together.

"I hope you don't expect one of these in return. You're turning me into mush."

"Good. You need a little relaxing."

"I admit that eleven months of sleeping on that lumpy pullout called a mattress has done horrible things to my muscles."

"I can tell." Slate shook her shoulders a little to emphasize his words. "Come on, relax a little. You know you're safe here."

Yes, she was safe. But it was still hard to let go of the stress caused by trying to free her brother. Stress and the guilt of being free when he wasn't.

"There you go again. Tensing up. Stop thinking about it." His strong fingers slid confidently across the loose shirt and the flesh underneath. "None of this is your fault. No matter how much you try to take the blame."

"For someone who wants me to forget about Victor, you sure are saying a lot to remind me."

"True."

Slate's fingers stopped kneading. She heard his booted footsteps leave his place behind the couch and go into the kitchen. Listened to the fridge open, to a glass clink.

Okay, so relaxation was over. She closed her eyes and tried to stop her brain. Stop it from racing down the path of helping her brother. That wasn't completely true. Her pulse was racing because of Slate's touch. Because she wanted more than a shoulder rub.

She desired the human contact he provided. Shoot…

she desired him. Back in Miami, she might have already invited him to dinner at her apartment. She might have slid her hands around his neck and suggested a long good-night kiss.

It was comical how much she wanted to just *be* with him.

Actually, there wasn't anything funny about her desire. All he had to do was sit next to her in his truck and her body trembled.

Aching for him was the easy part. Would there be a future? Did she have the right to think about what came next after Victor's trial?

"You're thinking about the case again." Slate offered her a beer.

"How can you tell?"

"You crinkle your forehead and flatten your lips." He gestured for her to scoot to the middle of the couch.

She moved, then took a sip of the ice-cold ale. "That look doesn't sound very pretty at all."

"On the contrary. I have a sister. I can imagine what you've been going through. I don't think I could put it on the back burner either." He turned to where his back was against the arm of the couch. "Come here."

She was surprised, but then again, she wasn't. She stood so one of his legs could stretch the length of the cushions, then she sat between his legs, resting against his chest.

They sipped their beers in silence.

Slate's free hand played with her hair, curling it around his finger.

The curtains blew away from the wide windowsill, cracked open to cool the sunshine that had been pouring into the living room. No one was around. Slate's parents were at the main house. Heath was at Company B headquarters.

Horses whinnied and the breeze blew through the trees. Other than something buzzing against the glass panes, there wasn't any noise. Very different from the low-income apartments where she'd heard every word of her neighbors. And very different from the apartment she'd had in Miami with the high-end stereo that drowned out every plane or argument.

Slate's fingers outlined the top of her ear, then the edges, drawing circles across her skin. She stopped thinking, concentrating on the early evening light shining on the hardwood floor. Once or twice, his finger swept across her forehead, checking on her tension. He softly smoothed her hair, again and again.

The next moment her eyes opened to a cooler and darker room. She must have relaxed. Completely.

The sun was setting, and brilliant colors beckoned them to watch through the front window. She could feel Slate behind her, awake. But he remained silent as they watched the shadows grow deeper.

The bottles had been set on the coffee table. Hers half-full, his empty. She began to sit forward when Slate's fingers lifted her long hair, draping it over her left shoulder. His fingers tapped across her shoulders before dancing down her spine, sending splendid shivers through her body.

His mouth grazed the side of her neck. Her head fell back, again resting on his chest, rolling to the left and giving him more access. As his light and teasing lips caressed her skin, he skimmed her shoulder with his knuckles before sliding his hands over the top of her arms.

Slate got up, laced the fingers of one hand with Vivian's, helped her to her feet and somehow twirled her straight into his arms. Their eyes connected and she was lost.

The first brush of his lips touched the corner of her mouth. A little hesitant. Was he trying to decide whether to continue or if she would reject him? She didn't dwell on the question, instead answered for herself. She turned her face slightly so their mouths lined up completely and pressed her lips to his.

The clean smell of his skin mixed with the smokiness of the fajitas. His breath was hot and created more wanton desire within her.

Each time their lips touched, the need inside her grabbed hold and wouldn't let go. It was anchored to something she didn't understand because nothing had ever reached that part of her before.

It scared her enough to run, yet spurred her forward at the same time. She tried to retreat and Slate deepened their kiss. His mouth was a warm haven, a taste that belonged only to him.

They'd been close to moving forward with the case and now they were closer to falling onto his bed. But she wasn't a fool. She could back away, douse this dynamite before it was ever ignited. They were still wearing all their clothes. All she had to do was take a step back.

He'd behave.

Just place her hand on his chest and step away from the only man who was helping her for all the right reasons. She'd be the only one to know what she passed up. No one would ever know how afraid she'd been to get involved.

She hadn't been close to anyone since moving to Texas, longer still because she'd been focusing on a career or in the army. What did one night making love with a man she actually respected matter?

All she had to do was say no.

Warning bells went off. Sirens louder than the fire trucks the night before.

She didn't want it to stop, but she forced the words that would keep their relationship at the same level.

"I should probably go to bed."

"Too early," Slate whispered, kissing her collarbone.

God, he was good at that.

"I'm not... I'm not really sure if we should be doing this."

He tugged her shirt down her arm, baring her shoulder more, and scraped his teeth across. Those luscious shivers that started in her core and traveled to every nerve ending encompassed her again.

"Do you think this is too dangerous?"

"Pretty much, yes." Her breathy words barely registered.

"It can't be as dangerous as a man trying to kill you."

Oh, I think I'm dying a little bit right now.

Vivian pressed her body closer. The cute borrowed top she wore was quickly tugged loose from her jeans. His was already free.

His calloused fingers smoothed the hot skin of her back. Hers explored the toned, muscular, sculpted man who had saved her. It would take very little maneuvering to shrug out of their clothes and into each other.

Imagining how she'd feel the morning after didn't compare to actually having his lips against hers, having his tongue tease in an age-old dance. Nothing was rational. She wanted to *feel*. Not think of consequences, threats or reality.

"How am I supposed to resist you?" she asked. Threats of fire and men swinging boards got pushed to the back of her mind when she timidly guided his hand to her breast.

"You want to?" he asked, his lips whispering on top of her own.

She answered with another kiss. No longer afraid of possible consequences or conflicts. He was man. She was woman.

The intensity of their kisses grew. They tugged each

other out of their shirts. They steadied each other as they shimmied out of their pants. Maybe it shouldn't happen, but it was happening. They explored each other's bodies with their hands and eyes.

Magnificent. A word she completely understood now.

Slate dropped to his knees, exploring further.

"I have an idea." Vivian heard her hoarse voice squeak the words when his thumbs hooked inside the edge of her skimpy underwear.

"I have one, too," he answered with an inviting smile. He turned her body until it relaxed on the couch.

Vivian's idea evaporated in the heat generated from Slate's caresses.

Chapter Eighteen

The adrenaline rush during the fight had kept him going through his shower. He'd begun to relax and slow down a little during the neck rub Vivian had given him. Then he'd touched her silky skin.

The rush was back and touching her wasn't enough.

He wanted all of her. Mind, body… Yeah, everything.

Slate swallowed hard at the realization of how much he was attached to Vivian. He'd known her two days and she was a huge part of his thoughts. He backed away, pushing the coffee table toward the television.

The look on his face had to be confusing her. She was squinting, asking what was wrong without any words.

"Nothing."

The corners of Vivian's mouth rose in a smile. First one side, then the other, along with a nicely shaped eyebrow.

"What color are your eyes?" he asked.

They looked smoky, sort of a grayish blue.

"What?" She seemed surprised and pushed the left strap of her bra onto her upper arm. "Probably gray. They change color."

"I thought they were different yesterday." He took a finger and lifted the right strap off her delicate shoulder to let it drape on her arm.

He stood, stretching his hands toward her. She took

them and he helped her stand. He led her around the couch, walking backward. His imagination was in overdrive but he moved slowly.

Vivian's expression changed more rapidly than his sex-seeking mind could keep up. Anticipation to quizzical to embarrassment—all in the time it took to move a step away from her. She dropped her hands, crossing her arms over her breasts.

"Someone's out there."

He spun around. It had to be Heath. No one else would be coming to the house. His parents would have called, not walked over.

"One of the horses—"

"A horse doesn't have a short beard."

Slate spun to face the front of the house. "Like the guy from—"

The door burst in, bouncing off the cabinet of DVDs. Vivian screamed in surprise.

"Get to the bathroom," Slate yelled.

She'd be safe there. But she didn't run. She only backed up.

His weapon was in the lockbox. His phone on the dining table. His shoes weren't on his feet. Hell, he wasn't even wearing pants.

"What do you want?" Slate asked him.

The man from the hospital was wide-eyed and crazy looking. He moved from side to side, almost indecisive about what to do next. The baseball bat in his hand slammed against the open door. Then slammed again, leaving a good-sized hole.

"Look, man. If I did something to offend you, let's talk. I'm sure we can work this out."

"Slate? Can he hear you?" Vivian asked, her hands on top of his shoulders.

"Not sure." He shrugged her hands away, preparing to defend himself. He lowered his voice to a whisper, "I need you to get to the bedroom or bath, Vivian. I'll do better if all I have to defend is myself."

"Can you get him into the living room corner? I could get to your phone and call 911."

"No. It'll take too long for them to get here."

"All right. I'll get out of your way then."

Slate took her at her word. With no idea why the guy was waiting to attack, he stepped onto the couch, ready to jump behind it and lure him away from Vivian. He waved his hand behind his back, indicating to her to join him, run and get to safety.

She raised a foot onto a couch cushion and the man grunted. Grunted like a cave man.

"What's with this guy?" Slate wondered aloud.

Vivian ignored him and moved in the opposite direction—she'd be trapped in the corner. The man turned the same way. She moved closer to the TV, dipping to the coffee table and grabbing Slate's shirt.

"Do you know him?" Slate asked.

"No," Vivian whispered. "Why doesn't he do something?"

"Can you keep his attention on you?" Slate waited for her to take another step away from him, then jumped lightly over the top of the couch to the floor.

The man blinked slowly but kept his gaze glued to Vivian. He grunted again. She took a step back. He advanced, swinging the bat.

Slate had one chance. He shoved off the end of the hall wall and tackled the man before he got too far into the room. Or too close to Vivian. The bat stayed locked in his hand.

Slate managed to stay on the man's back. The attacker

flung his arm—and the bat—from side to side as he rolled, trying to get free. Things crashed, breaking around his head. Slate tried to get a choke hold on the man, but he had to let go to block the bat from connecting with his head.

Slate saw Vivian cross the room. If she got his phone before running out the door, she wouldn't be able to unlock it.

The attacker growled, jerking the bat. Slate tugged it free from both their hands. It rolled under the couch. The man used that moment to shove Slate off his back. He scrambled to his knees and followed Vivian.

A split second later, Slate pursued both across the driveway, toward the main house. "Vivian," he yelled after her. "Back door!"

She ran.

The attacker followed, yelling like a madman.

Slate ran, the stones from the driveway better than the burrs and stickers he knew to be at its edge. They all kept running.

Damn, I wish I had my weapon.

He gained on the attacker, who was gaining on Vivian. She made it to the enclosed back porch, slamming through the screen door and dropping to the other side where he couldn't see her.

Slate was a body-length away from the attacker and dove. He caught the man around the ankles, tripping him to the ground. He just had to latch on until his father plowed through the back door. The man twisted, sitting and beating on Slate's back with both hands.

"Stop!" Vivian yelled from the steps, coming closer.

"Stay back!" Slate warned.

The man was pretty strong and still acting like he was possessed. He turned. Slate dug his fingers into the man's jeans, pulling himself closer as the man tried to crawl toward Vivian.

"What the hell's going on here?"

"Dad, help me stop this guy!" Slate yelled.

His father pumped a shell into his shotgun. The sound alone should have scared a normal man. But this guy was far from normal. He kept clawing at the ground to move inches, dragging Slate.

His dad raised the gun and used the butt to hit the man on the back of the head. All movement stopped.

"You all right, son?"

Slate stood, Vivian at his elbow. His father aimed the shotgun at the intruder, who was out cold.

"Yeah, I'm good." He turned to Vivian, who had managed to pull his shirt over her underclothes. "How 'bout you?"

"Nothing worth mentioning. Thanks for your help," she said to his dad.

"You calling the police?"

"Yeah. First we're going to tie this son of a bitch up. Mind getting some rope, Dad?" Slate held out his hand for the shotgun, which his dad passed to him.

"I'll call the cops on my way." His dad pulled out his phone and dialed as he headed to the shed next to the barn.

"You really okay?" Slate asked Vivian.

"My feet are sore. He never got a hold of me. Did you realize your knees are bleeding?"

"Slate? Everything under control now?" his mom asked from the porch.

"Yes, ma'am. We're good. Could you walk with Vivian back to my house?"

"She doesn't need to do that," Vivian whispered.

"Just let me get my shoes," his mom replied.

"Why did you ask her to do that? She's going to know what was going on. This is so embarrassing." Vivian covered her face.

"Sweetheart, I think they took one look at us and figured that out. Could you send back my jeans, boots and phone?"

The screen door swung shut and his mom dropped a blanket around Vivian's shoulders. "Come on, sugar. No need for everybody to catch their death out here. That storm last night brought in a cold front."

The women walked up the driveway. His dad returned with rope before the attacker moaned. Slate passed off the shotgun while he looped the rope and tied the guy up.

"Maybe you should hog-tie him to make him stay put," his father joked. "The local PD said they were ten minutes away. I sure am glad a Texas Ranger lives around here."

"Yeah, Heath's on an assignment."

"Where am I? What's…what's going on?" The man's voice shook, sounding confused and frightened.

Slate helped him sit up and lean against the porch, taking his wallet out of his back pocket. "So, Allan Pinkston. Why are you at my house and why did you attack me? Don't pretend to not know what's going on."

"I attacked you? I… I don't even know you. How did I get here?"

"I assume you followed us in the car you drove off in after you hit me with a two-by-four at the hospital this afternoon."

"No way, man. I don't even know who you are. Last thing I remember is being at the VA. Did you dose me or something?"

"What about Vivian Watts? You know her?"

"I've got no idea who that is. Why does my head hurt so bad?"

Slate could usually tell when a suspect was lying. Either this man was really, really good at it, or he was genuinely confused.

"You were attacked twice today, son?" his father asked.

"Yes, sir."

"By this guy?"

"Or his twin."

The stranger shook his head. "I don't have any brother and I didn't attack you. What are you going to do with me?"

"Let the cops sort it out," Slate answered. "If I were you, I'd insist on a drug test to see if someone did slip you something."

His mom returned with his pants just in time to pull on his boots before the Rockwall police arrived to take Pinkston into custody. They found a car registered to their attacker on the main road.

Sometimes being a ranger was a good thing. It limited the explanations needed to convince Rockwall PD to take a trip by the hospital to verify what Pinkston was high on before booking him.

Slate failed to mention Vivian's involvement. Pinkston didn't seem to remember anything. The charges were trespassing and assaulting a law enforcement officer. Slate needed to go by the station the next day to file a complaint.

"I hope you know what you're doing, son." His dad had his shotgun resting on his shoulder as they walked to Slate's house.

"I have to admit that this case is all over the place. Murder. A fire. An attack by a guy who seems to have amnesia. Weird."

"Yeah, weird. Mom and I will still leave tomorrow. That is, unless you need me to stay. I can watch Vivian if you need to chase a lead down or something."

Slate stopped to look at his old man. "Thanks, Dad. But I got it covered. Leaving probably is a good idea." They clapped each other on the shoulder, then finished their walk to the house.

"I sure hope you know what you're doing, Slate," his father repeated. "I know I'm not a cop, but you might consider keeping your boots closer."

In other words, he might do a better job by keeping his pants on. Slate agreed.

Before stepping into the house with his father, Slate called the man who got him into this situation.

"Wade, I think you, me and Jack need to have a conversation. I can be there in half an hour."

Chapter Nineteen

Wade threw another ball of trash into the far corner wastebasket and yes, pretended like it was a basketball. No one watched. No one was around. The nine-to-fivers had left for the day. He still had a couple more files to get through to meet his daily goal.

The door opened, the wind whipping it all the way back as Jack arrived.

"This better be good." He looked around at the empty office. "And hopefully on the books this time."

"I should be back out there, fighting criminals or helping on one of the weirdest cases of a lifetime," he said aloud, instead of just thinking it for once.

Sick of sitting behind a desk, Wade was living vicariously through his fellow rangers. Waiting on a call or information. Wanting to be right about his hunch. Setting up meetings between Slate and Jack.

"What you need to do is keep your nose clean until the major says otherwise," Jack told him. "We can handle things. Even the weird stuff."

The door opened again. Slate escorted a woman who must have been Vivian Watts to his desk across from Wade.

"You know I could run some of those names Heath sent you."

"No!" both Slate and Jack said together. They startled Vivian and both gave him a look like he was crazy.

"I can work the list," Jack said. "I'll be patrolling most of those neighborhoods anyway."

Obviously, Slate had already spoken to him about what needed to be done.

The outer office door burst open and Heath marched in, heavy boots on the worn linoleum. "Is my TV still in one piece?" he asked Slate, referring to the fight that had taken place in their living room.

"As a matter of fact, it's better than my head," Slate replied.

Vivian Watts sat on the edge of the conversation, obviously paying attention and purposely restraining her opinion. It was obvious since she had eyes only for her hero... Slate.

Heath gave her a strange look. Maybe he recognized the shirt she wore was one of Slate's. But what was strange about that? All her clothes were gone in a fire. And yet, Slate seemed preoccupied until Jack had mentioned the list they were waiting on from Heath. Then Slate had been quick to jump in that it had been Vivian's idea.

Dammit, Slate. You're falling for her?

"Have you found anything significant with Allan Pinkston's background check?" Jack asked.

"I guess Slate hasn't gotten to the *P*s on the sleep-study list."

"Pinkston's on it?" Slate asked. "This doesn't make sense."

"Do you think he's Subject Nineteen?" Vivian asked, turning all the men's heads toward her. Which in turn had them all looking at Slate.

"Maybe we should talk in the hall?" Jack suggested.

"Be right back, Vivian." Slate almost cooed.

"Stay." Jack looked at Wade with the direct order.

"Looks like I'm keeping you company for a while," Wade said to Vivian. "I'm Wade Hamilton and I assume you're Vivian. Guess they forgot we haven't met. You getting along with Slate okay?"

He already knew the answer. Her blush confirmed his suspicions as his fellow rangers disappeared into the hallway.

"Are they always this bossy?" Vivian remained in Slate's chair, sitting across from Wade. "So, why are you stuck here with me instead of with those three, making plans?"

"I'm supposed to have plausible deniability. They're trying to keep me out of trouble." Even though he was the one who'd started everything three weeks ago. By begging Jack to take his place and rescue Megan Harper— now Jack's girlfriend—Wade had gotten himself banged up and assigned to desk duty.

"Thank you." Vivian waved his attention back to the present. "Talking through what's happening should be helpful. I'm glad you could wait around for us."

"It's not like I have a lot to do." He patted the files living on the corner of his desk. "I'm officially off the streets."

And officially without a life.

"So you're the one who gave Slate my brother's case, right?"

"That's me."

"I can't thank you enough for what you've done."

"I didn't do anything except ask a question."

"I know Slate wouldn't be helping me if it wasn't for you. He told me as much when we met." She stood and began pacing the short open space between the desks on the next row.

Wade leaned back in his office chair, openly admiring

Vivian's shapely form. From what Heath had mentioned about Slate's interest, they were both pretty certain he would have found some reason to look into her brother's case.

"From what's happened around you in the past twenty-four hours, it's a good thing he's at your side. Slate's a good man."

She nodded in agreement and looked like she might cry. "I appreciate everything you've all done, especially Slate."

The guys came back into the office just as Vivian politely covered her mouth.

Vivian Watts had more than appreciation in her eyes. It was a look that represented something Wade could envy. The spark of love or something close to it. He'd seen it a couple of times now. Never aimed in his direction, though.

Did that mean he was ready for it? Nope.

Hey, he was a bachelor and proud of his status. The last thing he needed was a girlfriend. Or a serious relationship.

"We're out of here, man." Slate darted in the door, gathered Vivian under his arm and got out fast. "Thanks."

Heath ignored Vivian and kept walking out the door.

Jack waited for the others to leave then wandered to Wade's desk. He rapped a knuckle on the corner files. "It's another good hunch. This won't last forever. You'll be out there fighting the good fight soon enough. You should lock up and go home."

"Be cool," Wade said as the door shut behind his partner.

It was late. He should go home.

Instead, he flipped open another file, brought the number up on the computer and began the process of verification. He really should get a life. Or maybe at least go on a date. But one woman kept breezing through his thoughts, pushing all the others aside... Therese Ortiz.

Repaying the favor he owed her was the reason he sat in this chair instead of doing the work he loved. *Your pigheadedness got you stuck behind this desk. Not a woman.* He couldn't help his natural curiosity, he argued with himself. Was it his fault that he wanted to know more about her and what she did?

Therese was exciting. An unknown that he couldn't predict.

The broken ribs ached. He carefully sucked in a deep breath, expanding his lungs to capacity. Testing them. Disappointed in their reaction.

After two weeks, the swelling was gone from his eye and the bruise looked like a yellow stain on his skin. He'd tried to find out what had happened to Therese or where she'd gone after her arrest, but all records of her involvement with the Harper case had disappeared.

So had the number he'd contacted her through before.

Wade wasn't a patient man and hated to wait for Therese to reach out. But he knew without a doubt that she'd call.

And that he'd answer.

Chapter Twenty

"I want to help. I can be useful. You even told your friends that it was my idea to look up other veterans who may have had problems." Vivian had voiced all the arguments in the truck on the return drive to Slate's home.

He still hadn't told her what he, Jack and Heath had discussed in the hallway out of her earshot. In fact, he'd been very closemouthed since asking her if she was ready to leave Company B headquarters.

"Did I miss a key piece of information? Did they discover something you don't want to tell me?" she asked.

He shook his head and turned down the drive to his ranch house. It was completely dark at this end, but she could see the porch lights at both houses. There was no way to see a dark car parked along the road here. She hoped he wasn't blaming himself for Allan Pinkston's attack.

"You sure are quiet," she said.

He parked his truck, cut the engine and gripped the steering wheel so tightly she could see the blood leaving his knuckles. Whatever he was working up the courage to say wasn't going to be good.

"I have to apologize," he said.

"For what?"

"Letting my guard down like that could have cost you your life."

"I think we both let our guards down."

Somehow she knew that he'd withdraw even more if she extended her hand to touch him like she wanted. Going inside and trying to pick up where they'd left off would be awkward to say the least. Another intimate moment like that would bring up his need to apologize.

Yeah, it wouldn't work. The possibility of a relationship with this kind man had passed.

"If you could take me to the women's shelter in the morning, that would be great."

"I don't blame you for thinking... Hell, I'm totally at fault here. You lost your apartment and everything you owned. I should never have put you in a position where you thought you had to have sex with me."

"What?"

"I want you to know that you're welcome to stay here as long as it takes to get back on your feet. I spoke to my mom—"

"You think I was going to sleep with you for payment?"

He shook his head so hard the truck bounced. "No, not that. But a lot's happened you might have..."

"Go ahead. I dare you to say that I'm a poor little ol' female. So totally confused and overwhelmed by my situation that I'd sleep with the only *man* who extended me a kind word. Go ahead."

"That's not what I meant at all."

"You know, Slate, *you* approached *me*. I didn't ask for your help." She jumped down from the truck, slamming the door. She marched several steps before she realized she had nothing to collect from inside.

She really did own nothing, and her smoky suitcase was still in the back of the truck. She pivoted with her next step and saw Slate still inside the truck cab, mouth open, probably wondering what had just happened.

She got back inside. "I'm not staying with you more than it takes to drive me someplace I can stay tonight or drop me under a bridge with a cardboard box."

It was Slate who reached out and rubbed her shoulder. "I'm sorry."

"I'm serious."

"I know you are. I spoke with my parents before we left. We can sleep in the main house."

"No."

He pulled the keys from the ignition and shoved them into his pocket. "It's nonnegotiable. Heath and Jack agreed that it's too dangerous to stay here. Whoever's after you knows where I live."

"That means it's too risky to stay with your parents."

"My parents are leaving in the morning. The alternative is us in the same room at a motel." He shoved his hands through his short hair. "I know that's not a good idea. It makes better sense to be somewhere with more than one room."

"Just take me to a shelter."

He shifted, winced at the muscle strain and stretched his neck. She would offer to rub the kinks out again, but that's how this all started, with an innocent gesture.

"Look." He dropped his hand on top of her shoulder again. "If you insist on going somewhere… I get it. There's a motel back on Interstate 30, I'll get a room. You can take the bed and I'll camp out in front of the door. But I'd feel safer here with Dad's shotgun pointed out the window while I catch some shut-eye."

She'd forgotten that he hadn't slept much. For that matter, neither had she.

"We are already here. Is there something I could do? Like keep watch? I've done it before in the military. Or maybe some chores? I'd love to repay you and your family."

Was she giving in and accepting his charity because she didn't want to find a way to repay him for a hotel room? Was her mind actually working that way now?

Did it matter? She had few choices. Humbling herself to keep the rangers working on Victor's case hadn't been as difficult as before she'd kissed Slate.

"That's not necessary."

"My only goal at the moment is to get my brother out of jail. I'll worry about my life and Victor's after he's free and clear of these charges. So I need to accept your charity for now."

"That's not what I had in mind when I apologized."

"No apology necessary." She meant it. Whether it sounded sincere or not wasn't something she could correct at the moment. "I guess I should get the things you bought me together and move to your parents' spare bedroom?"

"That's probably best."

The gravel crunched under their feet as they got out of the truck and went to the porch. So much had changed since they'd made the short walk earlier that evening before dinner. Even after the attack at the hospital, she'd felt lighthearted and good for the first time in months. Now... not so much.

"Care to share what you guys talked about without me?" she asked once inside.

"A game plan of sorts." He went to the closet and got a gym bag, smelling the inside before handing it to her. "We split up the list. I didn't mean to segregate you."

"Oh, I realize that. Wade explained it was him you were trying to protect." That still made it sound like she was upset about being excluded. "I'm not angry or anything. Just curious what the plans are for tomorrow. When I should wake up, et cetera."

"Well..."

"Oh, no. I'm not waiting here with your horses while you discover who set up my brother. Please don't strand me here to wait."

"I told Jack you wouldn't go for it." He moved stiffly, attempting not to bend his knee.

"What's wrong?" She pointed to his legs.

"Just need a couple of bandages across my knees from when I fell earlier. I think the blood dried to my pants."

She was going to regret her next words. "Drop your jeans and let me see." Just stay angry, and they'd be safe.

"Nothing doing. That is *not* a good idea."

Vivian placed her hands on her hips for emphasis. "Do you honestly think I'd sleep with you after you practically called me a prostitute?"

"I didn't say anything like that. You've been through a lot of trauma whether you recognize it or not."

"Is that what your buddies at Company B told you?" She took a step closer to him and reached for his rodeo belt buckle to force him to comply.

He tried to jump back but stiffened in pain.

"Come on, Slate. You need help and I'm here. We are not going to sleep together. Ever. Not now. And it's not like I haven't see your plaid boxers before." She walked toward his bathroom. "Where are the bandages and peroxide? In here?"

"There's a first aid kit on the top shelf of the laundry cabinet."

She heard the sound of a large belt buckle hitting the floor along with a couple of curses. "I'm not taking my boots off and making it easy to undress."

"Suit yourself."

Finding the first aid kit exactly where he said it would be, Vivian took a second to look at herself in the mirror. She didn't look upset, insulted or homeless. She had a smattering of makeup left and her eyes weren't red from crying for once.

Since the rain had stopped, her hair was actually halfway decent, too. She washed her hands, grabbed a clean washcloth and towel, then returned to the living room.

Slate did indeed have his pants pulled down around his boots. His strong thighs were tan instead of the white that she would expect from someone who worked out in the sun instead of going tanning. He also had a pillow covering his lap.

"I'll clean up in here while you're getting your stuff together," he said.

She hadn't noticed that the living room was still a mess from the earlier fight. Had that really been just a few hours ago? She pulled the coffee table closer, opened everything and caught a look at Slate's knees.

"Those are pretty bad. There're rocks still in the wounds." She retrieved a bowl of warm water and a beer for the patient. "This is going to hurt. No way around it."

"Yeah, I figured."

The peroxide fizzed and she instinctively blew and waved her fingers at the white bubbles. She used the cloth to clean as much as she could before using the tweezers for the pebbles stuck in his skin. It was an intense experience and the least she could do for Slate after keeping Allan Pinkston from catching her.

Had Slate known he'd wreck his knees like this in the gravel?

He gritted his teeth, took a sip of beer and dug his nails into the pillow. But he never yelled out. Vivian hated hurting him and winced several times at what she had to do.

"Thank you," she whispered when she finished taping the second bandage in place.

"I think you've got that backward." He reached for the top of his pants but paused.

"If I were you, I'd get something looser than those jeans. At least for tonight."

He splayed his hands like he was stuck. She tugged the jeans up a bit, giving her access to the boots. Then she slipped each from a foot before pulling off the jeans, then folding them. She set them on the arm of the couch and extended her hands to help him stand. Much like he'd done for her before Pinkston had arrived.

He took her hands and when she tugged, his body rose to be next to hers. She couldn't step back because of the table. His arms went around her waist to prevent her from falling.

Close to him again, she felt all the tension leave her body to be replaced by anticipation. She wanted him all over again. His erection proved he wanted her, too.

"I'm sorry if I offended you back in the truck," he said softly. "I was embarrassed for the both of us. Not that we had anything to be embarrassed about. We're both adults. It was just that it wasn't fair to you that my parents…you know."

"We've already agreed that sleeping together isn't the most brilliant idea right now."

"Probably not. But you should understand that it's still on my to-do list. You're not getting away that easily."

"I didn't think I had been affected by everything in the past couple of days, but you may be right. I mean, right about being emotionally compromised." She sweetly kissed his lips and kept it short. "I don't mind being on your to-do list."

She was certain that could be misinterpreted, but she didn't care. They were friends again. She was curious about the potential between them and knew he understood. He stepped around her and gestured toward his boxers.

"I should probably get some running pants on before Dad comes looking for me."

"Couldn't we stay here? I hate to impose on your parents."

"No imposition. We're expected and we both need some sleep." He cupped her chin in his hand. "If we stay here, we both know sleep is the last thing we'll be getting."

He lifted his laptop.

"Is it broken?" she asked.

"Nothing a good charge won't fix. I'll pack it up so we can get the list update from Heath or Wade in the morning."

Slate got dressed, they gathered everything, straightened the room a little and then they settled in at the main house, where fresh brownies were waiting.

Vivian didn't have to wonder how Slate became such an awesome guy. She was blown away by the generosity of all of the Thompson family. She'd never be able to repay their kindness but she was going to try.

Chapter Twenty-One

Abby put the final touches into the white-noise program for the patients who would visit the EEG lab the next day. Her time was limited in the Dallas lab. Her next round of patients would be in Arizona. The movers had been hired to pack up the house.

Of course, her sensitive research would travel directly with her. Not in the moving trucks her father had scheduled for the end of the week.

Sometimes it was great to have her father's money. He was glad to pay for the move to her first job in Texas. Basically, it had been farther away from them in Florida. The Veterans Hospital in Arizona was one of the largest in the country and she wouldn't limit herself to a certain caliber of patient.

As soon as she programmed the last two names on the sleep-study list today, she'd be ready to leave Texas.

It was hard to add an activity to her routine, but she wanted to know if Allan Pinkston had carried out his mission. There wasn't a mention of an attack on a Texas Ranger, but she couldn't rule him out yet. There was still time before he'd been programmed to eliminate himself.

She looked in the mirror, but the woman there was silent.

No voice of reason. Only thoughts of panic.

How had she failed?

She needed her answers. Maybe switching to another facility with additional patients wasn't enough. She trimmed her cuticles, washed her hands, scrubbed under the nails and up her arms with her surgical brush. The stiff bristles indicated cleanliness. She strove toward that perfect sterile world and she'd get there soon.

Chapter Twenty-Two

"Slate Hansom, it's time for lunch. We'd like to eat and be cleared away before we leave for Oklahoma." His mom untied her apron and left it on the back of her chair. "Investigative work sure does look boring."

She'd cooked enough food to last them a week. She and his dad would be through Monday, and Slate really hoped he'd have this case wrapped up by then to keep his parents out of danger. Last night had been close.

"It not only looks that way, it definitely is," Vivian agreed.

"We've gotten a lot accomplished this morning. It beats knocking on twenty doors, driving all over the metroplex and hoping people are home. Now we've got three solid interviews lined up."

"Sounds good, son." His dad patted him across the back before sitting at the table. He'd already finished his chores, packed the car and showered.

His father had worked all his life. Hard work on the ranch, holding off selling any of it until it was evident that he and his sister didn't want to raise horses and give lessons.

"Did you get in touch with your half of the list, Viv?" Slate asked.

"We meet with the last one tomorrow at eleven during

his lunch break." She smiled and lifted an eyebrow. "You never did tell me why you're called Hansom."

"It's a family name," his mom chimed in. "Been in the family for generations. We think some family relative must have owned an English carriage. We haven't connected the genealogy back to the man who invented it, though."

"Oh, so you're named after a carriage not your looks," Vivian said for his ears only. She laughed and handed him her list.

It was good to hear her laugh, especially after the tragic stories he'd been hearing all morning. Together they'd found a lot of troubled veterans on the list. His call to the Rockwall PD wasn't encouraging either. Allan Pinkston still couldn't remember why he was stalking Vivian or why he'd attacked them twice. There was something about the wild look in his eyes that made Slate think he wasn't completely in control of himself.

After the police conversation, he'd begun calling the men and women on the list to ask if they were having blackouts, periods of time they couldn't remember getting to or from someplace. He sent a text message to the other rangers so they could add the question to their own lists.

Called to lunch a third time, Slate stopped at his dining table chair, sending another text about his and Vivian's progress.

"Honey, I know you're a grown man, but having your phone out at the table is just rude," his mother reprimanded. "You know how much I dislike it."

He turned his phone facedown and dropped his napkin in his lap. "If Heath or Jack call, I've got to take it, Mom. Just giving you a heads-up."

Lunch was more like a full dinner, including cloth napkins normally reserved for Sunday. Chicken strips, mashed potatoes and gravy, along with corn on the cob and biscuits. He'd smelled the chocolate chip cookies and snitched a couple earlier while they were cooling. He'd even shared with Vivian.

They passed the food and his parents kept looking at Vivian's almost-empty plate. "Aren't you hungry, dear?" his mom asked.

"I'm still full from the wonderful breakfast you made us. I'm not used to eating every meal of the day."

"Well, it's good you're with us then. We'll get some meat on your bones."

There was nothing wrong with the amount of meat on Vivian's bones. She was excellent and he hoped he got another chance to tell her, to show her.

"Come on, Mom. She's not ten. She'll eat if she's hungry." As soon as his plate was loaded, his phone rang. He picked it up along with a chicken tender and walked to the porch.

"Thompson." Unable to resist, he took a large bite of the tender.

"Jack and I are on our way to the ranch," Heath said, like that was the plan.

"Don't eat. Mom cooked." Heath would know there was enough here to feed an army. Slate's mother never cooked in half measures.

"Works for me. You're not going to believe what we've stumbled into."

"I think I will. What's your ETA?"

"Less than twenty."

Back at the table with his phone facedown again, he shoveled the food into his mouth. "Eat up, Vivian. The guys will be here to combine all the data. We'll clear and clean, Mom. You guys need to hit the road before traffic."

And before his coworkers arrived. His parents finished and hugged him goodbye. Then they hugged Vivian. No surprise. She was officially part of the household...almost family by his mother's definition.

"Good luck with your brother's case. We'll be thinking about you and praying that you both stay safe." His dad was normally the succinct man of few words. Sometime that morning, he'd gotten Vivian to talk about what they were doing.

"Take care of yourself, Slate. We told your sister to stay at school this weekend and we've canceled the riding lessons. Remember that you're in charge of the livestock."

"Yes, ma'am. Heath and I will take care of it."

"I'll help. You guys have a safe trip." Vivian waved from the porch.

And then they were gone. He was once again alone with Vivian. Not for long, but alone. He'd botched his apology last night and then she'd cleaned his knees. She'd insisted on taking a look at them this morning and debriding them again. His mom got a look and told him to go to the doctor.

The morning's events flashed through his mind in the couple of seconds it took to walk back up the three steps to the porch where she stood holding the screen door open. But a vision of the future beckoned to him of her doing the same thing.

Why? He barely knew this woman. But he wanted to know her better, wanted her to stay and be comfortable. Not only at his place, but also his parents' house. That meant something, right?

He wasn't a monk. Far from it. He'd had his fair share of dates and girlfriends. But never anything this intense, this fast. Proven last night when he'd forgotten about their situation and let his guard down.

Dammit. He liked Vivian Watts. A lot.

"Time to clean up?" Vivian asked.

"Huh?" He literally had to shake himself to stop dwelling on how fast this was hitting him. "Um, not yet. I told the guys there was food."

"I hope they have a plan. Victor is running out of time."

They went back to the den where they'd been making their calls. There was still a landline in this room for emergencies, which Vivian used. She checked the list and had the receiver up to dial.

"Wait," he said. "You know we're getting closer. Think where you were three days ago. You were just waiting for the trial to happen with no hope."

"All I can see is how far we still have to go."

"You have help now. People who care about making certain justice is carried out and that an innocent man doesn't stay behind bars."

He meant it. They both made another call. The families on the other end of the line were anxious to talk with someone about the injustices their loved ones had experienced. It was disheartening to listen to the same story—different variations, but basically the same story—about forgotten heroes.

The porch screen door squeaked open and closed.

"Do I smell chicken?" Heath didn't wait for an invitation to enter.

Jack followed Heath to the table. Both of his friends filled their plates and said no when Vivian offered to warm up the food.

"Something is definitely wrong with this sleep study. Almost half of the men and women on our list have had an altercation with the police in the past six months," Heath said, dipping his chicken into the gravy. "Man, your mom can cook. Let me see your list."

"It's about the same," Vivian said. "Almost half. We each spoke with a wife who had lost her husband in a murder-suicide. One killed a stranger and one killed a stranger off the street."

"I had one," Jack said. "He killed a grocery clerk for giving him the incorrect change, according to witnesses."

"What are the odds of that happening to three men in the same sleep study?" Vivian asked.

"Pretty damn low," Jack threw out.

"Are we one hundred percent certain that we have all the correct patients?" Slate put the question out there, but Heath nodded as he ate, acknowledging he'd done the work correctly. "Man, name after name kept coming up with a problem. One's involved with a brawl and the next is associated with a domestic dispute. By the time I got to the fifth name on my list, it was clear something was wrong."

"Good grief." Heath held up all three lists. "Did you realize that the only man affected out of alphabetical order is your brother?"

"Do the dates they had a brush with the law match alphabetically?"

Heath arched his eyebrows as he read and began nodding. "Pretty much."

"How can someone be getting these honorable men and women to break the law? Do you think it's without their knowledge?"

"Hypnotism?"

"Or something worse. It's a damn sleep study. What if someone's experimenting on them?" Heath was serious.

"That's ridiculous. It couldn't possibly happen without someone knowing about it," Vivian said. "Right?"

"I just looked it up and found a dozen sites on sleep programming to rewire your brain. I guess it's not so ridiculous." Heath kept typing on his laptop.

"Do you think Dr. Roberts was brainwashing veterans during a sleep study?" Vivian asked.

Heath shook his head. "The timing is off. Her murder was eleven months ago. The police reports don't go back that far."

"So we're still looking for Subject Nineteen," Slate pointed out.

"If you take Victor out of the equation, what's the connection? Who wants her dead?" Jack asked before munching down on another cookie.

"All of Dr. Roberts's associates were accounted for—they had alibis. She didn't have a boyfriend. She didn't have a husband or ex-husband or even an ex-boyfriend. We need to find Subject Nineteen. Male or female, this person is the key and probably the murderer." Slate paced around the room, very aware that everyone was listening.

"We have to go to the old man." Jack leaned back from the table. "This isn't just about seeing if Victor Watts is innocent. We need an official investigation."

"How long will that take?" she asked. Heath and Jack looked away. "My brother's trial begins Monday."

Slate barely had the courage to look her in the eye. "What choice do we have? We need an official investigation to get through the door, to ask doctors, nurses, janitors if they think something weird is going on."

"That might take weeks. If he enters a plea of guilty, he loses his right to appeal. No. There has to be another way."

"First, we get assigned the case. We talk with the VA OIG." Jack was the practical ranger. The one who knew the rules and how everything worked.

"Who?"

"The VA's Office of Inspector General. They'd handle complaints and investigations to see what's going on," Heath explained. "They don't like to share or play well with others."

"And if they say no? What then?" Vivian asked.

Slate crossed the small distance to stand next to her and face his friends. "She's right. Whatever happens with the bureaucracy, it'll be too late to help Victor. He's innocent."

"You *hope* he's innocent." Jack shrugged. "We all hope he's innocent but our hands are tied on this now. Whatever strange thing is happening in connection with the sleep study these veterans are a part of, we have to build a case by proceeding with authority. We need permission to get at those doctors and the rest of the staff."

"The VA inspector isn't going to cooperate." Heath shook his head before standing and ticking things off on his fingers. "The first thing they'll do is shut down the study. Then they'll drag their feet because they lack the staff or need to bring in a specialist from DC to ask the questions. In turn, that will alert whoever's messing with these veterans. They'll disappear before the investigation even gets started."

"That's not necessarily the case."

Slate shot Jack a get-real look. They all knew about government bureaucracy.

"What I meant…" Jack shrugged and continued "…is that we could get someone into the study undercover before we tell anyone."

"It's too late for that," Heath countered. "First, the person manipulating these people probably knows all about us. And second, the study's nearly over. They won't let anyone else enter it at this point."

"But my brother is out of time. Face it, this explanation doesn't sound believable enough for the sci-fi channel to make a movie about it. Who do we approach and how do we get them to believe us?"

"I think we should go to the old man with a plan. It's

too important to just wing it." Slate knew it was the only way. He'd call and set up an appointment. He would take all the heat.

No one would get in trouble for working on this case without authority...except Slate.

"We get Major Clements to convince them to send one of us in undercover. Has to be tomorrow. We find out what tests are required from the sleep-study patients, get us moved to the head of the line and get a handle on all the personnel."

"It should be me." Heath dipped his chin but raised a finger. "I'm the least likely to be recognized. They obviously know who you are, Slate. Jack, your father just won the senate race and you were in the news again last week. So it has to be me."

"Fine," Slate said at the same time Jack agreed.

"I've got all the data together and will print out the summary for Major Clements." Heath slapped Slate on his back on his way out the door. "By the way, you're not taking all the heat on this. I'll be at the meeting."

"So will I." Jack gripped Slate's hand. "We're in this together."

"You know, statistically, every ten days a murder is committed that won't ever be solved."

"Coming from Heath, that's probably true," Jack said before getting into his truck.

Vivian stood next to Slate, waiting for his friends to leave. Slate wanted to put his arm around her, to offer comfort. But that was too dangerous now that they were alone.

"Killing by a stranger. Do you really think someone is programming men to kill people they don't know? It's like *Strangers on a Train*. There'd be no way to connect the murderer to the murder."

"If it worked, if the veteran never remembered anything or if they commit suicide, then we might be looking at the perfect murder."

Chapter Twenty-Three

Vivian had reluctantly been allowed in the back of the major's office after she'd promised not to interject information or beg for her brother. It was hard, but she'd managed. Jack and Heath had also managed not to say anything, even with all the harrumphs the older ranger had made throughout Slate's convincing argument.

"Domestic violence, drunk and disorderly conduct, trespassing, voyeurism, and then there are the three murder-suicides in the past six weeks," Slate stated their case.

Or maybe it was a plea. If she'd been allowed to speak, Vivian would be crying and begging, attempting to convince the older Texas Ranger that her brother had to be innocent. There was a possibility that had occurred to her on the ride over to Company B. She didn't voice it out loud and didn't want to think about it. But her brother might have committed the murder after being brainwashed or reprogrammed.

However the Rangers wanted to refer to it didn't matter. She couldn't bear to think Victor was actually guilty. Judging him wasn't her job. Pleading for his innocence and being his sister was.

"That's why we need to get in there and find out what's going on, sir." Slate finished a very well-presented summary of their last week.

"Wade's behind this. He asked you to look into another one of his hunches," Major Clements muttered, but he didn't demand an answer.

Would the man in charge call it quits if Slate admitted that Wade was behind reopening the case?

"As I said, sir, I began looking into this on my own time. I met Vivian when I had lunch at the restaurant where she worked. After we were attacked a second time, I asked Jack and Heath for help to look at the situation more closely. That's when we discovered how many veterans had been affected."

Facts. He stated facts without involving Wade.

"You brought it to me." The commander leaned back in his chair, contemplating. "You know my hands are tied on this. I have to turn your findings over to the inspector general of the VA."

"We assumed that but were hoping—"

"What? That I'd convince the OIG to let you interview their doctors and patients? That's not the way things are done in government, especially at the VA."

Slate nodded but stood straight. No hand gestures, no fidgeting. And no looking around the room at her or his friends.

Vivian stood perfectly still, too. Trying not to draw attention to herself was getting harder and harder. Her lip was raw from biting down on it. What would she do if the major decided against fighting for her brother? Shout? Scream out? Cry?

Do it herself? Alone?

She would if she only knew where to begin. In fact, she would have already. Slate's comment at lunch about how far they'd come in the past couple of days was right. She'd been floundering on her own for months. Two days working with him and his friends, and they might actually get her brother freed.

It all depended on the man behind the desk. The man these rangers—standing around her, who had helped her—respected and trusted.

Major Clements rubbed his chin with his thumb and finger. "I respect you, Thompson. I'm going to make a couple of calls. No promises. And don't think this debate about how you came across this case is finished."

"Thank you, sir."

Jack and Heath turned, pulled the office door open and both put a hand on her back for her to go in front of them. She walked through with no idea where to go until she caught Wade's small hand wave in what appeared to be a break room.

"How did it go?" Wade asked under his breath, bringing his head close to hers.

"The major's at least making the call to the VA. That's hopeful." She kept her voice down, too.

"Sorry."

At first, Vivian didn't completely understand why Wade would be sorry. Then she caught a glance of Slate's expression. His eyes were drawn together, his brow wrinkled and strained, his lips pressed flat together...

Jealousy?

Wade winked at her and moved to the soda machine. Slate kept staring at him. And yes, it seemed like he was giving him the back-off evil eye. She'd seen the possessive look once or twice in her life. Just not recently.

It was a nice feeling and caused her to smile. She needed to be reminded that life went on, even if hers had practically stopped for the past year. She and Victor would come out of this ready to move forward. She'd be there for him this time.

She wouldn't let anything come between a new relationship with her brother. Sadly, that included Slate. He had a younger sister. He'd understand why Victor would come first in her life.

Wade, Heath and Jack all had assignments they needed to work. Slate was officially on paid leave. Vivian fiddled with her visitor badge while Slate looked at his phone.

"Mom and Dad checked in to their hotel."

"Glad they made it okay."

Vivian wanted to talk about the plan to help the VA's office find out what was happening within the study. Or talk about the look Slate had given Wade. Instead, she got into her head, thinking what would happen if she didn't free Victor.

"Do you think you should interview Victor?" she asked. "He might have some important information."

"Heath went to interview him yesterday. As the arresting officer, he set it up with that scumbag lawyer."

Slate was right about Ned Stevens, and after her brother was released, she'd file a complaint with someone...somewhere. After. Everything was about *after*.

"Thank you. No matter what happens. Thank you for everything you've done."

"Except the almost-getting-you-killed parts." He swiped a hand across his face, covering his eyes from her.

"No." She touched his hand, looking at him so he knew she meant it. "Those incidents made me remember where I'm from and where I've been."

"Which is where? You've met my parents and seen not only baby pictures but also goofy teen pictures when I was sweating in marching band. You practically know my life story."

"You know about the whole foster situation and I can't tell you it was all grand. Being separated from my brother was a relief at first. I mean, I was only sixteen and he was eleven—completely my responsibility. I wanted to hate them for separating us, but couldn't. But then I was crazy guilty. The only reason I joined the military was for the training and college opportunities. I couldn't take care of Victor without a way to provide for us both."

Their hands were still connected. He turned his palm up and laced his fingers through hers. It was comforting while they waited and got to know each other a little.

"I get the guilt. My story's different, but I'm not taking over my parents' dream. That's a lot of to be responsible for. Back to your story."

"Right. I stood in your living room more embarrassed than helpless. I served four years in the army. Basic was hard, but it toughened me up. I can fight, Slate. I won't be huddled in the corner next time."

He smiled and nodded as if he were wondering whether to believe her or not. This wasn't the time or place, but she'd like to get him on a workout mat. She could show him a move or two.

It was close to five o'clock when Major Clements gathered them back in his office. Once again, she stood near the door in the background, hoping no one would object to her involvement.

"It's a go. We've just got one hitch." The major looked at each of the men. "You need to find someone who's a veteran. We don't have time to go through all the channels to set up a fake history."

"What about James Diaz? Didn't he serve in the military?"

"I think Taylor White was in the National Guard."

"I can do it," Vivian volunteered quietly. She wasn't supposed to speak out. Doing so drew everyone's attention to her. "I served in the army."

"No way. The person behind this will know you on sight. What if you get programmed to shoot yourself?" Slate's attitude was full of emotion. He'd controlled himself throughout the day and especially the afternoon. His reaction was unexpected.

"You'll be with me to keep anything bad from happening. I'm the logical person, I know what to look for. And if it makes the person harming everyone run, then you'll all be there to catch them."

"No one has more at risk than her. And she's right. She does have us to look out for her." Jack spoke to the major, pointedly ignoring Slate's outburst.

"Doesn't it defeat the purpose of being undercover if the person we're after knows her?" Slate tried again.

"We're out of time, man." Heath looked at his partner and then at his commanding officer. "Sir, she does have military background. It's not the same as sending in an untrained civilian."

Major Clements had crossed his arms over his chest and looked at her while the men argued. It was his decision and his eyes locked with hers.

"Will it work?" she asked him.

"There are risks. You aren't law enforcement. Where did you serve?"

"Afghanistan for eight months and no, it wasn't in the typing pool." Everyone except Slate laughed. "I know my way around a weapon, but I won't need one in the hospital. I can do whatever's necessary. It's for my brother."

"Get it set up."

"But, sir, this—"

"You may not like it, Thompson, but you need to make it happen and be thorough."

"I'd like permission to accompany Miss Watts. I can

go in as her fiancé or husband. If the person behind this knows who she is, it won't matter if he sees me with her."

"You're right. As soon as he recognizes Miss Watts, he'll know why you're there. But being known as her husband would keep you close to observe not only her reactions, but the reactions of the staff." The major clapped his hand on Slate's shoulder.

"It's quicker to get you the necessary documents fixed up so you look like newlyweds than military records." Heath picked up his phone and made a call. "I suggest we give you a head injury, Vivian, and say you're having trouble sleeping."

"You don't have to do this," Slate tried again. "Give us an hour and we can find a ranger who is also a veteran."

"It's okay, Slate. I told you, I can handle it."

"Will you keep looking for someone more qualified?" he asked Jack, who just shook his head. "She hasn't exactly shown all this skill she claims to have."

"This is the best way, Slate. Posing as her husband, you can be there with her for every diagnosis and plan of action. There's no way we could set up that kind of scenario if it was Taylor White." Heath was still on the phone but slapped Slate on the back. "You know this, man."

"I might know it, but I don't have to like it."

Vivian stood next to Slate's desk. She'd intended to fill Wade in, but Slate's reaction had her confused. But she wouldn't let wondering about his intentions mess up how excited she was to finally participate in helping her brother.

"So…you want to marry me?" she whispered, gently sending an elbow into Slate's ribs.

"You might say that. But first we're hitting the gym."

Was he worried that she'd mess things up or worried that something might happen to her? Another crazy impression, but she got the feeling it was the latter.

Chapter Twenty-Four

"This isn't exactly how I envisioned our first date." Slate looked up from the floor mat into a pair of steel-gray eyes. "Can you change the color by changing your mood?"

"No. My eyes do whatever they want." Vivian laughed and extended a hand to help him to his feet. "How much longer do I have to show you that I'm capable of defending myself?"

"I believed you the first time my back hit this mat." He popped to his feet a little slower but ready to go again. "Nothing wrong with a little practice."

"Okay, but there's also a thing about rubbery arms if something happens for real."

Each strike he threw, she blocked correctly. The kick he sent her way, she dodged predictably. It was later in the day. No one was in the gym except them. No one would interrupt.

Slate needed to catch her off guard. See what she would do in an impossible situation. He pulled her to him, dropping his guard with his arms circling her waist. He latched his thumbs through her belt loops, trapping her arms at her sides. She tried to break free. This time, he didn't want her to get away.

"No fair."

"Get free." He tried to keep the smile off his face and laughter from his voice.

"Slate, attackers aren't going to hug me."

"Get free or say uncle."

"Um… I don't say uncle." She twisted.

He kept her next to his chest.

She raised a knee. He blocked with his hip but still kept his grip. She pulled, twisted, jerked and moved in ways that were a complete turn-on…but she still didn't get free.

Vivian brushed the back of her hand across his groin. He was expecting a reluctant word of surrender or apology when she tilted her face toward his and kissed him.

Thoroughly.

And again. Their mouths slashed, transferring the sparring energy from their bodies to their lips. Nothing but explosive energy between them existed. If his thumbs hadn't been hooked in her belt loops, he might have stood a chance. But this way? He couldn't untangle himself before she was paying him back for his torture of her the night before.

Exquisite torture he not only wanted, but craved.

Time and place didn't matter much when it came to male body parts. Tight blue jeans might have helped him from immediately expanding, but the loose workout sweats gave him room to grow.

Damn it.

Stopping her was what he should do. Okay, so he didn't really want to stop her, but this wasn't what he had in mind. Vivian's fingers skimmed over his collarbone. Then her fingernail scraped the outline of his earlobe.

When had her arms become free?

Vivian leaned into him, bringing her full body in contact with his. She turned her hip past the drawstring dangling from his pants. Full-blown erection. He had to keep her close in case someone walked in.

It didn't help his erection any that he'd wanted Vivian since the moment he'd seen her in the chicken wing uniform.

Remembering how she'd reacted to his touches didn't help his body respond any less either. He wanted to throw her to the mat and encourage those reactions again.

Their eyes met and he saw her smile—a smile of determination. No matter what she might say, she'd done that on purpose. But there were cameras.

"Uncle," he whispered. "The owners can see us."

They broke apart—too soon in his humble opinion—both still breathing rapidly.

He kept his mouth close to hers as he said, "I have to admit that was an unusual solution to your problem. No one I know would have approached it that way."

"And not a move that would work on everyone. Honestly, I don't know how that happened. I was thinking a head butt and the next thing I knew, I was leaning another direction." She ran her fingernails up and down his back.

He freed his thumbs and circled her slender waist with his fingers. She was free, but didn't move away.

"The head butt would have worked and was sort of what I was prepared for." He brushed her lips one last time, putting space between their bodies. "This was much more pleasant."

"I guess we should get cleaned up and head to the hospital. We don't have time for anything else. Right?"

"Time? Yes. Should we? No."

"Oh." She backed away with a disappointed look and he had to catch her hand, circling her back to him.

"Will it happen? Yes, absolutely, don't doubt it." He kissed her long and sumptuously, putting more of himself into the effort than he had for anyone. "That's a promise, ma'am. And I don't break my promises."

"Good to know, ranger."

SLATE DIDN'T THINK this operation would go south. He knew it would. They weren't prepared. They weren't in control. And he was crazy about the woman sitting next to him. As in, so major crazy it would cause problems if she were in danger.

He couldn't think straight and they hadn't done anything except fill out some papers for the hospital.

Jack and Heath waited in their vehicle a couple of blocks away. Wade was still at Company B headquarters. Their plan of action was to go through the emergency room and get most of the preliminary exams out of the way throughout the night.

Vivian had to be admitted the good old-fashioned way before their OIG contact could put her to the head of the line for the head-injury-specific tests. Tests that should be similar to those needed in the sleep study. Their contact would also make certain that the doctors performing those tests or exams were the same.

"I feel guilty taking time away from these men and women who need the care like my brother." Vivian was doing a great job acting nervous...or maybe she just wasn't pretending to be calm.

"What about the men and women who are a part of the study and not able to function in normal life? Just think about the three men who committed suicide and the many other innocent victims."

"Done. We're here for a purpose." She looked around the room. "Greater than my brother now."

"Damn straight."

They waited several hours before the basic tests began.

After being up all night, it wasn't hard to look tired or be discouraged that they weren't going home. Nine o'clock rolled around and they'd been in the hospital ten hours, seeing doctors for four of them.

No one could find anything wrong with Vivian. Of course, there wasn't anything wrong.

"How ya doing?" Wade asked during a phone call for an update.

"They're still digging around for answers," Slate said from the waiting room.

"Well, the people working on Vivian's case should be getting a couple of urgent care requests fairly soon."

They disconnected. Vivian was resting her head on his shoulder, so he kept the phone in his hand. Someone with a clipboard walked by, pointed to his phone and shook their head. This was one rule he'd be breaking. They'd given Jack's phone to Vivian in case they got separated.

God, he hoped this plan worked. Would they really be able to spook whoever was brainwashing patients? Hopefully spook them into running instead of doing something to Vivian.

"Watts. Vivian Watts," a nurse called her name, waking her.

She pushed up from his shoulder and they both walked to the door.

"Sorry. No one but the patient can go back."

"You can't make an exception?" he asked.

"No." The nurse held out a hand, stopping him. "She'll be fine. We'll take good care of her."

Slate pulled her to him for a hug and whispered, "Text me where you are. I'll find a way back there."

She nodded and he kissed her cheek. The door closed and once again he found himself praying that his gut instinct about this operation was wrong.

Chapter Twenty-Five

Abby got her list of patients for the day, dropped the clipboard and had to apologize. She quickly picked it up, holding it in her gloved hand, and just as quickly ran to the ladies' room.

"What is she doing on my list of patients?" She asked the question several times expecting the answer. Nothing came.

Was the woman in the mirror disappointed in the mistakes that had been made? Is that why she wasn't imparting the right path? Allan Pinkston was a disappointment, she thought, then said it out loud, attempting to begin the conversation.

"We do not have resources to waste at this time to eliminate her," the perfect voice finally answered.

"You know if she's here for a test, then he's not far away."

"If you run the experiment on her, then they'll find you. Our research will be over. We won't ever be together."

"But she must be eliminated."

"There are other ways. You have cash. Use it. You have access to drugs…procure them. Use your head, girl. Stop being a ninny."

That wasn't perfection. Those words were cruelty itself. Her father. The voice in the mirror was gone. She was on her own to find someone to deal with this matter.

She had until one o'clock before Victor's sister was getting nodes attached to her head. Abby hated to be off schedule. It would send her day into disarray. She wanted neatly run, smooth, orderly clockwork. Everything had a place. The things she did had a time to do them.

She could deviate from the daily schedule today in order to get the annoyance out of the picture. She used the stairs to arrive in the emergency department. She pulled her mask over her mouth and nose and ventured into the emergency room to recruit help.

Chapter Twenty-Six

Wrapped in a paper gown and blanket, Vivian sat in a hall for at least half an hour before anyone said, "Follow me." She went into a waiting room with lockers and was instructed to put her clothes and everything with her—including Jack's cell—into the locker of her choice. Each locker had a key that could be worn around your wrist.

"This is going to drive Slate so crazy," she mumbled to herself.

The idea of keeping in touch with him evaporated into the bad-smelling spray someone had used in the corner.

She was on her own—completely on her own—through the first test. But she'd had an MRI before. Nothing went wrong. Her brain was still there, according to the doctors. In an aside, the technician said everything looked good, but the doctor would give her the results later.

Vivian didn't find anything or anyone in the area suspicious. It didn't look like anyone would have an opportunity to brainwash a veteran. She wondered about that. Heath had mentioned sleep tapes. So whoever was possibly hurting the patients would need to have an extended period of private time with them.

It seemed like a logical conclusion. At least to herself. She'd have to go with it since there was no one else to ask. She was waiting to be escorted to her next test. The people around her seemed to treat her with kid gloves. She had to wonder what story the OIG had told to everyone.

She flipped through the only magazine on the table, reading just about every article and advertisement inside. She was starving and super tired, but she continued to wait. She slapped the magazine down on the table.

A lot of people had gone to a lot of trouble for today to happen. It didn't matter if she was hungry and wanted a certain bed in a certain ranger's home.

"Miss Watts?" a woman with a clipboard asked.

"That's me." She felt silly for answering since no one was in the waiting area with her.

"I was hoping you were here. Word came down to work you in for an EEG today. We're running ahead of schedule and thought we squeeze you in. Come this way."

Vivian followed the woman down the hall and into the elevator.

"What's an EEG?"

"It's used to monitor brain activity. Basically, we put gel on your scalp, connect a bunch of electrodes to your head and monitor you for a while. It's harmless and completely noninvasive. The worst part about my test is that you need to wash your hair afterward."

They got off the elevator on the fifth floor. Her guide opened a door and gestured for Vivian to go inside. "Abby will get you all prepped. I'll be back in a few minutes to get the test started."

"Oh, hi." Vivian recognized the woman who had spoken to her and Slate just two days earlier. "I think we met a couple of days ago."

"Oh, my gosh, you're the woman from the cafeteria. You were with that tall Texas Ranger. You know I'd never met one of them before. He's quite handsome."

"Slate is great."

"Were you both working on Rashid's case for some reason?"

"Actually, Slate is a friend. I mean husband. It's all so new. We just got married." Hopefully that explanation covered her mistake. "He brought me to the hospital because I fell and hit my head. While he was here, he got curious and started asking questions about the attack."

It was the story they'd agreed on. If anyone asked, they'd come here for her, not because of any case.

"I have to say that they got you in for testing fast. Your name must be on someone's favorite list. Things usually move real slow around here." Abby picked up a clipboard. "I have to ask you some boring questions that you've probably already answered. Everything's routine and I have to write it down again for our charts. Okay?"

"So that's the part you do?"

"Questions, and I get to attach the connector node goo. I've enjoyed working here and decided to go back to school to become a certified lab technician to perform the test myself. I find it very interesting. Now, you said you hit your head?"

"Yes, and I've had trouble sleeping since then."

"Any loss of consciousness or sign of a seizure?"

"No, I'm learning to ride horses and fell."

"Oh, my. I hope you got right back on it."

Vivian nodded and answered all the same questions about her head injury. The one difference in this department was that Abby used a clipboard with real paper. All the other departments had input the information directly onto a portable tablet.

She wanted to ask about it but was busy observing the assistant. There was an artificial awkwardness emanating from her movements and words. She smiled, but it was carefully in all the right pauses. She giggled, but it didn't quite seem real.

So was the assistant's behavior strained because she was covering something up? Or strained because she knew Slate was a Texas Ranger? It could be simply because Vivian as a patient had been labeled a VIP. Or none of it could mean anything and it could all be wishful thinking on Vivian's part.

How could a person investigating something on this scale tell which idea to follow? Make her own judgment call? Wait for feedback from the rest of the team? Perhaps she lacked the experience to discover anything useful after meeting all of these potential suspects. How would she narrow her impressions down to a manageable number?

Abby continued to part Vivian's hair and apply the spots of gel that would hold the electric nodes in place for the test. She was either concentrating very hard on a procedure that she'd done hundreds of times or ignoring normal conversation.

Why did the assistant's movements and expressions feel calculated? Was it just Vivian's desire that somebody she met today be worthy of an investigation? Or was it Vivian projecting her need to have someone seem guilty?

First thing, she had to calm down and go through all the motions. There wasn't a mirror, just a one-way glass at the end of the room. She looked very strange with her hair parted in rows, white gel that looked like toothpaste in dots across her head.

"So what happens now?"

"Lucy will be back any minute. She'll add the actual electric nodes and then she'll begin the test."

"What do I do?"

"Well, a lot of people fall asleep. We get the best results when you're relaxed."

"I've been up all night. A nap sounds extremely good right now."

"Would you like a bottle of water?" Abby reached into a small fridge and handed her a small bottle of mineral water.

"That would be great. Thanks."

Lucy came into the room and finished the preparations. She began the test, checked the EEG machine and told Abby she'd return in about half an hour.

Abby dimmed the lights and pulled the door almost closed. Vivian was thirsty and emptied the bottle of water. Then she closed her eyes and that was it. She awoke totally refreshed when Lucy touched her shoulder.

"My goodness, you were so sound asleep," the technician said. "Let's get you cleaned up now."

"I don't remember falling asleep."

"Well, apparently you needed a bit of rest. Good for you." She pulled wires, wiped the gel and then gave Vivian a disposable comb to pull through her tangles.

Abby waved from her desk when she left with Lucy to go back to the waiting area on the third floor. She walked into the room to find an almost frantic Slate.

He pulled her into his arms and hugged her, kissing her forehead. "Dammit, I've been worried."

"You look like you should have had that last test. I fell asleep and feel great now. Completely refreshed and ready for the next thing." She pulled away and looked at him. "I thought you were supposed to wait downstairs?"

"Yeah, well after the first hour that just wasn't going to work for me. I finally slipped through the doors. It took me a couple of hours to find this room."

"You must have just missed me before I left for the EEG." She ran her hands through her hair. "I feel like I have conditioner in my hair now. It's so greasy."

"Are you okay?" They sat in two chairs in the corner.

"Yes. I know my hair's a mess, but I feel great. Don't I look okay?"

"As a matter of fact, you do. It's just that…"

"I haven't found anything. Everyone's been nice and accommodating. They're treating me like a VIP…" she lowered her voice "…because they think I am."

"No one gave you any drugs or shots?"

"Nope." Vivian slapped her thighs, twisting in her seat, wanting to press her body next to this gorgeous man. *What am I doing?* "Slate, could we just get out of here?"

"Are you sure no one gave you anything?"

"Positive." She slipped her hand from her leg onto his thigh. "Maybe we could just find an empty room."

She did feel good. *Too good.*

"That's it. Something's wrong." He jumped up, leaving her alone in the corner.

Her skin felt all tingly. Not itching…just tingling and alive. What was wrong with him? She'd seen him in his plaid boxers. Why wouldn't he want to fool around?

Oh, God. Something was completely wrong with her.

Slate opened the door and shouted for a nurse. He pulled his cell from his back pocket and turned to face her again. "Where are your things?"

She lifted her wrist, unable to tell him her locker number in the dressing room behind one of the doors. Not the one he was standing at, but another door. There were lots of words on the tip of her tongue, but none would actually form to create a sentence.

Wow. My mind is totally not in control of anything.

It did wow her that she seemed like two people. One who just observed and one who was stuck, unable to really communicate. She couldn't even point. It was like being stuck in a nightmare, unable to wake up.

Slate rolled the keyring over her wrist. She tried to grab his hand, but he was too fast.

"I'm telling you, someone drugged her. We've got to get her out of here. What do you mean, take her to the emergency room? Whoever did this might be treating her. She's leaving. Meet us at the door."

She shook her head. Back and forth and back and forth until she was dizzy.

Oh, wait. She was more than dizzy…she was about to be sick. Extremely sick. She rose from the chair but fell to her knees.

"Vivian. Can you understand me? Can you even hear me?"

"Bath…" She tried to crawl toward the changing room. "Sick."

After clawing at the carpet a couple of times, attempting to drag herself to the dressing room, she gave up. She just wanted to pass out. Lying on the floor was a very good solution.

Slate picked her up around her waist and practically flew through the door. Her feet barely skimmed the floor he got her there so fast. And just in the nick of time. She lost what little there was in her stomach.

He stayed next to her and handed her paper towels, dabbing at her face and forehead until her own limbs began to obey her orders again. Her mind began clearing as embarrassment set in. Slate whispered into the phone again, probably telling the guys why they weren't downstairs.

He left her alone for a few minutes, and she overheard him talking to a nurse through the door. *My wife this* and *my wife that* didn't completely register as referring to her until Slate returned with towels to clean her up.

Which he did. Alone. He also had a clean hospital gown that he helped her slip into.

"I prefer my own clothes," she managed to tell him.

He ignored her since he didn't dress her. She could barely lift her head from resting on the tiled wall and couldn't argue.

"It's been years and years since I've thrown up. I feel like I've been drinking all night and have a hangover." Vivian dropped her head into her hands, totally at a loss as to why it felt so dang heavy.

"Feeling better?" Slate asked, towering over her.

She couldn't raise her head to convince him she was.

"We're leaving as soon as you can walk to the elevator."

"Clothes?" she asked hopefully.

"The nurse got your bag." He pointed to the one hanging on the back of the door.

"I can get dressed."

"Nope. Not waiting that long."

Completely humiliated by throwing up in front of someone she wanted to find her sexy, she let him wrap his arm around her and leave the waiting area. She was totally out of it. She couldn't even tell if the ties on the gown were done correctly or if the hospital gear was exposing her to the world.

Chapter Twenty-Seven

They were leaving. Walking out. Calling a halt to the operation. The team would punt. Slate was not going to risk Vivian's life again. Who were these monsters? He was about to call Wade and tell him to contact the OIG when the elevator jolted to a halt.

"What's happening? Why are we stopped?"

"Fire!" The shouts were clear even through two sets of steel doors.

Stuck in an elevator while the building was on fire. He checked his cell for reception. Nothing. *Right. Inside an elevator.*

"Do you think someone just pulled the alarm so they could leave the building without us seeing?" she asked.

"We can hope." He popped the emergency call panel open, pushing the button. "No one's answering. We might be on our own."

"Do we need to climb? Is there an escape hatch on the ceiling?"

"Only in the movies. Firefighters have keys, but when an elevator stops, the safest place is inside until they get it moving again." He kept trying the emergency button. The alarm was deafening in their ears, making it difficult to talk.

"Unless there's an actual fire."

"Yeah. But we don't know if it's real. Like you said, someone could have just pulled the alarm." Slate tested the door's open and close buttons again, just to be certain they weren't jammed.

"Either way, people are going to be hurt," Vivian said, sliding down to huddle in the corner. "What if someone is trampled or…or worse? Oh, my God, this is all my fault."

"You didn't pull the fire alarm or set a fire." He sat next to her. Hopefully the smoke would rise inside an elevator, too.

"Actually, you don't know that. I could have set the fire and not remember anything about it. Just like Victor…"

"Feeling any better?"

"Much. I can walk and most important, think." She hugged her hospital-issued plastic sack with her clothes inside.

The alarms were sounding in perfect time on the floors above and below them. They could hear people shouting and running. Everything was amplified inside the elevator shaft.

"Hey, anybody in there?" someone banged on the doors from the hallway. It was faint, but distinct.

They both shouted. Slate kicked their set of doors with his boots.

"Hey! Hey, man! Someone's still in there. Get something to help me!" the voice yelled.

Slate and Vivian waited on the floor, holding hands after a few minutes. As the doors inched opened, smoke poured inside, replacing the breathable air. They covered their mouths and noses as best they could, but Vivian was still in a hospital gown.

"No matter what happens, you do not leave my side," Slate ordered. "Got it?"

"But—"

"No buts. Just promise."

"Then you go out that door first," she said, matter-of-fact. "You go, you fight if necessary, then you pull me out."

Logical and right. He nodded. If someone had done this deliberately to get at them, then it made sense they would be waiting for them to escape or be rescued.

The fire seemed real. At least, the black smoke swirling above their heads did.

It circled inside the elevator.

The doors were pried and propped open, first in the hallway, then on the elevator itself. The whole process seemed to take hours, but it was just a matter of minutes.

"I'll reach in and get you," Slate promised. "I'll give you a thumbs-up."

She affirmed with a nod. He planted himself between her and the opening, hoping to shield her in case someone just opened fire with a weapon. That was where his mind had gone. Everyone in the hospital was a potential suspect.

But the men who'd pried the doors open were orderlies evacuating everyone off the floor. Good men who pulled him through the opening and helped him do the same for Vivian.

"You okay? Can you walk down the stairs on your own?" one of them asked.

"Thanks and yes," Slate answered, wrapping his arm around Vivian.

The smoke gathered like a fog at the high ceiling but it was still hard to breathe as they got closer to the exit. The sting blurred his vision and his eyes watered. Patients shoved, trying to get through the stairwell door, while hospital employees in scrubs helped those who had fallen or were in wheelchairs.

Slate held his ground, not budging, letting the crush sweep past them. They'd be safer if no one was around. He could protect Vivian better.

"Stay with me," he told her.

Vivian didn't answer so he turned back to check if she was okay.

He didn't see it coming, but he sure as hell felt it hit his shoulder. And it wasn't a stranger. The only person close to him was Vivian. Slate fell to his knees and lifted his arm just in time to deflect another blow from an IV pole that had been left by a patient.

Her eyes were blank, sort of crazy like Allan Pinkston. "Vivian!"

She threw a jab. He countered with a block. He tried to grab her arms, she evaded. It was like their practice the night before. Almost precisely. What if he repeated his last move?

He took one of her punches to his solar plexus. She wasn't holding anything back, that was for sure. He caught her left arm to her side and struggled to loop his around her right but managed it.

"Vivian!" he shouted, leaning back to avoid the head butt. "Get free, Vivian!"

After a few more seconds of struggling, of lifting her knee and missing, Vivian relaxed like she had the previous evening. There wasn't a kiss, but her head fell against his chest. Her body went slack and suddenly, Slate was struggling to keep her on her feet.

He swung an unconscious Vivian into his arms and joined others walking down the stairwell.

The bastards had gotten to her. Sometime while she'd been out of his sight, someone had hypnotized her or done something to make her attack him.

God, he hoped she could remember who. It might be the only way he'd forgive himself for not keeping his promise to keep her safe.

"What time is it?"

Vivian awoke, searching for the microwave clock that should have shown the time in its bright green illumination in the kitchen. She sat straight up, unsure where she was or who had a heavy arm across her midsection.

"You okay?" a male voice asked. "Have another nightmare?"

It all came back to her in the blink of an eye. No amnesia. Along with no possessions, no money and no bad guy. This wasn't a nightmare. It was real life. It was her living the hand she'd been dealt.

"Yeah, I'm fine." She glanced around, recognizing that they were in Slate's bedroom. "Shouldn't I be at the main house?"

"Heath's there. We came here because you were sick. It seemed the easiest way to get us both cleaned up."

An alarm clock across the room indicated it was around one in the morning. She felt like someone had beaten her up. And her mouth felt fuzzy with a hint of rubbing alcohol. "Do they know who set the fire at the apartment building?"

"You mean the hospital?"

She got out of bed with the intention of using her new toothbrush. She desperately needed some water and… *Oh, my gosh!* She needed clothes.

She stumbled to the bathroom and without turning on the light, found a towel to wrap around herself.

"Slate. I thought we—were we stuck in an elevator?"

"That's the last thing you remember?" He flipped on the light next to his bed.

There was blood on his pillow. She looked at his head, where a bandage was stained and leaking. He saw the direction of her eyes and touched his temple, then looked at his pillow.

"No reason to be upset. It didn't even need stitches."

"Who did that?"

His raised eyebrows gave her the answer. She had. And she couldn't remember any of it.

"Why are we naked?"

"*We're* not. You vomited a couple of times on the way home. The doctors said you probably would, but it still got all over us the last time. You really don't remember this?" He shifted the blanket aside, showing his sweatpants.

He looked around the bed, then over the side and pointed to the floor. "There's the T-shirt I had you in. You kept telling me you were burning in a fire."

"Nightmares?"

"Yeah."

"And you're sleeping with me because…?"

"You couldn't sleep without me. You coming back to bed?"

"I… I need…" She snatched up the large T-shirt and retreated into the bathroom.

After the time it took to take a shower—because something was making her hair a greasy mess—she expected Slate to be sawing logs in a dark room. But he wasn't. He was scrambling eggs in the kitchen.

"The doctors who looked you over said soft foods. Scrambled eggs are soft, right? You think you could eat?" He turned around, pan in hand, still stirring the eggs. He arched his eyebrows and grinned. "You look much, much better. I hope that's a good sign."

"Maybe. My teeth aren't furry and my hair isn't greasy anymore."

"Eggs?"

She put her hand over her stomach as it growled. "I think so. But if I stop eating, I'm sure it's no reflection on the cook."

"Well, that remains to be seen. But what self-respecting bachelor can't scramble an egg?"

He filled two plates already on the table. One place had a bottle of water and another had a beer. She took the place with the water bottle.

"So what happened?"

"You were obviously drugged. We won't know with what until the labs come back. Doesn't really matter since we don't know who did it to you."

She put her hand to her head. "Fuzz. It's all just a big blur."

"Sort of like Allan Pinkston and half of the sleep-study vets who had altercations for no reason." He smiled, but it was stiff and forced.

The humor was lost on her and she didn't quite understand what all the veterans had to do with her.

"So do you think that somewhere during the day someone drugged me and told me to—oh, God, you said I hit you. What did I hit you with?" She wanted to run to him, to get a closer look under the bandage at his temple.

"An IV pole. That was after the elevator stopped when the fire alarm went off." He shrugged like it was no big deal.

"So we were stuck in an elevator. Was there an actual fire? Did anyone get hurt?"

"Yes, we were. Yes, on the fourth floor. Only scrapes and bruises during the evacuation. And yes, they caught two vets. One set the fire and one pulled the alarm on a different floor."

"Two more men from the sleep study?"

He shook his head and took another bite of eggs. "You aren't eating and you should drink. They said you'd be dehydrated." Another bite. "No. These two are regulars in the ER. They said someone wearing a mask asked them to help with a drill."

"They believed that?"

"They were sort of out of it." He finished his last bite and started on his beer. "High on the oxy they'd been given."

She nibbled when he pointed toward her plate again. "Did I ruin everything?"

"Hell, no. We've got a list." He grinned, then pointed his beer toward her. "A limited list of people who had access to you. Whatever knocked you off your feet had to be ingested."

"But I don't remember anything."

"Believe me, Vivian. The rangers have worked with less. Whoever messed with you today underestimated just how good we are."

"And how humble."

He winked, tipping his beer at her. "Damn straight."

Chapter Twenty-Eight

Vivian loved seeing Slate's face smiling. In the past few days, when that deep furrow appeared across his brow, it had been because of her. Smiling was good. Smiling was great.

Avoiding her attraction to him wasn't. It made her feel all squishy inside. He was probably right about trying to begin something under these circumstances. But he was just so darn loveable.

And good Lord, that grin!

"Can I ask you a question?" She turned sideways in her chair to face him directly.

"Sure."

"When am I supposed to make a big deal out of being attracted to you? When's the correct time?"

"What? Where did that come from?" He looked totally surprised until he did his adorable eyebrow thing.

"From the fact that you are just so darn cute when you smile and waggle your eyebrows like that."

"Well, I don't think this is the best time. There's no telling if those drugs are affecting you some way."

She didn't care. At all. It was almost a compulsive need to be close to him. "I can write a note stating I'm of sound mind and drug free if you want me to."

"For what?"

"For now." She used her feet to push his chair away from the table and was quickly sitting across his lap.

There was just something about him. Something honest and refreshing and strong and safe. She wanted to discover everything and what made him who he was. So it made perfect sense to kiss him again.

And maybe again.

"Did I finally come up with a way for you to say yes?" she asked.

"Was I saying no?"

"Man alive. Each and every time we get close to releasing all this tension between us. There's a definite no from you."

She leaned in to kiss him and he leaned back. She shook a finger in front of his face, then pushed her body completely against his, holding him in place. He couldn't escape her lips connecting with his.

"Say yes," she pleaded against his lips.

Slate's chest began to rise and fall faster under her hands. "Bad, bad idea," he said before crushing his lips to hers.

The Texas Ranger in him might think kissing her was a bad idea, but the man hauling her hips to his left nothing but good sensations behind.

"If this is your idea of bad…" she whispered, leaving the rest to his imagination. "You are such a good kisser."

"You make me crazy," he said. His lips covered hers completely.

They stopped talking. He pushed her arms higher around his neck and stood, keeping her next to him with his hands under her butt as he moved them from the kitchen to his bedroom.

The bed was still disheveled from where they'd slept earlier.

"You're sure? This isn't a funny reaction to drugs or confusion or something like that?"

She nodded, afraid that answering him aloud would somehow make him misinterpret her reply. The luxurious kiss she gave him should be answer enough. She couldn't let him go this time. Just to be loved…even for a moment.

He laid her on the bed, tugging off her shirt as he did. He pulled his off quickly, then unbuttoned his jeans. He lowered himself on top of her, dipping his tongue into her mouth, then slipping across her chin and skimming…everything.

Frantic touching and hurried clothing removal got them completely skin to skin for the first time.

Heaven.

She tasted the salt on his skin, nipping the curve where his shoulder muscle met his neck. She tilted her head back, encouraging him to taste her more, sending additional shivers of anticipation down her spine.

He lightly scraped his teeth across her breast before settling into the hollow of her throat. He quickly replaced his lips with his fingertips, stroking the edge of her bra. Then he caught her mouth to his again, plunging his tongue inside. He captured her whimper as their hips pushed against each other, searching for more.

"There's no turning back."

"Ranger Thompson, are you going to kiss me or talk me to sleep?"

He didn't debate the situation after that.

Desire was evident from both of them. There wasn't any need to delay what they'd both wanted and needed. He shifted and was inside her, filling every bit of her with every bit of him.

There may be consequences in the morning, but at the

moment, all she could think about was the undeniable satisfaction. And how soon they could do it all again.

THE NEXT MORNING, consequences arrived with the dawn and a clear head. Only a couple hours of sleep for Vivian and then she was sipping coffee, watching the sunrise when Heath began feeding the horses. She joined him, pitching in without a word.

She'd volunteered to help. Heath treated her with what seemed like a little more respect. In spite of the fact that it was her fault Slate's roommate was taking on extra duties. Heath managed to feed the horses and chickens without much more than a grunt. But it was a respectful couple of grunts from the man of few words. He walked with her back to his house and kicked the couch as he passed to wake Slate up.

"You coming to work or going to sleep in?" Heath asked before going to his room.

Slate looked blurry eyed at his watch. "I've only been asleep a couple of hours. I came out here earlier to keep watch."

Heath didn't laugh much, but he did all the way into his room. Slate had to laugh since he'd fallen asleep keeping that so-called watch.

"We've got a psychopath to catch today," Heath yelled through his closed door. "But you can go back to bed if you want."

Slate was already sitting on the couch, rubbing his eyes, then stretching his arms above his head. "You doing okay?" he asked Vivian. "Get some shut-eye without fire nightmares?"

"Yes. I woke up about the time you fell asleep. Let me get you some coffee."

"Nice. Heath feed the horses?"

"We just finished." She handed him a cup and stepped back.

She wanted to know Heath's story. It seemed like he had one. But right now, today, he was very correct.

They had a psychopath to catch.

Vivian was ready to leave. It didn't take long to put on jeans, a pullover sweater and a pair of tennis shoes. Showers stopped as she cleaned the kitchen and tried to remember what had happened last night. She'd remembered most of what had happened in the waiting room and elevator.

No one had told her anything or pushed her to remember. Slate had explained that after Allan Pinkston, he'd been advised against saying anything to her. Anything that might create a false memory. But why couldn't she remember all of the tests the EEG lab had done on her?

As soon as Slate was out of the bedroom, she was ready to get started. He, on the other hand, was gathering his things and looking toward Heath's room.

"Why do you seem like you're waiting for backup?" she asked after several minutes. "I'm not being left behind. What if I remember something?"

He glanced at his phone again. "The guys are kind of worried you might hit them over the head with an IV pole."

"Oh. I hadn't considered that."

"Look." He gripped her shoulders. "You're not getting left behind, but we still don't know who's doing what. So we have to take precautions."

"That's understandable. I agree. I'll sit in the truck."

"I was thinking more like you'd sit in the office with Wade." He patted her arms, making her feel twelve.

"Okay, Wade can sit in the truck, too."

"Oh." He pointed a finger at her. "You're funny. Very funny."

"And serious. I might remember more if I'm at the hospital."

"Might. Might not. There's no guarantee you'll ever remember." Again, Slate didn't act too concerned. "We have units collecting all the remaining sleep-study patients. Even your brother's been put into a separate holding cell under surveillance."

She let his words sink in. It made sense. But he was keeping it almost too low-key. No one knew what the patients had been programmed to do if something went wrong. And no one knew what she'd been programmed to do.

Oh, God!

Last night, she'd made it back to the waiting area before she got sick. There was no telling what she might have done if a knife or gun had been available when she attacked Slate.

"I'm not going to hamper your investigation by doing something selfish and stupid. You don't have to worry about me."

Slate released a long sigh of relief, and right on cue, his phone rang. She heard Heath's phone buzzing and vibrating in his room.

"What's happened?"

"Let's get moving," Heath said, coming out of his bedroom. "Looks like you're going to the hospital. We all are."

Chapter Twenty-Nine

Vivian was left waiting in the truck at the front entrance of the hospital. The rangers were parked one after the other on the street. Police cars blocked the entrance and both roads coming to either side of the VA.

One of the sleep-study vets had walked into the hospital with his police escort. Shaking the policeman's hand, he'd overcome him, then taken his gun. Now he was in the admitting office, holding hostages.

The hospital was on lockdown and the rangers were assisting the OIG in any way they could. All the police escorts had been warned about the incident, so they hoped none of the other patients would react this way. But nothing was certain.

Everyone needed answers.

Especially her.

She wished she had a phone or even a notepad to gather her thoughts. There was nothing. Actually, she wished she had Slate to talk to. Or take a look at his smile and feel completely at ease.

But even on the ride over, he wouldn't talk about what had happened yesterday. He was more than serious about not forcing the issue. And since Heath had ridden with them from the ranch…there hadn't been any hand holding or a kiss goodbye.

She pushed those thoughts from her mind, admitting that it was very hard to do because their time together had been so exciting and a relief after the past few days.

She had questions and focused her mind on each conversation, each movement, each person who'd escorted her from one test to the next. No one had given her a pill. Not even an aspirin.

So what had happened to her after the MRI? Then she went to the fifth floor. What was there? Something that had made her hair oily. Another test to check her...brain waves. That was it, she'd had an EEG. Women. There were two women giving her a test.

One in a white lab coat and the other had...

She jumped out of the truck, locking it behind her. She needed to search for Slate or a police officer who could call him outside. One of those two women had drugged her. There was only one person who'd given her anything all day. Mineral water with a funny taste and that probably wasn't water at all.

Abby. The woman they'd met earlier in the week. She'd had a face mask hanging around her neck, disposable gloves on her hands. They'd even told her their names, asked her questions. How convenient.

And if it wasn't her? Well, then at least they'd narrowed the suspects down to two instead of more than a dozen.

"Excuse me, officer."

"You'll have to go back, ma'am."

"But I've got to get a message to one of the Texas Rangers. He'll be with the OIG."

The officer—or more like a security guard—wasn't going to help her. In fact, he was already ignoring her and concentrating on evacuating the emergency entrance.

Vivian knew enough about the hospital now to walk around to the employee entrance. There was a guard there, but she waited for him to help someone who'd stumbled and then she passed through the doors like a fish swimming upstream.

Each door she came to on that floor was locked. The elevators weren't running. Were the rangers spread out through the hospital?

Was there a chance that she'd find Slate at one of the doors? She really did have every intention of finding him. But she didn't exactly know how to get to the different floor levels of doors or where he'd be.

If she asked permission from one of the team, he would send her back to wait in the truck. Slate would probably escort her there himself. And if she told the others the truck was locked, he might turn her over to the police. She wouldn't put that action past any of them. By then, the EEG lab staff would probably be gone. So Vivian headed to the fifth floor.

Someone needed to stop the lab technicians responsible for all this chaos. She was available.

It was the perfect time to catch a psychopath.

THE SITUATION AT the VA Hospital was out of control. Totally out of control. And there wasn't a damn thing lowly Slate Thompson could do about it. By the time the rangers arrived, they were just more law enforcement officers under the direction of the hospital's OIG.

Investigating fraud or a physician's misconduct was completely different from a hostage situation. Very hard to explain that the rangers believed the veteran was under some kind of brainwashing. Or that the situation was a cover to get one or two people out of there without being caught.

The OIG couldn't contend with a possible scenario like that when they had a full-blown crisis actually happening.

They had procedures that would be followed this time. And of course, if it did have something to do with the sleep study and the fire set by two veterans the previous day, deviating from protocol had caused those problems. So the OIG was definitely not interested in allowing any additional guesswork.

Then when the hostage negotiator arrived…the hospital received a bomb threat. Unverified of course. But instead of employees and patients remaining where they were, everyone had to be evacuated.

Each Company B ranger who made it to the hospital took a different door to watch. Their commander tried to help the OIG handle the building evacuation. His second in two consecutive days, and according to Major Clements, he was madder than an angry hornet and more stubborn than a two-headed mule.

Chaos had nothing on the mass exodus from this place. Slate kept checking his phone, looking at the pictures of the men and women who had seen Vivian the day before. The hospital had confirmed that three of them weren't on the schedule, but that didn't mean they couldn't be in the crowd.

There were staff members on their suspect list, and searching those exiting had made his eyes cross for a while. But now the ambulance entrance was almost empty. Easy work compared to keeping his thoughts off Vivian.

How was he going to protect her if…?

"Exactly why you shouldn't have slept with her, you idiot," he told himself.

A silver-haired man in a white coat passed him and smiled knowingly. Slate's statement had probably been made by lots of men. Before he had to explain, his phone rang.

"Tell me something good, Wade."

"I'll tell you that I just saw Vivian run through the employee entrance and toward the stairs."

"Dammit. What's she doing?"

"You know I can't leave my post, man."

"Thanks for the heads-up."

He didn't wait for permission, didn't check in with his commander. He ran through the building, checking for directions along the way.

VIVIAN WALKED THROUGH a panicked hospital, asking directions, looking at signs. She hadn't passed additional rangers or law enforcement. Just confused patients and employees. She finally got close to the stairwell that should take her to the fifth floor when she noticed a woman in a lab coat wearing a mask.

When Vivian caught up with her, it wasn't Abby or Lucy. A sense of relief and disappointment swept over her as she entered another stairwell and continued walking to the fifth floor.

This set of stairs was the one a nurse had told her led directly to the wing where the EEG lab was located. It was a long process getting up the stairs while people were coming down. But the initial crowd had thinned.

Someone seemed to be running just below her, also heading up the stairs. She stopped a second later after she squeezed past a wheelchair wedged to hold the exit door open on the fourth floor.

She looked around for some way to defend herself and found nothing. She stepped behind a door that separated the elevators from the rest of the hall. The wheelchair stuck in the exit moved.

What would she do?

"Vivian?"

"Oh, God. Slate?" She ran out from her hiding place. "I can't believe you found me."

"Why aren't you in the truck?"

"It's the EEG lab. They gave me a bottle of mineral water. It could have been drugged. I remembered and I've been trying to find you. They wouldn't let me inside."

"Slow down, babe. They wouldn't let you inside because they've had a bomb threat."

"I thought it was a man with hostages."

He nodded. "What's this about the EEG lab?"

"It's either Lucy or Abby. You remember the woman who introduced herself in the cafeteria? My money's on her. She was curious about what we were doing and had one of those surgical masks tied around her neck. I saw it hanging around her neck both days."

He snapped his fingers. "The person who hired the veterans to pull the fire alarm wore a mask. Let me text their names to Heath."

"We need to go. Now. The women might still be in their office." She laced her fingers with his and started toward the stairwell. He didn't budge.

"I text first. Then we have backup on the way. Heath will call for background on both of the women." He squeezed her hand. "Don't worry. Both of them were already on our list. If they tried to leave, we would have seen them."

Slate's texting took longer than she thought it should. He was clicking his screen so slowly that she almost offered to type the message for him. But it was obvious he'd had some responses, maybe instructions.

When he put the phone in his back pocket, he took his badge out and clipped it to his chest. He also took his suit jacket off and removed his weapon from its holster.

"I hope they're not telling you to take me back to the truck or lock me in a broom closet."

"No closets. You're staying with me. It's the only way I can guarantee your safety. Afraid we're heading down to the first floor, though."

"Slate, please. You have to catch whoever's responsible for yesterday. For today. For all those men and women affected. Don't stop when you're so close. They're going to get away and—" She couldn't say that her bother would go to jail for murder.

They were so close.

And she was three steps ahead of him. She darted to the stairwell. He was right behind her, but at least he was still behind her. The stairs going up were clear, but he caught her just three steps from the fifth floor.

"Come on, Vivian. You know we can't go in there."

They were both breathing hard. She sank to the step, knowing he was right.

"I need… I need to rest."

He sat beside her. "Jack's checking it out. We'll know soon. But remember, we have to find evidence, babe. Without evidence we can't do anything."

"But I remember."

"You remember one of them handing you a water that could have been drugged by anyone with access to the lab. I'm not a lawyer, but that's a pretty big pool of people."

"I know it's the assistant. There's something off about her. She tries too hard."

He took her hand and stood. "Let's go." He led her back to the fourth floor to the two chairs in a waiting area near the elevator. "We'll stay here. But I swear, I'll cuff you if you run again."

"I won't. I promise."

His phone buzzed and she waited impatiently while he

silently read first one message, then another and still another. She bit her tongue, waiting for him to tell her what was going on.

"Jack's called for an emergency unit. The lab tech is unconscious."

"The tech or the assistant? Medium height or short?"

"He's got his hands full."

"It's safe now, right?" She walked toward the door. "We can go see."

He seemed to ignore her, checking his phone again. But as soon as he put it away, he rattled his handcuffs and led the way to the staircase. "You are staying in the hall. No exceptions. None. I'll see if I can identify her and you aren't doing anything. Please don't make me regret this."

"Thank you."

In spite of the bomb threat, an emergency team stepped off the staff elevator for transporting patients. They ran down the hall while she and Slate skirted the wall. The closer they got to the EEG lab, the harder it was to move her feet.

"I can't… I can't go."

"It's okay. Stay here and I'll go check."

"But—"

It was no use. A part of her mind kept telling her she didn't have an appointment. Her mind kept silently screaming that she couldn't return to the EEG lab without an appointment. She knew it.

She wanted to reach out and force Slate to take her with him, but nothing worked. Not her feet or her mouth or even her hands. She latched onto the handrail running the length of the hallway and hoped she didn't fall down.

It was a strange sensation that she'd never experienced before. But somehow she knew she had.

"Hello, Vivian. I was hoping we'd meet up today." Abby

Norman came out of an office across the hall. "Remember, Vivian. You don't have an appointment. Come with me."

Help. She could only shout the word in her mind. She couldn't call for Slate or anyone else. Abby's face was covered, she was in a lab coat that had Lucy's name on it and she had a wheelchair.

"This is going to be fun, Miss Watts. Lots and lots of fun."

Chapter Thirty

Vivian was in a state of complete numbness. Abby put a face mask over Vivian's nose and mouth, a knitted hat over her hair, tilted her head to the side and draped a hospital blanket across her lap. She used the elevator to go downstairs. Once in the lobby, Abby was joined by a man in a lab coat, and he escorted them out the ambulance entrance.

The man took over pushing the wheelchair. Abby bounced down the ramp, across the sidewalk and down to the street. Abby showed her hospital badge to the police officer there and they continued across northbound Lancaster Road.

"I can take it from here, Roger. See you tomorrow. Hopefully we'll get to work all day."

"See ya tomorrow." He waved and crossed southbound Lancaster.

"See, Vivian," the awful woman whispered in her ear. "Nobody has any clue that I'm responsible for everything that's happened. I literally wheeled you out of the hospital and no one even knows."

Vivian wanted to cry out. Scream. Yell. Pull the woman into the street and have a brawl that would gather a crowd. But she couldn't move.

Drugs or brainwashing or even a simple hypnotic suggestion…she didn't know which. She couldn't force herself to move.

Abby pushed her to the marked disabled entrance for the Rapid Transit. She was being so casual about everything. Her voice remained calm and in charge, but Vivian watched her adding a set of cloth white gloves to the disposable pair she already wore.

Speak, she commanded herself. Nothing happened behind the surgical mask.

Abby sat on a bench next to the wheelchair. "I can see you getting frustrated and upset. The more I try to understand the emotions everyone cares so much about, the more I'm glad they don't affect me. I hope you're smart enough to realize that I thought through my escape."

They were joined by two additional hospital workers, who waved at Abby as if they knew her. They weren't surprised Abby was there and if they were curious about her pushing a woman in a wheelchair, they kept the questions to themselves.

Vivian concentrated on lifting her hand, trying to reach out for the door or seconds later one of the poles within the train car. It worked until Abby saw her hand and moved it back to her lap.

"Stay there and obey." Two stops and Abby got them off the train. "I could leave you here, but I've been told you're my insurance policy. A guarantee that I get away. Personally, I don't see why you're worth the effort. But the advice is from someone close to me so I'll follow it."

The Rapid Transit station was on a hill. Vivian was grateful someone advised keeping her alive since Abby could have pushed her down what amounted to two flights of stairs.

There would have been nothing she could do except fall.

"YES, SHE'S MISSING. And yes, she left the truck earlier. But I'm telling you, sir, she didn't have a reason to leave." Slate had explained this to Major Clements, who had taken him at his word. It was the VA OIG who didn't believe him.

Slate was just outside the south side of the building in a command center. The hostage negotiator had successfully kept the sleep-study patient talking while SWAT stormed the office and took him into custody before he could kill himself.

Minutes were ticking off the clock that had begun the moment he'd stepped from the EEG lab. Lucy was dead of an overdose. They didn't know what had killed her, but the water bottle near her smelled of almonds so everyone assumed she'd been poisoned.

The building was being cleared floor by floor because of the bomb threat. Slate had unsuccessfully tried to get security to also look for Vivian. But his gut told him she wasn't there. She'd been certain Abby Norman was responsible. And now Abby's supervisor was dead.

Too much of a coincidence.

"Hey." Heath caught his attention.

"Did you get it?"

"She lives a couple of blocks from here. I'll text Jack and Wade where we're headed."

"No. Only one of us can afford to be fired. This is on me and me alone." Slate took his badge off and put it in his jacket pocket. "Text me the address."

"Don't do anything crazy, like get dead. Your mom will kill me."

"Give me fifteen before you tell the old man I'm gone."

"You got it."

The address came through and a couple of clicks later Slate was following the directions. Heath had been correct. Denley Drive ran parallel to Lancaster Road. He turned at the second intersection when the Rapid Transit train left the middle of the street.

He parked in front a gray house that was clearly built outside of the surrounding price range. Brand-new house on a block where the neighbors clearly didn't pay for garbage pickup. The end of the street just past the Rapid Transit lot was full of bags and loose trash.

Abby Norman's home was directly across from the Rapid Transit commuter parking. A person could drive straight from her driveway right into the lot. The yard was fenced off, surrounded by trees and groomed bushes. It had a detached garage but no sign of a dog. Which was good, since Slate had opened the gate to go to the front door and knock.

The suspect came to the door with a forced smile on her face.

"Miss Norman? I hope you remember me from the hospital cafeteria."

"Of course I do. You're the Texas Ranger who asked about Rashid. Did you discover why he went crazy like that? Did you need more information about his visits?"

"No, ma'am. That's not why I'm here."

"Oh?"

Her expressions had a well-rehearsed sense to them. He'd seen practiced sentences before, but this took it to a whole new level. Now that he was paying attention, he understood what Vivian had picked up on.

"May I come in?"

"Certainly. Do you mind if we have our discussion here in the foyer? I don't often have guests and don't have a formal room to entertain."

"I was wondering, Miss Norman, if you came to work today. There's been an incident."

"Oh, no. Not another murder."

"As a matter of fact, yes."

"After all the commotion yesterday, my patients—I mean the ones that come to the lab—were canceled. The hospital was fine with me staying home."

He stood, traditional hat in hand, trying to observe everything about the house. Looking for a possible struggle, listening for any signs of Vivian.

Nothing. He had no probable cause.

Nothing besides everything shouting at him that Vivian was here.

His phone vibrated inside his jacket. "Excuse me a second." He took it out and bent his head to read.

Slate didn't see what slammed into the side of his head. All he saw was a blur and had no time to duck.

Chapter Thirty-One

Vivian heard the casual conversation. Abby had invited someone with a deep voice—who sounded a lot like Slate—inside the house. Muffled words kept her from hearing what was said. Her present semidrugged state kept her from crying out. There was a crash and then a slam against the polished floor.

Oh, God. Oh, God. Oh, God. Was he unconscious or even…dead?

Vivian felt the bubble of panic forming in her chest. The cloth over her mouth helped keep her from hyperventilating. What wild imagination had ever convinced her she could find a murderer or help her brother? She should have stayed in the truck or better still, stayed at Slate's house.

Now she'd gotten him killed. He needed her help. Suddenly, the power of suggestion that she couldn't get up was gone. She was free. She could move. She felt sick, but she could move.

She ran to where she'd heard noises. It was Slate. Facedown on the floor, a silver tray and broken glass around his head. Abby was picking up the pieces and neatly stacking them in a trash can.

Vivian skidded to a halt as Abby grabbed one of the larger pieces and held it to Slate's neck. The madwoman pushed it just under his ear. It was sharp enough to draw a drop of blood.

"No! Don't…don't hurt him. I'll… I'll do whatever you want."

Abby handed her a small bottle of water like the drugged mineral water from the day before. She continued to pick up the glass and missed that Vivian poured most of the water onto Slate's pants leg. He had a huge knot on his head. She instinctively reached to help him, but Abby snapped to attention.

"She said we need to leave. We'll drive to the airport. I can change my ticket."

"Why are you doing this? What are you getting from killing all these people?"

"Remember, Vivian. You don't have an appointment. Do as I tell you."

Vivian sought Slate with her eyes but couldn't will her body to move toward him.

"My reasons are far above the intelligence in your average mind." Abby reached onto the credenza and pulled out a pair of disposable gloves, then handed them to Vivian. "Put these on. You can't contaminate my things with your germs."

Abby had done something to control her. A posthypnotic suggestion that was working.

"Remember, Vivian. You don't have an appointment. Come with me."

They left the house and slowly made their way across a new sidewalk. There seemed to be a certain place on each square that Abby had to walk. She didn't let anything touch her and the only thing Vivian had been handed was a single key to a car.

The garage door had a code, which Abby punched in. The door lifted to show some type of very expensive white sports car. Vivian was getting a little punchy. It was harder to focus than usual.

One piece of information kept repeating in her mind. *Do this and Slate is safe.* She pinched herself while getting into the car, trying to wake herself up.

"Good thing I'm not driving," she said, feeling kind of weird. Or drugged. She explained why automatically. "I can't drive stick."

Abby carefully put everything into the car. Vivian automatically latched her seat belt. Her abductor didn't for some reason, but Abby backed out of the building and the driveway anyway. She put the car in gear and took off.

It must have been fast because Vivian was pushed back in her seat for a second or two. "I need out of here." She tried to open the door, gaining more control of her mind. Pushing away the suggestion that she needed to obey.

Abby clicked the auto lock button.

"No. No. No." Vivian tried to reach across the other woman to unlock the doors. She tried to grab the steering wheel but her fingers slid. She stretched again, leaning against the other woman.

Abby screamed when she was touched, throwing up her hands. She lost control of the sports car, which went flying off the road.

Vivian was stunned. Literally. The seat belt jerked her backward. The airbags went off. A cloud of white powder coated everything, hanging in the air.

Abby began screaming hysterically. And kept screaming. Vivian covered her ears, it was so disturbing and bad. Horrible.

Even in a slightly drugged or hypnotic state of mind, Vivian could tell the older woman seemed to be having some sort of mental break.

"I need to be perfect. This can't be happening. My research. Everything's ruined. I'm ruined. Get out!" She pulled a knife and cut Vivian's seat belt, then plunged it into the airbag screaming, "Out! Out!"

Grabbing hold of Vivian's hair, she dragged her across the console and out the driver's side door. She kept the knife on her, holding her close.

"We've got to get to the train. I need… I need…my perfect death."

SLATE COULD FEEL…and he could still see. He pushed himself up from the floor. Or sort of tugged himself upright using the credenza that he'd been lying beside.

Putting his hand to his head, his fingers came away bloody.

Vivian! Where had they gone?

He stumbled through the small, sterile house. No Vivian. No suspect. He took out his phone and called Wade while he stumbled out the front walk. There across the parking lot at the corner farthest from him were the two women. Abby Norman led Vivian away from the station.

Toward the oncoming train.

He started running.

"Get out of the way! Train! Let her go!"

Chapter Thirty-Two

"No, Ranger Thompson. I won't," Abby shouted. "No one will see this for what it is. I need the perfect death and none of you are going to stop me from obtaining it."

Abby Norman was strong for a woman of her slight build. That or she'd drugged Vivian again. Vivian didn't have a mad, glazed-eye look but she wasn't struggling. Maybe it was part of Norman's programming the day before.

He saw the wrecked car at the end of the road. Vivian seemed sort of stunned. Then he saw the knife at her throat.

But she wasn't fighting back. Why? Was she in a trance like before?

"Vivian, honey, how did you get free?" he asked loudly, not caring if Abby Norman heard him or not. "If you get the chance, get free. Remember how you got free from me. Wake up!"

The Rapid Transit train whistle blew. It was at the previous block, crossing the intersection. They didn't have much time.

"Vivian! Fight!"

Slate ran across the parking lot for the stairs leading up the hill to the train stop, keeping his eyes on the women. No one was at the stop so he couldn't call for help. No one was there to stop a madwoman from walking onto the tracks in front of the train.

The steep incline up to the train stop was reinforced with a concrete wall. He couldn't climb it so he had to follow the sidewalk from the parking lot. Up two sets of steps and around to the loading area before he could run onto the track and follow them.

He was on the first set of steps. The whistle was blowing nonstop. The brakes were screaming, trying to stop...

"What are you doing? Let go of me." Vivian was alert and finally fighting. She knocked the knife out of her opponent's hand but couldn't get her hair free.

Slate hit the top of the second set of steps and began running. The fastest way was straight down the track. He waved, he shouted.

And he watched as Vivian threw several punches that her captor couldn't recover from. Abby fell, still holding Vivian's long hair and bringing her down to the track, too.

"The train is coming!"

Screeching brakes. Earsplitting whistle. Car horns blared. People screamed.

Vivian was on her knees.

Abby had a perfect smile on her face.

Slate got to Vivian with seconds left, just as the former army soldier kicked out and freed herself.

He grabbed Vivian around her waist and fell out of the train's path. It barely missed them. It didn't miss Abby Norman.

Lying on the track as she was, she died horrifically and instantly. The train slid to a stop. There was nothing the conductor could have done. People from across the street ran toward them. There was blood on the track under the train.

Slate dragged Vivian into his lap. She was crying and mumbling incoherently.

"It's okay. You're okay." He repeated the same words over and over again. While rocking her in his lap, he kept her face pressed into his chest, kept his hand over her eyes.

There was no reason for her to ever have a memory of what was in front of them. He'd keep the unpleasant scene in his head for legal reasons, but Vivian didn't need it.

She'd have enough nightmares based off of the actual event. The feel of having her abductor yanked from her hand, hit by the train. Hell, she was probably more equipped to handle the whole ordeal than he was. She'd been in the military. Had served overseas. No telling what she'd seen or had to do there.

But still… He could keep her from seeing this particular incident. No reason to force more into her mind.

Life had enough horror.

SLATE'S HEAD HAD A LUMP the size of Rhode Island on the side of it. Being hit with what felt like a brick wasn't pleasant, but he wasn't dead. The EMTs gave him a green light to be checked out by his own doctor. He might have stretched the truth a little about passing out.

So he'd be more truthful with his own doctor…but later.

He needed to get back to Vivian. He'd been keeping an eye on her, but she was sitting in the back of the major's SUV. At least the heater was running for her. Wade sat in the front but wasn't talking. He was actually texting Slate, who could only read and not respond.

She's fine. Doesn't want to talk about it. Wants to wait for you to give her statement. Would rather stay in the SUV until you're done.

Four texts, several minutes apart. If they'd moved her, Wade would have let him know.

"Sign here that you're refusing transport." The EMT stuck a clipboard and pen in front of Slate. "I really think you need stiches, Mr. Thompson. I'm taking a wild guess here, but I think you've got a concussion. So if you start vomiting or lose consciousness, find an ER, stat."

"Yeah. We good?"

The EMT shook his head but turned back to his vehicle. Slate hightailed it to the dark SUV.

"You can't be alone with her, Thompson. You know we have to take your statements independently," Major Clements said.

"I want her to have a lawyer."

"Good idea. So you think she needs one?" Jack asked.

"No. But it'll keep anyone questioning her in line. She shouldn't be alone."

"I'll call mine."

"Thanks. Now have Wade roll down the window." No, it wasn't a question asking for permission. It was a demand that he expected to be met.

The window went down without a word. Three rangers besides himself were listening to the conversation. Wade got out of the driver's seat and joined Major Clements, Jack and Heath in a semicircle that prevented anyone from interrupting them.

"I know what you're going to say," she said with very little emotion.

"You do?"

"This was all my fault. Abby would be alive if I'd just waited in the truck."

"I was going to say…" he pulled a twig from her hair "…they're going to ask you what happened. Be honest. Jack's calling his lawyer—"

"You think I need a lawyer?" she asked, panicked but still avoiding looking at him.

"No, I don't. I just don't want you to be alone." He wanted to open the door and pull her into his arms. He couldn't. Too many eyes were watching. "A lot of departments will be asking you the same questions. Don't get frustrated or hyperventilate. Having a lawyer there will help."

She should have reacted to his tease about hyperventilating. She didn't move, but the men around him did. Out of the corner of his eye, he saw their hands go up, heard his commander say, "Give him a second."

"I've got to go, Vivian. Jack will take care of you. All the guys will. I'll see you in a few hours."

She looked pale, unusually still as the window slid up between them.

"You sure you're both okay to face these guys?" Jack asked. "Maybe the hospital should be our first stop?"

"I think she's in shock. Any chance of getting the questions postponed?"

He shook his head. "You know this jockeying-for-position battle is out of my hands. I'm not leaving and will get her out of there as soon as I can." He nodded to a group of officers coming toward them. "You take care of business."

Chapter Thirty-Three

Done. Over. Another case for the files. And freaky as hell. Slate couldn't remember anything more weird or strange happening to people he knew.

Martha Abigail Norman Toliver had been a very sick individual. Major Clements and the VA OIG had notified her parents in Florida. He was curious to hear what they thought of their daughter.

Slate had changed and was at home when he called Wade for an update, knowing he'd be working his way through the punishment files so he could get off desk duty sooner. *His friend really needed a reason to leave the office.*

"Any word on the why?" Slate asked. "Clues to what motivated her?"

"The forensics team is still cataloguing items," Wade said. "This case is three jurisdictional-messed-up nightmares. Nobody knows who to report to so getting any information is crazy."

"But you went to the house. What was it like?" Slate had seen through the door. Everything was white, sterile. It almost looked vacuum sealed.

"Her parents verified that sessions with Dr. Roberts was part of their agreement with Abby to pay her bills. Dr. Roberts's office confirmed our mild-mannered lab assistant was a patient. She must have helped herself to the Subject Nineteen records. The circumstantial evidence against Victor was that he had an appointment with the victim. Then he confessed and everyone stopped looking further."

"That should clear Victor Watts. Vivian's going to want her brother out of jail pronto. How long do you think it'll take?"

"Days. But I don't think we'll have to wait long. But I got my doubts about sending him back on the streets."

"That's where I'm collecting on my favor, man. I did you one, now it's your turn."

"You got it."

"Take a look into Victor's attorney. I want to know if he's getting a kickback from the investigators he recommended to Vivian. She and her brother will need money to live on. And are there any places hiring where we can give them some recommendations?" Slate swallowed hard.

They'd known each other less than a week, but he didn't want Vivian to move back to Miami. A different city in Texas…he could handle that. Texas was a big state and rangers transferred companies from time to time. But breaking into another law enforcement agency in Florida…that was another story.

"You're using your favor on this? I thought you'd want something harder. Or the truth about Jack's girlfriend."

"This is important. It's going to be a fight to get her brother into a facility that deprograms minds—if there is such a place. In fact, all of the veterans who were exposed to Abby Norman are going to need it."

"I know, man. I've got your back and theirs. I'll make sure it happens."

Slate pressed his lips together and nodded. "Vivian will need to be checked out, too."

"Get this, the parents told us she had OCD and several

other phobias and disorders." Wade changed the subject. "And apparently, she had a psychotic break recently. No one confirmed schizophrenia, but it was suggested that's why she was being observed by Roberts."

"I don't envy the team having to look and sort through all that."

"Hey, before I let you go. Norman had several files on the laptop they found in the wrecked car. They seem to be different stages of her—for the lack of a better word—brainwashing files she played for the vets. Looks like she'd drug them and play the files while they slept."

"Hope that helps the doctors find a way to fix everybody." *Even Vivian.*

"Same here. Gotta run and I still owe you a favor."

They hung up just before she got out of the shower.

"Is it really over?" She laughed, shaking her hair free of its towel. "How soon do you think Victor will be free? Major Clements explained it would take a few days. I could go see him before that and tell him what happened. That deserves a visit, right?"

"I'll call County and arrange a time. I just spoke with Wade. It looks like there's corroborating evidence at Abby's house."

"I can't talk about this again." Her words had a frantic tone to them and didn't match the bright smile she displayed. Her actions were very casual, as if she were brushing everything off.

"You don't want an update?"

"Not anymore tonight. I'll leave the rest for the appropriate authorities to muddle through. Victor will be released and that's all that matters to me." She fluffed her curls, finger-combing as she tilted her head to one side. "Wipe the scowl off your face, Ranger Thompson. Do you have ice cream?"

"I don't think so, but we can run out for some if you want."

"Oh, wow. I just realized I haven't eaten since the scrambled eggs. I bet you haven't either. Did your mom leave any leftovers?" She popped off the couch and pulled open the fridge.

"Vivian!" His voice was louder than he'd planned.

"What? Do you want a hamburger instead?"

He held his arms open. She'd avoided him after the accidental death of Abby Norman. She'd pulled away from every pat on her shoulder offered by the team or by rescue workers. She'd avoided eye contact while speaking about it to each department head who asked her questions. And now she wanted to act like nothing had happened.

She shook her head. Her mouth opened and shut again, followed by flattened lips that looked determined not to say a word.

"You can't do this to yourself," he whispered. "Come here."

"I don't want comfort for what happened," she said finally.

The sky was darkening, causing the room to darken, as well. He waited while the light from the open refrigerator door illuminated this woman he'd come to admire so much.

"I've said this before, but you didn't ask for any of this to happen. You left everything behind to rush to the side of your brother. You've been going ninety-to-nothing with one goal and you accomplished it. Now it's time to take a moment. Come on."

He wiggled his fingers, taking a step toward her, but still not touching. He gave the fridge door a one-finger push and she let it close. He still had an open arm but used it to coax her to the living room.

Barefoot and in pj's, she grabbed the couch throw that

had been used more in that week than the year it had been draped over the arm of the uncomfortable chair in the corner. She curled her long legs into the corner cushions, leaving room for him on the opposite end.

Slate shook his head, refusing to be separated from her again. They'd been through a lot together in the past several days. He hoped she'd be around for several more. But it all depended on how he handled the next few moments.

He moved to the end of the couch behind Vivian, removed the cushion to make more room and squeezed his body in behind hers. She didn't give an inch until the last second. They sat there with no words. There weren't many that would mean much.

Vivian had almost been killed, and the woman chasing her, the woman responsible for all her pain of the past year, had died trying to finish her.

"It's okay to let it out, babe. We all do."

"I don't feel anything except relief," she whispered.

"That's okay, too. You have permission to feel that way. You also have permission to be glad you're alive. To be glad the train didn't hit you."

"I killed someone."

The only reason he heard her speak was because there weren't any other sounds in the house. She'd been in the military; hadn't she seen death before? Should he tell her how proud he was of everything she'd done today?

He wrapped an arm around the top of her shoulders, resting on the front of her chest, keeping her close and protected. Her cool fingers clung onto his forearm. She held on, dropping her forehead to join her fingers.

He didn't do or say anything else. He wanted to but training kept him silent. Or maybe it was experience from the way his parents had treated him and his sister. Either way…he waited.

Silent tears graced his arm. Then sobbing shook the woman clinging to him. He rubbed her back, offering what he could. But this seemed like one of those times it was better not to say anything.

"I was in the war. I've fired my weapon but I've never seen someone die like that. Maybe I should feel justified or vindicated. Look at what she did. She was horrible. All those deaths."

"You've been through a lot, Vivian. Give yourself time to take it all in, time to heal."

"But why?" She took a deep breath. "I don't understand how someone could do the things she did."

"We probably never will. Her mind wasn't all there. Some things just can't be explained."

"So many died. It's so sad."

She cried a bit more, and soon the sobs were just long, drawn, shaking breaths. She turned, lying on his chest, keeping his arm around her. He thought she'd fallen asleep.

Maybe he was the one who drifted asleep since he startled awake at her words.

"Pardon?"

"I don't know what to do now," she whispered a second time.

"You keep going. We keep going. And don't be afraid to ask for help if you feel you can't." He was proud of himself. He wasn't being a jerk. Wasn't being a typical man. This was his sensitive side.

Because the only thing he really wanted to do now was finish what they'd each started. After all, she was a beautiful, attractive woman who he wanted to stay around. He could think of something other than sex.

"You know you can stay here, Vivian. If you feel comfortable, that is. There's the extra room at the house and Mom could always use some help until you're back on your feet. It wouldn't be charity since you'd be earning your way."

"Your dad already called and offered me the spare room. I'm still not sure that's a great idea. And when Victor gets out, that's two of us. We can't do that to your family."

"Um… Wade's doing some research. We think that all the sleep-study patients will need some intense therapy. He's looking for a place to handle that. He's good at sweet-talking people to make things happen."

She turned her face and parted her lips but shook her head instead of stating any disappointment she may have felt. She rested on him again. "Maybe I should join them?"

"You need to be checked out for sure. But you weren't exposed the same. You're not getting any crazy feelings to bonk me over the head again. Are you?"

"I don't know. There aren't any spare IV poles hanging around." She laughed. "I can't thank you enough for the kindness you and your family have shown to me. I'm grateful. And especially to all you guys at Company B. You not only saved my life, but you've also saved my brother."

There it was again, the desire to kiss the luscious lips that tilted in a smile. So close to his. He wanted her like a desperate man, but the timing was all off. So he sucked it up and behaved.

Even if they would let down their guards.

And yeah, even if Heath was staying in the main house to give them privacy.

And sure, her fingers were drawing little circles and had unbuttoned the top button of his shirt.

Dammit, he needed to behave…didn't he?

It was hell being a man and not knowing when the moment was right. She was better now. Did she need him as much as he needed her?

There was one way—okay more than one—to find out.

But kissing her and discovering what she'd do afterward was the solution he chose.

Vivian's ever-changing eyes looked up into his again and he bent his head to capture her lips. She twisted around and kissed him back. Her arms went around his neck and across his shoulders.

Definitely an answer when she didn't pull back, didn't stop kissing. Her arms brought him to more of a sitting position, then she straddled his lap. And yet he found himself questioning if this was the best thing for her or for them.

Yeah, that was a head-scratcher. What red-blooded American male questioned if the timing for sex was right or not?

He cupped her shoulders, lifting her away from him. Their lips held onto each other until the last possible micron.

"Is something wrong? Should we move to the bedroom?" She managed to get off the couch before he could actually form a question.

Maybe he was having second—or even third—thoughts about asking the damn thing. He had his hand in hers and had followed her halfway around the end of the couch before...

"I'm going to hate myself, but are you sure this is a good idea?"

"What? Going to your bedroom? Do you need to put something on the door to keep your roommate out?" She began walking again.

Slate stopped and twirled her into his arms. He used one hand to keep her there and the other to tilt her face to his. Standing closer to the window and the porchlight, he could see the redness in her silver eyes from crying. He used his thumb to remove a smudge from the corner of her eye.

"Are you sure this is what you want? Now? Tonight?" he asked softly.

"You know I can get free from this hold."

"Please don't head butt me," he teased. Then he affectionately kissed the tip of her nose.

"Yes, Slate. I'm sure. I wouldn't have kissed you now or before for that matter."

"I just don't want you to feel pressured."

"Oh, please." She raised her hands and cupped his cheeks. "Do not insult my integrity or intentions again."

His hands went in the air in an act of surrender. "Whoa, believe me, I am not accidentally going down that road a second time."

She brought his mouth to hers in a beautiful, sexy-as-hell kiss before sliding her hand up his arm to take his hand. She led him down the short hallway.

"Then come down this one with me."

Epilogue

Two weeks later

"Relax. You're taking this ride way too seriously." Slate meant it. If she didn't loosen up in the saddle, she'd be sore all over.

"I've never been on a horse before." Vivian continued to sit stiff and straight. "At least not out of the paddock."

"You're doing great. I still don't understand why you won't let me give you lessons."

"Because we'd end up not having a lesson. I'm working them off, you know. Learning how to groom and clean the stalls. And in exchange, your sister gives me a beginner riding lesson. She's pretty good."

"I could do that. Teach you."

"We tried. Our one and only lesson ended up in the hayloft."

"Oh. I didn't think you were serious back then. Besides, it was going to rain." He remembered that afternoon. It was the last time he'd kissed her, stopping just shy of… "In fact, it rained all afternoon. I'm just saying, I could give you lessons now. I've got more time."

He slipped off his mare and was below her in a couple of strides, lifting her out of the saddle. She put her hands on his shoulders and slid down his chest.

Her cheeks were red from the winter wind. He'd already switched the ball cap from blocking the sun, turning it backward on his head. The thick jacket he'd started off in was draped over the back of his saddle. He hoped it was the sun heating his body and not nerves.

"Aren't you cold?" she asked.

"Sunshine and love are warming me inside and out."

"As your father would say, you're being downright silly." Vivian drew her jacket a little tighter, emphasizing that he should be cool. "I'm still not moving into your room. Or did you bring me out here to tell me it was time to get my own place?"

"Of course not. You know you're welcome as long as you want to stay. Besides, I kind of like having someone take my turn in the barn."

"So you brought me all the way out here to the edge of the property, Mr. Thompson. Do you have a specific reason?"

"First, I thought taking a ride today would be nice. It's the first day I haven't worked since you moved in. We haven't been alone since."

"Since the hayloft."

Vivian dug the toe of her used boots into the dirt. She'd barely been making eye contact with him recently. She lived in his old bedroom at the main house and he'd rarely been home. She was helping around the ranch and looking for a permanent business position in Dallas to be near her brother.

When everything was straightened out at the VA Hospital, another case had immediately required his full attention. He dived into work, trying to make up for all the ruckus raised by every official from here to D.C.

"And second?" she asked, wrapping the reins around her hand.

"It's the only way you'd agree to see me alone."

"True."

"Why? Did I do something?"

"You mean besides saving my life more than once, helping me free my brother, giving me a place to live? Oh, and let's not forget arranging for my brother to go to a hospital to make sure he wasn't still programmed by that horrible woman? And my treatment. Or maybe having Wade put in a few recommendations for my possible employment. Those things?"

"You know I meant did I do something wrong, Vivian." Slate took off his cap and scratched his head. He honestly didn't know what was going on. "I thought you liked me, sort of like we had a connection from that first glass of tea."

"We both got busy." She licked her lips. "And I do like you."

He unwrapped her mare's reins, which were now twisted in her hands, and looped them along with his around a low mesquite tree limb. He was sure the horses wouldn't run off. Not so sure about the filly standing in front of him.

Now that she didn't have the reins, he swept her hands into his and nudged her a bit closer. The fresh scent of her was on the breeze as vivid to him as rain on the horizon. He knew her...wanted her.

But he wasn't about to rush and mess things up the way he had when they'd first met.

"So I like you and you just admitted to liking me. Want to see a movie?"

"You're asking me on a date? Any chance you'd include dinner at a certain steak restaurant downtown?"

"Sure, I can arrange that."

"There's one more thing." She gently tugged her hands free and slipped them against his chest, then up around his neck. She tilted her head to the side slightly, looking at him invitingly.

He took her lips against his, tenderly at first, then more hungrily.

"What's your one more thing?" he asked against her lips.

"I'll need a good-night kiss."

"Oh, I can definitely see to that."

* * * * *

LET'S TALK
Romance

For exclusive extracts, competitions
and special offers, find us online:

f facebook.com/millsandboon

📷 @millsandboonuk

🐦 @millsandboon

Or get in touch on 0844 844 1351*

For all the latest titles coming soon, visit
millsandboon.co.uk/nextmonth